M000223590

Little Girl Lost:

The Return of Johnnie Wise

KEITH LEE JOHNSON

DARE TO IMAGINE
PUBLISHING

Little Girl Lost:
The Return of Johnnie Wise

Keith Lee Johnson

Dare to Imagine Publishing
PO Box 935
Maumee, OH 43537

ISBN 10: 1-935825-00-3
ISBN 13: 978-1-935825-00-5

Library of Congress Control Number: 2010931557

First Printing: July 2010

Printed in the United States of America

10 9 8 7 6 5 4 3 2 1

Recap: Books One, Two and Three

It was Christmas Eve when Johnnie Wise's purity was first compromised, but she had nothing to do with the extralegal transaction. She was a fifteen-year-old, born-again Christian who had aspirations of becoming an evangelist before her mother sold her virginity to a white insurance man named Earl Shamus during the winter of 1952. The color of the man who paid for the privilege and subsequently plundered the orchard that was reserved for one special man was not the issue. Had Earl been a black insurance man, the compromise would have been the same, only worse in that the crime would have been black on black—a slightly different rendition of dog eats dog. Humiliation, confusion, indignity, uncertainty, embarrassment, mistrust—all of these were the issue, and all of these shaped her future decisions, which culminated in a tragedy she, for all intents and purposes, wrote, produced, directed and starred in.

Because of all of these, she not only learned to accept compromise as a way of life, compromise became her strongest supporter, her trusted ally, her constant companion, and she learned to use it against the man who introduced her to it all. Earl took her innocence. Johnnie took his money. Along the way though, without realizing it, she became enamored with riches, which ultimately led to more compromising. Unbeknownst to her, the purity that once defined her slowly gave way to conniving manipulation. Before she knew it, she had learned to justify anything she did. But when she was being taunted by her classmates on the way home from school one day, she was rescued by a robust football player named Lucas Matthews.

The two fell in love.

Meanwhile, her love for money had grown, and she wanted more of it. Earl bought her a home in an affluent Negro parish called Ashland Estates. He even set her up with Stockbroker, Martin Winters, who she seduced to learn the ins and outs of the stock market, further compromising who she once was and who she wanted to become. But when Marguerite, her Creole mother, was killed by her most faithful customer, the Grand Wizard of the Ku Klux Klan, she turned to Lucas's boss, Napoleon Bentley, a ruthless gangster who would stop at nothing to have her.

As a ploy to win her heart, Napoleon promised to avenge her mother's death. Later, he went to her home and told her that Lucas was having an affair with his wife and he would kill him for that if she didn't give him the sweet revenge he deserved by giving him one night of pleasure. Johnnie quickly refused, but when Meredith Shamus paid her an unannounced visit and confronted her about her ongoing relationship with her husband, Earl, Johnnie was so shocked that she forgot Napoleon was still in the kitchen and could hear their conversation.

Meredith revealed it all. She even knew about Martin Winters. Napoleon then threatened to tell Lucas about the affair. She agreed to give him what he wanted, but she made it clear it would only happen one time, believing it would be a quick in and out encounter that she could easily forget and even pretend that it never even happened. But she was so enraptured by his sexual prowess that she couldn't get Napoleon out of her mind. Later, when Lucas saw Johnnie staring at Napoleon with longing eyes, he realized that she'd had sex with him. Johnnie responded with half truths and total lies—magnificent lies. Lucas believed her falsehoods because he wanted to believe her.

Later though when Lucas was presented with the prospect of selling drugs and making fast easy money, he seized the opportunity. Lucas didn't know that the whole operation was a set up by Napoleon to get him out of the way. Napoleon wanted Johnnie, and to show her what a wonderful guy he was, Napoleon talked to a judge he knew and got Lucas three months at Angola Prison and then three years in the Army. Lucas accepted the deal, having no idea he had been seriously set up.

While in prison, Lucas improved his reading skills, and one day he received a letter from Colonel Strong, who had played football for his high school coach. Strong was contacted by their mutual coach, and now he wanted to give Lucas the same opportunity he'd had. Strong also wanted him to play football for him in Germany. The Colonel pulled some strings and got him out of Angola Prison after serving one month. Lucas wrote a letter to Marla, his girlfriend on the side, Napoleon's soon-to-be ex-wife, who had left her husband and went back to Chicago. Marla and Lucas agreed to meet in an out of the way town far from New Orleans for one last romp.

After they made up for lost time at the hotel, Marla told Lucas a truth that deep down he knew, but didn't want to face. Lucas accidently killed the messenger who had delivered a strong dose of reality. He put her body in the trunk of her Cadillac and pushed it into the river. Before she died, Marla had told Lucas that Johnnie was being tried for the murder of her new stockbroker, Sharon Trudeau. Marla had gotten her the best attorney in Chicago to represent her.

Meanwhile, the Syndicate Commission decided to get rid of Napoleon Bentley. He had been warned to keep niggers out of the business and not to associate with them anymore. Bentley ignored their warnings, and he and Bubbles, his black lieutenant, paid for that mistake with their lives.

But when Lucas heard Meredith testify that Johnnie was having sex with her husband and Martin Winters, it broke his heart. Nevertheless, he still loved Johnnie. They had planned to leave New Orleans together, but something kept happening to prevent it. As a final act of love to ensure that Johnnie would leave New Orleans for good, Lucas set her house on fire. He didn't know that two hundred thousand of her money was hidden in the fireplace. He also didn't know that white Christians had decided to burn down Ashland Estates after he left even though he saw them heading that way as he left the prosperous community.

Johnnie was acquitted of murdering Sharon Trudeau, but she and the rest of the citizens who lived in Ashland Estates returned to the charred ruins of their once beautiful homes. Just as Lucas had hoped, Johnnie was about to leave New Orleans. And now, *Little Girl Lost: The Return of Johnnie Wise.*

Chapter 1

Leaving New Orleans

Looking through the rearview mirror as she drove away from her smoldering Ashland Estates home, the sight of seeing Sadie and her children standing in the street watching was far more than Johnnie Wise's young heart could bear. Sadie was the only friend she had left in New Orleans, in the world for that matter. She couldn't imagine what her life would be like without Sadie Lane in it. Oh, how she would miss hearing her friend's knock on the back door, her expectation of being let in to have a bite to eat and drink coffee. Oh, how she would miss their conversations about the men in their lives, the white folk they worked for, and the women who hated them for being beautiful—Mrs. Mancini, Mrs. Beauregard and her cook, Katherine.

As hard as she tried, she couldn't stop thinking about all the good times she and Sadie had shared. The trip to Las Vegas particularly came to mind. In her mind's eye, she could see them boarding an airplane for the first time, going into a casino, watching her brother, Benny, completely dismantle Paul "Sweetwater" Smith for six rounds before knocking him out, and then spending a few unforgettable hours with Napoleon Bentley, who she sweetly ravaged several times before returning to her own hotel room.

As the sight of Sadie and her children, who were probably still clinging to their mother, diminished while Johnnie drove farther away, she fought earnestly to control the emotion of losing a world that was hers and everything in it. But when the image of Lucas Matthews, her adoring boyfriend materialized in her mind, her eyes welled. When she saw him up in the balcony of the courtroom, looking down at her, knowing that she was more like her deceased mother than she cared to acknowledge, she lost control. She pulled her car over and parked as tear after tear rolled down her cheeks, lingered on her chin, and then eventually dripped onto her white blouse. With both hands on the steering wheel, she leaned forward and rested her head there while raw emotion forced her shoulders and back to hunch as she gave into the anguish of losing everything she had held dear.

She had other memories that were equally painful and difficult to forget. Just four weeks or so ago, she had been raped by Billy Logan, a boy who had teased her about her relationship with Earl Shamus because he thought she was too pretty to be involved with a white man on an intimate level. While she was coming to terms with that violation, she was violated again. This time by the law itself. She was arrested, tried, and fortunately acquitted for a murder she didn't commit. What made the arrest so egregious was that it was spawned by a vicious article in the newspaper. The prosecutor knew she was innocent, yet he tried to convict her anyway on the word of one "witness" who was not a witness because he didn't see Johnnie kill anyone, nor was she in Florida at the time of the murders. It therefore didn't matter if she killed Sharon Trudeau or not. Being a Negro and accused was enough for the grand jury to indict.

When she thought of how close she had come to death, not once, not twice, but three times, the law being her attempted executioner the second time, she cried all the more and wondered why God had spared her so many times when people in her family, black and white, were dying all around her. She had lost it all, and being dirt poor again left her feeling like her heart had been ripped out with no anesthetic to mask the radical surgery that had been performed. She had been poor before, and there was no honor in it. But now, she was in a worse condition because she didn't even have a place to lay her head. Image after image filled her mind as she thought about the beautifully furnished home she once owned, which had all the trimmings.

Without intending to, she thought about the clothes in her closet. She'd had so many outfits that she could go more than an entire year without having to wear the same garments twice. Now all she had were memories of the pampered lifestyle she lived, the clothes on her back, and the shoes on her feet. But when she thought the images couldn't get any worse, they did. While her shoulders and back were

still hunched, she saw the dilapidated dwelling in ruined Sable Parish—
the place that Marguerite called home and great uneasiness swept over
her as she contemplated the possibility of returning to that shameful
existence. The day she left that place with Earl came into focus as she
argued, and then physically fought with her mother prior to leaving
Sable Parish for good.

She had forty-five dollars and some change, which if she was
very thrifty, might last for a month, but what was that compared to the
two hundred thousand she had lost in the fire that demolished Ashland
Estates. Then, it occurred to her how she had acquired so much money,
and she wept all the more. She had sold her soul for ill-gotten gains,
and those riches were forever gone. She pulled away from the curb.
Then, she looked into her rearview, hoping to see Sadie one last time
before she turned the corner, even if it was for an instant and at a
distance that would make it impossible to recognize her. She didn't see
her, and if she did, she didn't recognize her because the distance was
too great and the number of people near Sadie made it impossible to
distinguish her from the rest of her former neighbors.

Chapter 2

"Bye, Mama."

Johnnie knew it was time to keep the promise she had made to herself when she told Earl Shamus off on Christmas Eve about four weeks earlier. She had told herself that she would need to have a similar conversation with her mother even though she was dead and in the tomb she had purchased for her remains. She had put the conversation off far too long. She wasn't sure what she was going to say when she parked her car and got out. Nor did she know what she was going to say when she reached the crypt, but she was determined to say whatever came to mind.

She entered the City of the Dead and tried her best to remember where her mother was. She hadn't been to the cemetery since Marguerite's funeral. She plodded her way through the graveyard, thinking she was close to the tomb, hoping she would soon find it. But when she neared the place where she and her brother had laid their mother to rest, she stopped in front of it, and seriously considered changing her mind. All of a sudden, she didn't want to go in. Even though her domineering mother was dead, Johnnie was still intimidated by her remains. She was about to turn around and go back to her car when she realized she would never be free until she told her mother the truth. With that in mind, she walked into the burial chamber and went to Marguerite's final resting place.

Now that she was there, it seemed silly to talk to the remains of what was once her mother, but she was determined to get it over with and get out of New Orleans for good. Hesitantly she said, "I love you, Mama, but I *hate* you, Mama." She closed her eyes and reflected for a few seconds, remembering all the events of the previous two years. "I was a good girl, Mama. I was a good Christian girl, pure before Almighty God, until you and Earl turned me into a whore. I know you meant well, but you were a jealous mother. You were jealous because I'm young and you were getting up in age.

"As far back as I can remember I could never do anything right for you. Nothing! Everything I did was wrong. Why, Mama? Why didn't you love me? Huh? Why couldn't you treat me like other mothers treat their daughters? Why couldn't you be nice to me more often than you were? Why did I have to fight you to get you to show me the same respect you wanted me to show you? Most of the time it seemed as if I was nothing but a meal ticket for you. If you didn't want me, why didn't you send me to my father? And why did you lie to me? Why didn't you tell me Sheriff Tate ran him out of town because he wanted to continue sleeping with you and my daddy wouldn't stand for it? Why did you have to paint such a terrible picture of him, saying he left you and never came back to see about us when you knew all along he was run out of town?" Her tears were flowing freely now as she purged her mind and her soul. "You could've been a better mother if you tried to be. You could've loved more if you tried to. You could've protected me if you wanted to. But you didn't, did you, Mama? And now, I've had to grow up quick and hard. Oh, and by the way, because of what you taught me, I had to end up killing my baby. I got pregnant, Mama. Pregnant! Pregnant before marriage, Mama. Do you have any idea what its like to give birth to children who don't have a name? Do you have any idea how embarrassing that is? Of course you do, and yet you did to me what was done to you. You knew better, yet you didn't do better by me. You took advantage of me for personal gain.

"How foolish can a mother be? You were supposed to protect me from the evil of this world, but instead, you forced me to participate in its depravity. Anyway . . . it was a little girl child, Mama . . . your granddaughter. Now that I've lost everything, I guess it's just as well that I killed her. And I guess you're happy now that I ended up just like you . . . broke and alone. I just hope the good Lord above forgives me for what I did. I'm not sure if I'll ever forgive myself though. But I know one thing, if the good Lord above gives me another child, I swear I'll never kill another one no matter what or whose baby it is." She looked at her watch, and then she closed her eyes and took a deep breath. "There's so much to say, Mama, and so little time. So, let me say this before I go. You were wrong about Lucas. Lucas was good to me, and believe it or not, I was bad to him and bad for him in so many ways. No, Lucas wasn't perfect, but he was better than most. If it weren't for that whore, Marla Bentley, I think he would have been totally true to me. I hope I run into her one day so I can tell her about herself. If you and Earl Shamus hadn't turned me out, I would have been good for Lucas, and we would have left this place long ago. I guess I'm more like you than I ever imagined. I guess sin is in the blood, and we are slaves to it.

"You once told me when we were at the Savoy Hotel, before those crackers burned it down, that I shouldn't blame you for the rest of my life. That I should do whatever I wanted to do from that time forward. Well, as of this moment, I'm through blaming you, and I'm through blaming Earl. I'm in control now. Whatever happens to me from this moment forward is on me. Well, I guess that's it. Bye, Mama. I hope you can rest in peace and somehow know that I've forgiven everything you and Earl did to me."

When she had finished speaking, she left the crypt. She saw a white woman clutching the hand of a little white boy who was holding a red balloon. The boy had the bluest eyes she had ever seen. When the woman's eyes met Johnnie's, it seemed as if the woman recognized her. The woman smiled pleasantly and tugged her son's hand, beckoning him to keep up with her pace. Johnnie forced herself to smile, too, even though that was the last thing she wanted to do. The woman walked faster as if she were all of sudden in a hurry, dragging the little boy with her into a nearby tomb. The name above the crypt read: PIERRE ST. JOHN.

Still looking over his shoulder at Johnnie, admiringly so, the boy let go of his balloon just before his mother pulled him inside. She could tell the boy thought she was pretty by the way he smiled and couldn't take his eyes off her. She thought the least she could do was retrieve his balloon for him. A gust of wind blew, and the balloon floated away. When she was on the verge of catching up with it, another gust of wind sent it on its way again, taking her farther into the cemetery and farther away from the crypt of Pierre St. John. Finally, the balloon floated over a wrought iron fence surrounding an expensive-looking mausoleum that resembled a miniature house with smooth cement columns. A winged angel of stone holding a sword and shield sat atop of the crypt while carved male and female lions guarded two bronze doors. She opened the gate and went inside, hoping she could get the boy's balloon this time. But when she reached for the balloon, another gust of wind caused it to rise where it hovered beneath the name BAPTISTE, which was chiseled into the stone facing.

Chapter 3

The Red Balloon

Seeing her family's name engraved in expensive granite sent an icy chill down Johnnie's spine and shook her like she was suddenly standing directly on the North Pole without a stitch of clothing to protect her from the frigid wind. She looked to the left, and then to the right. Seeing no one, she considered going in. In fact, every fiber of her being was telling her to go inside and take a look around even though she knew the crypt would probably be locked. Again, she looked to the left, and then to the right. Again, seeing no one, she looked up, hoping to see the balloon, but it was gone. She looked for it, but it seemed to have vanished as if by magic. Then, tentatively, she took a few steps forward, still looking around, hoping no one would see her going into what in all likelihood was another family's crypt as she was being pulled inside by an irresistible invisible force. On the chance that the crypt wasn't locked, she wanted to get inside and see if she recognized any names that might be in there.

She hurried up the stairs and hesitantly reached out for the bronze door on the right, fully expecting it to be locked while praying it wouldn't be. Her hand shook a little when she touched the door handle. Her heart was pounding. Holding it firmly, she closed her eyes and said, "Please, God, let it be open." She pulled the door, and it opened. Surprised, she immediately closed it. Again, she looked around, thinking it wasn't her family's tomb. It was probably another Baptiste family—a white one, given the expense it would have taken to build such a structure.

It occurred to her that a family member probably left something in the car and hustled back to get it and would return any moment now.

She turned around and was about to walk back down the stairs and leave when she again felt the invisible force that had guided her thus far. It seemed to be pulling at her flesh even more now, demanding that she enter and see what was in there. Her heart beat even faster as exhilaration threatened to consume her. She turned around and looked at the bronze doors. Then, she looked over her shoulder one last time. Seeing no one, she went inside before anyone could see her desecrating someone's sacred burial ground.

In the vestibule now, the light of the sun poured in from stained glass windows. Her heart was pounding so hard she could hear it. She told herself she would be in and out in a matter of seconds. Who would know that she had trespassed? She figured there were probably only a few names on the vaults. She went to the first vault. JOSEPHINE BAPTISTE was engraved in the vault's emperador brown marble facing. A burgeoning smile emerged and remained. She tried, but she couldn't remember her grandmother. She didn't remember when she died or even going to the funeral, but she was glad to finally make her acquaintance, albeit posthumously. At that instant, she remembered her grandfather, Nathaniel Beauregard, and the day he stood up and told his family the truth about who she was.

She was about to leave when something told her to look at the other names on the wall etched in the marble facings. She thought, *Why not?* She went to the far end of the wall, and then one by one, she read the following names: PRINCE AMIR BASHIR JIBRIL, LAUREN RENEE BOUVIER BAPTISTE. Amir and Lauren were together in a double vault. Beneath Lauren's name was another name in parentheses—IBO ATIKAH MUSTAFA. Next to them was the name: ROKK BAPTISTE, BELOVED HUSBAND OF LAUREN, STUDENT OF THE PRINCE. She continued on and read the following names: ANTOINETTE JACQUELINE GABRIELLE BAPTISTE, PHARAOH BAPTISTE, SETI BAPTISTE, RAMESSES BAPTISTE, and finally, JOSEPHINE BAPTISTE.

She noticed that only Prince Amir Bashir Jibril didn't have the Baptiste name. She wondered if he really was a prince, and if Lauren was married to Rokk, why was she in a vault with the Prince? She opened her purse, pulled out a pen and paper, and wrote all the names down so that she would remember them. Then, she left the crypt and descended the stairs. It occurred to her that she hadn't written down the dates of their births and deaths. She was leaving New Orleans for good and had no idea if she would ever return. She wanted to see all the vaults and all the dates again, but when she tried to open the door again, it was locked. She tried and tried, but she could not get back in. That's when she knew it was time to leave the city of her birth.

As she was leaving the cemetery, she saw the same white woman with the same little boy again, but this time they were about to come into the cemetery. The woman smiled pleasantly again as she and her blue-eyed son passed.

"Excuse me, ma'am," Johnnie said. "If you're looking for your son's balloon, I tried to retrieve it for him, but I couldn't. If that's what you came back for, I think it's gone."

The woman smiled and said, "There must be some mistake. You must have us confused with someone else. My son has a red balloon, but it's at home."

Johnnie offered a frown of confusion and said, "Are you sure, ma'am?"

"I'm positive. We just got here, so you couldn't have seen us. You must have seen another boy with his mother who happened to have a red balloon, too."

Johnnie was positive that this was the same woman and boy. The boy had the same blue eyes. She said, "Sorry for the mistake, ma'am. I could have sworn I saw you two going into a tomb that had the name St. John on it."

"Now that's truly interesting," the woman said. "My name is Caroline St. John, and this is my son, Trevor. It must be some sort of coincidence. Or, perhaps you saw one of my relatives. Now if you'll excuse us, I'm taking Trevor to meet our ancestors."

"Sure. I'm sorry to have kept you."

And with that, Johnnie took a few more steps toward the gate. When she realized she didn't tell the woman the balloon was red, she turned around, looking for the mother and her son, but like the red balloon, they had vanished, too. She shook her head and wondered if she had imagined seeing the woman and her son earlier, the red balloon, the Baptiste tomb, and the names of her relatives. She was about to go back and see if she was losing her mind. She opened her purse, grabbed the list of names, and read them again. Then she smiled, got in her car, and left town.

Chapter 4

"Can you wait that long, pretty lady?"

As Johnnie drove away, she couldn't help thinking about what she had seen and why it had been hidden from her for so long. She began to question a number of things she'd seen and heard recently and over the course of seventeen years. *I wonder who paid for that incredibly expensive mausoleum. I know my granddad, Nathaniel Beauregard, couldn't have paid for it because he wouldn't have been alive. The dates on the marble facing started in the late 1790s. There's no way he could have known whoever that Prince person was or any of my other relatives. And even if he had known them, why would a white man who had hidden his black family for years, spend the kind of money it took to build an edifice like that with the expressed purpose of memorializing the very family he'd hidden? And if he didn't pay for it, who did? Could it have been Amir Jibril? If he was truly a prince, wouldn't he have plenty of money?*

What about Josephine? I wonder why mama rarely talked about her mother. Was it because they didn't get along either? Mama said that she fell in love with a man named Michael, Benny's father. Maybe Benny knows something about all of this. I wonder if he knew our grandmother. If so, he may know who the other people in the mausoleum were, too. And who paid for it. I wonder if any of those people in there knew the Beauregards. If one of my relatives paid for that mausoleum, they had to be rich or close to it. If they were rich, what happened to all our money? How did my mother and her mother end up selling themselves and their daughters? It just doesn't make any sense. I bet Benny knows something. I'll give him a call when I get gas on my way to East St. Louis.

Two and half hours later, she pulled into Jackson, Mississippi. She had been there lots of times with Lucas on his drug runs, but they had never actually done anything in Jackson. It was always an in and out kind of thing when they came to town, and it was always at night. The gas tank was almost empty when she turned into an Esso gas station. The station was all-white and looked like a small house with two garage doors. She looked at the pump. It read twenty-two cent a gallon. She thought of the forty-five dollars and change she had and began to consider just how dire her situation really was, wondering how she would get to East St. Louis if Marguerite's car broke down on the way. She opened her purse and counted her change which amounted to eighty-nine cents.

A clean-shaven middle-aged white man came out and said, "What can I do for you, pretty lady?"

Still looking in her purse, Johnnie said, "Fill it up for me, sir."

"Yes, ma'am."

When Johnnie heard a white man call her ma'am, she looked at him and smiled, glad to get a measure of respect from a white man, being a stranger in that town. She quickly realized that she was an adult now and that people saw her that way.

The man put the spout in her tank and locked it so that the fuel flowed by itself. Then, he went to the front of her car and popped the hood. He took the oil stick to her and said, "Ma'am, you're going to need a couple quarts of oil."

"Really?" Johnnie said, impatiently watching the numbers on the pump continuously climb past a dollar fifty.

"Yes. See?" He showed her the stick. "You're just about empty. When's the last time you changed the oil?"

Embarrassed, she looked away and said, "Never."

"Never? You had to have had it changed at some point, ma'am. This is a 1947 Oldsmobile. It's a really good car, ma'am, but I don't see you going seven years without changing the oil. Did you just buy this car or what?"

"It was my mother's," she said, listening to the numbers click as the price for the gasoline continued to climb past two dollars. She now had $43.89 left and the numbers on the pump were still clicking.

15

"I see, and she gave it to you?"

"Well, see, sir, it was bequeathed to me."

"Be—what?"

Johnnie smiled and said, "My mother was killed, and she left me the car, sir."

"I see. Well, how far ya goin'?"

"All the way to East St. Louis, sir."

"You want me to pull it into the garage and check it out for you. I'll see to it that you make it all the way. I'll check your brakes, tires, engine, radiator, battery, everything."

"Sir, how much is all that going to cost?"

"The name's Jimmy, ma'am. Why don't we wait and see what it's going to cost? It may not be as bad as you think."

The pump clicked off. She looked at the price. It read: $3.52. She quickly deducted the sum. She now had $42.37, and Jimmy hadn't even put the much-needed oil in yet. Deflated, she wondered what she was going to do. Her stomach rumbled. She was hungry. She hadn't eaten since yesterday morning when she had breakfast with her attorneys before the trial began.

"Jimmy," she said pleasantly and with a smile, hoping her beauty would rule the day as it always had, "Is there someplace a girl could get something to eat around here? A place that serves coloreds?"

"Yes, ma'am," he said. "I suggest you go over to Lucille's. It's about a block or so up the street. They serve the best pancakes you've ever had, if that suits ya fancy. Tell 'em Jimmy sent ya."

"Are they expensive, Jimmy?"

"Not at all. And they pile your plate up high with plenty of grub, too. I eat there all the time. Lucille don't mind seeing my white face and others in there. We all love Hank's cookin'."

"So a colored woman owns the place?"

"Yes, ma'am. She serves whoever can pay. We have a nice little arrangement. I fix her cars, and she feeds me pretty good. She don't know it, but I'm getting the better deal. I get to eat for free whenever I want. Three square meals a day, if I want."

"How often does she bring her cars in?"

Jimmy smiled and said, "I'm the best mechanic around. Ask anybody. I keep those cars in tiptop condition. They hardly ever breakdown. I check 'em over every month to make sure they're in good condition. It's a great deal."

"I see."

"I'll tell you what. Go on over to Lucille's, and I'll take a look at your car. We can settle up when you come back."

"How long will it take to check everything out? I'm in a hurry to get to East St. Louis."

"Got a boyfriend waitin' on ya, huh?"

Johnnie thought of Lucas, lowered her eyes, and said, "No. No boyfriend. I'm going to live with my father."

Jimmy frowned and said, "Going to live with your father? How old are you, ma'am?"

Johnnie smiled and said, "Now Jimmy, you know better than to ask a woman her age. We can be very vain about these things."

"I reckon."

"So, how long will it take to fix everything?"

"Oh, about an hour or so, I'd say, depending on what I find. Can you wait that long, pretty lady?"

"Jimmy, I don't have any other choice. But I gotta tell you up front, I don't have much money."

"I'll do the best I can as quick as I can for ya, ma'am, but I don't know what it's going to cost."

Chapter 5

"What can I get you, sugar?"

Sleigh bells rang out when Johnnie pushed open the glass door and walked into Lucille's Restaurant. Muddy Waters', "I'm Your Hoochie Coochie Man," filled her ears, along with numerous conversations, lots of laughter, and the sound of grease popping in a deep fryer. Lucille's looked like any other eatery that had hamburgers and hotdogs on the menu. Its booths were pressed tightly against the walls beneath large picture windows. Tables for two or four were strategically placed in the center of the black-and-white checkered floor. Red leather-covered swivel stools were anchored in front of the counter.

The restaurant was filled with Negro men and women with a few liberal-minded whites sprinkled in. Her immediate impression was that Lucille's felt like home, only not. It reminded her of what she had left in New Orleans, specifically, Walter Brickman's, but unlike his place, none of the faces that stared into hers were familiar. With the exception of Muddy Waters, everything stopped for a few seconds as the patrons stared at the beautiful stranger who had come to their town and found her way to the best café in it and stood at the entrance, looking at them as they looked at her, mesmerized by the stunning visual she offered. Her long, wavy black hair draped her slender shoulders, and she was still wearing the lavender-and-black skirt suit she had worn to her trial yesterday.

Other than Herbert Shields, a friend of Lucas' who sold marijuana for him, she was completely unknown in Jackson and being examined by Lucille's customers made her feel a little uncomfortable. She inhaled deeply, partly to gather herself, being the center of attention again, but mainly because the smell of delicious food lingered in the air. Her heels clicked loudly and in cadence to Muddy's smooth vocals, making it even more difficult not to stare as she made her way over to the empty booth she had spied from the entrance. She slid into her seat and looked at the collage of faces that were still staring at her through the reflection of the window. They had no idea that she was staring at them, too, watching the interaction of the men and women as they talked, frequently looking at her, subtly tilting their heads in her direction, which let her know that she was the topic of many ongoing conversations as the place was alive again with buzzing chatter now that she had taken a seat.

Over the years, she had gotten used to the attention she normally attracted from males and females wherever she went, especially from men, married or not. But now she was in a different place, another city. The attention felt different. Still looking at their reflections, she watched as the level of jealousy continued to rise and reveal itself on the faces of colored women who envied her beauty and manner of dress. What she found interesting was that the women who hated her not only didn't know her, but they had virtually no under-standing of the curse that walked side-by-side with beauty. What clearly ate at the women, she deduced, were the wanton looks their men wore and the fact that they couldn't keep their eyes off the beautiful stranger though they were clearly doing their best to appease the women they were sitting with. While she would never ever exchange her pretty for unpretty, pretty was often burdensome because it kept her from having female friends. Sadie Lane, who was much older and comfortable with her own pretty, was the only exception to the rule so far in her young life.

It was eleven-fifteen, making it eight-fifteen in San Francisco. . She decided to give Benny a call. She had also hoped he'd gotten his prize money from the fight he'd had in Las Vegas. If he had gotten his purse for the fight, she thought he could perhaps wire her the money she would need to not only fix any necessary repairs her car required, but a little extra to get the things a woman needed, like a fresh pair of panties, a bra, and other toiletries she needed. She could also use some more clothes and at least one pair of flat shoes.

"Hi, sweetie," a mid-range female voice said, "I'm Lucille, and this is my restaurant. What can I get you, sugar?"

Chapter 6

"So, y'all don' been to college, I see."

Johnnie swiveled her head to the left and looked at the woman who had offered to take her order. She began to size the woman up immediately, looking into her large, brown eyes, attempting to see if there was any jealousy in them, and if so, what level of jealously it was. The woman was tall, about five-feet-nine inches. She was endowed with rich-brown skin. She saw no wrinkles, no crow's feet, no gray hair—just alluring, flawless skin, covering high cheekbones. She was thick, but not heavy, and her friendly smile seemed genuine and inviting.

"Hi, Lucille, I'm Johnnie," she said and offered her hand. "I'm just passing through, and Jimmy over at the Esso filling station told me to tell you he had sent me over here and that you would take good care of me."

Lucille took her hand, shook it firmly, and said, "Jimmy told you that, sugar? Well, bless his heart."

"Yes, ma'am, he did. I hope he told me the truth."

"He did. I'll take good care of you. You can trust, Lucille. Now what'll ya have?"

"I'm not sure. What do you recommend?"

"Well, Hank, that's muh husband, his specialty is the fresh perch and fries. He's got his own homemade sauce. I just know you gon' love it. And since Jimmy sent y'all over here, I'll make sure Hank gives ya a double portion of everything, okay, sugar?"

"Thank you so much, Lucille. I haven't eaten since yesterday morning, and I'm starving. So a double portion would hit the spot, I'm sure. And may I have a glass of lemonade?"

Lucille wrote the order down and then said, "You haven't eaten since yesterday morning? Were you on a fast or something?"

Angrily, she said, "No, I'm from New Orleans, and them crackers down there burned down my house. I lost everything. I mean everything, including my life savings. I don't even have a change of underwear. All I have is the clothes on my back, and the shoes on my feet. They burned down our whole neighborhood. Everybody lost everything."

"Ahhhh, that's so sad, sugar. I'll bet you're short on money, too, huh?"

"Yes, ma'am, I am."

"What are you going to do? Do you need a job?"

"Well, I'm on my way to East St. Louis to live with my father for a while . . . just until I can find a job and get on my feet. But I had to stop for some gas and found out that I was out of oil, too. Jimmy's checking the car over for anything else that might be wrong with it."

"You're in a terrible fix, sugar. How 'bout I give you your meal on the house. Would that help?"

"It sure would, but I have enough to pay for the food, Lucille. I'm just concerned about what it's going to cost to fix my car. All I have is what I had in my purse when I left New Orleans—$45.89. But when I deduct the price of filling the tank and the oil and whatever else he finds wrong with my car, I'm afraid I'll be whipped out. So the cost of your husband's delicious specialty is inconsequential."

"It's what, sugar?"

Johnnie smiled and said, "What I meant to say was that the cost of the meal is of little importance, ma'am. It's a much smaller issue when I look at the big picture."

"So, y'all don' been to college, I see."

Johnnie laughed out loud, remembering that there was a time when she used to say that when she didn't understand words. But she had grown significantly since those days, and now her vocabulary was such that she now knew that people were viewing her the way she viewed Sadie.

"No, ma'am, I've never been to college, but I hope to attend someday."

"Well, I'll put your order in. Is there anyone you can call to help you? Can you call your father and tell him about your situation? If he can't help, you can work here until you have enough money to get to East St. Louis."

"That's so sweet of you, Lucille. The folk here in Jackson are so nice and friendly, but I don't want to put you out like that."

"You won't be putting me out at all. In fact, you'll be helping me out, sugar."

"Huh? How would I be helping you?"

"When word gets out that Lucille don' hired herself a beautiful new waitress, all the men folk will be runnin' to get a peek at you. That's what everybody's talking about right now. And see, sugar, when the men folk come runnin', the women folk won't be far behind 'cause they'll have to keep an eye on their men and get a look at you so they can see what they have to compete with. So, ya see . . . you won't be putting me out at all. Give it some thought."

"Okay, I will. Let me call my brother in San Francisco. He'll know what to do. I'm sure he has some money that I can borrow. He's a prize fighter."

"Oh, really? My Hank used to box when he was in the Army. He listens to the fights on the radio all the time. I bet Hank knows who your brother is if he's any good."

"He might. He just had a fight in Las Vegas a little while ago."

"Really? What's your brother's name?"

"Benny Wise."

Lucille swiveled her head to the left and said, "Hey, Hank?"

"Yeah, sweet thang, what is it?"

"Ya ever hear of a fighter named, Benny Wise?"

Chapter 7

"Boy, that musta been somethin', huh?"

A short man with wide shoulders and hard muscles came out of the kitchen. He had a square chin, and he wore a wide smile underneath a thick mustache. His white chef's smock was stained with a variety of foods. He said, "You mean the Bay City Terror? That Benny Wise?"

Lucille looked at Johnnie. "Is that what they call him, sugar?"

"Uh-huh, and they call him The Body Snatcher, too."

Skeptical, Lucille said, "What other names do they have for him, Hank?"

"They call 'em The Body Snatcher because he don' knocked so many niggas out with body shots! Benny be breakin' ribs and shit. I'd hate tuh fight his ass. Nigga be pissin' blood for a week after a few rounds with him."

Excited, she said, "Ya don't say. Well . . . don't look now, but The Body Snatcher's sister is about to have lunch right here in Lucille's! Her name's Johnnie."

Hank fast walked over, wiped his hands on his smock, and shook Johnnie's hand rapidly. "Is Benny Wise really your brother?"

Johnnie suddenly felt like a celebrity. She smiled and said, "Yes, he is."

"I won two hundred dollars when he fought Sweetwater. I knew Benny was gon' kick that nigga's ass."

"I was at the fight," Johnnie said.

"Really? In Las Vegas?"

"Yes, sir."

"What was that like?"

"It was hot mostly, but they have cool air conditioners in the casinos and hotels."

"Boy, that musta been somethin', huh?"

"Yes, sir. It was."

"Well, I tell you what . . . any sister of The Bay City Terror is a friend of mine. You're food is on the house." He took the ticket out of Lucille's hand. "I'll go cook this up for you right away, sweetie." He walked off, shaking his head. "Um, um, um. The Body Snatcher's sister is right here in Jackson, in our restaurant no less! Yes, Lawd, its gon' be a good day today!"

Now all of a sudden people were looking at Johnnie differently, like she was royalty, like she was Dorothy Dandridge or somebody—all because of her brother's growing fame. Even women who only minutes ago had looked at her like they'd like nothing more than to take a straight razor to her face were now smiling and nodding, like they approved of their men gawking at her, even though she could have been lying. But there were a few women who still looked down their noses at her, like they knew she was all talk.

Johnnie looked at Lucille and said, "I think I'll try and get Benny on the phone. Hopefully, he'll have plenty of money left. If so, I'll get him to send me some of it."

"You go right ahead, sugar, and give him a call. Your food'll be ready by the time you finish."

Johnnie walked to the back of the restaurant, her heels clicking loudly as every eye in the place followed her. Women looked her up and down as she passed while men were trying to see as much of her figure as they could. The men were unable to stop their heads from swiveling as she passed them, leaning at angles, focusing exclusively on her hind parts. It was as if she was somehow emitting a heavy dose of her pheromones and the dogs, disguised as men, were on the verge of howling as they inhaled her inebriating scent. When she entered the booth, she looked out into the restaurant. She saw lots of men looking at each other, nodding vigorously and smiling, apparently letting each other know what they thought of the beautiful stranger without saying a single word.

Chapter 8

"Is that what you're telling me, Brenda?"

Johnnie closed the phone booth door and sat down. She looked at Hank who she found quite gregarious as he was still smiling from ear to ear, no doubt thinking of her famous brother and that his sister was in a restaurant that he and his wife owned. She remembered that Lucille had said that Hank had been in the Army, and that made her think of Lucas again. Spontaneously, the courtroom scene played out in her mind. The look of betrayal on Lucas' face surfaced, and she felt the full weight of her guilt. She wanted to talk to him. She wanted to explain although she didn't have an explanation, none that she thought would change his mind anyway. She exhaled hard, wishing she could go back in time and change it all, knowing it was impossible.

She exhaled hard again and dialed zero. Before long, she heard a nasal female voice say, "Operator."

"Operator, I'd like to make a long distance call to San Francisco, collect."

"Sure. What number?"

She gave her the number.

"Whom shall I say is calling?"

"Johnnie Wise."

"One moment, please."

The phone started ringing.

"Hello."

Johnnie recognized the voice right away. It was her sister-in-law, Brenda.

"This is the long distance operator, ma'am. I have a collect call for anyone from Johnnie Wise. Will you accept the charges?"

"I sure will."

"Go ahead, ma'am," the operator said.

"Johnnie? Where you been, girl? Benny's been worried sick since he read in the newspapers that you were on trial for murder. We've called the house a million times and no one ever answered. Now it's not ringing at all, like it's disconnected or something."

"I didn't answer because they put me in jail, Brenda."

"What? They kept you in jail the whole time? They wouldn't let you out on bail or anything?"

"They let me out, Brenda, but I was in jail for a whole day when Sheriff Tate arrested me. Most of the time, I was with my lawyers, trying to figure out why the police thought I killed Sharon Trudeau, but I had nothing to do with her murder. Nothing! Ever since y'all left, all kinds of things have happened to me. Ethel Beauregard tried to kill me twice."

"What?"

"And that ain't all, Brenda. A boy that liked me raped me when he found out they put my boyfriend in jail."

"Raped? Oh my God. Did they catch him?"

"Well, sort of."

"What do you mean, sort of? Did they catch him or not?"

"I mean someone did. He's dead. Someone beat him to death."

"Uh-huh. So it was your mobster friend, huh? What's his name, Napoleon something or other?"

"Brenda, I don't know who did what to whom in either case, and I don't want to know. I just know that I didn't do anything to anybody, period."

"Uh-huh. Okay, so what happened with your friend Lucas? What's he in jail for?"

"Selling drugs. But he's out now. It's been one thing after another. All kinds of stuff has been happening to me."

"Well, are you alright?"

"Yeah, I'm okay, but at the same time, I'm in a little bit of trouble. Is Benny there? Them crackers have lost their minds. They burned Ashland Estates down. They tried to burn it down over the summer, but the white men who had black women living there put a stop to it. It was different this time though. They kept their plans quiet and they waited until my trial started, knowing the courthouse would be full of Negroes from Sable and Baroque Parishes."

"What?"

"Yeah. And Brenda, all my money burned up in the fire. I had two hundred thousand dollars."

Alarmed, she said, "Two hundred thousand dollars? Where'd you get that kind of money, Johnnie?"

"Investments. I had two hundred and fifty, but I gave my friend, Sadie, fifty thousand so she could start a new life, too. Detective Meade made Sadie have sex with him. He told her that if she didn't, he was going to arrest Santino Mancini for raping me when he knew all along that Santino had nothing to do with it."

"Who is Santino Mancini, and what did he have to do with any of it?"

"Santino is the father of Sadie's kids."

"Uh-huh. Don't tell me this was a white man, Johnnie."

"Uh-huh."

"And he's married?"

"Uh-huh."

"So, Sadie has a history of lying down with married men, huh?"

"What do you mean, Brenda?"

"Don't play dumb, Johnnie," she snapped. "I know she was sleeping with Benny when we were there. And you know it, too. If Benny wasn't your brother, you would have told me what was going on behind my back."

Silence.

Brenda inhaled deeply before saying, "Nevertheless, she didn't deserve to be raped and neither did you."

"Brenda, Detective Meade didn't rape her. She did it to keep Santino out of jail."

"It's the same thing, Johnnie! She didn't want to do it, so it was rape plain and simple. The fact that she was coerced into doing it only reveals the deep depravity of Detective Meade and Santino Mancini."

Silence.

"Well, Benny caught a plane out to New Orleans this morning," Brenda continued. "He would have come sooner, but he blew almost all

27

the money he won in the Las Vegas fight. He had to borrow some money to come down there to see about you."

"What? He lost all the money?"

"He didn't come home after the fight. He stayed in Las Vegas for two whole weeks. Only God knows what he was doing."

"What did he make on the fight?"

"I don't know for sure, but it had to be at least six thousand dollars . . . maybe ten thousand."

"He lost that much money, Brenda? How?"

"He said he lost it gambling, but you know your brother. I bet he spent it all up on women and drinking and his good-for-nothing friends who always disappear whenever he runs out of money."

"I wonder what really happened."

"Me, too. So, where are you?"

"I'm in Jackson, Mississippi now."

"What are you doing in Jackson?"

"I'm on my way to East St. Louis, but I ran out of gas and found out that I didn't have any oil in the car. The mechanic is checking it out right now. I'm in a restaurant called Lucille's."

"Well, I haven't heard from Benny. I hope he's alright. You know how them whites can be down there."

"Yeah, especially since they burned down Ashland Estates. The good thing is Lucas got outta town before they burned it down."

"Yeah, he was in jail. I never thought I'd say jail was a safe place for a black man, but thank God he wasn't there. Who knows what might've happened."

"He's out now. He's on his way to Fort Jackson in South Carolina. They let him out early."

"When did he decide to join the Army?"

"The judge offered him a deal, and he had to take it. Otherwise, he was looking at fifteen years."

"Fifteen years? What was he selling, heroin?"

"Yeah."

"What? Where would he get heroin?"

"They set him up, Brenda. It's a big mess."

"Um. I guess it is. So, what are you going to do for money?"

"Depending on what it's going to cost to fix my car, I'll probably have to stay here and work. I was just offered a job by the lady who owns the place. I guess I can be a waitress for a little while. I'm about to call my father and see if he can help me."

"Okay, if he can't, let me know, and I'll send you what I have. I've been putting away a little extra because Benny don' blew most of ours, and he just got it. Every dime he wins in that ring, he spends like its water, and there'll always be plenty of it. But one day it's going to run out, and where we gon' be then? It's a shame what the devil is doin' to ya brother. Can you talk to him and get him to straighten himself up? We've got a baby now, Johnnie. Jericho needs to see a strong black man he can look up to. It's time to stop this wild livin' before we lose everything we have, too."

"Brenda, no. You keep your money. God knows you can't depend on my brother to do right with the money. I can't take your last when I just got offered a job right here in Jackson. I'ma hav'ta work for a living, and I might as well start now. As for talking to my brother, I don't know what good that's going to do. I'm not making any excuses for him, but I don't think the man knows any better. I think it's just in him to do the things he does. All I can tell you is to keep praying for him."

"Will you let me know what you decide, so I can let Benny know when he comes home?"

"Yeah. No problem, Brenda. Before I let you go, can you ask Benny if he knows anything about the Baptiste mausoleum in the cemetery?"

"The Baptiste mausoleum?"

"Yeah, I was there earlier this morning before I left. I wanted to say my goodbyes to my mother. It was the strangest thing, Brenda."

"What do you mean?"

Johnnie hesitated for a moment before saying, "I think I saw some angels."

"Angels? What makes you think that?"

"I saw this white woman and this little boy with these blue eyes going into a crypt. The boy had this red balloon. I didn't think much of it at first, ya know? But then, the boy let go of the balloon and it kept floating and stopped at the Baptiste mausoleum. I went in and looked at the vaults and saw what I believe was our ancestors, going all the way back to . . . wait a minute . . . I wrote the names down and put it in my purse."

"Aren't those crypts locked?"

"Yes. That's the strange thing. This one was unlocked. Ah, here's the list. Josephine Baptiste was the only name I recognized, but there was this woman named Lauren Renee Bouvier-Baptiste, but underneath that name was another name in parenthesis: Ibo Atikah Mustafa. Sounds African, doesn't it?"

"Uh-huh. But you say the other names were Baptiste, and the woman's last name was Bouvier-Baptiste?"

"That's what was on the vault. And another thing . . . she was in a double vault with a man named Prince Amir Bashir Jibril."

"What's strange about that? He was obviously her husband."

"I don't think he was her husband."

"Why not?"

"Well, his name was Jibril. Her name was Bouvier-Baptiste."

"And you say they were in a double vault together?"

"Yes, and there was another man next to them. A man named Rokk Baptiste. It said that he was the husband of Lauren. I guess they had a bunch of kids or something because all the other names are Baptiste."

"What were the dates on the vaults?"

"Funny you should mention that, Brenda. I had forgotten to write down the dates when I left. But I thought it would be important, so I tried to go back in and the door was locked all of a sudden."

"What?"

"Yeah. I couldn't get back in. It was like I was lead there so I could see these names, but I only had one shot at it. And then, when I left the cemetery, I saw the same white woman and the same boy coming through the gates. I figured they had come back to try and find the boy's balloon. I stopped them and told them I had tried to find it and couldn't. I was just trying to save them some time, ya know?"

"Uh-huh."

"Anyway, the woman said it couldn't have been them because they had just gotten there. She also said that the boy had a red balloon, but it was at home. They didn't bring it with them. So, I said I thought I saw you and your son going into the St. John crypt. The woman agreed that they were going there, but she maintained that she and her son had just gotten there. I left it alone and walked on, right—"

"Uh-huh."

30

"But the thing bothered me, so I turned around, and they were gone, too. Just like the balloon. It was like they disappeared, too. So when I got into my car, I realized that the woman had mentioned a red balloon, but I never said the balloon was red."

"You didn't? Are you sure you never told her the balloon was red?"

"I'm positive, Brenda."

"Um. I think you're right."

"So, you think they were angels, too?"

"Well . . . that's an incredible story to me. You know I believe in the Lord, so I don't have a problem believing that it happened. Apparently, the Lord wanted you to know what was in that mausoleum."

"Why? I mean, everybody in it is dead. That's why they're there, right?"

"I'm not sure why, Johnnie, but I'd say you just had an encounter with the celestial."

"If that's true . . . why me, Brenda?" she asked.

"Why any of them, Johnnie," Brenda said. "Why any of the chosen Old Testament men? Why Mary the mother of Jesus? Why Elizabeth, Zachariah, the high priest's wife, who was too old to have children? Why Hannah? Why Deborah the prophetess and judge? Why Ruth the Moabitess?"

Hank knocked on the phone booth door. "Your perch and fries are ready, Johnnie. Come get it while it's hot."

Johnnie put up her index finger and nodded. "You sure do know the scriptures, Brenda."

"Hmph! I have to know 'em to stay married to your brother. It's the only way. Otherwise, I would have been gone years ago, Johnnie."

"I can believe that. You married into a family of whores, Brenda. And when you do that, you can expect us to do what we do."

"I didn't mean you, Johnnie."

"I know you didn't, Brenda, but the truth is the truth. I'm starting to realize that more and more." At that instant, she remembered the words of Richard Goode, who had been killed at her behest. *You can't change what you are!* "Maybe someday I'll be more like you, Brenda."

"You can be more like me now, Johnnie. You have free will."

"Do I? I wonder about that especially when things happen to me like what happened to me today. Like my mother selling me. Like Billy Logan raping me. Like Ethel Beauregard trying to kill me, and she was family. I mean stuff like that happens more than seeing celestial beings, if in fact that's what they were, ya know? I mean, God lets too many bad things happen to me."

"How much of it is your own doing, Johnnie? God's got a law. It's called sowing and reaping. And there's no escaping it. Most folk are only worried about reaping what they've sown because they've sown far more bad things than good. But the law of sowing and reaping works equally well when we do right, Johnnie. Make doing right a habit and the law of sowing and reaping will work on your behalf, too."

"So you're saying it's my fault I got raped, Brenda? It's my fault my mother sold me to Earl Shamus? Is that what you're telling me, Brenda?"

"No, I'm only saying that you should consider your ways, Johnnie. Consider the things you've done and leave what others have done to you in God's hands."

"Okay, Brenda. I gotta go. The cook said my food is ready. I'll talk to you later."

Brenda was saying something more about God when Johnnie forcefully hung up the phone.

Chapter 9

"Have you spoken to him?"

"Shake, Rattle, and Roll" filled the restaurant when Johnnie returned to her booth. She was breathing heavily as the anger she was feeling threatened to boil over. She took a sip of her ice cold lemonade, hoping it would help cool her off and gain a better perspective, but it wasn't working. The more she tried not to think about Brenda's comments, the more they invaded her mind. Her eyes narrowed as she replayed the conversation she'd had with her sister-in-law. She liked Brenda, and in some ways she felt sorry for her because she married a man who wasn't husband material. She was a woman of God who had wanted a man walking in lockstep with the devil. In other words, she found the devil very appealing; so appealing, in fact, that she married him. Now she wished she hadn't.

Nevertheless, it irritated her that Brenda was suggesting that she had brought much of what had happened to her on herself. She looked out the window. She could still see the reflection of the restaurant patrons. One woman in particular had been watching her like she wanted to hurt or humiliate her in some way. She was hoping the woman would come over to her booth and say something, so she could give her a piece of her mind. She turned around and locked eyes with the woman to let her know that she knew she was staring at her and that if she wanted to try something, she was ready for whatever happened, whether it was a verbal exchange, or heated words that led to a physical altercation. She stared back, but eventually, the woman looked away. Only then did Johnnie stop staring at her.

Hank brought her perch and fries to the booth and set them on the table. "I see how the women are looking at you, Johnnie. Don't worry about them. They're the ones with the problem, not you."

"Thank you, Hank. I really needed to hear that. I get so sick of having to deal with women who have a problem with themselves."

"How's ya lemonade? Is it cold enough for you?"

Johnnie took another sip and said, "Yes. Thanks!"

Hank pulled out a bottle of hot sauce from his smock pocket and sat it on the table. "Enjoy!"

She looked at Hank, forced an uncomfortable smile, and said, "I'm sure I will, Hank. Thanks for bringing it out. Where's Lucille?"

"Oh, yeah. I knew I was forgetting something. Lucille told me to tell you she was going to talk to Jimmy to make sure he takes care of your car for you. And by the way, she told me what happened in New Orleans, and that you don't have much money. So, how did things work out with your brother?"

"I didn't get to speak with him. I talked to my sister-in-law. She told me he took a plane to New Orleans this morning. For all I know he might be there right now."

"So, do you think he'll be able to help you out? We've got a Western Union right up the street."

"I don't think so. My brother and his wife have problems of their own. They've got a baby now. His name is Jericho. From what Brenda just told me, they need all the money they can get right now. If he was the champ, I guess I would ask for his help, but he's just a contender, still trying to get a title shot."

"I see. So, you're going to accept Lucille's offer to work for us then?"

"It depends on what it's going to cost to pay for my car. East St. Louis is only about five or six more hours away. I'm sure my daddy will take me in."

"Have you spoken to him?"

"Actually I haven't. I was going to call him, but you said my food was ready, and I didn't want it to get cold. My daddy can be long-winded sometimes."

"I see. Well, if it don't work out with your father, consider workin' for us. And if your car cost more to fix than you can afford, we'll pay for it, and you can pay us back by working here for a week or so. Who knows, you might get to like it and stay right here in Jackson. Good-lookin' girl like you won't have no trouble findin' a man. That's fo' sho'."

Johnnie smiled. "Thanks, Hank. I might just have to take you up on your offer.

"I hope so. We'd love to have you around. Anyway, go ahead and get started on your food and let me know how you like it."

"I sure will, Hank. And thanks again."

Chapter 10

"Is Florence on her way, Johnnie?"

Johnnie picked up the ketchup and squirted some on her fries. Then she sprinkled some salt on them and put one into her mouth. "Mmm," she heard herself saying. Then, she picked up a piece of fish, broke it in half, and dipped it in the homemade tarter sauce. She opened the hot sauce and put a few drops on the perch to determine which way tasted best. She thought both ways tasted wonderful, but she couldn't fully enjoy her meal because she kept thinking about what Brenda had insinuated.

I'm not perfect, and I never claimed to be. Brenda's being ridiculous. I can't help that I'm beautiful. I didn't ask for this face. And I certainly didn't ask for this body. God gave them to me, and He had to know that by making me look like this, every man who saw me was going to want me. I had nothing to do with that. I never asked to be born in this evil, crazy world either. I didn't ask for a jealous mother who would sell me to some child molester. But somehow all of this is supposed to be my fault. All I did was accept the money Earl gave me. I didn't ask him for the money. He put it on my pillow. And truth be told, I didn't spend a dime of it for almost a year, I think.

I didn't tell Meredith Shamus to offer me all that money. She did that on her own after she had Tony Hatcher follow her husband. If she couldn't control her husband, that was her problem, not mine. And I also didn't have anything to do with Napoleon Bentley's lust. That was on him. I didn't want to get involved with him until after he blackmailed me that first time. After that, then I wanted to. So, if he didn't blackmail me, I would have never done it with him.

The one thing I do take full responsibility for is my tryst with Martin Winters. I did lead the man on when I realized he couldn't take his eyes of my breasts, but I just wanted to learn about the stock market. He didn't have to act like he didn't know who I was. He could have told the truth in that courtroom. He didn't have to lie. He knew I was looking at life if they found me guilty. And what about all the good deeds I've done?

I've been good most of my life. I didn't go around wrecking peoples lives. I tried to do right. And I was a good girlfriend to Lucas even though I did a few things behind his back. And he did some things behind mine, but I never stopped loving him. I never stopped being good to him either. Besides all that, I treated people right even though they did me wrong. I had just given Sadie fifty thousand dollars. I sang in the choir for years. I never gave my mother any trouble. I was a very obedient child. I was an above average student, too. That's gotta count for something! And if I've sown good seeds by doing those things, where's my reward for that? And since I had been a good girl for fifteen years, where's my reward for all those years? I mean if Brenda's right, I oughta have fifteen years of good coming my way. Where are they? I've only been bad for two years. So we're talking fifteen years of goodness versus two years of badness. Where's the reaping for all the good?

She took another sip of her lemonade, and when she set the glass down, her mind was suddenly transported to that Thanksgiving Day when the Beauregard men were killed. Hovering above the room like an angel, she watched it all play out again in slow motion, and she was powerless to stop it, as if the questions she was asking were now being answered. She saw her uncle, Eric Beauregard. He had his hands around her throat, choking her. His eyes were bulging out of his head it seemed as he tightened his powerful grip. As she looked at herself, she could tell that she was at the cutting edge of death. Her eyes had rolled so far up into her head that she could no longer see the pupils.

She watched as Ethel took the gun out of her favorite son's hand after he had blown his brains out. Then, slowly, methodically, she put the gun to the back of Eric's head and blew his blood and brains all over her. Eric released his death grip and fell to the floor. She watched herself gasping for air, heaving heavily, desperate to get some air in her lungs. While she was sucking in as much oxygen as she could get, she saw Ethel, who was only three or four feet away, point the same gun in her face. Ethel's face was covered with wicked determination. The scowl she wore looked so intense and so malevolent that it was as if she had been possessed by a demon before pulling the trigger.

The bullet came out so slowly that she could see it moving through the air. She watched the Johnnie in the room close her eyes, accepting her death as if it was rushing up to her for an autograph. The bullet continued moving in slow motion moving toward her forehead, but just before it entered her head, it disappeared. A half a second later, the bullet reappeared behind her head and entered the wall. She watched the Johnnie in the room open her eyes, turn around, and look at the hole in the wall. That's when she realized that she had reaped for the good years. The next vision transported her to her home in Ashland Estates just a few hours ago when she was holding the only page of the Bible that didn't burn in the fire. It read: I will never leave you nor forsake you.

"Johnnie?" Lucille said. "Are you okay?"

"Huh," she said, looking at Lucille, as she came out of the fog of spontaneous remembrance. "What did you say?"

"I said are you okay?"

"Uh, yeah. Yeah, I'm okay."

"Looked like you were gone for a minute there."

"No, I was just in deep thought. Anyway, what did Jimmy say about my car."

"Well, I've got good news and bad news. What do you want first? The good or the bad?"

"Give me the bad first," Johnnie said and resumed eating her perch and fries. "How much is it going to cost me?"

"The cost ain't the bad news. We can cover the cost with no problem."

The problem is you need a new radiator and four new tires. He says the tires are bald. Jimmy thinks those are the original tires. Are they?"

Johnnie shook her head and hunched her shoulders. "They probably are."

38

"Well, he's got four tires, but he doesn't have a radiator. It's going to take at least three weeks to get one shipped here from Michigan. He said it may take as long as four or five weeks."

"So, I'm stuck here?"

"For a little while. But if staying here bothers you that much, I'll buy you a bus ticket to East St. Louis. And then when the car's ready, you can come back and get it. It's up to you."

"Let me call my father. Maybe he can come and get me. I hate to put you out like this, Lucille."

"I told you it wouldn't be a problem. You can work here if you like."

"But I would need a place to stay, which is going to cost money. Plus, I need clothes, underwear, and other personal things, if you know what I mean."

"Is Florence on her way, Johnnie?"

Johnnie frowned and said, "Florence?"

Lucille smiled. "Yeah, Flo, the sister that visits once a month. We all have a sister by that name."

Johnnie smiled. "Yeah, Lucille. Sister Flo could be here any day now. Is there a store near here where I can pick up the things a woman needs to feel fresh?"

"Finish your food, call your father, and then come into the kitchen. I think I have something to tide you over until we can go shopping, okay?"

"Thanks, Lucille."

Chapter 11

"Don't be late."

"Looks like I'll be staying in Jackson for a few weeks," Johnnie said after entering the kitchen where Hank and Lucille were a half hour later.

"Your father couldn't help you out either, huh?" Hank said.

"Either I wrote down the wrong number or his phone is disconnected," Johnnie said. She exhaled hard and continued, "When do you want me to start, and how much is the pay?"

"You can start tomorrow morning," Lucille said enthusiastically. "And the pay is something we can discuss on the way to Woolworth's. We gotta take you shoppin' to get you all the things a woman needs. Can you handle it while we're gone, Hank?"

"When are you leaving? After the noon rush, right?" Hank said.

Lucille frowned and exhaled hard. "You can't handle it by yourself?"

"No. I'm not takin' that many orders, cook the food, and serve the people. I do the cookin'. You take the orders, and you serve. That's our arrangement."

"Well, couldn't you do it all just this one time, Hank? Please."

"No. I'm not gon' be runnin' 'round this restaurant like a chicken with its head cut off while y'all havin' a good ol' time shoppin' at Woolies. You ain't foolin' me. You just wanna take advantage of the January sale, is all."

"Ah, Hank . . . please. It's just a couple hours."

"Fine, but you need to be back in this restaurant by four-forty-five, no later than five o'clock."

"Maybe we can make it back by five-thirty."

"If you're not back here by five sharp, I'm lockin' the doors and puttin' up the closed sign. Whatever shoppin' y'all need to do, don't have to get done in one day. She just needs a few things. She can get the rest later."

"Okay, Hank," Johnnie said. "In the meantime, I need a place to stay. Is there a hotel here where coloreds can stay?"

"Come on," Lucille said. "I'll take you over to the Clementine. It's only about a mile or so from here. Maybe two."

"Johnnie," Hank said. "The Clementine is on Wilshire. That's only six blocks up Blakeslee Street. Turn left on Wilshire and go another half a mile or so and you can't miss it. But you might wanna go on over to Woolworth's first. It's right around the corner from the Esso fillin' station where your car is. That way you don't have to do so much walkin' in them heels."

"Why can't I at least take her to the Clementine and get her checked in and then over to Woolies? It'll only take a few minutes, no more than a half an hour. I'll be right back. I promise."

Hank's eyes narrowed before he said, "Because I know you, Lucille. A half hour will turn into an hour, and an hour will turn into two hours. In the meantime, customers will be complainin' to me. She'll be just fine by herself. She don' drove all the way from New Orleans by herself. Surely, she can find a store and a hotel without yo' help, Lucille." He looked at Johnnie and said, "Can't you, Johnnie? You don't need Lucille with you, do you?"

Johnnie looked at Lucille, and then at Hank and said, "I don't want to cause you two any problems. I can handle everything on my own. You're right, Hank. I made it this far without any help. I can find the hotel, and the store on my own. I just appreciate the help and the job."

"Good, good," Hank said. "I'll call Mr. Saunders and tell him you're coming, and he'll put whatever you buy on our tab. Mr. Saunders'll know what you need, and you can get a few other items, too."

"Okay, thanks."

"Are you a church-going girl?" Hank asked.

Johnnie couldn't remember that last time she was inside a church. But she said, "Yes. I sing in the choir and play piano."

"You don't say," Lucille said. "Well, you might need to find four or five dresses that you can wear to church just in case you decide to go."

"I want both of you to know that I appreciate everything, and I won't let you down. I'll be here in the morning ready to work."

"Just remember, you can spend as much as you like," Hank said, "but it all comes out of your paycheck at the end of the week. So, if you're in a hurry to get to East St. Louis any time soon, I suggest you spend as little as possible. But, if you think you're going to be here a while, spend accordingly. You're welcome to stay as long as you like."

"What time does Woolworth's close?"

"Eight o'clock," Lucille said.

"Okay. I think I'll do just like you said, Hank. I'll head over to Woolworth's and then check into the Clementine." She yawned and stretched. "I've been up all night, and I'm starting to get sleepy. What time should I be here in the morning?"

"We open at six sharp, but we need you here by five-thirty," Lucille said.

"Don't be late," Hank said. "Closing time is eight o'clock. So, ya got a long day ahead ya."

Johnnie yawned again. "Okay. I'll see you both at five-thirty then."

Chapter 12

I'll make a deal with you, Lord.

Johnnie had gotten a block and half away from Lucille's when she realized that she never found out how much it was going to cost to fix her car. Hank had said that Woolworth's was around the corner from the Esso filling station. She had decided to stop in and find out. Jimmy had told her the total price including gas, oil, tires, and a new radiator would cost $67.45. While she didn't show it, she was thoroughly disappointed because not only would that sum absorb everything she had, but she would still owe nearly $20.00. Even after paying the whole amount, she would still need more money to buy gas and other items. However, the way Jimmy looked at her, she got the feeling that the cost to fix her car would be erased if she were willing to compromise herself again. As her heels clicked loudly against the pavement, she began to consider her position and the choices before her. That's when she realized that she might be stuck in Jackson for a very long time, given the fact that her father's phone was disconnected and Benny had blown all of his prize money.

One more compromise won't kill me. I mean, I guess I could give him what I know he wants, and then I'll at least keep the money I have in my purse. It's strange how life can turn on you. Yesterday morning, I was rich. I had more money than I would ever need. Twenty-four hours later, I'm as broke as my mother was. Maybe this is what she was facing. Maybe Josephine was facing the same situation. Maybe something happened to them, and all they had was their bodies. Maybe they felt exactly how I'm feeling right now. Maybe they didn't want to do it either, but they felt they had to do it or starve to death. If it weren't for Lucille and Hank, maybe I would have offered myself to Jimmy. I don't know.

Oh, my God! What if mama was broke, and she had to sell me? What if that was the only choice she thought she had? And if I'm even considering compromising myself now, and I have a job waiting for me with good people helping me, what if mama didn't have anybody? What if it was just her . . . all alone? What if she talked to her friends and the Beauregards and they shunned her? What if a job didn't fall into her lap the way it fell into mine? What if Earl Shamus offered her the easy way out when she was at her lowest? She probably thought about what Josephine did to her and maybe then she understood her mother the way I'm starting to understand her. What if mama was just like me when she was my age? What if she used to go to church and sing in the choir, too? What if she was a virgin when Josephine sold her, too? Maybe that's why she made me go to church. When she fell in love with Benny's daddy and that didn't work out the way she thought it would, she probably lost all hope of living a better life. Maybe she thought that living in Sable Parish was as good as it was ever going to get for her and that made it easy to sell herself. That's why she tried to stop me from falling in love with Lucas. She didn't want me to end up like her.

Is this what happened to all the women in my family? Is that what mama meant when she said, "All women go through this?" Have we all been in impossible situations and found it easier to give into depravity rather than to do what's right? Here I am seriously considering compromising myself again. Here I am telling myself that one more compromise won't kill me when in fact it might. It just might. If I compromise myself now, when and where will it end? If I compromise myself now, will I end up like my mother or worse? I'm in a new town where no one knows me. No one knows my past. Who knows, I could start all over here. I could start off fresh. Everyone deserves a second chance. I sure do, and I need a second chance. I've made up my mind. I'm not going to compromise myself again. I'm going to take the hard path this time. I might have to work for Lucille for a year to pay her back, but I will not compromise myself. I'm through with that. Who knows, maybe Hank is right. Maybe I can find myself a good man here.

I guess Jackson's as good a place as any. Maybe Jackson can be my new home. Besides, I'm stuck here for a while. Let's see how things play out. Maybe I can start school here. If I work hard, I can rebuild my investment portfolio and get rich again. If Job lost everything in one day and got everything back, maybe I can, too. She looked to the sky. *I'll make a deal with you, Lord. Send me a good man to help me turn my life around, and I promise I'll do right. I know I'm not perfect, so he doesn't have to be perfect either. Just make him a good man with a good heart and good job, kinda like Boaz from the book of Ruth, and that'll be enough for me.*

Chapter 13

Reality

Lucas Matthews had been driven by a searing cauldron of rage, pain, and disappointment all rolled into one when he left the courtroom where his sweetheart stood trial for murder. Not only was Johnnie Wise the love his life, he loved her more than life itself. While his fierce love for her was stronger than the bond that exists between a woman and the child she bore, he was incredibly weak when it came to Marla Bentley, who had given him the succulent fruit that patiently waited for him in the midst of her hidden secret garden. Marla was his living, breathing Delilah—the dragon he chased, but could never apprehend because not only was the dragon a larger than life myth, but blindness of heart was the grand prize the pursuit gave way to. He, therefore, could not see nor know how his relationship with Marla would affect his future with nearly every woman of interest that crossed his path.

As he was riding the bus to Ashland Estates, the last conversation he'd had with Marla at the Red River Motel played out again in his mind. In short, she had told him that Johnnie was not who he thought she was and that she was no different than any other human being when it came to desiring physical love. She went on to tell him that they were two of a kind, trapped by their own inability to say no to the same temptations that all men and women face. That truth had been far too much for his fragile ego, but when he heard that salient truth for himself, in a court of law from a witness duly sworn to tell the truth, the whole truth, and nothing but the truth so help her God, he snapped.

After setting Johnnie's house ablaze, he drove his 1941 Chevy over to the apartment building he had lived in to get a few of his things. The Army pretty much owned him for the next three years, and he wasn't sure when he would return to the Crescent City, if ever. The place of his birth offered far too many painful memories. It was January 1954, and Mardi Gras was rapidly approaching. He hated the idea of not being there, in the French Quarter, being in the midst of it, watching the gala pageantry of it all—the parties, the food, the influx of tourists, and all the money he had planned to make selling heroin during the celebration.

He went into the building, clumped up the stairs two by two, entered his home for the last time, and headed over to the closet. He looked at all the suits and shoes he had purchased, trying to decide what he wanted to keep and what he'd leave for the next man who rented the apartment. Napoleon Bentley had been paying the young man of eighteen years a hundred dollars a week; a substantial sum at the time, all of which he deposited into his bank account.

Still looking in a closet full of suits, ties, shoes, and other accessories, he couldn't decide what to take, but he knew he couldn't take it all nor did he want to. Nearly all of his suits reminded him of what appeared to be better times when he and Johnnie were connected to the Syndicate through Bubbles, Napoleon's Negro lieutenant. Lucas and Johnnie were living the life that American couples dreamed of. They each had more money than they needed or knew what to do with. More important than their money was the great love they had for each other. Both of them were prisoners of passion, and they thought their love and their money would never diminish.

He looked at the black suit Johnnie had bought him for her mother's funeral, and vivid images of that day flooded his mind. The suit took him back to what happened before the ceremony began, when the men of Baroque and Sable Parrish's wanted to kill white men, women, and children for what Klan Leader, Richard Goode, had done to Marguerite. He decided to leave the suit. It reminded him too much of the woman he still loved, even though he was still very much wounded by her latest betrayal.

He touched the blue suit, which reminded him of the night he and Johnnie went to see the play *No Way Out* at the Sepia Theatre. Some people didn't want the play to come to town because of its provocative theme and because it ended with a destructive race riot, much like the riot the city had experienced when Richard Goode was murdered. After the play he and Johnnie had made sweet love. It was so good, so right, so perfect for them both. Then, he reached out for the gray suit, and when he touched it, Marla Bentley came to mind.

He remembered a phone call he had gotten from Johnnie while he and Marla were in bed together. He had told Marla to never come back to his apartment, but he didn't mean it. Sex with Marla was good, too, but he knew it had to stop. His life was on the line. To make matters worse, Napoleon forced him to drive Marla to Shreveport to get a new car. On the way back, she seduced him again, promising him it would be the last time they met for a lustful romp. Out of control, he had pulled over on a deserted highway and went up in her again. He couldn't take that outfit either.

He continued perusing his suits. All but three had a story all its own. He took them along with the accessories and neatly laid them out in a suitcase. Then, he put in a few pairs of slacks, shirts, underwear, socks, cologne, and toiletries. After that, he went into his bedroom and took seven thousand dollars he had earned from selling heroin and marijuana. The money was in his mattress along with his former stock portfolio. *One day I'll reinvest. Maybe there's a brokerage in South Carolina,* he thought. Having taken everything of value, he left his apartment and headed over to the bank, where he drew out eighteen hundred more dollars, closed the account, and left New Orleans.

Chapter 14

Welcome to Fort Jackson

After he was a couple hundred miles east of New Orleans, Lucas pulled into a gas station and told the attendant to fill the tank. The filling station reminded him of Preston Leonard. Preston was the young man Napoleon had used to get him involved in the drug trafficking business. While he waited, he wondered how he let it all happen to him and to Johnnie. He reexamined everything while he was in prison, and now he would do it again, hoping to not only avoid the pitiful mistakes of the past, but to somehow acquire wisdom and turn himself into something he would one day be proud of.

He thought about Preston Leonard and wondered what happened to him. Bubbles had told him that he was going to kill Preston. He wondered if Napoleon would go that far to cover his tracks. He also wondered if he wanted Johnnie badly enough to kill an innocent man to get her. If he would kill Preston, why didn't he just kill him instead of constructing a complex plot to first, put him in jail for three months and second, get him to accept a three-year stint in the Army? He paid the station attendant, and then drove all night to Columbia, South Carolina, stopping and refueling two more times.

He was about to enter Fort Jackson at about five in the morning, oblivious to the fact that the fire in Ashland Estates was just starting to burn itself out. He wasn't required to go on active duty for another two weeks, and his original plan was to spend fourteen days with his sweetheart. But after hearing Meredith Shamus testify that Johnnie had been having a relationship with her former stockbroker,

Martin Winters, he knew his relationship with her was over. On the ten-hour drive, he thought mostly about Johnnie, but he also thought about Marla Bentley.

The conversation he'd had with Marla kept replaying as he was powerless to stop it. She didn't deserve what she'd gotten, he knew, but it was too late. As much as he wanted to, he couldn't raise her from the dead. He had loved Johnnie with all of his heart, and he couldn't believe how wrong he had been about her. He told himself he would never ever put that much faith and trust in any woman again. It was just too painful when the ugly truth surfaced. And in Johnnie's case, the ugly truth had surfaced three times with three different white men. The thing that bothered him most was that Marla had been right all along. He told himself that if he had listened to Marla the first time, or at the very least the second time she'd told him what kind of girl Johnnie was, maybe he wouldn't have accidentally killed her.

But he didn't listen, and now a woman who had been honest with him, a woman who wanted to join him in Columbia, South Carolina, and then in Germany, was dead and gone. And the memory of both women would be forever seared into his conscience. He promised himself that he would make it up to Marla by finishing what she started in him. He was going to educate himself. He was going to take her pearls of wisdom and make her proud of him. In his heart, he knew she had forgiven him because she, too, knew that he didn't mean to do it.

During the thirty days he spent at Angola Prison, he read the books Marla sent every day. It was a struggle at first, but he worked hard to overcome his dyslexia by reading daily and markedly improved his reading speed and skill. He even improved his vocabulary and penmanship. Clancy "One Punch" Brown, an unschooled, but wise fellow prisoner, had taught him that prison was for fools. He promised himself that he would never be a fool again and that decision would keep him out of cement cages for the rest of his life. He was going to pull himself up by his own bootstraps.

He stopped at the guard shack where a couple of uniformed guards were on duty. He pulled up to the black-and-white striped gate and said, "I'm Lucas Matthews. I was told to come here for basic combat training."

The guard grabbed a clipboard and looked it over. He looked at Lucas and said, "You must be in some kinda hurry, boy."

With a New York accent, the other guard said, "You're not supposed to be here for another two weeks."

He didn't like being called boy, and he certainly didn't like being talked down to, especially by a white man with a Yankee accent, but he didn't have anywhere to go. He was new in town, and he certainly had enough money for a hotel, but there was no guarantee the Columbia, South Carolina crackers were any different than Louisiana crackers. He was supposed to be at Fort Jackson. They had to let him in if he kept his cool and let the guards get away with calling him boy. He said, "I know, sir, but I was told I could come early if I wanted."

"They can't process you in yet," the New Yorker said. "Nothing's open until 7:30, boy. But I suppose you could go on over to the Mess Hall and put some SOS in ya belly."

Lucas frowned. "SOS? What's that?"

"Shit on a shingle, boy. Don't you know nuthin'?" the New Yorker said.

Lucas frowned again, wondering if part of the training meant that's what he had to eat. "Is that what I have to eat for initiation or what?"

The guards looked at each other and laughed themselves silly. "Yeah, boy. We eat it every mornin'. It'll put hair on ya chest."

Chapter 15

"What's your name, son?"

Following the directions he had been given by the guards, Lucas drove over to the Mess Hall. He dreaded eating SOS, but he figured that if everybody had to do it, particularly those two white boys he'd just met, he would, too, thinking it must make soldiers strong or something. Otherwise why would they eat it? He parked his car and went into the Mess Hall. The place was packed with uniformed soldiers. The Mess Hall reminded him of a much larger version of Walter Brickman's restaurant in Baroque Parish. It, too, was probably full of people, he thought. As far as he could tell, he was the only person wearing civilian clothes. It seemed as if every soldier in the place had to eyeball him before they continued their meals or conversations.

He didn't know what to do, so he watched to see how things worked. He saw four soldiers come in, all of them with stripes on their sleeves. He followed them at a distance, having decided to do whatever they did. He watched them grab a tray and silverware. Then, they disappeared around a corner. He did the same thing. He kept hearing all the soldiers ordering shit on a shingle. That's when he realized that it was all true. The guards had told him they ate SOS every day. He didn't know why, but he figured all the soldiers must love it. The strange thing was that the SOS didn't smell the way he thought it would, like a stable or something. Another thing he didn't get was that there seemed to be plenty of bacon, eggs, potatoes, sausage, pancakes, toast, and oatmeal in addition to the SOS. Yet four soldiers in a row, when asked what they wanted, said, "Shit on a shingle."

The cook looked at him and said, "What'll it be, newbie?"

Lucas looked around, thinking the cook was talking to someone else.

"Yeah, you, newbie," the cook said.

"Oh, I didn't know you was talkin' to me," Lucas said. "My name is—"

"I don't give a shit, newbie. All I care about is the order. Now what'll it be?"

Lucas looked at the other soldiers, exhaled deliberately, and said, "Shit on a shingle, I guess." Then, he eyed the cook and said, "And if you talk to me like that again, I'm gonna come over there and turn you into whatcha servin'. I'm from *New Orleans.*"

The cook stared at him for a long few seconds, trying to ascertain the seriousness of the threat. He looked at the other soldiers in line. They were waiting to see what the cook was going to say. The cook figured the best thing to do was to defuse the situation and give the kid what he ordered. The kid obviously didn't know he couldn't threaten soldiers at Fort Jackson, but he would soon find out.

"What's your name, soldier?" the cook asked.

"I'm not a soldier yet. I just got here a little while ago, but I can see right now that I'ma have tuh kick some ass before the day is finished tuh get some respect around here."

The cook stared at him again and said, "What's your name, son?"

"My name is Lucas Matthews, and don't call me son. I kick ass, and I take names, especially when a man calls me son and he's not my father. Now . . . do we understand each other, or do I hav'ta explain it to ya on the other side of this counter?"

The cook looked at the soldiers standing there, watching it all, listening to the civilian threaten a fellow soldier, waiting for him to make a move on the cook so they could stomp his ears together. He hoped that one of them would put the kid in his place, but they didn't. When he realized that none of the sergeants were going to say or do anything about the upstart, he grabbed a couple pieces of toast with tongs, placed them on a plate, and then poured a couple helpings of a grayish mixture over the toast and handed it to Lucas.

The cook then looked at the soldier who had come in behind Lucas and said, "What'll it be?"

Chapter 16

"First Lieutenant."

Lucas followed a couple soldiers to the milk and orange juice stand and did what they did, grabbing one of each. Then, he looked around for a place to sit, while the buzz of numerous conversations filled his ears. There were only two open tables left, and the four soldiers with stripes on their sleeves who had just come in had taken one of those. He saw a woman sitting at a table alone. She acknowledged him with a warm smile. She was wearing an all-white nurse's uniform with thin silver bars on her shoulders. He didn't think there would be women at the post. And he certainly didn't think there would be a good-looking Negro woman with a perfect smile sitting in the Mess Hall.

He figured she must be married to one of the soldiers or something. He looked at her left hand. No ring. He smiled and sat at the table near her, thinking she must have a boyfriend or something. She was far too beautiful not to be with someone. Then, he noticed that she, too, was eating SOS, and she seemed to love it. He looked around the room and nearly all the soldiers were eating the SOS heartily, but most of them also had the other food the cook served, too.

He looked at his plate, swallowed hard, and then looked at the soldiers and the woman again. He smelled the SOS. There was no foul odor, no stink of any kind. He figured the cook must have put some kind of seasoning in it to get rid of the smell. That was a good thing, he thought. He picked up his fork, determined to dig in like all the other brave soldiers in the room, but he couldn't do it. It was shit on a shingle no matter how it smelled. That wasn't something he thought he should eat no matter what. He figured he'd get back in line and get the bacon and eggs. Just as he was about to get up, he saw the woman looking at him, staring actually. She smiled and nodded slightly, offering him a friendly greeting. He returned her salutation in like manner and was about to get up again when she said, "Is there something wrong with your food, newbie?"

He was thinking, *newbie?* He locked eyes with her. "My name is Lucas Matthews, not newbie. And I'm from New Orleans."

The woman picked up her tray and moved over to his table. "Mind if I join you, newbie?"

"I don't mind. But again . . . my name is still Lucas Matthews, not newbie. You need to get that straight before you say anything else and definitely before you sit down."

The woman put her tray on the table, sat down, smiled and said. "So you're a tough guy, huh?"

"Tough as nails. You gotta be when you collect money for the mafia. I had to kick a lotta ass and I take names back home."

"Uh-huh," she said, smiling, figuring he was making it up to impress her. "Well, I like tough-as-nails guys. I like to soften 'em up."

Lucas locked eyes with her, full of glee, glad she had opened the door for him to use one of his fancy new words on her like he'd heard Johnnie do many times. "Is that a sexual overture?" He had more fancy words for her if the conversation lasted long enough.

The woman's smile vanished. "It most certainly was not, Mr. Matthews."

"Hmph! Then, you couldn't soften me up if you lived to be a hundred."

"I couldn't, huh? And was that a double entendre?"

Lucas had no idea what she was asking, but he was determined not to let her know that. He decided to hide the fact that he didn't understand by answering the first question only. "No, you couldn't soften me up. So don't waste your time."

"It's my time to waste, is it not?"

"You talk real fancy. Where you from, girl?"

"I'll be glad to tell you where I'm from, *boy*. But, first tell me what's wrong with your food."

Lucas was about to say, "It's shit on a shingle," but he was in the presence of a very pretty lady who apparently had high moral standards, so instead he said, "It's SOS. That's why, and I don't see how you can eat it, especially being a woman and all. But I guess everybody in the Army has to eat it, huh? It's like a rite of passage or something, right?"

"What do you mean by that?"

Lucas frowned. "Don't you know what SOS is? It doesn't smell bad or anything, but don't you know what you're eatin'?"

"Yes. I'm eating creamed beef over toast."

Frowning, Lucas said, "Creamed beef over toast?"

"Yeah. What did you think it was?"

"The white boys at the gate told me it was shit on a shingle. I heard the other soldiers ordering it, too."

The woman laughed from her belly and said, "That's why I called you newbie. You're green. You're wet behind the ears. You don't know the ropes yet."

"So they were just kidding with me then, huh?"

"Yes and no. It *is* called SOS, but it's just an acronym, silly. This must be your first day, huh?"

"Yeah."

She offered him her hand. "I'm Cassandra Perry, First Lieutenant."

"First Lieutenant, huh?"

She laughed again. "Yeah . . . as opposed to Second Lieutenant, newbie."

"The name's *Lucas Matthews.* I'm from New Orleans."

"If newbie bothers you, wait until you meet your Drill Sergeant, and you better hope it isn't Limitless Cornsilk. He saw action in World War II and The Korean War. He's a mean SOB. That's son of a bitch, by the way." She laughed a little.

"I know what SOB means, Miss Perry. I'm from New Orleans."

"Uh, that's Lieutenant . . . First Lieutenant, Perry, Lucas Matthews from New Orleans. I earned these bars, newbie. And you damn well better respect 'em."

"So, you're a tough girl, huh?"

She laughed and said, "Yeah . . . tough as nails. I kick ass and I take names."

"So, look at us . . . a couple of tough customers, having SOS together, but with no sexual overtures to speak of."

She looked into his eyes and said, "So . . . you knew what SOB meant, but you didn't know what SOS was, huh? Is that what you're telling me, newbie?"

"The name's still Lucas Matthews, and I'm still from New Orleans, girl. When you gon' get that through that pretty little head of yours?"

"Proud to be from the Crescent City, aren't we?"

"Yeah. Where you from?"

"I'm originally from, Des Moines, Iowa, but I lived in Daytona Beach, Florida for about four years before I went to Tuskegee, established in—"

"1881 by Booker T. Washington."

"So . . . he reads, huh?"

"I do."

"Really? So, what have you read lately?"

"I read a couple books while I was in prison."

"Titles and authors please."

"I read Booker T. Washington's autobiography and a book about blacks in the military by William Wells Brown."

"So . . . being in the military was a lifelong ambition of yours?"

"No. Playing football was, but I had trouble reading, and that made taking tests a crapshoot. So, I got into collecting money for the mafia."

"You're serious?"

"I am."

"Hmm . . . so what made you join the Army?"

"It wasn't up to me. I was selling drugs, and the cops busted me. It turns out that it was my boss who set the whole thing up because he wanted my girlfriend."

Disappointed, Lieutenant Perry said, "So you were serious about being in prison?"

"Yeah, why wouldn't I be? Who would joke about a thing like that?"

"And you collected for the mafia? You were serious about that, too?"

"And I was very serious about kicking ass and taking names, too. I got paid to do that and more."

She silently stared at him for a moment, letting the fact that she was having breakfast with a man who admitted to being in prison for selling drugs settle in. Then, something else he had said occurred to her. "Oh . . . so you have a girl waiting for you in the Crescent City, huh?"

"No, we're through. Far as I know, she's with my former boss right now. I'm free to see who I please. What about you, Lieutenant? You married?"

She shook her head.

"Got a boyfriend?"

She shook her head again.

"So, you're free, too?"

"I am."

"Pretty thang like you? How can that be?"

"I wouldn't put out, so he broke it off."

"Is he still on post? I would hate to havta kick his ass because I made you mine."

"My, my, my . . . aren't we awfully presumptuous?"

"I'm new in town. Why don't you show me around tonight? They gotta movie theatre in this town?"

"They do, but you don't even know if I like movies, Mr. Matthews."

He stared at her for a moment or two and said, "Do you like movies, Cassandra?"

"Soldier, did I tell you it was okay to call me by my first name?"

"No."

"No . . . what?"

"No, you didn't tell me I could call you by your first name, *Cassandra*."

"That's no, ma'am when addressing a female officer," she said, smiling.

Lucas smiled and said, "What do you expect from a *newbie*?"

"Well, I declare, Mr. Matthews," she said with a pseudo-southern drawl. "I guess y'all do have a sense of humor inside y'all after all. I think I've taken a likening to you, sir."

"You have, have you?"

"I have indeed. Finish your shit on a shingle. When you've finished every mouthwatering forkful, I'll escort you to reception and they can get your paperwork started. Have you been sworn in yet?"

"No."

"We'll take of that, and then we'll get you a bunk in the barracks before I go to work."

"Thanks a bunch. I was wondering where I was going to sleep. I'm a couple weeks early."

"Do you wanna get started, or do you wanna wait two whole weeks?"

"Might as well start now. No point in waiting. The sooner I get done, the sooner I can get outta here."

"What's the rush? You just met me, and you're ready to run off already?"

"I've got plans, Lieutenant."

"Oh?"

"Yeah, girl. As soon as I'm done with basic combat training, I'm going over to Germany to play football for Colonel Strong. Ever heard of him?"

"Can't say I have."

"Yeah, well, he pulled some strings and got me outta that hell-hole they called a prison in Angola."

"So, how did you get here? Please tell me you drove."

"I sure did. Drove all night long."

"In a hurry to leave, huh?"

"Nothing left for me there now."

"So, you loved her, huh?"

"Still do. Nothing I can do about it either. If I could, believe me I would."

"Thanks for being so honest with me, Mr. Matthews. That's a rarity these days. I wish more men would just tell the truth no matter how bad it may be."

"I've got nothing to hide. I am who I am. I did what I did. I paid the price for selling heroin, and I paid the price for loving a girl who loved money more than she loved me. But I left all that behind me, and I'm looking forward to getting over to Germany and playin' some football again."

"You're a good man, Lucas Matthews from New Orleans. I can tell."

"Can you now?"

"Yes, I can. What kind of movies do you like?"

"Anything that has some action in it. I like to see some fightin' and stuff. I love pirate movies and stuff like that, too. What do you like?"

"Romance."

"Is that a sexual overture, Lieutenant?"

She laughed. "No, Mr. Matthews, it isn't."

"Oh, okay. I was just checking."

"So . . . can you drop me off at the hospital after we get you settled in?"

"Sure, but I'm wondering if Columbia has a stock brokerage firm. I've got some money I need to invest. But a bank will do until I find one. Do you know of any in town?"

"No brokerages that I know of, but I can take you to a bank when I get off work."

"No, I need to get to a bank right away."

"How much money do you have, Mr. Matthews?"

"Don't worry about that," he said, smiling. "Just show me where the bank is, and I'll handle the rest."

"No problem. If you pick me up from work, we can have a bite to eat at this nice little restaurant called, The Blue Diamond. They served the best catfish and collard greens and cornbread you've ever tasted."

"Hmph! Better than New Orleans?"

"Uh-huh."

"Let me ask you something, *Lieutenant* Perry."

"Go ahead."

"Have you ever been to New Orleans?"

"I can't say I have, Lucas Matthews."

"Uh-huh. And uh, who's supposed to pay for this little soiree?"

"I can pay my own way, Mr. Matthews. I know how hard money is to come by."

"It truly is. I had to do time for what I have, and I don't plan on blowin' it all on you, and it has nothing to do with you not putting out.

I've got plans, Lieutenant, and those plans don't include spending all my loot on anyone, not even my self, understand?"

"I do, Mr. Matthews."

"But tonight is on me. It's the least I can do for all the help you're going to provide."

"Not to mention my bubbly personality, my pleasant conversation, my expertise on SOS, and other culinary delights you've yet to devour."

Lucas smiled and said, "I think I like you, Lieutenant Perry. In fact, I'm sure of it."

"I guess that means we can see *Rear Window,* huh?"

"*Rear Window?* I guess so, if that's what you want. So who's in it? A pretty girl, I hope."

"Grace Kelly and Jimmy Stewart. Do you think she's pretty?"

"I'll have to let you know after the show, but I'm sure that no matter how pretty she is, you'll be the most beautiful woman in the theatre tonight."

"Uh-huh. It's official."

"What's official?"

"I'm likin' you a lot."

"Same here. So, uh, what's it about?"

"I don't know for sure, but it's an Alfred Hitchcock movie so you know its going to be suspenseful. I hope you like mysteries."

"You obviously like them."

"Yeah . . . is it a date?"

"It is."

Chapter 17

"I get so sick of you niggers . . ."

Feeling good about the decision she had just made, a smile emerged. Just then, she saw F. W. Woolworth's across the street. Several white women pushing baby strollers were going in and coming out. Woolworth's seemed to be a lively place. She walked across the street and pushed the door open. The store was abuzz with spirited chatter. The smell of fresh popped popcorn demanded her attention. A broad smile crept across her face when she realized that Hank was right not to let Lucille leave the restaurant.

She realized he was right about the January sale, too, when she saw a sign that read: 40% OFF MOST ITEMS. She knew she could shop all day, given the vast selection of goods and having a deep discount didn't hurt either. Still smiling, she stopped at the candy counter and saw an assortment of chocolates, peppermints, licorice, jellybeans, orange slice candy, cashews, pistachios, peanuts, macadamia nuts, sunflower seeds, and gums, all of which could be purchased according to weight. She wanted to buy a little of everything, but forced herself to move on, remembering that she was on a very tight budget.

As she browsed the merchandise, she thought deeply about what she was going to do. She was no longer feeling lost with nowhere to go and no one to turn to. For all she knew, her father had moved into another house, which meant the address she had was probably no good. With no valid phone number and no way to know for sure where her father was, it didn't make sense to continue on to East St. Louis. It also didn't make any sense to go back to New Orleans. There was nothing there for her either. While she was looking at a pair of shoes, she saw a young man. From the back, he reminded her of Herbert Shields, Lucas's friend who played football for Jackson College. She thought it would be nice to know someone in town, someone her own age. She walked over to see if it was Shields, but it wasn't. She turned around to go back to the shoe department and bumped into a white woman.

The woman looked at her watch and said, "I've been watching you for the last twenty-six minutes and fifteen and half seconds. If you're not going to buy anything, you're going to have to leave the premises."

The memory of being molested by the store detective back in New Orleans surfaced. She also remembered Marla Bentley. Not that the woman looked anything like Marla, who was drop dead gorgeous. All Johnnie saw was another white female who was trying to steal something like Marla, Cynthia, and Sharon Trudeau had. Three different white women sure, but they all had the same attitude as far as she was concerned. But Marla Bentley was the worst of them all because she had stolen a piece of Lucas, which was the equivalent of stealing a piece of her heart. Now another white woman was attempting to rob her of what little dignity she had left.

As all the negative incidents with white men and women flashed in her mind, Johnnie glared at the woman and said, "But *I am* going to buy something, ma'am. I just haven't made up my mind yet. And I'm quite sure there are a number of white women that have been here longer than the twenty-six minutes and fifteen and half seconds you say you've been watching me. And not only are they still here, they haven't purchased anything either. Now . . . I was told to ask for Mr. Saunders. Is he here?"

"Mr. Saunders is a busy man. He doesn't have time for the likes of you. I get so sick of you niggers coming in here and stealing us blind."

Chapter 18

"You're not married, are you, Linda?"

Johnnie took a deep breath and blew it out hard before saying anything, while at the same time, looking around the store to see who was watching, attempting to avoid a destructive scene that would get her kicked out of the store before she bought anything. But she was incredibly frustrated and very tired. To be accused of stealing when she had never stolen anything in her life was insulting, particularly since she had been rich. The irony of it all was that white folks had always stolen from her, starting with her virginity, which was far more precious than any dollar amount assigned to it. A white woman had stolen her money. A white woman had stolen her man, too. All of this was clinging to her at that moment and it took all of the strength she had to keep from slugging the woman. She conveniently forgot about the white men she had stolen from white women.

"I'm not here to steal, *Mrs. Woolworth*. I have money. Besides, Mr. Saunders is expecting me, ma'am. Hank over at Lucille's called and told him I was coming over to pick up a few items and that he was to put it on Lucille's tab. But if he didn't call, as I said, *I have money*."

"I'm not Mrs. Woolworth. I'm Linda Schumacher. And—"

"What? You mean you aren't the owner of this establishment?" Johnnie said, driving home her point, knowing full well she wasn't Mrs. Woolworth. "Are you the store detective then?"

"No. I'm just—"

"Then maybe you should just do your job. I'm a customer, and I expect to be treated like one."

Cackled laughter burst forth before Linda Schumacher said, "Let's see your money! Otherwise, you'll have to leave immediately."

Again, she remembered what it was like to not only have plenty of money, but to have the full weight of Napoleon Bentley getting her the kind of respect from white folks that other Negroes only dreamed of getting. She felt weakened, reduced in stature, and insignificant all at the same time. She now knew that a loss of money equaled a loss of power. She also realized that while being in a new town offered a new start, it also meant she had to build a new reputation. Her pride told her to walk out the store at that very instant, but her sensibilities quickly vetoed the notion of a boycott as she knew that being broke and Negro meant that she had to endure a certain level of indignity from white folks who were often in a worse financial situation than she.

Having been thoroughly cowed, Johnnie angrily snatched open her purse. When she pulled out her last forty-five dollars, a folded piece of paper fell to the floor. Without opening the paper, she instantly knew that it was the five-thousand-dollar check bequeathed by Nathaniel Beauregard, her white grandfather. She showed the woman the cash, and then she picked up the folded piece of paper and handed it to her.

"What's this?" the woman asked.

It's a note from the principal you dumb bitch! "Open it," Johnnie said softly, trying to control her anger and frustration.

When the woman opened it, her eyes nearly bulged out of her head. "Five thousand dollars?" she blurted out without thinking. "It would take me seven years to make that much money."

Sarcastically, Johnnie said, "Seven years, huh?"

"It says this check belongs to Johnnie Wise. Are you Johnnie Wise?"

Totally frustrated, Johnnie rolled her eyes and said, "Who the hell else would I be you simpleminded Caucasoid?"

"What did you say?"

"Nothing. May I have my check please?"

"Not so fast."

"You're not married, are you, Linda?"

"Why no, I'm not."

"Hmm, I wonder why."

After that comment, Linda Schumacher's face twisted into an ugly scowl. She said, "We'll have to check this out with Mr. Saunders."

Chapter 19

"You hear me, Johnnie?"

Johnnie snatched the check out of her hand and was thinking, *You do that, Simple Simon.* After that final exchange with Linda Schumacher, Johnnie searched for a phone booth, smiling and speaking to everyone she saw. Now that she had found a life preserver in the form of money, she was filled with energy. Having money in her purse had a unique way of relieving stress that was better than many of her sexual encounters. Money made financial worries disappear. Sex made problems insignificant as long as the participants were in the moment, but when the moment was over, not only were the problems still there, so was the stress. She needed to tell her sister-in-law the good news. She wanted Brenda to know that even though Benny had blown his prize-fighting purse, they were not destitute, not yet anyway. They still had one card left in the Seven-card Stud game aptly titled, *Life.* She knew she had a new lease on life, and if she handled her money properly, in a few years, much of her fortune would be restored.

She had allowed Martin Winters to use her body in exchange for financial knowledge. The time had come to put that hard-earned knowledge to use. While she searched for the phone booth she was about to enter, she enthusiastically planned the rest of her day. The first step to rebuilding her fortune was to purchase a Wall Street Journal, which had been in existence since July 1889. Martin explained that the paper had been founded by newspaperman, Charles Henry Dow, who later sold it to Clarence Walker Barrow in 1901. Martin further explained that she needed to read the Journal regularly and had started a subscription for her. First, she would finish shopping. Second, she planned to go to the bank to open a savings account. Third, she planned to call New York, where the Journal was printed, and give them her new address immediately after checking into the Clementine Hotel.

A few minutes later, she was on the phone again with Brenda, telling her what happened. "Anyway, Brenda, the main reason I called back is because I have great news!"

"Really? What happened?"

"I found my inheritance check!"

"Your inheritance check?"

"Yeah. Benny has one, too. Has he called?"

"No. Not yet. Now what is this about an inheritance check?"

"Remember when I was telling you about my grandmother, Josephine?"

"Yes."

"Well, I met Nathaniel last Thanksgiving at the Beauregard house."

"And . . . what were you doing there?"

"I was working for them."

"You were what?"

"Sadie told me Ethel needed a housekeeper, so I took the job when she offered it to me. She had no idea who I was. She just wanted a Negro woman to clean her house for her. Probably made her feel like it was the good ol' days when we worked for nothing. I just wanted to meet them. I heard mama talk about our white relatives from time to time and how well they lived and how unfair it was for us to live a life of squalor. Anyway, he died on Thanksgiving. Later on, I found out that our grandfather loved us enough to put us in his will. He left me and Benny five thousand dollars each. I had so much on my mind that I completely forgot about the check."

"Really?"

"Yeah. So Benny might as well collect his share while he's there. When he calls, tell him to find an attorney named Parker Jamison. I'm sure he has an office somewhere in the financial district. He should be easy to find. He's supposed to be the best lawyer in New Orleans. Anyway, Jamison has a check for Benny, too. And Brenda, tell him to bring it straight home to you. Tell him that if he doesn't, you're going to leave him and take baby Jericho with you. That'll get his attention."

"I sure will."

"Make sure you tell him I'm in Jackson, Mississippi. I'll be staying at the Clementine Hotel for a while. I haven't checked in yet, so I don't know the number. But just in case he calls before I get there, tell him he can call and leave me a message. I'm sure the operator can find the number."

"Okay, but did you ever get a hold of your father?"

"Unfortunately, I haven't."

"Why not? Did you at least try to call him? I think he'd love to hear from you since your mother and that good-for-nothing Sheriff ran him outta town and made it impossible for him to see you."

"I called, but his line is either disconnected, or he's moved, or I wrote down the wrong number. I'm not sure which. So I'm just gonna stay here in Jackson for a while."

"Why don't you come out to San Francisco? I'd love to have you here, Johnnie. And I know Benny would too."

"I can't afford to come out there now, Brenda."

"But I thought you said you have five thousand dollars."

"I do, but I can't spend that money."

"Why not?"

"I've got to reinvest what little I have left. I can't just spend it. I have to work for a living now. I suggest you do the same thing with yours. Invest at least half the money. It's a way to make some real money."

"I don't think I can do that, Johnnie. We need money now. I can't put money into stocks and wait for it to grow. We have a child now, and I already told you about your brothers' spending habits."

"I understand, Brenda. I do. When things ever change for the better, let me know, and I'll try to help you, if I can. But listen . . . I've gotta go. Here comes that simple-ass white woman again with a white man. Maybe it's me, but it seems to be so much easier dealing with a white man than a white woman. You know what I mean, Brenda?"

"Yes. But you keep your temper in check. Let the Lord lead you, and you'll be just fine even down there in Jackson, Mississippi. You hear me, Johnnie? Keep your temper."

"Okay, I will, Brenda. They're almost here. Gotta go. Bye!"

Chapter 20

"Then, let's do business, sir?"

Still watching Linda and the white man she had hoped would be Mr. Saunders coming toward the phone booth, Johnnie assessed their faces. Linda was smiling from ear to ear, like she was expecting to witness her destruction up close and personal. As far as Johnnie was concerned, it was personal for Linda, and it was certainly personal for her. She was sick of white women. As she looked into the gleeful face of her immediate nemesis, she remembered that her mother had told her two years ago that black women and white women didn't get along. Given this latest incursion, and the string of similar incidents, she knew Marguerite was right again.

Focusing on the man now, she knew he was the weaker of the two because his eyes would betray him. She knew that once he got a gander at her, he would be hers to do with as she pleased. Her history with white men had proven this. She decided to be the aggressor this time. She was going to take charge from the opening bell. She pulled the handle on the door, stepped out of the phone booth, offered a phony friendly smile, and said, "You must be Mr. Saunders. Did you get a call from Lucille's husband, Hank?"

"I did. But there's a matter of a five thousand dollar check. I'd like to see it, if I may."

Johnnie looked into his eyes, which told her that Mr. Saunders was like any other man who found her attractive. He could be easily handled if she smiled and talked sensibly, unlike Linda Schumacher, who coveted power. "May I ask why you need to see my check, sir?"

"Well, we just want to be sure it isn't stolen," Mr. Saunders said.

Johnnie took a deep breath and said, "Mr. Saunders, you've spoken to Hank. Does he have an account here, or doesn't he? If he doesn't, I'll gladly leave your store. But if he does, and he told you to let me put a few items on his account, I'm not sure why you're asking me about money that belongs to me exclusively."

"I see, and I fully understand your trepidation, but five thousand dollars is a lot of money."

"Come now, Mr. Saunders. Let's not mince words. You mean five thousand dollars is a lot of money for a woman, particularly a Negro woman, right? Lord knows, Linda here, who works for you couldn't possibly have that much money, and she's a white woman. You're skeptical because I'm a Negress. If I were white and male, you and I both know we would not be having this conversation. And so does Linda."

Saunders looked at Linda, who was now looking at the floor, then back at Johnnie. He offered an insincere laugh before saying, "I just want to be sure the money's yours and not one of our customers who may not yet realize they've lost it. I'm sure an obviously educated and articulate woman like you can understand my concern. Besides, it doesn't make any sense that Hank would tell me you're down on your luck if you have a five thousand dollar check, does it?"

Still looking into his eyes, taking advantage of her beauty and his weakness, she smiled again and said, "Point taken. May I ask you a question, Mr. Saunders?"

"By all means ask. I'm as anxious to resolve this as you are."

"When you spoke to Hank, did he happen to say who was coming over here to get a few items?"

"Yes. A woman named Johnnie Wise."

"And did he describe me to you?"

"He did."

"And do I resemble his description, sir?"

"You do."

She looked at Linda. "Mrs. Schumacher, what name did you see on the check?"

"It's *Miss* Schumacher."

"That's right," Johnnie said, smiling. "You've never had a husband. Only God knows why. A charming woman like you should have the men folk lined up around the corner. But could you please tell us what name was on the check?"

Looking at the floor, she offered a barely audible, "Johnnie Wise."

Johnnie looked at Mr. Saunders. "You see, sir. There's no reason to see my check. Hank said a woman fitting my description would be here to buy clothes and shoes and a few other items. I have a check with the name of the person who was supposed to come here and according to you, I fit the description you were given. Come now, sir, you're an intelligent man. Does it make sense to you that another Negress fitting the description you were given would somehow assume my identity, sir?"

"Actually it doesn't, but—"

"Then, let's do business, sir."

"Absolutely! The customer's always right! Right this way, Miss Wise. And just so there are no hard feelings about this little incident, I'll give you my twenty-percent discount."

"Are you offering me your personal discount in addition to the January sale discount?"

"I am. Again . . . the customer's always right!"

"Thank you, sir," she said and wrapped her arm around his. Then, she glared at Linda as they strolled down the aisle together. "I was wondering, Mr. Saunders," Johnnie continued, knowing they were being heavily scrutinized by shocked white female eyes, "if you could tell me what kind of shoes I'll need to work at Lucille's. I'm going to be their new waitress for a while."

"I'll be happy to show you our fine selection of shoes, Miss Wise."

"And Mr. Saunders, can you tell me where the bank is so I can open an account."

"Certainly. Now, since you're going to be on your feet for long periods of time, I'm going to suggest you buy the same shoes I see nurses buying. They're right over here in our vast shoe department."

Chapter 21

A New Lease on Life

It had been a long night in Ashland Estates, a longer drive away from New Orleans, and an even longer day in Jackson, given that Johnnie hadn't had any sleep, and she'd had more bad luck in the last twenty-four hours than she thought she deserved. After a night fraught with bitter misery, the sweetness of hope was on the horizon, and she could almost taste its delicious fruit. Just when she thought the mighty thunderstorms of life were about to drown her in the depths of despair, the sun was now poking gaping holes in the clouds of desperation, and she felt invigorated. And because a new day was dawning, she was able to see the good in her bad, and she was already embracing her new beginning.

The glimmering light of hope began to shine when Hank and Lucille offered her a job. Finding her forgotten pot of gold when she thought she had lost everything, ushered in a confident expectation that put her at ease. Another reason for hope that her life would change for the better was the unanticipated generosity of Saunders. When she told him what had happened to her in New Orleans, he felt sorry for her and made sure she got everything she needed. A smile, a good attitude, and keeping her anger under control when she was clearly being singled out because she was a Negress were instrumental in getting his personal attention and the twenty-percent discount that was normally reserved for employees. Another unexpected benefit that overshadowed Linda Schumacher's unfair behavior was that Saunders didn't require quid pro quo for his philanthropic spirit; he made no unwanted advances.

Johnnie was accustomed to men seeking sexual favors for their "benevolence." She found that school of thought particularly prevalent among the white men she had met in New Orleans and thought it must be true of all white men. While Saunders enjoyed her company, he was the antithesis of what she had come to know as standard operating procedure. He was never inappropriate with her even though she could tell he found her incredibly attractive. She kept expecting a proposition that never came. He was a happily married man, firmly rooted and grounded in his Christian beliefs.

She had spent a little under a hundred dollars, but due to the double discount she'd received, she had gotten over two hundred and fifty dollars worth of merchandise, all because she had heeded Brenda's wise counsel. When she left Woolworth's, she felt as if her feet were no longer touching the ground, as if she was walking on air. And even though the bank teller tried his best to steal her bubbly joy by acting as if he was doing her a favor by allowing her to open an account, she was unmoved by his attitude. His snide remarks found no home and simply bounced off her insult-proof exterior and went to that place where impotent words go once they've lost their power. She refused to let one man destroy what might one day prove to be the best day of her life.

She knew she would be staying at the Clementine for a while, and for the first time in her life, she would be alone and completely on her own. All the men she had come to depend on had been surgically removed, as it were. Finding her inheritance check at the last minute had been such a joy that she decided to splurge just a little by buying a bag of Brach's orange slices candy and several Agatha Christie novels. Having been tried and ultimately acquitted of a homicide, she found the idea of murder mysteries oddly appealing.

Chapter 22

"Hold your horses, Missy."

While Johnnie was innocent of the charges levied against her, she knew who had killed Sharon Trudeau all along. How a Negro had managed to kill Sharon in a well-known hotel chain full of white guests without being seen piqued her curiosity. She had never read a murder mystery before and Saunders had said that Agatha Christie was the best ever at writing them. Saunders was to some extent an expert on Christie's books and her life. What intrigued Johnnie from the outset was Christie's life story, which she believed paralleled hers just a teeny tiny bit.

She loved the fact that even a famous woman like Agatha Christie had hardships in her life. Archie Christie, Agatha's first husband, left her for another woman around the same time her mother had died. Agatha then disappeared for three weeks. She had gone to a hotel to get away from her troubles, Saunders had assumed. One thing Johnnie loved about Christie was that she had never been to school. She believed Christie must have had a wonderful mother who took the time to educate her daughter at home with the help of a number of governesses.

Another thing Johnnie loved about Christie was that adversity didn't deter her. It had taken five years to get her first novel published. She also admired the fact that Christie had studied music and could have been a concert pianist were it not for her nerves. More important than everything Saunders had told her about Christie, she loved that Christie was a wildly successful woman in a man's world, and that was the main impetus for purchasing *And Then There Were None, Murder on the Orient Express,* and *The ABC Murders.* She had read the first page of *And Then There Were None* in Woolworth's, and she was totally hooked. She then bought a brand new dictionary and a thesaurus, so she could continue building her vocabulary.

By the time she finished shopping, she had twelve bags full of merchandise from Woolworth's. Saunders was gracious enough to allow her to leave her items in the store behind the counter until she returned to pick them up. After returning to the store, she called a cab to take her over to the Clementine Hotel. Even though she had seen a vacancy sign, she was nevertheless apprehensive because the Clementine wasn't a Negro owned establishment, which meant that there was no guarantee she would be allowed to be one of its guests.

She pushed the door open, and she and her cab driver walked in. She had a bag in each hand, holding them by the straps. So did her cab driver, only he had four. While the cabby went back to retrieve the rest of her bags, Johnnie walked up to the counter where a white woman of more than forty years was sitting comfortably in a chair, reading a book. She looked for a sign that would indicate whether or not she would be allowed to stay there. She didn't see a sign that specifically said the hotel didn't allow Negroes. An unnoticeable sigh of relief escaped her lips. "The Adventures of Superman" was on the television even though the proprietor wasn't watching.

The woman was so engrossed in her book that Johnnie assumed she didn't hear her come in. She just kept turning the pages while Johnnie patiently waited. The cabby had come and gone several times, but Johnnie remained silent, thinking the woman would serve her when she finished the chapter that had obviously captivated her. As a reader, she knew what it was like to be deeply involved in a tale, to be in full escape mode, and then be interrupted by some fool who should have known better. She understood that when she was reading, unless somebody close to her had died or the house was on fire, she did not want to be disturbed. So, she respected the proprietor's space. But the woman proceeded to the next chapter, which Johnnie could clearly see. Johnnie inhaled, remembering that she needed a place to stay, and she had to take what the woman was dishing out. She cleared her throat to get her attention.

Without looking up from the book, the woman said, "Hold your horses, Missy. I heard you come in. Patience is a virtue. I'll get to you in just a minute."

Chapter 23

"You're good . . . very good indeed."

Johnnie watched the woman read several more pages of the book. She was trying to be patient, but she was quickly losing the battle, fully expecting the woman to give her a difficult time once she finished reading and realized that a Negress was seeking lodging for an undetermined amount of time. Normally, she would have prepared for the catfight, but this time she would have to be very humble because unlike the bank and Woolworth's, money wouldn't be enough of a reason for the woman to rent her a room. If money were reason enough, there would be no signs that let people of color know where the boundaries were.

The only color a store or a bank cared about was green. If she had that color, she could acquire whatever she wanted from either venue. In Mississippi, and in most of the southern states, a Negro could have all the gold in the world, but it couldn't buy him the use of a bathroom, or a bed, or a seat at a restaurant counter if whites owned it. Those necessities were parceled out at the owner's discretion. Johnnie understood that quintessential truth and kept her mouth shut because she was too tired to look for another hotel that might have a *No Coloreds Allowed* sign in the lobby. Besides all that, her cab driver had just pulled off. So, she waited. And she waited some more.

A few minutes after the driver pulled off, the woman laughed a little, turned another page, and then continued reading for another minute or so. Then, she dog-eared the page she left off on and stood up. She looked at her potential guest over the cateye glasses sitting on the bridge of her nose and said, "Double or single occupancy?"

Johnnie offered a bright energetic smile, determined to be as friendly as humanly possible, wanting to make a good first impression. She took a couple hurried steps forward and said, "Hello. My name is Johnnie Wise, and I'd like single occupancy please. I'd also like the biggest room you have, preferably one with a kitchenette. As you can see, I have a lot of bags. I'm planning to stay awhile."

The woman removed her glasses and let them dangle by a silver chain against her burgundy blouse. Then, she quickly examined Johnnie, looking her up and down, judging her appearance, her femininity, and her articulation, before saying, "Are you married, Miss Wise?" Her voice was strong, commanding, and midrange in tone.

"No, ma'am, I'm not."

Still looking Johnnie up and down, she said, "I don't condone fornication in my hotel. Are you expecting a boyfriend? One of those college boys, perhaps? Hmm?"

"No. I'm here alone."

"Trying to get away from your man, are we? Is he beating you? Is that why you're here alone, young lady?"

"Ma'am, I don't have a boyfriend . . . not anymore. We broke up yesterday. He's in the Army now. Just starting boot camp, I guess."

"Um-hmm. You don't say. Were you running around on him or something?"

Johnnie hesitated for a moment, looking the woman in the eyes for a fleeting second, knowing she was never supposed to make eye contact with white folk. When she wasn't angry, she generally adhered to the social norms of the south. But in this particular case, she needed a room and the woman standing before her had the power to turn her away. Therefore, staying in Negro character, giving the respect expected, and swallowing her pride whole was necessary to gain access to a world that paid no attention to the historic documents that brought about its existence. Racial protocol notwithstanding, she felt the need to examine the woman's motives in the fraction of a second that she'd looked into the windows of her soul. Unable to discern her thoughts, she said, "No. I'm not that kind of woman." She returned her eyes to the floor.

"Why did he join the Army then? You're a pretty girl, wonderfully built. No man in his right mind would leave you unless you're damaged goods. Are you damaged goods, Miss Wise?"

She lifted her eyes and said, "No, ma'am, I'm not."

"So, then you're still a virgin? No pickaninnies runnin' around without a nigger father to speak of?"

Feeling the sting of the insult, Johnnie smiled to maintain control, looked into the woman's eyes and said, "Ma'am, I just need a place to stay for awhile. I just drove in from New Orleans, and I'm very tired."

"So, you're a virgin?" the woman repeated, staring directly into Johnnie's eyes, into her soul, if it were possible, looking for any signs of emerging anger or an imminent lie.

Johnnie lowered her eyes to the floor before saying, "Ma'am, I'm really tired. It's not my intention to disrespect you, but are you going to rent me a room, or do I have to call another cab?"

"There's a phone booth about a mile and a half south from the end of my property. That's a long walk for someone as tired as you say you are. And to carry all those bags, too?"

"May I use your phone?"

"Well, I declare . . . you sure do speak proper for a nigger woman. Been to one of them nigger colleges, I'll bet."

"No, ma'am."

"Never been to college, huh? Where'd you learn to speak so fancy then?"

Johnnie smiled. "My good friend, Sadie Lane, taught me."

"You don't say. Well . . . I suppose I could let you use my phone, but I'd have to charge you."

"I understand. How much?"

"Five dollars a call."

Johnnie's mouth fell open, and she inhaled deeply before saying, "Excuse me, ma'am, but it only costs a nickel to make a call."

"You heard me. Five dollars a call. If the line's busy, and you need to make another call, it'll be another five dollars."

"Ma'am . . . again . . . I mean you no disrespect, but I'm no fool. Now, I'm willing to pay you fifteen cents, but no more. If the use of your phone costs more than that, I guess I'll have to walk the mile to use the phone booth then. May I at least leave my bags here until I return?"

"Sure. Five dollars a bag per hour."

Johnnie exhaled again, but she kept her mouth shut. Then, she started picking up her bags.

The woman said, "You can't be too tired if you're willing to carry twelve bags a mile up the road and had time to shop at Woolies."

"I had no choice. My house burned down last night. I've lost everything. And I'll walk ten miles before I pay you five dollars to use your phone."

"And you just happened to come to Jackson, Mississippi, on the way to where?"

Johnnie exhaled again. "I was going to East St. Louis, but now I think I'll be staying in Jackson for a while. Now that I've answered your questions, may I at least use your restroom before I go? I'll gladly pay you."

The woman smiled, and then said, "You're good . . . very good indeed."

Stunned by the woman's sudden reversal, Johnnie frowned and said, "Excuse me?"

"Forgive me, Johnnie, but I had to see if you could keep your cool under pressure. It is essential if you are to be a guest of Hotel Clementine."

"What do you mean?"

"I purposely ignored you for about ten minutes or so to see how you would respond," the woman said. "Then, I asked you questions that don't really concern me and you handled those questions well, too. I don't mean to offend you, but from personal experience, a lot of Negro women in your position would have made a number of incendiary remarks and stormed out, but you didn't. They would have felt good that they told a cantankerous white woman off, but they wouldn't have a place to lay their heads. And I know you wanted to do the same thing. I'm impressed, Johnnie. The point is, you never lost control, and if you persevere, you'll go far in this world because you are not easily shaken."

"May I ask why you were testing me—Miss—"

"Gloria Schumacher. You met my sister-in-law, Linda, over at Woolies."

Chapter 24

"Even if they call you a nigger."

Johnnie's heart sank as the memory of what happened at Woolworth's flooded her mind. In an instant, the whole scene replayed itself. Now it all made sense to her. She realized that the woman wasn't giving her a hard time because she was colored. She was giving her a hard time because of what her sister-in-law had told her. In the instant that the incident flashed, she imagined that Linda Schumacher probably had embellished the story, making it more sensational than it was, all in an effort to justify her racist attitude. She had met people like Linda in New Orleans, and she knew what they were capable of. Without another word, she started picking up her bags to leave.

"I don't particularly care for my sister-in-law," Gloria said, extending her hand. "So, don't worry about the incident at Woolies. If you've got the money to pay, and I know you do, you've got yourself a room—the best room I have. And I won't charge you one cent more than I would if I didn't know you had five thousand dollars."

Johnnie took her hand and shook it. "So, you know about my check?"

"By now the entire town knows. Linda couldn't wait to tell me what happened when you were there, and she knows I don't like her. She called a few hours ago. If she took the time to call me, knowing I have very little regard for her, I'm sure she told everyone in Woolies. I never expected you would be coming to my hotel though. That is until your brother Benjamin called."

"Benny called?"

"Sure did. He called about an hour ago, wondering if you had made it here, and if you were alright. Your brother sure knows how to charm the ladies, I'll bet."

"That's one of his problems, Mrs. Schumacher. He's got a great wife, but he's too stupid to realize it because he's always got a lady that needs charming."

"That's what your sister-in-law finds attractive about him, right?"

"Probably."

"Benjamin's part of the reason I'm gonna take you in."

"Really? How so?"

"When I told him I wasn't going to let you stay here because of the Woolies incident, he told me who he was and that you were the sweetest girl he knew and that Linda had probably provoked you in some way, which was very easy to believe."

"So, he told you he was a prize fighter, huh?"

"Uh-huh. I love watching a good fight, in or out of the ring. I'm too much of a lady to tell you why. The only time I don't like fighting, whether it's verbal or fisticuffs, is when it has even a remote chance of affecting business. And business is synonymous with money—my money. Understand?"

"I understand on both counts—money and charm. My brother has that affect on lots of women. He always has. Did he leave a number where I can get a hold of him?"

"Yes, I wrote it down for you. He told me you would be coming here after you finished shopping at Woolies."

"Thank you, Mrs. Schumacher. I've met so many wonderful people here in Jackson."

"Hmph! How many of 'em are white?"

"Most of them."

"Really? Well, you be careful here in Jackson. It can be a very dangerous place for pretty girls, black or white."

"I will, Mrs. Schumacher. And thanks for the compliment."

"Call me, Gloria. I suspect we're gonna get along just fine, Johnnie."

Smiling again, she said, "I do, too, Gloria. So . . . what were you reading?"

She held up the book. "Agatha Christie. *Death in the Clouds.* I let Mr. Saunders talk me into buying it the last time I was in Woolies. Didn't take much to convince me though. I just love her books."

"He talked me into buying three of her novels, too."

"Really? Are you a reader?"

"I'm starting to be."

Excited, Gloria said, "Which of her novels did you buy?"

Johnnie showed her the novels.

Gloria said, "Of those three, I've only read, *Murder on the Orient Express.* Great reading. Great ending."

"I was thinking of starting with, *And Then There Were None.*"

"I'm sure that's a good choice as well. Perhaps I'll pick it up, and we can read it together. I'm here all day by myself with nothing to do but read and watch television."

"What about your husband? Does he come by and visit?"

"That ol' fool up and died ten years ago."

"Oh, I'm so sorry. I didn't know."

"Don't be sorry. Good riddance. Anyway, I know you're tired after all you've been through. I hope you don't mind, but I'm going to put you on the second floor. I think my guests will give you less of a problem up there. But you'll have the best room in the hotel. It has everything you'll need."

"Thank you, Gloria. I really appreciate it."

"Just remember one thing. I'm running a business here. If one of my guests gets out of line, keep your mouth shut and bring the matter to me. Let me handle it, even if they call you a nigger. Don't say a word. Just go to your room and call me. Most of my guests are out-of-towners, and I can kick 'em out without too much of a backlash. They'll just move on to the next town, and that's fine with me."

"What do you mean a backlash?"

"If white folks in Jackson knew that I kicked a white guest out for mistreating my Negro guest, they would burn down my hotel. I'd all of a sudden be what they call a nigger lover. To them, that's worse than committing murder. That's how primitive my neighbors are. That they would equate southern hospitality to murder boggles the mind. I guess the thing that kills me is every last one of 'em will be in church praising the good Lord the following Sunday while my hotel is still smoldering."

"I understand. I promise I won't make any trouble for you, Gloria."

"I'm sure you won't. So, do we have a deal?"

"We have a deal."

"I'm not sure how long you plan to stay, but when I open the pool, unfortunately, I can't let you swim in it—at least not when I have guests, but that's usually in the evening. They generally stay the night and checkout in the morning. I don't have a problem with you swimming, but my guests might have a problem with it, and I make money off my guests, so I try to keep them happy. As long as they don't get unruly, they can stay, and so can you. If anyone asks you if you're a guest, tell them you're the maid and you live in the apartment on the second floor. Otherwise, I might be forced to kick you out. It wouldn't be personal, Johnnie. It would be a business decision. You're only one guest. I've got over a hundred rooms. At an average rate of two dollars a night, that comes to two hundred a night at full capacity. That's nearly six thousand dollars a month—more than that check you deposited. You understand?"

"I do. And thank you, Gloria."

"Great. Now . . . let's get these bags up to your new home."

Chapter 25

"It'll cost you four thousand dollars to find out."

Johnnie and Gloria climbed the stairs and walked along the L-shaped hotel on the grayish cement and entered her home for the next three weeks. She was very impressed with her spacious accommodations. The room had a couch, a dining table, a colored television, a small kitchenette, a dresser, a bathroom, and a queen-sized bed in the adjacent room. The walls were sky blue. Emerald carpeting covered the floor everywhere except the bathroom and the cooking area. It wasn't nearly as nice as the Bel Glades Hotel in New Orleans, but it was better than what she expected. They hustled back down to the lobby and brought up the rest of her things.

"I suppose you're ready for a nice long sleep," Gloria said.

"Yes, ma'am. Right after I call the Wall Street Journal and my brother."

"The Wall Street Journal?"

"Yes, ma'am. My stockbroker told me to read it every day."

"He did, did he?"

Johnnie nodded.

"Never had much faith in the stock market since it crashed in 1929," Gloria said.

"May I ask how old you were when you got married?"

Gloria smiled and said, "You gotta be quicker than that, Johnnie. I'd much rather you ask my age than try to extrapolate based on an educated guess minus the date of the crash."

A smirk revealed itself before she said, "Okay. How old are you, Gloria?"

"Now, Johnnie, you know better than to ask a woman her age."

Johnnie laughed and said, "Okay, Gloria."

"Now, back to the stock market. Will you give me some pointers?"

"I most certainly will. But it's going to cost you some of the six thousand you make a month."

"Are we bartering here, young lady?"

"I suppose we are. You're a businesswoman, and so am I."

"How do I know your advice is sound?"

"You don't. That's the chance you take, but I'll tell you this: I acquired over two hundred thousand in two years."

"What?"

"I had two stockbrokers . . . a woman and a man. Both of them were white, Gloria, if that means anything." Johnnie placed her hand on the Gideon Bible sitting on the dresser, put her hand over her heart, and said, "With God as my witness."

"What happened? Did your boyfriend steal it or something?"

"My stockbroker stole it."

"What?"

"Yeah, it's a long story. Perhaps I'll tell you about it someday. I still remember what stocks I had, but I'll have to start all over because the cost of the stock has increased exponentially since I originally bought them. But . . . I bet several of them haven't ripened yet, and I can still get them pretty cheap."

"You say your stockbroker stole your money?"

"Uh-huh."

"Of the two, it was the man who stole your money, wasn't it?"

"Actually, it was the woman who stole my money. She stole over a million, I think. Of that amount, two hundred and fifty thousand was mine."

"Two hundred and fifty thousand, huh?"

"Yes, ma'am."

"In two years?"

"Yes, ma'am."

"So, what would I have to pay you to get your advice?"

"It depends. What are you charging me for this room?"

"I was planning to charge you the standard rate, but since we're bartering for stock futures, I think I'll have to charge the regular rate."

"Which is what?"

"Three dollars a day. What are you planning to charge me?"

"Oh . . . not much . . . just the cost of my room and a small percentage of your earnings."

Smiling, Gloria said, "So let me get this straight. You want to pay absolutely nothing for the room, and I pay you for your advice?"

"Yes, ma'am."

Gloria doubled over as laughter spilled out of her mouth. She stood erect again and said, "Why that's highway robbery. You know that, don't you?"

"Yes, ma'am, but some folks might say three dollars for this hotel room is highway robbery. I guess it depends on one's point of view and the value of the services rendered."

Gloria stared at Johnnie for a few seconds, trying to determine if she should take the word of the woman in front of her. She thought about the amount of money Johnnie said she had made and thought it sounded too good to be true. "How long are you planning to stay in Jackson?"

"I'm not sure. But, we'll need a contract, so that no matter where I am, I can manage your stock portfolio, and I can get paid."

"What do you mean get paid? You just said you wanted a percentage of the earnings."

"Yes, but I need money to live on, too. So I'll need eleven hundred dollars up front to take you on as a client for one year."

"Eleven hundred dollars?"

"Yes, ma'am."

"You're serious?"

"I am. It'll be my retainer. We can go over to the bank some time this week and set up an account that will disburse my fee the first of every month."

"What if I pay you in cash? If we setup an account together, it wouldn't look good for a white woman to be doing stockbroker business with a Negro. Please don't be offended. That's just the way things are right now. Perhaps in the future blacks and whites won't have to hide their relationships, business or otherwise, if you follow what I'm saying."

"Gloria . . . I understand, believe me. Any way you want to do it is fine with me. I have no problem with cash. In fact, I prefer it."

"How about we try it for a couple of months, perhaps three? What would you charge me then?"

"I'll do it for four hundred plus a percentage and the cost of my rent. But after that, I'll have to charge you more, based on how your stocks are doing."

"Talk about highway robbery."

"Think of it this way . . . for two nights of revenue, you're going to make a fortune. Besides, I'm down on my luck right now. I need to make as much money as I can to rebuild what I lost in the fire."

"I'll have to think about it some, Johnnie."

"I understand, but the price of stocks fluctuates daily."

"How much was your initial investment?"

"I started with four hundred and maybe six months later, I received a dividend check worth four thousand dollars, I think, and then I reinvested it in the company."

"And what company was that?"

"It'll cost you four thousand dollars to find out."

They both laughed.

"I like you, Johnnie. I really do. But listen, I have to get back downstairs. I may have guests. By the way, what are you doing for dinner?

"I'm not sure. I need to sleep."

"Okay, when you wake up, if you're hungry, there's a restaurant up the road from here called the Flamingo Den, but be careful. The food is excellent, but the place attracts riffraff. To be safe, just knock on my door, and I'll get you something to eat. Besides, they may not serve you there."

After Gloria left, Johnnie picked up the phone and told the operator to connect her to the Wall Street Journal in Manhattan. A woman answered.

"My name is Johnnie Wise and I have a subscription with you. I've moved from New Orleans to Jackson, Mississippi, and I'd like you to send my paper to my new address."

Chapter 26

"It automatically locks after you open it."

After contacting the Wall Street Journal, Johnnie sat on her bed and looked around the room, taking it all in, saying within, *This is a temporary situation. I'll only be here for a few weeks.* It wasn't home, but it would be home for the foreseeable future, and she told herself she would make the best of the situation she found herself in. She then thought about the possibility of being a stockbroker for the first time. She didn't have the experience of Martin Winters or Sharon Trudeau, but she didn't think she needed it. She thought she had acquired the skill and knowledge she needed from both of them. After looking at a display of televisions in a department store, she had concluded that it would be a smart play to invest in broadcasting companies, not Martin Winters. She then remembered that it was her idea to invest in Sears after being accosted by the store detective who had tried to feel her up. She realized she had good instincts and that she needed to spread her wings a little and fly on her own.

It occurred to her that if she could land Gloria Schumacher, a woman who had plenty of money to invest, if she made the right investments, she just might be able to get her fortune back much sooner than she thought. The trick though was not to mention investing to Gloria again. Once her Wall Street Journals arrived, sooner or later, Gloria would ask about investing. And when she did, she would try to tell her it was too risky to invest. She thought Gloria would then ask her if she was still investing, to which she would answer in the affirmative. She believed that if she played it right, Gloria would then think that it couldn't be too risky if she was investing and beg her to get in on her investments. It was all set, she thought. It was just a matter of time before she collected a hefty retainer from her very first client.

Lying on her back, smiling, she thought of the brightness of her future. Before she knew it, she had drifted into a deep satisfying sleep, having a vivid dream about the love of her life, Lucas Matthews. She was at the University of San Francisco, about to register for classes when she literally bumped into Lucas, who was coming out of the Men's room. He was wearing his Army uniform, which was covered with medals and ribbons. Gold clusters were on his shoulder straps. They were both incredibly surprised to see each other. They embraced and held on tight, lost in the moment as memories flooded their minds. As they held each other, for whatever reason, wedding bells started chiming.

Her eyes shot open. She quickly turned her head to the left and looked at the phone. It was ringing. She looked around the room and knew that it wasn't all a dream. She was at the Clementine Hotel in Jackson, which meant she had really lost a quarter of a million dollars. Still in the haze of sleep, she picked up the phone, and with a scratchy throat said, "Hello."

"How ya doin' little sister? It's ya big brother, Benny!"

She took a moment to gather herself. "Hi, Benny. How you doin'?"

"I'm good. Gloria told me she gave you my number. Why didn't you call?"

"You know what, Benny? I closed my eyes for just a second, and the next thing I knew, I was in the dream world. I was planning to call you though. Did you get your money?"

"Yes, Lawd. I got that nice check, and it was right on time, too. It's about time we got something from them white niggas."

Surprised to hear Benny call the Beauregards white niggas, Johnnie said, "Benny, do the Beauregards have black blood in 'em?"

"The hell if I know. All I can tell you is this: the Bible says the two shall become one. Since Nathaniel was havin' his way with Josephine, he became one with her. And if we niggas . . . they niggas, too." He laughed uproariously. "Then, he went back and had kids with his wife, making him one with her. They all niggas as far as I'm concerned . . . whether they look like it or not."

Johnnie laughed with her brother and said, "You know, Benny, there is a certain logic to all that."

"I know. But I'm telling you, it should've been a whole lot more than five grand. You know that, don't you? After all, the Beauregards are rich, and we had to live like recently freed slaves. We deserve a whole lot more."

"I agree, but this is all we got. We gotta make due with it. Ya know?"

"Yeah, I know, but damn, they got all that money!"

"I told Brenda y'all need to invest it. Give it a few years and make some real money."

"I wish I could, little sister, but I need every dollar these days. I had to borrow money just to come to New Orleans to see about you."

"Didn't you just win that fight in Las Vegas?"

"Yeah, but I owe people. In order to make some real money, I'ma hav'ta fight a couple fights a month to pay bills and put bread on the table."

"It would help if you didn't spend so much on your worthless friends and good-for-nothing women that just wanna help you spend all you make."

"Who told you that shit? Brenda?"

"Are you questioning the veracity of my statement or the moral turpitude of the envoy who delivered it?"

"Am I what? Speak English, goddammit!"

They both laughed.

"I said, is it true or not?"

"Listen, little sister, I put a lot of time in at the gym, preparing for fights. I deserve to enjoy the fruits of my labor. When mama died, I saw the house you was livin' in. You obviously was enjoying the fruit of your labor. When I step into the ring, my life is on the line. I oughta be able to spend some of the money *I* earn on my friends, if I want to."

"You're right, but your wife and Baby Jericho come before your friends and before you, Benny. If you wanted to spend all your money carousing, you shouldn't have gotten married."

"So, you're gonna lecture me about my life when you wasn't doin' right yourself, Johnnie?"

"I don't have a husband and a little child, Benny. You do."

"Listen, I'ma 'bout to let you go. I just called to see if you was alright. I see you are. You go ahead and live your life the way you want to. And I'll live my life the way I want to. And we can call it a day."

"Benny!"

"What!"

"I'm sorry, okay? Just put some of the five thousand away for the future, okay? We're the only ones left in our family, unless you know of others."

"Yeah, we got other family, but I don't know where they at, and I don't know how to contact 'em. Right now it's just you and me."

"That's all the more reason not to argue. Now, Benny, I oughta be able to tell you the truth without you getting all mad. And you oughta be able to do the same with me, right?"

"Right, right."

"I'm just looking out for you, Benny. You're my only brother."

"What about daddy's kids? I think Jasmine don' had about four kids, right?"

"Yeah, but daddy's phone is disconnected. Have you heard from him?"

"Not since I saw him at the funeral."

"Oh, yeah . . . that reminds me. Have you ever been to the Baptiste Mausoleum?"

"Yeah. Grandma Josephine used to take me there before you was born. She used to tell me about a prince and some African woman. She had one of them Nation of Islam names. When Grandma Josephine died, I guess the stories died with her because mama didn't want to talk about it much. She used to say that was in the past, and it didn't make any difference now how we got here. But Grandma Josephine gave me the key to the mausoleum before she died. I visited her one last time before I left New Orleans to go out to the coast. I'm not sure why. I guess I was just paying my last respects to all the people in there, ya know. I wish I could remember all the stuff she used to tell me about the people, but I can't."

"Did you lock the door of the mausoleum?"

"It automatically locks after you close it."

"Really?"

"Yeah, why?"

"Because it was open yesterday."

"Open? How?"

"I don't know how, Benny. It just was."

"So, did you go in?"

"Yeah. That's why I'm asking you about it."

"Well, how did you get in? Far as I know, I've got the only key."

"I told you the door was open. But when I left, it locked automatically like you said. I'm trying to figure out who left it open in the first place."

"You can't leave it open, Johnnie. I can't explain what happened yesterday, but I'm telling you. You can't leave that door open. No way."

"Hmph."

"So, Brenda told me you lost all your money and everything. And since you can't get a hold of daddy, why don't you come out to San Francisco now? Brenda told me that Lucas is in the Army now. Why don't you come on out. We'd love to have you with us."

"You know what, Benny. I'ma stay here for a while. I just gotta job yesterday. And you met Gloria over the phone. Isn't she the sweetest white woman you've ever met?"

"Yes, Gloria is alright. Did she tell you I talked her into letting you stay there?"

"Yeah. I appreciate that. Otherwise, I don't know what I'd do."

"Well, listen, this call is costing me a fortune, little sister. I'm gonna stay the night, cash my check in the morning, and fly on back to San Francisco. If you change your mind about coming out, let your big brother know, okay?"

"Okay. Give Brenda and Baby Jericho my love."

"I will. Get some sleep."

"I will. Goodnight."

Johnnie turned off the light, but she could not get back to sleep. So, she started, thinking, planning how she would fortify her stock portfolio.

Chapter 27

"Make sure one of 'em is a female."

Private Detective Tony Hatcher, who was originally hired by Meredith Shamus to follow her husband, Earl, had been following Johnnie since she left Ashland Estates earlier that morning. Hatcher was in the courtroom when Meredith was killed by Ethel Beauregard. He was a surprise witness who was supposed to testify that he had bugged Johnnie's house and had her under constant surveillance. But when Johnnie's attorney, Jay Goldstein, tripped Meredith up during a brutal cross examination, she left the witness stand and ran at Johnnie with the intention of killing her. Instead, Meredith caught a bullet in the head. Hatcher was then rehired by Earl and had been told to follow Johnnie wherever she went, no matter how far, and to report all his findings, no matter how small. Money was no object.

At first, Hatcher felt a little strange working for Earl Shamus, particularly since he had been initially hired by Meredith to follow him. Hatcher's testimony, had it been given, would have exposed him as the person linking Meredith to the person who leaked the stories about Johnnie's relationship to the Beauregards, which ultimately led to Meredith's death. Fortunately for Hatcher, Earl wasn't at the trial. Otherwise, Earl would have known about the role he'd played in the whole sordid ordeal.

When Hatcher saw the light go off in Johnnie's room, he went down the road to The Flamingo Den, a roadside bar and grill. The Flamingo Den was famous for its scantily clad busty women who served ice cold beer and other spirits to truckers, bikers, and unsuspecting visitors from another state who didn't know that The

Flamingo Den wasn't the place to bring their wives and children. He ordered fish and chips and a bottle of Pabst Blue Ribbon beer. He took his food and beer into the phone booth and called New Orleans.

"Mr. Shamus, Tony Hatcher here."

"Yes, Mr. Hatcher. I take it you have something to report."

"I do, sir. As you know, sir, her house burned down last night."

"Yes, go on."

"Well, sir, she left what was left of Ashland Estates and went over to the cemetery."

"She wanted to say her last goodbye to her mother, I take it."

"I would assume so, sir. She had a brief conversation with a woman and her child before leaving the cemetery and left New Orleans."

"I take it she didn't talk to anyone else while she was in the cemetery?"

"No."

"Okay, and where is she now?"

"She's in a hotel called the Clementine in Jackson, Mississippi. It looks like she's in for the night. Her car needs a little work, so she's going to be here awhile. She spent several hours in Woolworth's buying some new threads to replace the ones she lost in the fire. She had a verbal altercation with a woman named Linda Schumacher."

"Where was this verbal altercation, Mr. Hatcher?"

"I'm sorry, sir. The altercation was in Woolworth's. Miss Schumacher works there. From what I could tell, she was looking around and Miss Schumacher confronted her about something. I think she thought Miss Wise was there to steal something from the store."

"I see. And was she attempting to steal something?"

"I'd have to say no because she bought about two hundred dollars worth of merchandise."

"So, it's true. She was involved in the murder of Sharon Trudeau. She does have the two hundred and fifty thousand the papers said was missing in the Fort Lauderdale Hotel."

"I seriously doubt that, sir."

"Really? Why?"

"If you'll allow me to finish my report, I'm certain everything will become clear."

"By all means, Mr. Hatcher, continue your report."

"Yes, sir. After the verbal altercation, she went to a phone booth and made a call. It could have been a local call, but I'm thinking it was long distance. As you know, she has a brother in San Francisco. It makes sense to me that if she lost everything, she would call him for help."

"So, you think she called, Benny, huh?"

"Perhaps. It appears that she was going to live with her father who lives in East St. Louis. As you know, much of what I know about her, I learned when your wife hired me to find out all there was to know about Miss Wise."

"I remember, Mr. Hatcher. Please . . . continue with your report."

"When she came out of the phone booth there appeared to be another verbal altercation with Miss Schumacher, but this time the store manager, a Mr. Saunders, was there, apparently to investigate what Miss Schumacher undoubtedly told him. They all exchanged words, and after that, Miss Wise and Mr. Schumacher walked off, arm in arm."

"What?"

"Yes, sir. Miss Wise was very friendly with Mr. Saunders."

"Is there something going on between them?"

"I don't know, sir. Only time will tell. After she left Woolworth's, she went to the bank and made a deposit. I don't know how much."

"Find out how much, Mr. Hatcher. I told you I want to know absolutely everything she does, who she meets, what she eats, everything. Do you understand?"

"If you want that much information, I'm gonna need another guy or two on the job. If I do that, this is going to get really expensive, sir."

"Get as many as you need, but I want to know everything there is to know."

"No problem."

"What's she doing right now, Mr. Hatcher?"

"Sleeping, I guess."

"Mr. Hatcher, if you have to guess, there is a problem, and the problem is you. I'm not paying you to guess. I'm paying you to know."

Hatcher doused a couple fries in ketchup, and then put them into his mouth. Smacking, he said, "No problem. Consider it done."

95

"How many men do you think you'll need?"

"At least three, possibly four. The trick is to be able to watch her without her knowing, but the problem is that there are other people who will see us and ask questions. We've got to eat and sleep, too. We stick out like sore thumbs around here. But we'll get the job done."

"And you'll do it without alerting her to your presence, right?"

"Absolutely."

"Good. Now what else do you have to report."

"She'll be starting a new job tomorrow in a dive called, Lucille's. She had lunch there earlier today."

"You don't say. A job, huh? Then, she really doesn't have the two hundred and fifty thousand. I wonder what happened to it."

"Maybe she never had it, sir."

"Oh, she had it alright. I don't know what she did with it, but she had it. She may have reinvested or something. I don't know, but she has that money."

"Forgive me for asking, sir, but if she has that kind of money, why would she work in a dive like Lucille's when she doesn't have to?"

"Perhaps her money is tied up. She's a very smart girl. She's not going to touch that money until she has to. Now what time is she supposed to be at work tomorrow?"

"Lucille's opens at six. So, I'm sure she has to be there before that. I'm thinking some time between five and five-thirty."

"What about the boyfriend, Lucas Matthews? What do you have on him so far?"

"The kid's probably on his way to boot camp. He heard testimony that his girlfriend was sleeping with several white men. That couldn't have set well with the kid. At some point, Johnnie looked up in the balcony and screamed his name. So, I'm sure the kid heard everything. After hearing that, no man would want any part of her—at least not on a permanent basis. I can put a man on him, too, if you like."

"No. Leave the kid alone. But if you're wrong, and he didn't join the Army, and he comes back into her life, follow him, too."

"No problem."

"Good job so far, Mr. Hatcher, but in the future, I want every detail, no matter how miniscule. Go to the Western Union tomorrow, and you'll have enough to cover your expenses for three weeks. If she leaves Jackson, we'll make arrangements to pay you and your people wherever she goes."

"How long do you want her under surveillance?"

"Mr. Hatcher, I want her under surveillance until I don't want her under surveillance. Do you understand?"

"I do."

Hatcher hung up the phone and guzzled his Pabst Blue Ribbon. Then, he doused his fries with ketchup again and put them in his mouth. He picked up the receiver and called New Orleans again. "Hawkins, Hatcher here. I need you to get a couple people up here in Jackson pronto . . . yeah at least two. Make sure one of 'em is a female. I think she'll be able to hide in plan sight much easier . . . no, not tomorrow, tonight . . . right now . . . move your ass!"

Chapter 28

"You sure you wanna know the ugly truth, Cassandra?"

Lucas Matthews and Lieutenant Perry had seen *Rear Window,* and now they were in The Blue Diamond Restaurant, sitting in a cozy booth in the back, waiting for their waitress to serve their meal. Throughout the movie, Lucas kept thinking of Johnnie, specifically his first date with her. They had gone to the Sepia to see *A Street Car Named Desire.* He had come a long way since those days. At that time, he didn't have a car, money, or the apartment he left. Johnnie had to pay for everything until he took the runner's job Napoleon offered him. Now he had everything Johnnie had the first time he went to the movies with her. He wondered what she was doing now that her house had burned down. He hoped that she had finally left New Orleans. He had no doubt that she would land on her feet, but he wanted it to be in another place; someplace where Napoleon couldn't reach her. It occurred to him that even though he was over eight hundred miles away from her, she still had his heart, and he wondered if he would ever get over her.

"So, did you think she was pretty, Mr. Matthews," Cassandra said.

"Huh?"

She stared at him for a moment and said, "Where are you, Mr. Matthews . . . in New Orleans with your former girlfriend?"

"Uh, no. I was just thinking."

"About?"

"Just thinking.

She rested her back against the booth before saying, "You must've really loved her, huh?"

"Who?"

"You know who . . . that woman in New Orleans. What's her name, so I can at least know who I'm competing with? I had hoped my competition was Grace Kelly. I could compete with her. She's not a living, breathing rival. She's just an actress on a movie screen. You have no fond memories of her. I could easily win that battle. But I don't know that I can compete with a memory."

He smiled and said, "Is that a sexual overture, Lieutenant?"

She laughed out loud. "Is everything sex with you, Mr. Matthews?"

"Not everything, no, but it has crossed my mind on more than one occasion since we met this morning."

"Uh-huh. I see."

"So, the truth easily offends you, is that it?"

"Offended? I'm not offended. I'm just perplexed by the males' preoccupation with reproduction."

Lucas recoiled a little and said, "Hey, I never said anything about making babies."

"Excuse me, Mr. Matthews, but that's exactly what you said."

"I never said a word about any babies, Cassandra. Not one word, and you know it."

"Did you use the word babies, no? But you've used the phrase 'sexual overture' three times now."

"So, you're keeping track of what I say?"

"I am. My father says that not only is a man's word his bond, but whatever comes out of the mouth of a man reveals what's in his heart. So, I pay strict attention when I listen to people, especially men."

He smirked and said, "Hmm, okay, so from what I've said, I've got babies in my heart, huh?"

"No . . . you've got the act of reproduction in your heart. Just the act, Mr. Matthews."

"Same thing."

"Exactly."

The waitress brought their catfish, greens, macaroni and cheese, sweet cornbread, and a couple bottles of Coke. She set it all on the table and disappeared.

Cassandra bowed her head and blessed her food while Lucas watched. When she started eating he said, "I see what this is all about now."

"What do you mean?"

"You're one of them holy rollers, aren't you?"

"If you're asking me if I believe in God, I do, but do you have to believe in God to replicate yourself, Mr. Matthews?"

Lucas exhaled. "There you go again," he said, avoiding the God question. "I'm not trying to replicate myself. I don't see what's wrong with having a little fun."

"My sister wasn't trying to have children either, but nine months later that's exactly what her and her boyfriend did, who by the way, left her as soon as he found out she was pregnant. They made a copy of themselves even though they had no intention of doing so. Now isn't that an interesting thing, Mr. Matthews?"

"So, that's what this conversation is about. Your sister has a baby, and you're afraid you'll end up just like her."

She locked eyes with him for a brief second, picked up the bottle of Frank's RedHot Sauce, shook a few drops on her catfish, and said, "Actually, no, my sister doesn't have a baby, Mr. Matthews."

Lucas stopped eating and looked Cassandra in the eyes. "But you just said she has a baby. Now, which is it? Does she have a baby or not?"

"My parents have the baby."

"Okay, why is that?"

"You know what, Lucas, let's change the subject. How's your catfish? Isn't it divine?"

Lucas nodded. "It's pretty good, but it's better in New Orleans." He ate some of his cornbread and said, "So, why do your parents have your sister's baby?"

"You sure you wanna know, Lucas?"

"Yeah, I wanna know. Why wouldn't I?"

"Because the truth can be an ugly thing sometimes. Sometimes it's better not knowing, I think. Knowing a thing, knowing the truth can be a burden sometimes, ya know?"

"Yeah, it can be, but whatever happened in your family is obviously bothering you. It seems that we both have precious things on our minds that we wish we didn't. I told you about my former girlfriend."

"Actually, you didn't, Mr. Matthews."

"Oh, so it's Mr. Matthews again, huh? A minute ago it was, Lucas."

"Yes. It keeps things *official* until they're no longer official."

"Uh-huh. Well, *Lieutenant*, what would you like to know about her?"

She smiled and said, "I wanna know everything there is to know about her. Are you willing to tell me absolutely everything, Mr. Matthews?"

"We could be here all night."

"Is that a sexual overture, Mr. Matthews," she said, smiling, looking at her watch.

Lucas laughed. "No, Lieutenant, it isn't."

"That's good to know. The restaurant closes in about forty-five minutes. So, we definitely won't be here all night. But if you wanna talk, there are places we can go and talk. And no, that's not a sexual overture, Mr. Matthews."

"If *I* wanna talk, huh? *Me?* You're the one who wanted to know everything there is to know about Johnnie."

"So, that's her name, huh? Tell me, does this Johnnie have a last name?"

"Yes. Her last name's Wise."

"She obviously can't be too wise if she got involved with your boss, can she?"

"I said her name was Wise, not that she was wise. But the truth is she's a really smart girl."

"Is she now? What evidence do you have of that? I mean, besides the brilliant decision to get involved with her boyfriend's boss. I gotta believe that if you love her as much as you say still, she had to love you, and yet look at her actions."

"You know what, Cassandra? You don't know anything about her, okay? You don't know what he did to make her do what she did with him."

Cassandra leaned forward and rested her elbows on the table. "So, wait a minute. She actually tried to make a replica of herself with him?"

Lucas cut his eyes to the left.

She folded her arms and leaned back against the booth again. "And you think that was a smart move, huh, Lucas?"

Lucas exhaled hard and said, "You weren't there, okay? You don't understand!"

"Touchy. Touchy," she said, looking into the windows of his soul. "You're right, Mr. Matthews. So far none of this is making any sense. None of it. Help me understand this nonsense."

"You sure you wanna know the ugly truth, Cassandra?"

"Yes, Mr. Matthews. I do. Enlighten me."

"You first. Why are your parents taking care of your sister's baby?"

Chapter 29

"That's so sad."

Cassandra cut her eyes to the left for a moment or two, and then she looked at Lucas again. Her eyes were glassy. One tear from each eye raced down her cheeks. Resurgent thoughts of her sister surfaced and reminded her of everything that her sister went through when she got pregnant. Her sister's life was full of promise. They were planning to attend Tuskegee together, but when she missed a first and then a second menstrual cycle, they both knew in their hearts that could only mean one thing. She remembered the first time her sister came to her and mentioned getting rid of *it*. Aborting the unwanted child sounded like the best way to hide the pregnancy and move forward with her life. Who of consequence would know? She had even planned to visit a woman who performed the delicate procedures in the basement of her home. At that instant, she remembered walking over to the woman's house after school and standing out front. They were about to open the gate when her sister decided she couldn't kill her baby. She had said that she would keep her baby and deal with the consequences.

The atmosphere had suddenly become thick and dark, as if a cloud were hovering over them, threatening to rain on their dinner. Feeling the weight of what she was telling him, and the emotion of the moment, he said, "Are you alright?"

"I'm fine, Lucas." She locked eyes with him. "Alexandra's dead. She died giving birth to my nephew, Alexander. We were identical twins. She was older than me by one minute. That's why she got the "A" and I got the "C". She's gone, Lucas, and she's never coming back. And that good-for-nothing, so-called man she decided to open her legs to doesn't even know the name of the child he sired. So, my mom and dad are saddled with *his* responsibility. It's so unfair to them, ya know? They raised the seven children they brought into this world. Alexandra got pregnant when it was time for my parents to sit back and enjoy the rest of their lives, ya know? I know people make mistakes, Lucas, but when you decide to be reckless with your body in that way, it's your responsibility to rear the children you bring into this world, ya know? It isn't your parents' job. It isn't your neighbor's job. That job belongs to the risktaker exclusively." She wiped her eyes. "I'm sorry, Lucas. I told you the truth was ugly."

As Lucas listened to Cassandra's story, his heart went out to her. He knew that he could very well be in the same position with Johnnie or Marla, or a couple of other teenaged girls he manipulated into taking off all their clothes. He thought he understood where she was coming from and why she didn't want to engage in the act.

"You ready to hear my ugly truth now?"

Cassandra picked up a napkin and dried her eyes and nose. "Yes. I wanna hear it."

"It's pretty ugly."

"Good. The uglier the truth is, the greater the need to expose it."

Lucas finished off his food, and then washed it down with several swallows of his Coke. The waitress came back, took their plates, and left the bill. Lucas looked at the bill, turned it face down, then peeled off five dollars and placed it on the table. He looked at Cassandra again and said, "First of all, I fully understand how you feel about what happened to your twin sister, and I'm very sorry."

"Do you really understand, Lucas?"

"I think I do, Cassandra. I think I do because my own father did the same thing to my mother. I've never even seen my father, and I don't know his name."

"That's so sad."

"It is sad. If it had started and ended with me, I guess that would be easier to deal with, but it didn't end with me. What made matters worse was that several other men came into my mother's life, promising her this and that and never delivered. She thought all three of them would be her risen savior, and not one of them kept their word to her. So, I understand what you mean about a man keeping his word, too."

Chapter 30

"Marla made me do it to her."

Lucas paused for a second and stared at Cassandra. In the brief moment that he paused, visions of the last two years of his life passed before his eyes. He remembered confronting Billy Logan on the way home from school when he teased Johnnie and called her all kinds of dirty names. He could actually hear Logan ask her if she sucked Earl Shamus' dick, which brought tears to her eyes. Next, the first fight he'd had with Logan materialized. He had made Logan apologize to Johnnie on his knees. After that, he walked her home, and she invited him in so she could put ice on his swollen face. But Marguerite came in and started screaming, making accusations that were not true. Next, he saw Johnnie at the playground, waiting for him, and they went to her new house—a house that Earl Shamus had purchased for her. And now, Cassandra had just reminded him of Johnnie's fling with Napoleon. Hearing her point of view on the relationship was like pouring salt on his open wound.

He said, "You know what, Cassandra . . . you have a way of putting things that people might find offensive."

"The truth is always offensive, Lucas. People kill and get killed over the truth. Mothers abort their babies because of the truth. In their case, she has to risk her life by getting the abortion because she was playing a dangerous game of Russian roulette, hoping there wasn't a bullet in the chamber with her name on it. I watched my sister agonize over the decision for weeks before she decided to do it, and then later, at the last minute, change her mind. Husbands kill their mistresses because of the truth he refuses to tell her; that being he's never leaving his wife, and while he loves gambling with both their lives, all she would ever be to him is a warm wet receptacle. When the mistress realizes this, when she comes to terms with what she's allowed herself to become, she threatens to tell the wife, and in so doing, hastens her own death. Wives lie to their husbands, telling them that junior is his son because the truth revealed would in all likelihood get her kicked out of the house with nothing to show for ten, perhaps twenty years of marriage. Depending on pride and how fragile her husband's ego is, truths' reality might get her brutally killed because for years she had passed off junior as his legitimate heir. All of these scenarios are a very real reality as I have seen them all come to pass."

"Wait a minute. You know of people who have been killed over this?"

"I do. I'm baffled by why you're so surprised. Murders are committed every day. I would bet a year's salary that there hasn't been a murder committed that truth was not a central reason for the execution. It seems that death and reproduction are not only syncopated, but the relationship between the two is wholly ironic, don't you think?"

Having no idea what she had said, Lucas rolled his eyes and said, "You tend to ramble on, you know that? Anyway, before you go on another rant," he rolled his eyes again to hide his lack of knowledge and his inability to keep up with her soaring intellect, "let me say this. My mother will probably end up pregnant by the man she's currently living with, and I've already got three half brothers." He looked away for a moment or two, and then continued, "Now what happened with Johnnie and Napoleon is partially my fault."

"I find that hard to believe."

"Just hear me out. You want the ugly truth? That's exactly what you're gonna get. You can blame Johnnie if you like, but the truth of it is, I was doin' some things with Napoleon's wife that I shouldn't have been doin'."

"Reproducing, Lucas?"

He nodded. "Yes, reproducing, since you insist on calling it that."

Shaking her head, she said, "So how did all of this happen?"

106

"Marla made me do it to her."

Cassandra laughed before saying, "C'mon, Lucas. Do you really expect me to believe that a white woman made you lay down with her? I mean . . . she is white, right?"

"Yes, she's white, but no, I don't expect you to believe me, but that's exactly what happened. I'll never forget it. It was the craziest thing."

She leaned back and folded her arms again. "I gotta hear this. She musta looked like Grace Kelly, huh?"

"She looked better than Grace Kelly."

Skeptical, she said, "Really? And I suppose she was better looking than Elizabeth Taylor, too, huh?"

"No. Elizabeth Taylor had Marla beat by a country mile. She wasn't a close second either, but Marla was a good-looking woman. And it's a good thing she didn't look better than Elizabeth Taylor. I might be still in that situation or dead if she looked better than even her."

Shaking her head, "And at no time were you concerned about castration or the hangman's noose?"

Lucas locked eyes with her and said, "So . . . you're a virgin, right? You must be a virgin to say something like that."

"I am."

"Uh-huh. I see."

She leaned forward again and laced her fingers under her chin. "You see what?"

Chapter 31

"I guess you're ready to take me home now, huh?"

Lucas leaned back and folded his arms. His first thought was to defend his actions, but then he thought he had just said that part of what happened between Johnnie and Napoleon was his fault, and he knew a smart woman like Cassandra would take issue with that contradiction. He then remembered that earlier that day, in the Mess Hall, she had repeatedly called him a newbie, meaning that he was inexperienced. She had actually told him he was wet behind the ears, but he knew that if he said the same thing to her, there was a good chance her feelings would be hurt, even though she had used those very words when describing his lack of knowledge concerning military protocol and culinary delights.

He said, "I see that there's no way you can understand sex and the hold it can have on the man and the woman involved. The thing just gets crazy. It really does."

"Sure I do, Lucas. I understand slavery just fine. There's nothing difficult to understand about slavery in all of its forms."

"Slavery? What does releasing a little pressure and slavery have to do with each other?"

"If I have to tell you, Lucas, you're the worst kind of slave because you don't even know you're a slave."

Frowning, he tightened his folded arms a bit more prior to saying, "What do you mean? I'm no slave. I'm free. I do whatever I want."

"Didn't you hear me? I just said you're the worst kind of slave because you don't know you're a slave. Did you hear me say that, Lucas?"

"I heard you, but that's not true. I'm not a slave, and I never will be either. So, I really don't understand what you mean."

Shaking her head, she leaned forward a little and whispered, "You talk just like a fool. You know that them crackers down there in Louisiana will castrate you, hang you, or turn you into a human torch, and you still went up in a white woman whose husband is in the mafia? Listen . . . if you can't stop doing a thing . . . any thing . . . a thing that you fully know and understand that can lead to castration and death . . . and you can't stop yourself, you're a slave, Mr. Matthews. And get this . . . it's the worst kind of slavery because it feels so good. I'm told that once you engage in that kind of activity . . . after awhile . . . not only can't you get out of it . . . you don't even wanna get out of it. My sister and I thought that my father was going to be so angry when he found out she was with child that he might kill her, but he was just the opposite. He understood what happened to my sister."

"Yeah, but Alexandra could have died even if she had waited until she got married."

"True, but she wasn't married, was she? And my nephew doesn't know who his father is, does he? So, we dare not justify what they did and how it all ended. Later, after my sister died, I realized that anything that feels that good and might lead to your death is not good for you no matter how good it feels. You might as well be smoking opium or shooting the heroin that you were selling to others into your own arm."

Lucas looked at her for a long minute, contemplating her conclusions, examining her accusations, wondering what she saw that he didn't, knowing there was a truth that she knew and understood, but he couldn't fully grasp. "You said that I couldn't stop, right?"

"Right."

"Well, I can stop, Cassandra. And if I can stop, then I ain't no slave."

"Really? Okay, so then, you're going to stop reproducing until you're ready to reproduce, right?"

He looked at her for a long minute and said, "I don't wanna stop, Cassandra."

She unfolded her arms and laughed out loud.

Lucas said, "What's so funny?"

"You just proved my point. Slavery is so deeply woven into your psyche that you would rather stay in it because the idea of slavery isn't anathema to you. In fact, for you, slavery is the sweetest delight, and you wouldn't give yourself permission to be free of its diabolical tentacles. And even if you did, the call of that kind of slavery would chase you down for the remainder of your life, threatening to make you one of its captives again. That's how far gone you are. And again, you don't even know it."

"I'm not hurting anybody, Cassandra."

"Really, Lucas? If you believe that, then the men who left your mother with four boys that obviously needed their fathers didn't hurt you, your mother, or your three brothers, right? I suppose the fact that you ended up just like the man who brought you into this world, the man you say you've never met, means your father's legacy, the blood that flows in your veins, didn't hurt you either, huh? I mean, crackers with sharp knives with eyes for your privates don't even frighten you."

Lucas quieted himself and reflected for a few moments, trying to figure out how to respond to a woman who had clearly thought the subject through. Then, as if he had found the Holy Grail, he said, "But what if I don't make any babies? What then? Would I still be a slave if I didn't make any babies?"

Amazed by the level he was willing to go to justify his illicit behavior she said, "You know what, Lucas . . . I hate to say this, but you're damaged goods."

"Damaged goods? What do you mean by that?"

"I mean that even though you've never met your father, he duplicated himself in that his attitude was reborn in you, which is why I insist on calling it reproducing. How you think and consequently how you behave are evidence of this. I mean you are more like the man you've never met than you could possibly imagine, at least in terms of attitude, because you're doing what he did to your mother. The fact that you have no offspring, given all the sex you've been having, in no way obfuscates that fundamental truth. I would bet that your Johnnie Wise is from the same sort of damaged stock, given that she was sleeping with your boss no matter what her reasons were. I feel sorry for both of you to be honest. You both returned to the cesspool that birthed you.

110

The sad part about it is, when you've been in the cesspool long enough, the smell of it doesn't even bother you anymore. You just float around amongst the defecation and the urine, which probably look like fish and other aquatic creatures in champagne. After awhile, you'll grab a floating piece of excrement, thinking its prawn and eat it whole, and then wonder why you're vomiting and running back and forth to the latrine. The thing boggles the mind."

Lucas looked out the window into the dark night, searching his soul for arguments to refute her penetrating observations, but none surfaced. "You know what, Cassandra? You're different."

"What do you mean, 'I'm different?'"

"I mean, you're smart, and you know things that lots of folks never even think about. How did you end up in the Army?"

"I didn't end up here. People without clear direction always end up someplace, usually someplace they didn't intend to be. I chose to be here. My oldest sister was one of the Ten-percenters of the Women's Auxiliary Army Corps stationed at Fort Des Moines, Iowa back in 1942. There were four hundred white women and forty black women. I wanted to serve my country, too, and so I joined. Simple as that."

"I suppose you wouldn't be interested in a guy like me, huh?"

"You mean for a husband?"

"Yeah. I don't mean now or anything. We just met, but what if we had known each other for a few years. Would you be interested in me then?"

"I'm interested in you now, Lucas, but at the same time, I'm not interested in you now. I'm interested in you because you're a very attractive man, and one day you'll have lots of potential, but right now, you're a slave. And if you can't control yourself prior to marriage, why would I ever believe you could somehow control yourself after marriage?"

"I'd be committed to my marriage."

She rolled her eyes and said, "Yet, you're not committed to freedom, and you've already violated a marriage. Frankly, I think you'll do it again sometime in the future because that's who you are at this point in your life. Face it Lucas, you've got a lot of work to do. Maybe its providence that brought you to the Army now. Maybe you'll learn how to control yourself. My guess is you won't because as you said, slavery feels good. I know those weren't your exact words, but that's what it amounts to. And until your mind is free, you won't have the will to be the kind of husband I need."

Lucas raised his hand to get the waitress's attention. When she came over, he gave her the money and the bill and told her to keep the change.

"I guess you're ready to take me home now, huh?"

"Yeah, I start training tomorrow, and they might start early. I wanna be ready. I heard basic training can be tough. So, I wanna get as much sleep as I can. I've been up all night and all day."

"So, you don't want to see me anymore, right?"

"I'd love to see you again, Cassandra. Like I said, you're different. We can go out again, if they let us."

"Well, I'm an officer, and you're an enlisted man. We're not supposed to date, but I'd be willing to see you off post and out of uniform. You'd have to wear something like what you're wearing now. I love the way you dress, by the way. The suit looks like it was made specifically for you."

Lucas smiled. "It *was* made specifically for me. Me and Bubbles, the guy I reported to, had the same tailor. Well . . . if you're ready, I'll drop you off."

"So, you really were involved with the mafia?"

"Yeah . . . I really was."

It was a quiet ride back to Fort Jackson. Cassandra wondered if Lucas wasn't talking because she had said too much in the restaurant. She really liked him, but she felt that she had offended him because she was so outspoken. When he stopped in front of her barracks, she said, "I'm sorry I offended you, Lucas."

"It's no problem."

He walked her to the barracks door, but he didn't try to kiss her. He waited until she was safely inside, and then he returned to his car and drove over to his quarters. For the next thirty minutes, he thought about Cassandra Perry and everything she said, searching his soul, while vainly trying to fend off her piercing words. He thought that if he was damaged goods as she had asserted, a woman like Cassandra would be the balm that would cure whatever ailed him.

Chapter 32

"Ya comin' in, little lady?"

It was approaching nine o'clock when the phone in Johnnie's hotel room rang. She had been asleep for nearly five hours prior to Benny's call. She tried to sleep again, knowing she had an early start at Lucille's, but couldn't. She wanted to make a good impression on her first day at her new job by being on time. Unable to sleep after lying in the bed for half an hour, she felt her stomach rumble. It demanded that she put something in it, hopefully something delicious, followed by a sweet soft drink. She remembered that Lucille's closed at eight and that Gloria Schumacher had said that there was a restaurant up the road. She also remembered that Gloria didn't recommend going there. She hadn't had a meal in nearly twelve hours.

All she had to eat was her orange slices candy, a quarter pound of salted cashews, and a box of popcorn that was fresh when she bought it. At first, she was going to eat the orange slices, and if she was still hungry, she would start working on the cashews. Then, it occurred to her that she didn't have a beverage to wash down the nuts as the salt would add to her thirst. That's when she seriously considered disregarding Gloria's advice about the restaurant up the road. She turned on her light and waited for her eyes to adjust to the sudden brightness. Then, she went into the bathroom and cleaned up.

She considered asking Gloria if she had anything to eat, but quickly rejected the notion, not wanting to be a bother despite her earlier offer. Gloria had done enough by letting her stay in her hotel. She thought the restaurant couldn't be that bad, and even if it was, her stomach was in command. It was making the decision to go in there.

Prior to opening her door, she pushed the curtains aside. She figured that the Clementine was filled to capacity when she saw so many parked cars. Gloria had made her two hundred dollar quota. She opened the door and walked out onto the veranda. She felt a cool breeze prick her skin and went back into her room and grabbed a sweater to keep the chill off and to help hide her large bust, sensing it could be the catalyst for any trouble she might encounter. Then, she made her way down the stairs, and then down the road to the restaurant.

From a distance, she could see a pink neon sign flashing: the flamingo den. A neon replica of the thin, long-legged, s-shaped neck birds were on both sides of the sign. The parking lot was full of trucks, cars, and a few Harley Davidson motorcycles. There were countless vehicles with licenses plates from Nashville, Philadelphia, Atlanta, Santa Barbara, Key West, Detroit, and numerous other places. She had hoped that the lateness of the hour would deter most hungry customers, but apparently lots of people were driving at night instead of stopping at a hotel. She walked past a window and looked inside. The place was packed. She was hoping to see a few black faces, so she would feel comfortable going in, but she only saw white men and women, complete with preadolescent crumb snatchers.

The Flamingo Den appeared to be a place for Country and Western lovers. She could hear Hank William's "Your Cheatin' Heart" as she approached the restaurant's entrance. Apprehensive, she looked through the windows again and saw a cowboy hat or two. Again, she remembered what Gloria had told her about the restaurant. She was about to turn around and go back to the Clementine when the door of the restaurant opened.

A white man held the door open for her, tipped his hat, and said, "Ya comin' in, little lady?" His accent was unmistakably Texan.

Chapter 33

"I don't need your kinda trouble."

Johnnie looked at the man holding the door open for a few seconds, trying to decide what to do, watching him as he shifted a toothpick from one side of his mouth to the other. He reminded her of John Wayne who had starred in John Ford's, *Rio Grande*. She had seen the movie when she was thirteen, and over the years, had grown quite fond of westerns. The man leaned against the door, waiting for her to accept his gracious invitation. She took him in with her eyes for a few more cautious seconds, examining his outfit, which consisted of a beige felt Stetson, a rust-colored shirt, a black leather vest, Levi Strauss jeans, and tan Lucchese boots. He was a cowboy all right, and he was a long way from home, she thought. She wanted something to eat, but at the same time, she sensed trouble.

"Go on in, little lady," the man said with a mild Texan twang that added flavor to his rugged good-looks. "Try the chili and grilled cheese sandwiches. It's the best thing on the menu. The chili's kinda hot, but it sure hits the spot. If you don't like chili, I recommend the barbecued ribs, corn on the cob, baked beans, potato rolls, and whatever cool drink you prefer to wash it all down. Whenever I roll up this way from Houston, I make sure I stop in for a bite to eat. I'll tell you what, little lady, the smell of the potato rolls'll have your mouth waterin' in no time flat."

Her stomach rumbled again. She was hungry enough to try them both, especially the potato rolls, but she wasn't sure she should go in.

The Texan shifted the toothpick again, and then reached out and gently, yet firmly grabbed her arm. She resisted his touch, but his hands were powerful and easily overcame her defiance. "You'll be just fine, I promise."

She looked at his face, trying to see his eyes, believing that in them she could gauge his sincerity, but it was too dark, and the brim of the Stetson was in the way. He was tall, about six-four, and lean. He looked like he could handle himself in a fight if he had to. She decided to go in, but she was going to be cautious, knowing that at any moment, all hell could break loose. Looking at the ground, she said, "I'm very hungry. I just wanna get something to eat. If I go in, will you wait until I get my dinner, sir? I don't want no trouble."

"Pretty thang like you . . . sure. I'd be honored. If you want, I'll stay in there while ya eat. Make sure nobody bothers you if you don't mind me starin' a bit."

"Thank you, sir, but I'll just take it with me. I don't think they'll let me eat in there anyway."

"They won't, huh? So, you've been here before?"

"No, sir."

"Then, how do you know they won't?"

Still looking at the ground, she said, "You know why, sir."

"You think they won't let you eat here because you're a Negro?"

She looked for his eyes again for a quick second and nodded.

"Well, we'll see about that," he said and dragged her into The Flamingo Den by her right arm. Loud country music, complete with six string acoustic guitars and banjos rang out as a rollicking number filled their ears.

"I told you I don't want no trouble, sir," she said, still resisting as he pulled.

"There won't be no trouble, little lady. And if there is, I'll make sure it goes away right quick. Now come on and get some of this delicious grub." Still holding her by the arm, he pulled her up to the bar and said, "Scotty, look at this woman."

Scotty didn't bother looking at Johnnie. He continued looking into the Texan's eyes, wanting to tell him to leave his establishment, but afraid to.

Keith Lee Johnson

"Go on, boy. Look at her. Ain't she the prettiest thang you ever did see?"

Scotty continued eying the Texan and said, "Listen, Preacher, I don't want no trouble in my place. I'm tryin' tuh run a respectable business. I don't need your kinda trouble."

When Johnnie heard the bartender call the Texan "preacher," she wondered if that was his name, or if he was a minister of the Gospel. If he was a man of the cloth, she wondered why anyone, let alone a bartender would be afraid of him. The memory of Reverend Staples shot through her mind, the man who had been killed while trying to stop white folk from rioting. He was an excellent example of what a clergyman should be. She focused on the exchange between the Texan and the bartender again. Her eyes shifted back and forth between the men. She felt the atmosphere thicken. Even though Scotty was being contentious, showing his frustration with the Texan bringing her into his restaurant, she felt safe with the Texan, but she wasn't sure why.

His powerful presence alone had gotten Scotty's attention, and she could tell that he was afraid of the Texan. If the owner was intimidated by him, he probably had good reason to be, which conjured up images of Napoleon Bentley and Lucas Matthews, her former lovers and bodyguards. They had both protected her at crucial times in her life, when she needed protecting. And when they were unable to protect her, a young attorney named Jay Goldstein picked up the baton. Now, it seemed as if she had found another guardian, one who would stop evil, malicious men if they tried to harm her.

"Scotty, listen, buddy. You know I would never start trouble in your respectable restaurant. It's the yahoos you serve spirits to. If you keep the yahoos in line, I'm sure this beautiful creature will be on her best behavior, too." He looked at Johnnie. "More so, won't you sweetie?"

Johnnie smiled and nodded several times.

"What's your name?" the Texan asked.

"Johnnie Wise."

"Hello, Miss Wise. Pleasure to make your acquaintance. Paul Masterson's the name. And this is Scotty the bartender and owner of The Flamingo Den." He looked at Scotty. "Now . . . Johnnie here thinks she can't eat here. That's not true, is it?"

117

Scotty cut his eyes to Johnnie for a second or two. She looked just as afraid of what might happen as he felt. He knew it wasn't her idea to come in there and start trouble. It was Masterson's idea. His body tensed and became rigid when he thought about going for his double barreled shotgun, but he knew that if he so much as flinched, he would feel Masterson's fists long before he saw them coming, having seen him dismantle men bigger and tougher-looking right there in his restaurant. He looked at Masterson who was smiling from ear to ear, like he knew there was no way he would say no to him. If he did, Masterson would break his jaw, go into the kitchen, make whatever he wanted, bring it to his colored friend, and then watch her eat it in his restaurant. He felt the eyes of his customers watching. He looked at them and smiled, hoping there wouldn't be a mass exodus before they paid their collective bills. He looked at Masterson again. Fear registered. "I suppose it'll be okay *today*, Preacher."

Masterson smiled devilishly, shifted his toothpick, and said, "Now, Scotty, that don't sound friendly at all. What if I'm still in town tomorrow, will it be okay then, too?"

Scotty nodded once. "As long as you're with her, she can eat here whenever she likes."

Masterson said, "See, Scotty, I just knew you could be hospitable. Since you've had a change of heart, she'll have a nice bowl of your scrumptious chili and a grilled cheese sandwich. And if it's not too much trouble, throw in a few bones of your delicious barbecue." He looked at Johnnie. "What are you drinkin,' sweet thang?"

"Lemonade."

Masterson looked at Scotty, shifted his toothpick, and said, "Make sure it's ice cold. We'll be over there," he tilted his head, "in that booth by the window. Is that okay with you?"

Scotty nodded once. "It'll be up in a second. And please, Preacher, leave as soon as she's finished. I don't want no trouble, okay?"

"Sure, Scotty, sure," Masterson said, smiling, and then pulled Johnnie over to the booth he spied from the bar. He waited until she sat down, then he removed his Stetson and set it on the table. "So . . . you ain't from around these parts, are ya, honey?"

Johnnie looked at the table and said, "No, sir. I'm from New Orleans."

"Ahhhh, I thought I recognized the accent. "So what y'all doing up here in Jackson? Can't be visitin' relatives, right? They would know better than to let you come to a joint like this by yourself."

"Just passing through, sir," Johnnie said, still looking at the table.

"Okay, I've had just about enough of that," Masterson said forcefully.

"What, sir?"

"I expect you to look at me when you talk," Masterson said. "I'm no better than you, ya understand?"

She looked at him and said, "No, sir, I don't. White folk don't like for us to look them in the eye."

"Now you listen to me . . . any white man, or woman for that matter, that requires you to look at the ground, the table, or anywhere when addressin' 'em, is weak on the inside, and they know it. So, as long as you don't look 'em in the eye, they can feel superior, but not in the eyes of Almighty God. Ya understand, little lady?"

She looked him in the eyes for the first time and noticed that they were a hypnotic, grayish-blue. She said, "Mr. Masterson . . . can I ask you a question?"

"Go right ahead, but I know what you're gonna ask before you even open your pretty little mouth."

"Really, sir? What am I going to ask?"

"You wanna know if I'm a real preacher, right? You heard ol' Scotty call me preacher, and you heard me call the Creator, God Almighty. So, you put two and two together, right?"

She nodded. "So, are you, sir?"

"I'm an evangelist, Johnnie. I travel around the country preaching the word of God." He smiled and said, "Now you wanna know why Scotty's so afraid of me, right?"

She smiled and nodded several times.

"He's not really afraid of me. He's afraid of what his stupid customers might do. Here comes several of 'em now. Excuse me a second, sweet thang."

Chapter 34

"If anything else happens tonight, don't hesitate to call."

Tony Hatcher was still in the phone booth, talking to his people in New Orleans when he saw Johnnie come in with the tall man. He had seen the tall man finishing his meal when he was making his calls but didn't pay much attention to him. He was just one man in a restaurant full of people. He even noticed when the man paid his bill and was leaving the restaurant. He was about to leave the phone booth when he saw the man and Johnnie come into the restaurant together. He sat back down, dipped his fries into some ketchup and stuck them into his mouth while he watched the man and Johnnie go up to the bar, exchange what looked like a few uncomfortable lines, and then walk over to the booth and began another conversation. Now, he was watching the three bikers he had passed on the way into the restaurant. They looked like they were looking for trouble when they walked over to the booth Johnnie and the tall man were sitting in. They were wearing sleeveless leather biker vests. The leader looked like a small head on a thick mass of muscle. He was bald and had a long, black goatee. Hatcher remembered seeing a tattoo of a bikini-clad girl on his right bicep, and what looked like an Ace of Hearts on his chest. He opened the phone booth, so he could hear the conversation. Before speaking, the leader flexed his chest muscles and said, "The nigger can stay, but uh, you gotta go, Tex."

All three bikers laughed.

The biker on the leader's right said, "We gonna take her out back and party with her for awhile."

The biker on his left looked at Johnnie who had laced her fingers together, clasping them tightly and said, "Yeah, you'll love it."

The tall man said, "Gentleman, I advise you to return to your seats before someone gets hurt. Or, better yet, why don't you three sissies get on your Harley Davidson's and ride on outta town?"

"Goddammit, Masterson!" Scotty yelled. "I told you I don't want no trouble in my place. Get her outta here. Now!"

Without taking his eyes off the biker leader, Masterson said, "Johnnie's not going anywhere until after she eats her chili, the grilled cheese sandwich, and the ribs. I suggest you corral these she devils before I have to put a serious hurtin' on 'em." He looked at Scotty for a quick second. "And don't let me hear you take the Lord's name in vain again."

All of sudden the bikers stopped laughing. The leader looked into Masterson's eyes. What he saw in them made the hair on the back of his neck stand up. He looked at his guys and said, "It's not worth going to jail over. Let's hit the road, boys. We gotta get to Memphis by mornin'."

They turned to leave.

Johnnie's smile lit up the room.

"Not so fast, boys," Masterson said.

The leader turned around and said, "What did you just say?"

"Who me?" Masterson said, smiling broadly.

"Yeah you, Tex," the leader said.

Smiling again, Masterson said, "I feel like you heard me. But just in case you're as stupid as that unkempt goatee makes you look, I said . . . not so fast, punk. I'm afraid I can't allow you to leave without a sincere apology."

"They don't have to apologize," Johnnie said, fearing for Masterson's life and whatever sacred honor she had left. She had been raped before, and she knew that's what they intended to do once they dispensed with Masterson.

"Don't worry, Johnnie," Masterson said without looking at her. "These she devils are sissies, sodomites that like men, not women. That's why they were trying to walk away. They know deep down that they like to stick their hard flesh into unnatural holes. And that's why they don't have the courage to stand up to a real man. There are three of

121

'em, and they know I'll clean their clocks—every last one of 'em . . . me . . . all by lonesome. That's why they're goin' to apologize."

The leader unleashed a quick right that landed flush on Masterson's square chin and would have flattened nine out of ten men. Masterson saw the blow coming. He expected it, but he didn't bother ducking or slipping the punch. Instead, he stood there, watching the leader put as much power behind the punch as he could. The blow sounded off when it landed. Smack! By taking the blow, he sent all three men a clear message. He wanted them to know that he could take the best punch their leader delivered, and then they would have to deal with a man they could not hurt—intimidation.

Masterson's head barely turned when he absorbed the blow. Instead, he smiled, turned his head to the left, offering his attacker the other side of his face and head. Again, he saw the blow coming, but he stood there and waited on it. Again, it sounded off. Smack! Masterson looked at the leader who had thrown the punches. His eyes bulged as he took a step or two backward. Masterson took two steps forward, anticipating the attack from the man on his left. He caught the blow in the palm of his hand and squeezed until the man screamed. Then, Masterson twisted the man's wrist, which forced his elbow to rise as he bent over in an attempt to alleviate the pain in his wrist and shoulder.

The biker on Masterson's right moved forward to attack, but caught a left hook for his trouble. His legs carried his upper body backward until he fell against the bar counter. The biker he was holding was still screaming. The leader went for Masterson's legs. He let the biker go and brought his elbow down on the back of the leader's neck a couple times. Then, he kneed him in the stomach, knocking the wind out of him. He grabbed the leader by his vest and stood him up. He was about to punch him in the face when he saw the biker he'd just let go about to swing. Masterson turned the leader into the blow. Teeth landed in several customers' food. The leader was on the ground— dazed, groaning, and holding his mouth as blood squeezed through his fingers.

Masterson faced the two bikers still standing. He waited until the first one came forward. When the biker swung, he stepped to the side and hit him with a left hook that landed on his chin. He was out cold before he hit the floor. The remaining biker screamed, "I'm gonna kill you, man." He ran at him full speed, pushing him across the room and up against a wall. The biker swung. Masterson ducked and brought his knee into his stomach. Then, he hit him with an uppercut that sent him reeling backward. Masterson pursued the biker and hit him with several more uppercuts, knocking him out. He looked at the three bikers. All of them were out cold. He went back to the booth where Johnnie was waiting and sat down.

Hatcher closed the phone booth, called New Orleans, and told Earl Shamus everything he'd seen.

"Find out everything there is to know about him," Earl said. "Everything."

"Mr. Shamus, that's going to cost a lot more money and I'm going to need more people on this."

"Whatever it takes, Hatcher."

"Then, I can expect a significant increase in pay when I go to Western Union tomorrow?"

"Don't worry. The money will be there. And it'll be more than enough to cover all your expenses and the expenses of your people. Now . . . when can I expect a report on the man she's with?"

"A few days. Maybe a week or so."

"Fine. If anything else happens tonight, don't hesitate to call."

"Yes, sir."

Chapter 35

"Yeah, but you're glad I did, right?"

Paul Masterson slid back into the booth across from Johnnie and looked into her sparkling eyes. He had never seen a woman more beautiful than she. A waitress brought out a piping hot bowl of chili, a grilled cheese sandwich, and six ribs with thick meat on the bones, soaked in zesty, mild barbecue sauce. She placed a glass of cold lemonade with a straw on the table and said, "Enjoy." Then, she winked at Masterson and said, "I get off in a half hour, Preacher. You're welcome to come home with me, if you like."

Masterson acted as if he didn't hear the waitress. He didn't even bother looking at her, nor did he acknowledge her invitation. Instead, he smiled at Johnnie until the waitress walked away. Then, he said, "Now . . . where were we?"

Johnnie said, "Why didn't you accept her invitation, Preacher?"

"The invitation didn't come from her, Johnnie."

Frowning, Johnnie said, "I heard her offer. Didn't you?"

"Yes, but the offer came from the devil. I doubt the woman had any idea she was being used by invisible spiritual forces. Again, where were we?"

"You were telling me that you're a traveling evangelist," Johnnie said and started working on her ribs. "But that can't be so."

"Why not?"

"Preachers don't go around starting fistfights, sir." She took another bite of her ribs. "And even if they did, they wouldn't enjoy it as much as you seem to."

"How are those ribs, Johnnie?"

She finished cleaning the bone, smacked a few times, and said, "All I can say is, I'll sure miss you when you leave town, sir."

"Call me, Paul, Johnnie. That's what I prefer."

She took a deep swig of her lemonade and said, "Okay."

"Now . . . why will you miss me when I leave town?"

"As long as you're here, I'll be able to come to this restaurant and be treated like any other human being. Quiet as it's kept, we Negroes are actual humans. We're not animals, and so we actually have feelings, same as white folk. It's unfair that I can't come here and eat when I have money to pay like everybody else. I could see if I were like you, coming in here, starting trouble. Yet you can come in here again and again. I've done nothing, and I cannot do that. So, as long as you're here, I plan to take advantage of whatever hospitality I can get."

"So, you think I started trouble, huh, Johnnie?"

"Yes, sir. You know the rules, yet you insist on breaking them."

"What if the rules are wrong, Johnnie? What then?"

"What do you mean, *if*, Paul? You, Scotty, the waitress, the bikers, and everybody else in here know the rules are wrong."

"And if I try to change the rules, I'm wrong for at least trying to change them? Is that what you're saying?"

She picked up another bone and started working on it while she thought about what her new friend had said. "Is that what you were doing, Paul . . . changing the rules?"

"What else would I be doing?"

She washed down the barbecue with some more lemonade. "You could have been trying to impress me."

He smiled and said, "Why can't I do both, Johnnie?"

She picked up her spoon and dug into the chili. She put the spoon in her mouth, shook her head and smiled as it went down. "Oh, my God, this is delicious."

"Next time, take a bite of your grilled cheese, and then put the chili in behind it. It's even better that way."

She tried it the way Masterson suggested and groaned, "Um, um, um. This is so good. It's a shame I won't be able to come back after you leave."

"Nothing I can do about that."

"Sure you could, Paul."

"What could I do more than what I just did?"

"You know other preachers, don't you?"

"Yeah, so?"

"White preachers have to tell their white congregations to help us get the same freedoms they have. Otherwise, nothing will change, Paul. Don't you know that? The white church is the main problem."

"You don't think I've done that? You don't think I've begged these guys to stand up for what's right?"

"Well, why aren't they standing up, Paul? Aren't they men of God? Don't they have a holy obligation to do what's right in God's eyes?"

"Most are too weak to get involved, but a few think that only the Gospel's message can change the hearts of men and women. And that's an argument that's hard to deny."

"But it's the white Christians that are killing coloreds, Paul. Don't you know that?"

"I know they're saying their Christians, but that don't mean they are."

She finished her chili and grilled cheese, and then started working on the remaining three bones, thinking about the church she used to attend before being sold to Earl Shamus, wondering how she would measure up if Paul knew who she was and all she had done over the course of two years.

"What's wrong?" he asked.

"Nothing."

The three bikers were still groggy as they staggered past Masterson and Johnnie's table. Masterson said, "Excuse me, gentlemen. I still can't allow you to leave without an apology to my friend here."

The bikers looked at each other, shrugged their shoulders, and staggered over to their table. The leader said, "Preacher, you're one tough son of a bitch." He looked at Johnnie and said, "We're sorry for ruinin' your dinner, ma'am. Goodnight."

The leader looked at Masterson and waited for his approval. Masterson looked at Johnnie. She looked at the biker leader and said, "Apology accepted." The biker leader looked at Masterson again, hoping that would be the end of it, having lost several of his front teeth, which he had retrieved. Masterson nodded and the bikers left quietly.

"Well, it's getting pretty late, Johnnie," Masterson said. "Is there someplace I can drop you?"

"Yes. I'm staying at the Clementine Hotel. It's right up the road."

"What a coincidence. I'm staying at the Clementine, too."

"Really?"

He nodded.

"Perhaps we'll get to know each other while you're in town, Paul. I'm thinking we should have dinner again tomorrow, right here in The Flamingo Den. What do you think?"

"I think that's a splendid idea, but it would have to be before the tent meeting."

"The tent meeting?"

"Yeah. I'm a guest preacher for the revival."

"So, you're a real preacher then?"

"I am."

She shook her head. "You're not like any minister I've ever met."

"Well, thank you, I think."

"So, why do you go around starting fistfights? Doesn't that go against the Bible, Paul? Aren't you supposed to turn the other cheek? Aren't you supposed to be humble and self-effacing?"

Chapter 36

"I thought we could be friends."

"Self-effacing, huh? That's a mighty big word, little lady. But to answer your question, didn't you see me take two blows before I defended myself?"

"I did."

"Then, there you have it."

"So, you think its okay to fight?"

"I most certainly do, and so does the Lord. He's been havin' a perpetual war with the devil for thousands of years, has he not? And if He fights for what's right, what's holy, and what's good, should I be any different? Should I not whip the devil's children when they have every intention of raping a defenseless woman? People always ask, "Where's God when you need him? I say He's right here, among us, but most of us won't lift a finger to help each other, but we expect God to do everything. I have two arms and two legs, and I'll use them to help anybody I can, anytime they need it. If people wanna criticize me for that, that's criticism I'll take."

"You mean white Christians won't help black Christians when they have the means to do so? You mean white Christians will send ten thousand missionaries over to Africa, but they won't so much as smile at a black Christian, let alone help him? Let me ask you something, Paul. How many Christians do you think are in this restaurant right now?"

Masterson looked around the room and said, "Well . . . the United States is a Christian nation, so I'd have to say ninety percent of the people in here probably have at least an affiliation with the church."

"Yet, not one of them said anything to the bikers that wanted to rape me. Christians had the bikers outnumbered about twenty to one, and they just sat there on their hands, watching it all. Why should colored people take you seriously? Why are there no good Samaritans in your flock, Paul?"

"See, that's where you're wrong, Johnnie. One did help you. Namely me."

Johnnie laughed. "You helped me, Paul?"

"Yeah."

"As I recall, you were the one who dragged me in here against my will."

"Yeah, but you're glad that I did, right?"

She nodded and smiled, "I am glad."

"If you're ready, I'll take you on back to the Clementine."

"Okay, let's go. And thanks for making it possible to eat here."

About ten minutes later, Paul and Johnnie were making their way up the stairs and to her hotel room. When they reached her door, she expected him to kiss her, which she wasn't against because the region beneath her waist had been seriously stimulated since she watched the preacher pummel her would-be rapists. She finally realized that she had a thing for roughneck men, no matter what color skin they were in. While she would not let him into her room, she would let him kiss her because she wanted to kiss him. As he drove her back to the Clementine in his hunter green Ford pickup truck, she wondered what his lips and tongue tasted like. She wondered what it would be like to be held by his strong arms, and so she waited for the inevitable. However, Paul didn't try to kiss her. He waited until she opened the door, and then he turned to leave. That intrigued her all the more because he was a white man, and white men always wanted to kiss her and any other thing she allowed them to do.

"Paul?"

He turned around. "Yeah."

"You wanna come in?"

"I most certainly would like to come in there, but I can't do it. I appreciate the offer though. Goodnight and sleep tight. I'm in Room 107, if you need anything."

"Seriously, Paul, you're not coming in?"

"Seriously."

He turned and walked a few paces down the veranda.

"Paul?"

"Yeah."

"You're not going to at least invite me to revival?"

"No. You made it clear that you have a real problem with Christians."

"It's just white Christians."

"Goodnight, Johnnie."

"Usually white women Christians, if you must know. Most of the men really like me. I'm sorry, you don't. I thought we could be friends."

"We'll see ya tomorrow, Johnnie."

"You mean it?"

"I mean it."

Chapter 37

"Welcome to the Army!"

Lucas Matthews entered the empty barracks and switched on the light. The bay was filled with more than forty beds of iron, lining both walls. He could almost see himself in the glossy floor. He walked down the center aisle, looking at each bunk and footlocker in front of it and standing locker behind it. He had heard many times that boot camp would be a much stronger version of football practice, where hazing was a part of the ritual for freshmen. He remembered when he first joined the team and how he was targeted because he was so much bigger than all the first-year high school players. He figured he would be a target here, too, and had prepared for it. He looked at the clock. It was 9:30. He took a quick shower, and thirty minutes later, he was sound asleep.

The signal to rise, boisterously articulated by the Reveille bugle, sounded about ten minutes after Lucas had fallen asleep. At least that's how long it felt to him. Actually two hours had passed. Bright lights stung his eyes even though they were still closed. When he was finally able to focus, he looked at the clock. It was 12:01. Wondering if he had really slept fourteen hours, he looked out the barracks window and saw the cover of night. That's when he realized it was just after twilight. The sergeant who had processed Lucas had lied when he said that his class would start at noon. There was no way he could get twelve noon and twelve midnight mixed up. Nevertheless, basic training was starting right now, he realized. As he struggled to get his bearings, he felt his bed being lifted, rising higher and higher, until it toppled over with him still in it. Then, he heard the sound of people running into the barracks along with several commanding voices screaming, "Move you candy-assed bastards! Move it! Move it! Move it!"

Still groggy, Lucas was trying to get to his feet when he felt two powerful hands on his T-shirt, pulling him up, then pushing him backward swiftly, and slamming him into his locker. The sound of his back hitting it echoed throughout the barracks.

"What's yo' name, son?" the sergeant who had literally snatched him to his feet screamed.

Alert now, his eyes found the man the hands belonged to. He was a short man compared to Lucas. The sergeant was about five-seven in his spit-shined combat boots. The man had fire in his eyes, and it wasn't from too many shots of whiskey. He looked around the room and saw about forty to fifty men and about ten other sergeants he presumed was there to back the play of the man holding him against the locker like he was the prime suspect in the murder of a good ol' boy. Most of the sergeants were white, two were black, and one Hispanic, but they were all dressed in heavily starched fatigues, with tight creases in their short-sleeved shirts and khaki pants. They were all wearing round headgear with wide stiff brims, all of them clean-shaven, and from what he could tell, practically bald, showing very little hair above their ears.

"Did you hear me, son?" the sergeant screamed.

His eyes found the man shouting at him. "Lucas Matthews."

"Lucas Matthews what?" the sergeant screamed.

He shrugged his shoulders and nonchalantly said, "Just plain Lucas Matthews."

The sergeant let him go and put his fists on his hips. "Are you mocking me, son?"

Lucas was about to answer when the sergeant punched him in the stomach. The blow landed a little below the belt line, exactly where he intended it, which gave the sergeant an air of strength he really didn't have. To all the recruits, it looked like a shot to the belly, but hitting a man anywhere below the belt had the same affect on the body, which is why the sergeant's aim was true. Lucas dropped to one knee and coughed. It was the hardest he had ever been hit in his life.

Still standing over Lucas who was struggling to get air into his lungs, the sergeant said, "My name is Sergeant Limitless Cornsilk. And

I want all you dim-witted sons of bitches to listen and listen good. You will address me as Sergeant or sir. Not Sergeant, sir! Not sir, Sergeant! Either Sergeant or sir. Never together! Have I made myself clear?"

"Yes, Sergeant," the men nearest Lucas said, fearing they would be next to feel his invisible fists.

"When I ask you sons of bitches a question," he looked around, offering the men a menacing glare, his fists back on his hips, "I want everybody to answer in unison with military precision. I wanna hear you say, 'Yes, sir.' Have I made myself clear?"

"Yes, sir," the men screamed in unison.

Cornsilk looked at Lucas, who was still on one knee coughing. "Stand yo' ass up, Matthews! I barely touched you. You're supposed to be a tough cookie. You were the star running back for your high school football team, and ya ran numbers for the New Orleans Syndicate. Ya sold dope to heroin fiends and did time in a meet grinder called, Angola. Time in Angola alone should have toughened you up." Looking down at Lucas, he said, "I know Colonel Strong pulled some strings to get you out of prison two months early. I also know you think that if you make it through boot camp, which means making it pass me, you've got a free ticket to Germany to play football for the Colonel while these other boys might have to do some real fighting when another war comes along. But you won't hav'ta fight, will you, Matthews?" Lucas couldn't seem to stop coughing. "And if you cough one more goddamn time, I swear to God you'll spend the next two weeks in the infirmary." He turned around and walked down the center aisle, eyeing the recruits, looking for the fear that they should all have by now, considering their introduction to the man who would own them for the next four months. When he saw fear on their faces, he put his fists back on his hips again and said, "Welcome to the Army!"

Chapter 38

"You'll do what I say . . . when I say . . . how I say . . ."

Lucas forced himself to stand erect even though he hadn't caught his breath yet, gasping for air, desperately trying to refill his lungs, constantly resisting the urge to double over and let the catfish and the rest of the dinner he had eaten spill all over the polished floor. The delicious dinner he'd had with Cassandra seemed like a distant memory now that his training had started. He eyed Sergeant Cornsilk, wondering how he knew so much about him and why he would tell everyone about his life in the New Orleans underworld. At the same time, he was glad that the sergeant had stopped short of mentioning his tryst with Marla Bentley, who for all he knew had been found in her Cadillac by now. The more he looked at Cornsilk, the more recognizable he became. He was one of the men he had been in line with in the Mess Hall less than twenty-four hours earlier. The scene between him and the cook played out in his mind again. He now knew that the sergeants in line with him were just waiting for him to carry out his threat against the cook and they would have beaten him to within an inch of his life.

All of a sudden, he was glad the cook hadn't called him a newbie again. He was also glad that he hadn't jumped over the counter and whipped him to show him he was all the things that Sergeant Cornsilk had just told everyone. Still watching Cornsilk, Lucas now understood to some degree why they called him newbie and why Cassandra had told him he was wet behind the ears. Sergeant Cornsilk knew exactly who he was, what he had done, and where he was planning to go. And if he knew that much, he knew about Napoleon,

Marla, Bubbles, and Johnnie, too. He had stood in line with his drill sergeant, right next to him in fact, yet he had no idea where the man who had ordered SOS before him was from or how he knew about the newbie who had constantly bragged about being from New Orleans.

Sergeant Cornsilk said, "Now . . . when I say atten-hut, you will all snap to it! You will bring your heels together at a forty-five degree angle. You will suck in your gut and stick out your chest. Do you understand?"

"Yes, sir," they screamed.

"I can't *hear* you!"

"YES, SIR."

"Atten-hut!"

The men stood up straight and stuck out their chests.

"What the hell was that? I wanna hear one sound and one sound only. It will be the sound of your heels clicking together. Now at ease. For you dumb bastards from Cheyenne, Wyoming or wherever the hell you sons of a bitches are from, that means you are to return to whatever you were doing prior to me calling you to attention. Understand?"

"Yes, sir!"

"Now let's try that shit again. Atten-hut!"

The recruits came to attention again, but they still didn't do it the way Sergeant Cornsilk wanted it done. He made them do it ten more times, which was when he heard one sound and one sound only.

"While at attention, you will keep your eyes forward at all times. For you simpleminded, backward-assed hicks from the sticks that don't know any better that means as I walk around the barracks, your eyes are not to follow me as I move. Understand?"

"Yes, sir!"

"As I said, my name is Sergeant Cornsilk, and this ain't no playground. The work I have to do is serious . . . serious business! This is my domain. I rule here. Understand?"

"Yes, sir!"

"For you moose-ridin' bastards from Fairbanks, Alaska, that can't read or write that means for the next sixteen weeks I'm your mother and your father, your sister, your brother, your uncles, and your aunts. Understand?"

"Yes, sir!"

"I want all you son of a bitches who've come from every corner of the fruited plain to know that you have not come to me by accident. Providence has brought you to me. For you dumb bastards from Raleigh, North Carolina, that means that Almighty God brought you here. He brought you to me so I can teach you girls how to fight and win wars. I want all you bastards to know that the United States Army is not a democracy! You don't have any rights. You have no say. You have no vote. This is the Army! We are warriors.

"For you cheese-eatin' bastards from Green Bay, Wisconsin, that means that when our Commander-in-Chief, the President of the United States, decides it's time to go to war, we will hunt down our enemies, and we will kill them. The United States Army is a dictatorship. For you Italian hot-dog-eatin' bastards from New York City, that means you'll do what I say . . . when I say . . . how I say . . . or you'll visit the infirmary for two weeks! Understand?"

"Yes, sir!"

"And if you have to visit the infirmary for two weeks, when you get out, we'll have to start this little dance all over again, girls. And we'll keep starting over until I'm satisfied that you dumb bastards from Hollywood, California, learned to do everything, and I mean everything, the Army way. You will not be kicked out. And you cannot quit. We'll think about letting you out when your three-year commitment is up. In the meantime, you'll eat the Army way. You'll drink the Army way. You'll shit the Army way. And by God you'll fuck the Army way. Understand?"

"Yes, sir!"

Chapter 39

"Ya ever see such a poor class of recruits in your life?"

Sergeant Cornsilk's heels clicked as he walked the floor, looking in the eyes of each man he passed. "I see you sons of bitches looking at me, wondering where I'm from, what race I represent. Some of you smart bastards that went to college probably think I'm a Native American. Listen up! I am not a Native American. The title makes me sick to my stomach. It implies that the land was always called America. It eradicates my ancestors' birthright as being the only indigenous people here long before Christopher Columbus supposedly discovered it, long before it was named after Amerigo Vespucci. Both of them dumb bastards were lost. Columbus thought he had found India, which is why they call my people Indians. And Vespucci, that dumb fuck, thought he had discovered Asia. Understand?"

"Yes, sir!"

"I'm a full-blooded Apache. A direct descendent of Geronimo. That means all you sons of bitches are foreigners to me. Especially you pale-faced bastards who stole my land in the first fuckin' place. Don't believe that bullshit you see in cowboy movies. Understand?"

"Yes, sir!"

"Listen up you dumb bastards! We just finished a war with North Korea six short months ago, but know this: There will always be another war to fight. Understand?"

"Yes, sir!"

"My point is that you poor bastards are here for one reason and one reason only. My dilemma is whether or not to ask you why you *think* you're here. I'm tempted not to ask you dumb bastards anything because I know the answers will reveal just how stupid you really are. But I'll give it a try." He walked up to tall white recruit and said, "Where you from, son?"

"Lynchburg, Virginia," the young man said in a mousy voice.

"Lynchburg, Virginia, what?" Cornsilk screamed after getting into his face. Without telegraphing the blow, Cornsilk hit him just below the belt line. He dropped to one knee, much like Lucas did. Standing over him, Cornsilk yelled, "Is Lynchburg full of sissies like you? And sound off like you got a pair. Are you a man or woman?"

He coughed several times before shouting, "Lynchburg, Virginia, sir!"

"Lynchburg, huh?" Cornsilk repeated, looking at Lucas. "Ya hear that, New Orleans? This patriot might wanna lynch you and your people." He looked down at the recruit again, who was still coughing, still trying to get air in his lungs. "Ain't that right?"

Wheezing, the man said, "No, sir."

"Stand up!"

The young man stood up and returned to attention, but everything in him wanted to double over and continue coughing. His eyes filled with water and a tear slid down his face.

"What the hell is this? Are you crying, Lynchburg?"

"No, sir! I'm just trying to catch my breath, sir!"

"What's your name, son?"

"John O'Reilly, sir!"

"O'Reilly, huh? That's Irish, ain't it?"

"Yes, sir!"

"Uh-huh. So, that means ya mama and daddy are drunks, ain't that right?"

"No, sir!"

"John is a religious name. So, tell me, John . . . are you of the religious ilk?"

"Yes, sir. I'm a Presbyterian, sir!"

"Proud of it, too, I see."

"Yes, sir!"

"And do you practice your religion, son?"

"Yes, sir!"

"Uh-huh. Tell me, John . . . why are you here in my barracks?"

"I'm here to die for my country, sir!"

Cornsilk turned around and walked into the center aisle and said, "Whoever agrees with John, raise your hand."

Cornsilk looked around the room and saw that Lucas Matthews was the only one who didn't have his hand raised. He fast-walked over to Lucas, got in his face, nose to nose, and screamed, "You dare disagree with a fellow recruit when everybody agrees with him?"

"Yes, sir," Lucas shouted with conviction.

"Outstanding." Cornsilk said softly and walked back to the center of the barracks. "Okay, New Orleans, I'll bite. Enlighten us. Tell us why you're right, and all these other dumb bastards are wrong."

"The purpose of the United States Military is to kill as many of our enemies as we can and to blow up all their buildings and equipment, sir! I'm not here to die for my country! I'm here to kill for my country, sir!"

"Outstanding, son. That's exactly right. You just might be officer material after all. Look around this room, New Orleans. Ya ever see such a poor class of recruits in your life?"

"No, sir!"

"Me neither, New Orleans. Me neither." Cornsilk started walking the floor again, his heels clicking, looking at the men who were still at attention. "Do we have any more *Christians* here? If so, raise your hands."

Half the men raised their hands.

"Those of you that raised your hands have no doubt heard of King David. Not only did he kill Goliath with one stone, but he killed tens of thousands of men. Now what that means is this: I don't wanna here nuthin' about you bastards not fighting for religious reasons. You will not be assigned to administrative duties. You will not be assigned to the kitchen. You will not be assigned to the motor pool. You will fight, and you will kill just like David did. Any man who will not fight for religious reasons is a coward, and I will not have any cowards saying that I trained them. Understand?"

"Yes, sir!"

"Outstanding!"

Chapter 40

"Victory starts here, gentlemen."

"Now," Cornsilk continued, "I want you white bastards to look at the black bastards across the bay from you. I also want you to look at the Mexican bastards, the Puerto Rican bastards, and the Asian bastards standing at attention next to you. Do it now." The men looked at each other. "I want you to think of all the racial names you've heard your mama and daddy and minister call 'em at the dinner table after church. I want you to call them those names on my command. Understand?"

"Yes, sir!"

"Now . . . all you nonwhites, I want you to do likewise to the whites on my command. Understand?"

"Yes, sir!"

"Now . . . if any man so much as touches a man that's not of his race during this exercise, I will personally see to it that he spends the next two weeks in traction. Understand?"

"Yes, sir!"

Cornsilk walked down the center aisle, heels clicking with each step. When he reached the entrance, he grabbed a chair, brought it to the center of the barracks, and sat down. Then, he looked at them and said, "When I raise my hand, it all stops. Understand?"

"Yes, sir!"

"Once I raise my hand, if I hear another word, or if I think I heard another word, where will you end up?"

"In the infirmary, sir!"

"For how long?"

"Two weeks, sir!"

"Outstanding." He pulled out a stopwatch and said, "Begin!"

For the next fifteen minutes, the recruits called each other the worst names imaginable. And they were quite animated, gesticulating with their hands and fingers, grabbing their crotches, talking about each other's mothers and sisters and girlfriends. Before long, they brought extended family members, schools, teachers, and a lack of education into it. And that was what the blacks were saying about the whites. Then, they started badmouthing each other's city and state.

Laughing uncontrollably, Cornsilk raised his hand and silence filled the barracks. He stood up, having regained his military bearing and said, "Now . . . I want all you bastards to know something. In July 1948, President Truman signed Executive Order 9981. Executive Order 9981 eliminated segregation in the Armed Forces. That's why all you bastards are in the same barracks now. From this day forward, from this very moment, you will not use the word nigger, spic, wetback, cracker, chink or any word that means the same thing. Understand?"

"Yes, sir!"

"Any man who disregards what I just said starting right now will spend two weeks in the infirmary. Before I'm finished, you will be brothers in arms—warriors! The man you just called nigger or cracker or wetback or chink will one day save your life on the field of battle. Understand?"

"Yes, sir!"

"You will therefore value his life as your own, understand?"

"Yes, sir!"

"Outstanding. When we go to war, we will kill our *enemies*, not each other, and we will keep killing our *enemies* until they surrender or there's none of them poor bastards left. Understand?"

"Yes, sir!"

"Victory starts here, gentlemen. Victory costs and is paid for in blood. Victory demands a heavy price. And tomorrow you start paying, long before you ever step on the field of battle. I will get you in the best shape of your lives. That, I guarantee. Starting tomorrow, for ten hours a day you will learn military courtesy, you will drill, and you will practice personal hygiene. For all you dumb bastards that don't know what personal hygiene means, it means you will wash your ass daily! I know some of you funky bastards only bathe once a month . . . hell, I'm being generous. Some of you only bathe on Christmas and Easter. But from now on, you will wash your ass every single day, or you will spend two weeks in the infirmary! Understand?"

"Yes, sir!"

"You will be awakened by the Reveille bugle and you will go to bed by the Taps bugle, understand?"

"Yes, sir!"

"Every night, before you go to sleep, you will sing one stanza of 'America the Beautiful' or 'My Country Tis of Thee' on alternating nights, lest you forget what this is all about. Understand?"

"Yes, sir!"

"Sergeant Davis. Sergeant Miller. Sergeant Williams. Sergeant Garcia."

All four sergeants came forward holding what appeared to be large white rolled up scrolls.

"Show these poor bastards what this is all about," Sergeant Cornsilk said.

All the sergeants unrolled their scrolls in front of the men. They were blown up photographs of Elizabeth Taylor, Dorothy Dandridge, Marilyn Monroe, and Rita Moreno—all of them in tight, two-piece bathing suits. The eyes of the recruits lit up, and big bright smiles filled the room.

"That's right. We're here for them. We fight for them. Everything else is a bunch of bullshit. We're here to protect our women, your mother, your sister, your aunt, and your grandmother . . . all of them. The things that are going through your minds right now as you look at these women are going through our enemy's minds, too. And if they come in here, if they make it to these shores, the first thing they're going to do is fuck your mothers and your sisters. Some of them horny bastards will even fuck your old-ass grandmothers. All conquerors do it. It's been that way since men started killing each other for personal gain. As quiet as it's kept, we do it, too. And we can't let that happen, can we?"

"No, sir!"

"New Orleans!"

"Yes, sir!"

"You played running back for your high school football team, did you not?"

"Yes, sir!"

142

"Did your school have cheerleaders?"

"Yes, sir!"

"And what was there purpose?"

"To motivate us so that we would be victorious on the field of battle, sir!"

"For you dumb bastards who didn't fully understand what New Orleans just said, I'll explain it to you. Football players and cheerleaders are symbols. Hundreds, perhaps thousands of years ago, when warriors invaded, the men fought to protect their property, their food, and most important, their women and children. The women knew that if their men lost, they were going to be invaded, so they cheered when their men won. But if they lost, a cry of lamentation rang out loudly because the women were immediately invaded and impregnated by the foreigners. That . . . gentlemen, is the price of defeat. And so we fight, we kill, we maim, until we have complete and total victory. Understand?"

"Yes, sir!"

"Outstanding. Now, let's hear the first stanza of 'America the Beautiful.'"

Standing at attention with his hand over his heart, Cornsilk led them in the song, and they all sang out loud and proud.

"America! America . . . God shed His grace on thee . . ."

"New Orleans!" Cornsilk shouted.

"Yes, sir!" Lucas answered.

"Lynchburg!" Cornsilk shouted.

"Yes, sir!"

"Front and center . . . both of you!" Cornsilk shouted.

Sergeants Davis and Miller brought their pinup posters and handed them to Cornsilk, and then they went back to where the other sergeants were standing at parade rest. He handed one to Lucas and the other to John. He looked at Lucas and said, "I want you to tape this to your locker." Then, he looked at John and told him the same thing.

"New Orleans!" Cornsilk shouted.

"Yes, sir!"

"Show your brothers in arms who you'll be protecting."

Lucas unrolled the poster. He smiled and showed everyone Elizabeth Taylor's bikini pinup. A loud groan swept through the

143

barracks as the white recruits felt the sting of Taylor hanging on Lucas' locker.

"Pipe down, you horny bastards," Cornsilk shouted. He looked at John and said, "Show the boys yours, Lynchburg."

He unrolled his and showed the recruits a picture of Dorothy Dandridge. Another loud groan swept through the barracks. This time it came from black recruits.

"What about Rita Moreno?" a recruit called out.

"Yeah, and what about Marilyn Monroe?" another recruit called out.

"Who said that?"

No one responded. Cornsilk walked up to Sergeant Williams and Sergeant Garcia and took the pinups of Monroe and Moreno out of their hands. Then, he walked over to one of the recruits and said, "Where you from, son?"

"Spanish Harlem, by way of Puerto Rico, sir!"

"Uh-huh. You don't say. Here . . . you get Marilyn Monroe."

Another groan from the white recruits bounced off the walls.

Cornsilk doubled over, laughing. When he regained control, he said, "I know you pale-faced sons of bitches don't like it, but that's too damned bad. The founding fathers thought of the United States as a melting pot, an amalgamation of people—E pluribus Unum. That's Latin for 'Out of many, one.' So, you might as well get used to it. This is our future. New Orleans!"

"Yes, sir!"

"Since you were the only one with enough guts to disagree with Lynchburg earlier, you're the barrack's chief. You're in charge when I'm not here. That means you're responsible for everything that goes wrong and everything that goes right. If a man's shoes aren't shined properly, I'm gonna blame you. If a man fails an inspection, and I don't care if it's a surprise inspection, I'm gonna blame you. If a man doesn't know his left from his right when we're in formation, I'm gonna blame you. Understand?"

"Yes, sir!"

"When you've heard Taps, and its time to hit the rack, I expect you to lead the others in one of the songs I mentioned. You will call the men to attention, put your hand over your heart, and you will sing loud enough to be heard at the front gate. Understand?"

"Yes, sir!"

"Lynchburg!"

"Yes, sir."

"You are second in command when I'm not here. You will remind New Orleans of his responsibilities, and you will back him up. If there's even one racial incident, I'm going to blame you. If I have to demote New Orleans for any reason, I'm going to blame you. If one white recruit refuses to obey his orders, I'm going to blame you. Understand?"

"Yes, sir!"

"What do you think'll happen if I blame you, Lynchburg?"

"I'll lose my position as second in command, and I'll end up in traction, sir!"

"Outstanding." Cornsilk looked around the barracks and said, "Did everyone hear my orders?"

"Yes, sir!"

"If you have a problem, you will not speak to me about it. You will first take it to Lynchburg. Lynchburg will take your problem to New Orleans. New Orleans will determine if I need to know about it or not. And gentlemen, if any, and I mean any bullshit gets to me, God help you. Understand?"

"Yes, sir!"

"I've just given you what we call the chain of command. You never ever violate the chain of command. Understand?"

"Yes, sir!"

"New Orleans!"

"Yes, sir!"

"You and Lynchburg are squad leaders. Pick two others." Cornsilk looked at the recruits and said, "If you are picked to be a squad leader, the men under you will report any problems to you. You will then take them to Lynchburg and so on. Understand?"

"Yes, sir!"

"Alright. That's it for now. After New Orleans selects the squad leaders, hit your racks and get some sleep. You're gonna need it."

"New Orleans!"

"Yes, sir!"

"Just because you answered the question right don't mean that you've got it made. This ain't high school football, son. This is the Army, and I'm gonna ride you into the ground. I'm gonna ride you until you become everything Colonel Strong thinks you can be. If you're not officer material, I'm gonna find that out. Understand?"

"Yes, sir!"

"Outstanding. Take over."

"Yes, sir! May I ask a question, sir?"

"What is it, New Orleans?"

"What about Rita Moreno, sir? Who's girl will she be, sir?"

Cornsilk looked at the pinup for a quick second. Shaking his head wantonly, he said, "Um, um, um. I forgot I was holding her. She's my favorite of the four. Must be a psychological thing." Still looking at the poster, he shook his head wantonly again and offered it to Lucas. "Here, you decide who gets her."

"Yes, sir!" Lucas shouted.

Chapter 41

"I would be honored, sir!"

Lucas waited until all the sergeants left the open bay. When he heard the barracks door close he said, "All right you simpleminded mutha-fuckas! You heard 'em! If I lose my job as barracks chief . . . if I have to fire Lynchburg . . . if I have to fire one of my squad leaders, I will personally see to it that you end up in the infirmary! If any of you muthafuckas doubt that shit, step up now, and I will beat the living shit outta you! You heard the sergeant. I was with the New Orleans Syndicate. I had to kick ass on a daily basis. My mentor was a Negro named Bubbles. We used to collect debts. And when a muthafucka couldn't pay, we took it outta his ass. We used to beat muthafuckas to within an inch of their lives. I loved that shit! That means that not only will I beat the shit outta every man in here, but I'll enjoy doing it. Understand?"

"Yes, sir!"

"UNDERSTAND?"

"YES, SIR."

"Alright then. Lynchburg!"

"Yes, sir!"

"Pick two squad leaders, and if they fuck up, it's yo' ass!" Then Lucas walked over to the only Asian recruit in the platoon and said, "Where you from, son?"

"Chinatown! San Francisco, California, sir!"

"The girl I was gonna marry has a brother that lives in San Francisco. Perhaps you can tell me all about it someday. What's your name?"

"Nicolas Lee."

"Here you go, San Francisco. You get Rita Moreno. Protect her, son."

"I will, sir! With my life."

"Can you fight, San Francisco?"

"Yes, sir! I'm trained in Wing Chun Kung Fu, sir! I've been practicing for fourteen years."

"You don't say. You think you can take me, San Francisco?"

"I can do either, sir?"

"You can do either? What do you mean you can do either?"

"I mean I can take you, or I can protect you, sir. Your choice."

Lucas looked into Lee's eyes for a long minute, attempting to find fear in his heart. He didn't see any fear, nor did he sense any. He knew then that the man from Chinatown could probably do exactly what he said he could. "How would you like to be a squad leader, San Francisco?"

"I would be honored, sir!"

Still looking into Lee's eyes, Lucas shouted, "Lynchburg!"

"Yes, sir!" O'Reilly shouted.

"How many squad leaders have you chosen?"

"Two, sir!"

"Get rid of one 'em. Lee's gonna be a squad leader. He understands loyalty. He doesn't know the meaning of betrayal. I can see it in his eyes. So, we only need one now."

"Yes, sir!"

Chapter 42

"Not many people want them in this town."

Johnnie's alarm rang out with the ferocity of an alert klaxon at four the next morning. She hit the button, and the bells stopped ringing. Quiet filled the room. She hadn't slept nearly as long as she wanted to. She wished she could go back to sleep and stay in that condition for another six hours or so, but now that she was broke, she no longer had the luxury of sleeping as long as she wanted. The lack of money demanded that she abandon any notions of sleep, so she could pursue gainful employment to ensure that she ate, paid her bills, and invested in her future. Nevertheless, lying in a comfortable bed and being in complete darkness was a sweet temptation to continue sleeping, and she almost fell into its trap.

She turned on the light, hoping its brightness would keep her from falling back to sleep. The last thing she wanted was to be late for work on her very first day. Still lying in bed, letting her eyes adjust to the light, she took a deep breath and exhaled as the memory of her house burning down washed over her. The smell of ashes suddenly filled her nose as the picture of charred remains filled her mind. It was still hard for her to accept her new position. Life had dealt her another unfair hand, she thought. She took another deep breath and told herself that it wasn't too late to start all over.

She encouraged herself with a new picture—one that offered the promise of regaining the fortune she had lost. She used her imagination to conjure up a future she could believe in. She thought that if she could see it in her mind, she could have whatever she saw. She pictured herself having a bigger and better house, a bigger and better car, a whole new wardrobe, and a closet filled with nothing but shoes. What she saw in her mind's eye seemed real because seeing those things made them believable, and therefore attainable. Suddenly, Gloria Schumacher came into focus.

It soon occurred to Johnnie that Gloria Schumacher and people like her who had disposable money could be the key to her success. The prospect of having white folks as potential clients would have seemed impossible a year ago, but now that she had lost everything and everyone that held her in New Orleans, she began to wonder if the old paradigm, the old way of thinking, that success belonged exclusively to whites, was true. At sixteen, she had already debunked that theory by amassing a quarter of a million dollars with her initial investments. Upon realizing this, a smile emerged, and nearly obliterated the memory of the wasteland that Ashland Estates had become. Where she once saw wreckage, misery, suffering, and regret, she now saw opportunity, possibility, hope, and good fortune.

Feeling good all of a sudden, Johnnie hurried into the bathroom and hopped into the shower. Having a real, almost tangible vision for a future that could be hers if she pursued it, gave her a burst of energy that she had never felt before. The vision put a smile on her face, gave her something to strive for, and it would keep her moving forward until the vision became an authentic reality. A half hour later, she was on Wilshire heading toward Blakeslee, briskly walking over to the restaurant, and hoping to get there before Lucille and her husband. She had a lot to prove to the people who had given her a job, and she had a lot to prove to herself.

When she reached Blakeslee, she was still a block or so away, but she could see the glow of light pouring out of the large picture windows and the glass door. Lucille and Hank were already in the restaurant. A little disappointed that she hadn't beaten her employers to work, she walked faster, still hoping to make a good first impression. Having reached Lucille's, she pushed the glass door, but it was still locked. She looked inside and saw Lucille and Hank talking. They looked angry, like they were having an argument. Lucille had her arms folded. Hank was shaking his head, and then he threw up his arms. She was about to knock on the window to let them know she was there bright and early and ready to earn her pay, but she hesitated, thinking she should just wait until five-thirty, which was when they were expecting her. She walked farther up the block, where she saw a white newspaperman setting up his shop, preparing, she assumed, to sell papers, magazines, and books. She smiled, thinking he might have a Wall Street Journal.

"Are you open for business, sir?" Johnnie asked.

The man looked at her briefly, and then seriously looked at her a second time, stunned by her beauty and voluptuous womanhood. He smiled and said, "You must be new around here."

She smiled and said, "I am, sir. I just got here yesterday. I'm going to be working for Hank and Lucille. Today is my first day, and I'm really excited."

"I see. I know Hank and Lucille. They make the best breakfast around these parts. I suppose I'll be seeing you regularly. My name is Franklin Hill. I don't usually open before six-thirty, but since you're already here, what can I get you?"

She looked around for a moment or two, hoping to spot the periodical she was looking for, but when she didn't see it, she said, "Do you carry the Wall Street Journal?"

"I carry a few. Not many people want them in this town. But I get about ten a day, just in case. Would you like one?"

"Yes, sir, I would."

Chapter 43

"I probably could, but it's a big risk."

Johnnie paid Franklin, and he handed her a Wall Street Journal. She smiled and tried to read the first page even though it was still dark. She moved under the streetlight and read for awhile. When she felt Franklin's eyes staring at her ample backside, she turned around and locked eyes with him, letting him know that it wasn't okay to gawk. When he looked away, she realized her point had been made without a single word. Then, she turned around and headed back to the restaurant, still trying to read the paper in the dark. Just as she was about to push the door again to enter the restaurant, it occurred to her that Franklin had said that not many people in Jackson wanted the Wall Street Journal. She figured he meant white people didn't want it because she didn't know any Negroes who invested their money.

A bright smile covered her face when she realized that she might be the only stockbroker in Jackson. Her smile fled almost as quickly as it arrived when she realized that it might be difficult to get people to invest with her because she was new in town. They might think she was some sort of flimflam artist. She knew that was an obstacle she would have to overcome. She understood that she needed people to trust her with their money, and that it could prove to be a very difficult feat because money ruled the world, and those who had it were its monarchs. Herbert Shields, Lucas' friend, who lived in Jackson and played football for the college came to mind. He knew her, and he probably had lots of money from selling marijuana. She figured that if she made him money, his word alone would get plenty of customers.

Smiling broadly now, she pushed the glass door to enter, but it was still locked. She looked at her watch. It was close to five-thirty. She saw Lucille and Hank. They were still in the kitchen, but they were no longer arguing. She knocked on the window. She saw Hank look at her, and then at his watch. She saw him look at Lucille, tilt his head toward her, and then he looked at her again and smiled. She wondered what was going on as he made his way over to the door and let her in. "You made it on time, I see," Hank said, still smiling. "I told Lucille you'd be here bright and early."

Johnnie wanted to ask why Lucille would doubt her punctuality, but instead, she said, "Actually, I was here about ten minutes ago, maybe fifteen."

"Really? So, you saw me and the Missus having a little spat, and you left, huh?"

"Uh-huh. I was early, so I went and picked up a copy of the Wall Street Journal."

"Really? Funny you should mention Wall Street. I understand that you were quite the investor in New Orleans. Is that right?"

Frowning, Johnnie pulled her head back a little and said, "What do you mean, Hank?"

"I mean, we know who you are," Hank said, still smiling. "How long did you think you could keep who you really are a secret?"

"You know who I am, huh?"

"Yeah, and you ain't just Benny's little sister either the way you made it seem yesterday. You're the Johnnie Wise that all the papers are talking about right now. They're saying you were acquitted of murder charges and that the crackers were so mad that they burned down the black community. Is that right?"

"Yes, sir, it is."

"So, did you really lose two hundred and fifty thousand dollars like the papers say?"

"Between me and you, yes, I did, sir."

"Lucille," Hank called out over his shoulder.

"Yeah," Lucille replied.

"Come on out here, girl. We don' found ourselves a bona-fide businesswoman who can take us where we wanna go."

Lucille came out of the kitchen. She was drying her hands with a white towel. Her face was wrinkled by growing anger. "Hank, I don' told you I'm not getting involved with no investments. I'm not gon' lose my restaurant trying to play the stock market."

He looked at her and said, "Well, I am." Then, he looked at Johnnie and said, "I've got some money saved up, Johnnie. Do you think you can help me make the kind of money you made?"

Although she was elated by the prospect of yet another potential client, Johnnie looked at Lucille before speaking, knowing that husband and wife were at odds on the issue. "Uh, I don't wanna come between you and your wife, Hank. I told y'all they stole all the money I made anyway."

Practically ignoring what she said, Hank persisted and said, "Yeah, yeah, I know, but you can do it again, cain't you? I mean, if you did it once, you could do it again, right?"

Johnnie looked at Lucille again. She could tell she was getting angrier by the second, which told her that they had been arguing about her and investing when she saw them earlier. She looked at the floor and didn't answer.

"Johnnie, don't let Lucille scare you, okay?" Hank said. "She's not going to do a damn thing to you. And if you're worried about losing your job with us, don't worry about it. Lucille doesn't have the vision that you and I have. She's a good organizer, and she keeps everything clean. She even knows how to stretch a dollar, but she thinks small-time. I think big-time, and I know an opportunity when it comes my way. Sure, she knew it would be a good idea to open this restaurant, this is small-time compared to the fortune you made. The restaurant is doing okay, I guess. I mean, we don't miss any meals, and we pay our bills on time, but we ain't no closer to a fortune than we was when we started. We get here at five in the morning, and we don't lock up until eight. By the time we get home, we tired as hell, and we go straight to bed. Then, we get up at four the next morning and start the process all over again. I think those investments can put us on easy street."

Feeling the pressure, Johnnie said, "Hank, please, it's not that simple. There is no guarantee that you'll make any money. Not one dime. In fact, you could lose it all."

"I know, but listen. If you do a thing one time, you can do it again, right?" Hank repeated.

"I probably could, but it's a big risk."

"How much of that five thousand are you going to invest?" Hank asked.

Chapter 44

"What do you mean *our* money?"

Johnnie stared at Hank for a long minute as what Gloria Schumacher had told her the previous day washed over her. She closed her eyes for a second or two, thinking about her business being all over town in a matter of minutes, it seemed. She opened her eyes. Hank was still staring at her, trying to keep from laughing. She shook her head and laughed before saying, "Does everybody in this town know about my check?"

"Mm-hmm," Lucille said. "The place has been buzzin' since you left Woolies and went to the bank to make the deposit. We had hoped that you'd come back before you went over to the Clementine. It would've been good for business if you had. You're probably the most famous person in Jackson, at least right now anyway."

"Yeah, I'm thinkin' we could put that fame of yours to good use," Hank said. "We can all make a fortune. I expect the place will be buzzin' with people today. All you have to do is smile, and when the people ask you about the trial, share a few stories. You can even make up some stuff if you want. Nobody will ever know. Then, they'll go out and retell the stories and we'll get even more customers and make even more money to invest. It'll be great! Will you help us out?"

Before Johnnie could answer, Lucille said, "I don't care how much money we make. I'm not investing in no stock market. I'm not doin' it, Hank!"

"You don't have to, Lucille," Hank said. "But I am. I believe this girl is the answer to muh prayers. And she's Benny's sister tuh boot!"

"By the way, I finally spoke to Benny when I got to the Clementine," Johnnie said.

"Really?" Lucille said, skeptical that she was even Benny's sister now that Hank was all excited about investing.

"That's good," Hank said. "Is he coming to town? Will I get a chance to meet him?"

"He's probably back in San Francisco by now," Johnnie said, "but who knows, he may just call the restaurant one day looking for me. If he does, I'll let you speak to him, okay, Hank?"

"Really? That would be so nice. I wish I could go to one of his fights." He looked at Lucille and said, "The way things are going, I'll never see 'em fight. I'm in this restaurant from sun up to sun down six days a week, and I never get any time off. You'd think that Lucille would catch the vision that I have, but she hasn't, and I don't think she ever will."

Johnnie looked at Lucille, and then back at Hank. "Again, investments are risky, and they take time to grow."

"How much of the five thousand are you going to risk, Johnnie? I bet it's enough to keep you working for us until you can get back on your feet, huh?"

"Hank, I don't mean to offend you, and I do need this job, but I don't discuss my finances with anybody, and you shouldn't either. But, since you and your wife are helping me get on my feet, I'll tell you. I'm going to invest a substantial amount of the five thousand."

"Then, that must mean you believe you can do it then, huh?" Hank asked.

"I think I can, yes, but that doesn't mean I can, understand?"

"Yeah, I understand, but I'm willing to risk double what you risk."

Incredulous, Lucille screamed, "Have you lost your mind, Hank?"

"No," Hank said. "Not only haven't I lost my mind, I'm willing to trust this young lady with a good portion of my money. I believe she can make something happen with it. I've got plenty saved up, but not nearly enough to be on easy street."

Lucille said, "And if you ain't careful, you'll lose it all on a foolish flight of fancy."

"No guts. No glory! My first sergeant used to say. Now . . . I'm willing to risk ten thousand hard earned American dollars to try to get what you got, Johnnie. Will you please help me?"

"If ten thousand is all you have, let's invest half that amount," Johnnie said.

"I've got more than ten, Johnnie. I've got a lot more than ten, but my wife could be right. And even you said it was a risk."

"How do we know you're not going to take Hank's money and skip town?" Lucille said. "You can't get a hold of your father, and for all we know, you never did call your brother. How can we be sure we can trust you with our money?"

"Our money?" Hank asked, looking at Lucille. "What do you mean *our* money? I got this money from my mama and my daddy when they died. They left me a nice sum of money and some land. Now all of a sudden it's *our* money, and you don't wanna make it grow."

"Fine, Hank," Lucille screamed. "It's *your* money! You can blow it any way you want, I suppose. But just know I tried to warn you."

"This is precisely why I would rather not do this," Johnnie said, eyeing them both. "I don't want to come between y'all."

"How long you planning on staying in town, Johnnie?" Hank asked. "I mean, my wife does have a good point. No offense. But we don't know you all that well. You seem nice enough and all, but we really don't know you. Can you give me any assurances that you won't run off with my money?"

"Hmm, well, I suppose I could just set up a portfolio for you, and you can handle your own money. That way, I never have access to it and can never steal it. Yeah! I like that idea. I had a fortune stolen from me, and I would never want the temptation of stealing somebody's money because it was staring me in the face every day. That's probably what happened to Sharon Trudeau. She probably had lots of bills to pay, and the temptation to steal from her clients got the better of her, and we all lost our money."

Hank looked at Lucille and said, "See, there . . . all I need is one of them there port . . . port . . . whatever she said, and I'm in business. You've got some money, Lucille. Come with me on this. Who knows when we'll get another opportunity like this? It's worth a shot."

"I don't know, Hank. I just don't know. Ten thousand is an awful lot of money. I mean, what would your mama think if you lost it all?"

"I prefer to think of winning, not losing, Lucille," Hank said. "And when I win, I think she's gonna be proud her son. That's what I think. I don't think about losing, I think about winning. That's what Benny says when he gets into the ring. It works for him, and I think it'll work for us, too. He says he lets his victims think about losing and how much damage he's gonna do to 'em."

"She still hasn't answered the question, Hank," Lucille said.

"What question?" Johnnie asked.

"How long are you staying in Jackson?" Lucille repeated.

"Since I don't know where my father is or how to get in touch with him, I'll probably be here for quite awhile."

Hank looked at Lucille and said, "Good . . . good. When can we get started?"

"Right away, but there's the matter of my fee for managing your portfolio."

Chapter 45

"That's cheating me out of my fee."

Hank frowned and stared at Johnnie for a long minute, trying to gauge whether she was serious about being paid for managing his stock portfolio. He looked deeper into her eyes and saw her resolve and the confidence she had in her ability to not only reacquire what she had lost, but to also amass an even larger fortune. He looked at Lucille, who was standing there shaking her head with her arms folded, like she was disgusted that the young woman they had offered to help was now asking to be paid for a venture that could prove to be unprofitable and perhaps a sham. He took a deep breath, determined to work something out because in his heart, he knew she could do it again, and he wanted in on it this time. To him, Johnnie was like finding a rich vein of gold or an oil well that might never run out of oil.

"How much we talkin' about, Johnnie?" Hank asked, stone-faced.

"Well, I spoke to Gloria Schumacher about investing yesterday, and I told her she'd have to give me a free room for as long as I'm here, a percentage of the profit, and a fee of eleven hundred dollars as a retainer for a year."

"What?" Lucille shouted. "So you make money no matter what happens?"

"I know it seems unfair, but just remember, I had to pay my stockbrokers, too."

"How much?" Lucille said.

"Didn't you hear her say she doesn't discuss her finances?" Hank said. "What's the big deal, Lucille? She's charging us less than a hundred dollars a month. That's nothing when you look at what we could make in the future."

"Hmph, sounds like a racket to me," Lucille said.

"I know this is going to sound self-serving, but Hank is right," Johnnie said. "This is business and business is about money." She looked at Lucille. "Just yesterday you were telling me how much I would be helping you by working here to bring you more business, which amounted to more money, right?"

"Right," Lucille said hesitantly.

Johnnie looked at Hank and said, "And you told me just a few minutes ago that you could make even more money now that people know that I'm supposedly famous, right?"

"I sho' did say that, Johnnie," Hank said, "I sho' did say that."

"Well, it seems to me that you two were willing to make money off me when I had forgotten about my inheritance check, and I didn't care because I needed the money. Yesterday, when I came in here, all I had was forty-five dollars and eighty-nine cents to my name. At least that's what I thought. Now that I don't really need the job, I still showed up, and I'm prepared to keep my word to you two. Finding my grandfather's check hasn't changed my mind at all. I'm just saying we could all potentially make money together. It's up to you."

"And I suppose you want to be paid for being our waitress, too," Lucille said.

Johnnie frowned, folded her arms and said, "I most certainly do expect to be paid for that as well."

"How much we talkin' about, Johnnie?" Hank asked.

"Well, let's see, you two were willing to help by giving me a job and paying to have my car fixed. And whatever you paid came out of my check at the end of the week, right?"

"Right," Hank said.

"So, then you agree that you were helping me, but not for nothing, right? I mean I had to work off my debt, right?"

"Right," Hank said.

"So, then you don't expect me to help you for nothing, right?"

"Right," Hank said and cut his eyes to Lucille, and then back to Johnnie. "So how much we talkin' about, Johnnie?"

"I need a dollar an hour more than what waitresses make at The Flamingo Den."

"A whole dollar?" Lucille screamed, incredulous at the outlandish sum.

"Yes. A whole dollar."

"I'll tell you what," Hank said. "We're going to pay you minimum wage until we see if there's a difference in our profit. If we make a lot more because you're here, you'll get that dollar, and then some."

"Fair enough, Hank, but I get to keep all my tips, and I only work six hours a day, three days a week. Deal?"

"Six hours a day, three days a week?" Lucille questioned.

"Yes, ma'am," Johnnie said. "If I'm going to manage Hank's portfolio, I'll need to have enough time to pay attention to what's going on with the market. It's not like I can just pick the stocks, and then never look at them again. This is a daily thing, like working from sunup to sundown, going to bed tired as hell, and then starting the whole thing all over again at four o'clock the next morning. Besides, regular stockbrokers don't have two jobs. They have one. I have to stay on top of everything. The first thing I'm going to do is invest in a stock ticker. Then, I have to get to a library or someplace and look at some old newspapers. In other words, I have to study the market, look for new investments, and new ideas, new inventions, new trends, everything. All of that takes lots of time. I can't be stuck in the restaurant from sunup to sundown. If I manage people's financial portfolios, I have to have the time to do it. So, is it or deal, Hank, or not?"

"Deal," Hank said. "Now, when can we get started with the investments?"

"As soon as I get my eleven hundred dollar retainer."

"Fine. The bank opens at nine. If we're not too busy, Lucille can take you over there and get the money."

Lucille put her hands on her hips and said, "Oh, so now you can all of sudden spare me now that you got a scheme to make some money, huh?"

"I sure can. And I'll tell you why? Yesterday was about shopping for you. Today is about business, and like Johnnie said, 'business is about money.' I'm ready to make my fortune, and whether you know it or not, you're gonna wanna spend what I make, right?"

Lucille smiled and said, "That's right."

"I can cook if either of you need to leave," Johnnie said.

"Can you now?" Hank said. He looked at his watch. "We got about fifteen minutes before we open the doors. Grab an apron and show me what you can do. If I love it, I'll let you handle the orders until I come back from the bank."

"Uh, I'm the waitress, Hank," Johnnie said, smiling. "If I have to cook, too, and miss my tips because Lucille is getting them, I'm gonna need a raise."

Laughing, Hank said, "I like you, Johnnie. You're alright."

"What if I wanna get in on them investments, Johnnie?" Lucille asked. "I've got some money saved up, too."

"Well . . . if you go in with your husband, I'll just charge the eleven hundred for one portfolio. But if you decide to wait until I get him set up, you'll have to pay eleven hundred, too."

"What?" Lucille practically screamed.

"Yes, ma'am. It's the same amount of work. If a surgeon has to do two surgeries to remove a cancer, you don't get both surgeries for one fee. He's not working at a discount. Why should I? Why should you for that matter? I'm sure you're charging your customers a certain amount to make a profit. I'm only doing what you do. You have expertise, and so do I. Again, this is business and business is about—"

"Money," Lucille finished her sentence.

"So, what are you going to do, Lucille?" Hank asked.

"Oh, I don't know. Eleven hundred dollars is a lot of money, Hank."

"It's less than a hundred dollars a month. We make more than that amount in a day . . . sometimes three or four times that a day. And if this girl can bring in the customers like we think, it could go as high as thirty or forty . . . maybe even fifty! The sky's the limit, Lucille. Don't you see?"

Lucille folded her arms and thought for a few seconds. Then she said, "Did you really have two hundred and fifty thousand dollars?"

"Yes, ma'am."

"And is Gloria Schumacher going to invest with you, too?"

"Actually, she said she would have to think about it first."

"So, she's not investing?"

"Not at this time, no, but I think she'll come around when she learns that we're all making good money."

"Can I think about it, Johnnie?" Lucille asked. "This is a mighty big step for me. I don't have the adventurous spirit like Hank. See... his people come from Tulsa, Oklahoma, in the Greenwood area. Ever heard of it?"

"No, ma'am."

"Well, his people had money before them crackers burned it all down like they did y'all. Every time we get a little somethin', them crackers come and snatch it right out from under us. It's like they're afraid of us getting ahead or somethin'. It's like they think they'll end up workin' for us, and we'll treat them the way they've treated us. So, they steal everything we create, and then pass it off like they created it. They're stealin' our music, our inventions, everything, with no shame of what they're doin'."

"I know, but the one thing they can't steal, unless we let them is our money. That's why we'll all manage our own investments. I'll set everything up and tell you all what to do. And Hank, I don't want you telling your wife what stocks I get you either. That's cheating me out of my fee."

"I understand. It's no problem, Johnnie. Just make me some money, so I can retire in style!"

Chapter 46

"But it'll cost you an additional eleven hundred, Lucille."

Less than an hour later, Lucille's was packed with customers, many of whom were white and curious about the pretty colored girl they had read and heard so much about. The sleigh bells that hung over the door seemed to ring every few minutes, letting them know they had another hungry customer. Johnnie could hear them whispering about her as she walked by their tables. She loved every minute of the unsolicited attention, offering friendly smiles in return for the compliments and money she received from the customers she served. She didn't know that a waitress could make so much money in tips. She had plans for all those coins and dollar bills she slipped into her apron, which jingled as she walked. She had goals and a plan that she was going to stick to. She didn't know how long it would take to get rich again, but she planned to get there, and this time on her own terms.

However, Lucille still had mixed emotions about it all, even with the unusual influx of customers, old and new. She was glad to have so many customers, particularly the new faces, hoping they would become regulars. There were so many customers that she had to run out and buy more food for Hank to cook, but at the same time, she didn't like the fact that her regular customers where leaving Johnnie much bigger tips than they ever left her. From what she calculated, Johnnie had already made over forty dollars in tips before nine o'clock. She figured that she'd have well over a hundred dollars before she left at 11:30. And they were going to have to pay her more than a dollar an hour due to the enormous influx of people, but when it occurred to her that they had made over two hundred and fifty dollars before eleven o'clock, which had never happened, she smiled, walked up to Johnnie, and embraced her.

Johnnie laughed heartily and said, "Do this mean you're going to invest?"

"Well, let's just say I'm seriously thinking about it," Lucille said. "When do you think you'll have Hank's portfolio set up?"

"Tomorrow at the latest," Johnnie said. "I leave at 11:30. That's six hours."

"What?" Lucille questioned, thinking about all the money she and Hank could make if she stayed longer. They had already made two months of the retainer fee Johnnie required to take Hank on as a client. She was thinking Hank had been right—at least about how quickly they could recoup their initial fee. She thought that if Johnnie stayed another couple hours, they might have four or five hundred dollars. And if that happened for a full week, it would be as if they hadn't paid her a dime to handle their portfolio. "Can't you at least stay until the lunch rush is over? What if people continue coming in, Johnnie?"

"But we agreed, Lucille," Johnnie said.

"What if we pay you two dollars an hour to work from 5:30 to 1:30?" Lucille asked. "Would you stay then?"

"I don't know. A deal is a deal."

"Think about all the tips you could make. I know you got about fifty dollars in your apron in three hours. Would you stay if you could get the raise and make another fifty or so in tips?"

"I might, but looking at what you're making, I think I'll need at least three dollars an hour. But like I told you and your husband, I need time to study the stocks and stuff, so I don't think I could work much longer than eight hours," Johnnie said. "I also have to figure out a way to get a stock ticker. I would ask Western Union to let me buy one of theirs, but they might want to know why I need one. They might ask a bunch of questions and start trouble, you know?"

"What if they wanna become customers, too?"

"You mean investors?"

"Yes!"

"At first I wanted some white clients, but now that they know who I am and what happened in New Orleans, I don't think I want to deal with white folk that I don't have a relationship with. Gloria is one thing, but to get white folk involved might start some unforeseen trouble. Let's just stick with our own people and Gloria if she wants to get involved, okay?"

"Suit yourself. Money is money. I say get all you can while you can. Look at all the white folk in here today."

Johnnie turned around and saw lots of whites sitting at her tables, her booths, smiling at her like they wanted to meet the famous colored girl who had been accused and acquitted of murder. As she scanned each face, the men and the women, she began to consider the possibilities. The what ifs? She looked at Lucille. "And what if the stocks don't make them money, and they lose? Who do you think they're going to blame? Themselves?"

"I see what you're saying. Then, you have to make sure you make them money. What did Hank say? Didn't he say he doesn't think about losing? Didn't he say he thinks about winning? What if Hank is right? What if you win?"

"That's impossible. I can't guarantee success, not even for myself. Even white folk can't do that. Otherwise the market wouldn't have crashed in 1929, would it? But if a nigga calls herself a stockbroker, she better make them crackers money, or they'll turn her into a human torch."

"So, you're going to continue to think about losing?"

"Listen to you, Lucille. You're telling me to think about winning, and all you're doing is thinking about losing. You haven't even decided to invest yourself. Yet, you tell me I'm thinking about losing?"

"I'll tell you what: Given what I've seen so far, I'm more inclined to invest. But I'll admit I'm a bit squeamish about investing. So, here's what I'm willing to do. Seven is the Lord's number. If we have seven straight days like this, I'll invest. How about that?"

"But it'll cost you an additional eleven hundred, Lucille."

"I know, and I'll gladly pay it. It'll be worth the risk at that point. And we'll have a track record of people coming in regularly. Your fame may have brought them in, but Hank's cookin' is gonna keep 'em comin' back for more. In seven days, at upwards of five hundred dollars a day, we'll more than make back the fee we're gonna pay you. Plus, we'll be making back our initial investment, too. And think of the possibilities. If people come in like this for a month, we're looking at making about fourteen thousand. If we subtract the twenty-two hundred dollar fee, that still leaves us almost twelve thousand. If we subtract Hank's initial ten thousand from that, we're still over a thousand to the good! That's why I don't mind waiting and seeing, and then investing. It's worth the wait and the extra eleven hundred as far as I'm concerned."

Johnnie smiled and said, "So, you've thought the thing through, huh?"

"Yes, I have."

"Well, I can't argue with your plan. Let's see how things happen for seven days, and we'll get you started, too. I'll go ahead and make you a separate portfolio now since we're expecting to win and not lose!"

The sleigh bells rang out, indicating that someone had either left or a customer had just come in and would need a menu.

"Pick up," Hank yelled.

Johnnie said, "Well, Lucille, I gotta get back to work."

"I know. Can you handle things until I run over to the bank for Hank?"

"Sure, but please hurry back, okay?"

"I'll do my best," Lucille said, taking off her apron.

Johnnie turned around just in time to see Paul Masterson pull off his Stetson and slide into a vacated booth.

Chapter 47

"What's my compensation going to be?"

Seeing Paul Masterson was an unexpected, but welcomed surprise—a treat even. Meeting him the previous night at The Flamingo Den immediately came to mind. They locked eyes and smiled warmly. "Pick up," she heard Hank yell a second time. She looked at the stainless steel grill counter. Two plates of food were ready to be served. She looked at Masterson again and put her right index finger in the air. Masterson nodded politely. Then, he picked up a white coffee cup and showed it to her. Johnnie nodded, letting him know she would bring the coffee as soon as she could. "Pick up," Hank yelled again. She looked at the grill counter, and now there were three plates instead of two.

She rushed over to the counter and picked up the order slips. She couldn't help looking back at Masterson, who was still looking at her, patiently waiting for her to get to him. She didn't know why, but she was nervous now that he was there. She also didn't know why she wanted to impress him with her newly acquired waitressing skills. She looked at him again. He was so handsome that she couldn't help but stare. "Pick up," Hank yelled a fourth time and set yet another order on the grill counter. Johnnie forced herself to concentrate as she read the orders before picking up the plates and delivering them to her customers. While doing so, she could feel Masterson's eyes following her from table to table, back to the grill counter, and then to another table.

Of all the eyes following her around the restaurant, only Masterson's eyes interested her. He had fought for her honor, and when he did, it made her want to get in bed with him and do lots of naughty things she knew the church wouldn't approve of. The fact that he was a preacher did nothing in the way of stopping the images of them being in bed together, nude and intertwined, moving in a smooth cadence that they both enjoyed. Just as she was making her way over to Masterson's table with a fresh pot of hot coffee, Hank yelled, "Pick up!" She quickly made her way over to Masterson's table, poured his coffee.

"Fancy meeting you here," Masterson said.

"How did you know I would be working here?"

"I didn't. I stopped to get a paper and I saw people coming in. I thought I'd come in too."

"Pick up!"

"I'll be right back to take your order, Paul."

"So, you remember my name, huh?"

Johnnie locked eyes with him, smiled sweetly, and said, "I remember everything, Preacher. Absolutely everything."

"I see. I'm looking forward to having dinner together some time soon."

"When?" Johnnie said, anxiously, like she would love to leave with him at that very moment.

"Pick up!"

"Can you be a little patient with me, Paul? As you can see, we're very busy."

"Take your time. I got all day long, and I'll wait all day if I have to."

Johnnie smiled again and said, "Figure out what you want, and I'll get it for you in a few minutes."

"I don't have to figure out what I want. I found it last night at The Flamingo Den."

"Pick up!"

Smiling, Johnnie said, "That's so sweet of you to say."

Masterson leaned forward and whispered, "They weren't just words. I've been thinkin' about you all night long."

Johnnie smiled and said, "I'll be right back, okay?"

"Take your time," Masterson said and opened his paper.

As Johnnie walked over to the counter, she looked at the clock above the grill. It was only 10:26. That meant she still had another three hours of work to do instead of one. She wished she hadn't told Lucille she would work until 1:30. She wanted to hear whatever Paul

Masterson had to say. Nevertheless, part of her wanted to stay until they closed because she had made so much money in tips. She thought that if she stayed until eight, she would take two hundred dollars in tips back to the Clementine. That was enough money to pay for car repairs and nearly all the things she bought at Woolworth's the previous day. She thought the novelty of being the new girl in town, the check that everyone knew about, and the talk of being accused of murder would eventually die down and things would return to normal, whatever normal was in Jackson, Mississippi. For all she knew, today might be the only day that she could make that kind of money.

When she returned to the grill counter, Hank said, "Johnnie, we're having a great day. I think I'll make all the money back, including the ten thousand in a week or so if this keeps up."

"Yeah, that's what Lucille was saying. I think she's going to invest, too."

"Thanks for coming to town. I've been waiting so long for this to happen to me. And now, it's finally happening."

"Thanks, but um, Lucille wanted me to stay until 1:30 from now on, starting today. I told her I'd do it, but I needed three dollars an hour to do it. Is that okay with you?"

"Yes, but only when the place is packed like it is now. Deal?"

"Deal. And if we're having a slow day, I work six hours, and I'm finished for the day, right?"

He nodded and said, "Now . . . who is that white man—that cowboy I see you getting all friendly with?"

"Oh, that's Paul Masterson. He's a preacher. I met him at The Flamingo Den last night."

"What? They let you in there?"

"Well, yeah. Paul insisted, and when three guys threatened to rape me, he protected me."

"Wait a minute, are you tellin' me a white man got you into The Flamingo Den, and when three white men tried to rape you, he fought them off?"

"Yeah, but how did you know they were white? I never said what color they were."

"You didn't have to. First off, ain't no black folk supposed to be up in there. Second, white men are always tryin' to rape our women. That ain't nuthin' new."

"I suppose you're right on that one. White men have always wanted to have their way with me. Since I was twelve years old."

"Yeah, that's how them cracker men are. All the time tryin' tuh get up in our women. I suspect that preacher ain't no different."

"He might be different. When he took me back to the Clementine, he didn't try anything."

"He didn't, huh?"

"No."

"Hmph! Well, that don't mean nuthin'. He brought his ass up in here lookin' for ya, didn't he?"

"Maybe he wants something to eat, Hank?"

"I just bet he does. Them crackers cain't wait to get their pale faces between a black woman's legs. That's the kinda eatin' he wants to do."

Johnnie just stared at him without blinking.

"Uh . . . so . . . uh . . . They won't let me in there, not that I wanted to go in any way. I cook better than anything they're makin'. So . . . um . . . what was it like?"

"The food was good. I had chili and grilled cheese and a few bones of barbecue. They play lots of country music in there. It's nothing like here."

"You don't say. Well . . . listen . . . there's a big game this weekend. The Tigers are playing Alcorn. We always stay open until midnight when the Tigers play. Can you work that long for us?"

"Until midnight, and then come back at 5:30?"

"Yeah. Come on. If me and Lucille can do it, surely a young girl like you can do it."

"But Hank, I don't know if I can do all that and stay on top of the stocks and stuff."

"Sure you can, Johnnie. It's only two days a month. The other two days they're on the road."

"I'll think about it, Hank. When is basketball season over?"

"March, but then there's track and baseball, and then there's football. I'm thinkin' when them college boys get a look at you, we're going to clean up fo' sho'!"

"What's my compensation going to be?"

"Your what?"

"My compensation . . . my pay for drawing a crowd."

Hank folded his arms and said, "Your pay for drawing a crowd?"

"Yes."

"Do we have to pay you for everything you do around here?"

"Yes. Business is business, and I lost a fortune. The only way to get that money back is to work, save, and invest. You wanna use my good looks to bring in the crowd, which in essence means you want me to bring in money. I expect to get paid for that."

"I see what you're saying."

"Good. I hope we don't have to have this conversation again. If you and Lucille want me to do anything that brings in money for your pockets, I expect to line my pockets, too. That's only fair. Otherwise, you'd be using me. I've allowed myself to be used before, but that was in the past. I'm not going to allow that anymore. I hope you understand, Hank."

"I do, Johnnie. I do. What's fair is fair."

"Thanks so much for understanding. I've learned that a girl has to stick up for herself or be run over. I'm sure you wouldn't want someone running over your wife. So, please, don't take advantage of me. I'll do my part, and you do yours by compensating me for my pretty. That's a fair exchange, don't you think, Hank?"

"Well . . . I hadn't thought about it like that. But when you put it that way, I have to agree with you. So, I'll make sure we compensate you for your pretty and your work, okay?"

"Thanks!"

Chapter 48

"When do you need an answer?"

It was approaching 10:45 when Johnnie saw Lucille coming down the street through the picture window. She had been gone for less than twenty minutes, which meant that Johnnie could catch her breath since Lucille could take orders and serve. The breakfast crowd was thinning out, but Hank had told her that the lunch crowd would soon find their way into the restaurant about ten minutes after eleven. She knew Lucille would be entering her restaurant any minute, and Johnnie wanted to collect all her tips before she put her apron back on. That way, there would be no confusion as to which tips belonged to whom.

She was just making her way over to Paul Masterson's table when she heard the sleigh bells ring out, letting her know that Lucille had entered. She looked up to confirm that it was her, just in case another customer had entered with her. Lucille was alone, so she stopped at Masterson's table, coffee pot in tow. He was finishing off his thick, cheesy western omelet, French toast, and grits.

"So did you enjoy your meal, Mr. Cowboy Preacher," Johnnie said. "You sure can put it away. Somebody must have their hands full trying to prepare enough food for you three times a day."

Masterson took a swallow of his coffee and said, "Actually, I cook for myself."

"Do you now?"

"I've been cooking since I was a little boy. Perhaps I can whip up something for you before I leave town tomorrow."

"I'll probably be working tomorrow when you're ready to leave. I start at 5:30, and I don't get off until 1:30. I guess I'll have to wait for you to come back to try out your culinary skills."

Masterson put his cup to his lips and guzzled down the last of his coffee before saying, "It'll be worth waiting for I can tell you that."

She filled his cup again. "Uh-huh. And what's your specialty, Mr. Cowboy Preacher?"

"My specialty? I don't know that I have a specialty, but I can make just about any dish you have a hunkering for."

"Why can't you make something for me tonight?"

"I've got revival tonight."

"Oh, yeah. I forgot. Don't revivals normally last a week?"

"Normally, but I'm a one-night only kind of guy."

Johnnie smiled and said, "Why does everything you say have a double meaning, Mr. Cowboy Preacher?"

Masterson frowned. "A double meaning? What do you mean by that?"

"My sentiments exactly!"

"Tell me what you're talking about. You're obviously the only one who has a clue as to what you're driving at."

"You said you're a one-night only kind of guy. Are you trying to imply something? Are you trying to seduce me right here in this restaurant? Or what?"

Frowning, Masterson said, "What?" No! Of course not. I'm an evangelist."

"Yeah, but are you a real one, or are you just some jack-legged preacher trying to make a living off the good Lord?"

Masterson poured some cream into his coffee, and then put in a couple teaspoons of sugar. He looked at Johnnie. She stood there patiently, waiting to hear his answer. "I'm a real evangelist."

"You sure don't talk like one."

"I don't, huh? How does a real evangelist talk?"

"I don't know. But I'm sure real evangelists don't make sexual innuendos, do they?"

"So, you're saying I made a sexual innuendo when I said I'm a one-night only kind of guy?"

"Yes."

Masterson smiled and said, "If you believe I meant something sexual when I said that, perhaps it says something about you. Have you considered that?"

Johnnie pulled her head back and frowned. "What do you mean it says something about me?"

"Well, the fact that you would think that I was talking about a single night of sex with you tells me that it's been suggested to you before. Given your beauty, I'm now thinking it's been suggested to you regularly, if not verbally, nonverbally. Even when a man doesn't mention it, his eyes are no doubt screaming it, I'm sure. It also says that if it could so easily roll off your tongue in the presence of a clergyman, you've accepted an invitation or two, or you've seriously considered accepting a proposition or two. The only question remaining may be an inappropriate one to ask."

"Which is?"

"Did you accept any of the offers?"

"What would you think of me if I did?"

"I don't know you, so I wouldn't think anything of you."

"Really, Mr. Cowboy Preacher? If I did I bet you wouldn't be nearly as attracted to me as you are. And you certainly wouldn't have thought about me all night long, would you?"

"I think any man would have trouble getting you out of his mind. You're absolutely stunning."

Johnnie smiled and said, "So, who was I in your dreams last night, Mr. Cowboy Preacher? Was I Tamar? Perhaps I was Rehab? I know it wasn't Ruth, was it? Oh, I know. You think of me as Bathsheba, the wife of Uriah, the Hittite, right?"

Masterson picked up his cup and took a swallow, carefully thinking about his response before opening his mouth and inserting his foot. "Is this a test, Johnnie?"

"You tell me, Mr. Cowboy Preacher."

"How about I tell you over lunch at the Clementine?"

"See there you go again."

"What do you mean there I go again?"

"I mean, that sounds like an invitation to sexual exploration to me."

"Why? Because the Clementine's a hotel?"

175

"Yes. Where they have plenty of rooms with beds. And you know how you white men are when it comes to laying down with a black woman. Preacher or not, white men can't help themselves. You know that."

Masterson ran his hand down his face before saying, "I most certainly don't know that."

"So, you're different from the rest, huh?"

"I don't know what the rest are, and neither do you. You may know a few, but there are a hundred million or so of us white men here in the continental United States. There are several hundred million more in Europe and Australia. There are even a sizable number occupying parts of Africa. Are you telling me you've been with all of them? And I'm the only exception . . . me? If you are, not only are you revealing a lot about yourself, but you've inadvertently answered my question concerning why your mind immediately embraced the underbelly of an activity that was originally meant for good."

Unfazed by his denial and his provocative logic, she said, "So, you have no sexual proclivities, Mr. Cowboy Preacher?"

"Pick up!"

"I can see that this is a conversation that needs more time. How about I pick you up at 1:30 when you get off? I'll take you back to The Flamingo Den for lunch."

"I'll think about it, Mr. Cowboy Preacher. When do you need an answer?"

"Pick up!"

"I'll tell you what . . . I'll be out front at 1:30. You know my truck. If you wanna have lunch with me, get in. If not, don't."

Chapter 49

A New Lover on the Horizon

Lucas Matthews had been lying in his bunk, fully awake for half an hour before the Reveille bugle would blare, signaling the new recruits to get up and get into formation in front of the barracks. While he listened to his fellow Army recruits snore, he wondered if the cops had found Marla Bentley yet. It had been three days since he had killed her while they were naked and in bed at the Red River Hotel. While he knew it was an accident, images of their last night together stayed with him, torturing him, making him afraid, wondering when the police would show up and haul him off to Angola, where he would have to explain to Clancy "One Punch" Brown how he ended up back in prison after their lengthy conversation. He wondered what he would do if the police had found Marla and had learned the awful truth—that he was having an affair with her while she was married to a notorious mob figure that had known of the dalliance and did nothing to stop it. It was such a fantastic tale that no one would believe it; let alone a jury of twelve angry white men who no doubt couldn't wait to get a noose around his thick neck and send a message to all Negro men who dared plunder one of their untouchable women.

Johnnie was still on his mind, too. He still loved her in spite of herself. He was still hooked on her, but no longer wanted to be. He knew it was stupid to continue loving a woman who would behave the way Johnnie had, but love demanded that he make excuses for her. And when he couldn't make any more excuses, he set her house ablaze, hoping to obliterate all ties to New Orleans. He hoped he had been successful while wondering where she was at that very moment. The answer to that troubling question came to mind, lingered, and then angered him when he realized that even though he had hoped to set her free, what he had really done was send her into the arms of his rival— Napoleon Bentley. He suddenly realized that even though Bubbles had gotten her money back, instead of leaving, she went to Napoleon, and they were probably making love at that very minute, laughing at him, talking about how big a fool he had been and still was.

The thing that bothered Lucas most was that he had told Lieutenant Perry about Johnnie, and she had said many of the same things Marla had said. What he found interesting is that Lieutenant Perry was far more forthcoming, far more direct with her appraisal of Johnnie and the situation itself. Not only had she called him a slave, but she had called him the worst kind of slave because he didn't know what condition he was in. He began to wonder if he was damaged goods as she had said. And if he was, what if anything, could he do about it? According to Lieutenant Perry, his father's legacy, the blood that coursed through his veins, would in all likelihood determine his ultimate fate, which unnerved him.

Lieutenant Perry's theories about who he was and what he would eventually become made him search his soul for a truth he had not yet considered. According to her, his life was a burgeoning cesspool that he floated in along with the rest of its foul smelling inhabitants. So vivid was her description of him, what he was on the inside that he began to wonder if he had been in the cesspool so long that he had gotten used to the filth floating around in it. The power of her commentary made him question whether he was as out of control as she had asserted. He didn't think so. He still didn't see anything wrong with lying down with a woman that he wasn't married to, even if she had taken an oath and was committed in holy wedlock. That was her problem, not his. It wasn't like he had committed murder or anything. After all, murder was definitely wrong. But sex with a beautiful woman felt good. Therefore it was good, and he was going to get himself another piece as soon as he found a willing female even if she was married.

Besides all that, there was another lover on the horizon, and she needed his full attention. Her name was spelled A-R-M-Y. Although he had only had a taste of basic training, he did love it so. The Army reminded him of the coaches that taught him the game of football back home in New Orleans. They, too, like Sergeant Cornsilk, were no nonsense men—leaders who first saw greatness in their players, demanded nothing less, and somehow got it out of them. Not only was there a daily structured regimen, they had taught him to believe in the gifts God had given him and to use them on the gridiron. He had purchased their philosophy, what they believed about him, and he battered his opponents with their philosophy every Friday night during the season. He had excelled at football, and after meeting Sergeant Cornsilk a few hours ago, he knew he would excel in the Army, too. From what he could tell from the initial introduction, Sergeant Cornsilk would get greatness out of him, and one day he would make an excellent officer. While he wasn't perfect, he was confident that there was something good about him on the inside.

Chapter 50

"Do they understand their responsibilities?"

Having convinced himself that he was a good person, he got up and went to the latrine. On the way, he looked at the clock. It was 4:45. The bugle would sound in fifteen minutes. When he finished in the latrine, he went over to Lynchburg's bunk and woke him up. Whispering, he said, "The bugle's gonna sound in about ten minutes. Get the squad leaders up and have them wake up the men. I want the men ready when Sergeant Cornsilk returns. We're gonna sing 'My Country Tis of Thee' when he comes in. Understand?"

Still groggy, Lynchburg said, "Okay."

Lucas whispered loudly, "Okay, what?"

Frowning, Lynchburg tried to focus and said, "Aren't you taking the barracks chief thing a little too far?"

"I'ma say this shit one last time because you obviously didn't hear the sergeant a few hours ago. This is not a democracy. You don't have a vote. Whatever the sergeant says goes. He put me in charge, and you're under me. He told you to back me up. If I hav'ta to tell you this shit again, I'ma kick yo' ass. Now get the squad leaders up and have them get the rest of the men up. When the sergeant walks in, I'ma call all the men to attention, and then we will sing. Understand?"

"Yes, sir!"

"On second thought, I'll wake up San Francisco. You wake up Cheyenne."

Lynchburg, bare-chested and still in his white shorts, hustled over to Cheyenne's bunk and woke him up. Cheyenne's real name was

Chauncey McKenzie. They immediately started waking up the other recruits.

"San Francisco," Lucas said.

"Yes, sir," he replied.

Lucas smiled. "How long have you been awake, recruit?"

"Long before you woke up, sir."

"What were you doing?"

"Watching your back and my own, sir. I heard what Lynchburg said. He can't be trusted, sir."

Lucas smiled and said, "Help me get the men up and ready to go before Sergeant Cornsilk gets here."

"Yes, sir!"

Two minutes before the Reveille bugle sounded, the barracks door opened and closed. They could hear the sound of Sergeant Cornsilk's combat boots clicking. He turned on the lights.

Lucas came to attention, and then shouted, "Atten-hut!"

There was but one sound that rang out; that being the sound of nearly fifty men bringing their heels together synchronously. Then, in one voice, they sang the following words:

"My country tis of thee . . . Sweet land of liberty . . ."

Sergeant Cornsilk came to attention and held his hand to the brim of his headgear in a salute as they sang. They finished singing just before the Reveille bugle sounded. When the barracks was quiet again, Cornsilk shouted, "Alright sissies. We gotta busy day today. And don't think for a second you impressed me. You didn't. From this moment forward, you will do everything as a unit. You will do everything with military precision. First, we're gonna march over to the Mess Hall and get you some chow." He looked at Lucas. "There will be no talking in the chow line. Understand?"

"Yes, sir!"

After you get your SOS, that's shit on a shingle for you dumb bastards from Fort Lauderdale, you will find an empty table. You will set your tray on a table and wait at attention until three other recruits join you. Is that clear?"

"Yes, sir!"

"Then, you will all sit together, bless your food together, and then you will eat together. Is that clear?"

"Yes, sir!"

"And I better not see anybody acting like they're at their favorite restaurant eating French cuisine. You will eat quickly, and you will leave the Mess Hall. You will then wait outside in formation for the rest of the platoon. Understand?"

"Yes, sir!"

"After that, we're gonna march over to the barber shop and get your haircuts. After that, we'll march over to the hospital, where you'll get your shots. Then, we'll go over to the quartermaster's office and get your uniforms, underwear, socks, and boots. From there, we'll go to finance and get you broke bastards some money to purchase the items you'll need. Then, we're going to the Post Exchange, where you will buy toiletries, including toothbrushes, toothpaste, razors and blades, and a shoeshine kit. Understand?"

"Yes, sir!"

"New Orleans!" Cornsilk shouted.

"Yes, sir!" Lucas replied.

"Have you chosen two more squad leaders?"

"Yes, sir!"

"What are their names?"

"Nicolas Lee aka San Francisco. And Chauncey McKenzie aka Cheyenne."

"Do they understand their responsibilities?"

"Yes, sir!"

"Outstanding!" He looked at the men and said, "Well, what are you waiting for? Get into formation in front of the barracks. Move!" He looked at Lucas and said, "New Orleans. Stick around for a second."

"Yes, sir!"

"Who's idea was it to get the men up early and sing?"

"Mine, sir!"

"Are you tryin' to impress me, son?"

"Yes, sir! I'm planning to go to officers' training school, sir!"

"Hot damn, son! You keep that up for sixteen weeks, and you just might make it. Now get out there with the rest of the men. We gotta long day ahead of us."

Chapter 51

"Your car won't be fixed for three weeks, right?"

Johnnie walked out of Lucille's at exactly 1:30, expecting to see Paul Masterson's pickup truck with him in it and the engine idling. She had been thinking about him since he offered to take her back to The Flamingo Den for lunch. She liked him, but she wondered what he would think of her if he knew her past; especially given her age, being only seventeen. She knew and understood that men didn't like women that had more than a man or two in their secret place. Even when a woman has had a man or two, men prefer that she was married to the men, not some woman that easily opened her legs. Men thought women who did that were whores, and no man wanted a whore for a wife.

She thought that since she had invited him into her hotel room and he had declined, he would have much higher standards than the average man, but quickly reminded herself that even if he had come inside her room, she would not have let him inside her. Entering her hotel room was one thing, but entering her was quite another. Besides, the invitation was more of a salve for her bruised ego when he, being a white man, didn't even try to kiss her. That intrigued her as it did most women, color notwithstanding, because women had to say no to men ten times a day, even if they were ugly. Beautiful women had to suffer through twenty or more invitations to sex and a myriad of salacious looks in a single day. So, when Paul Masterson didn't try to kiss her and rejected her invitation for presumed sex, she wanted to find out what made him so different.

A few seconds later, Paul's truck stopped in front of Lucille's. She looked in at him, smiled and said, "For a minute I thought you had turned me down a second time, Mr. Cowboy Preacher."

"Talk about sexual innuendos," Masterson said, "I think it's you that's trying to seduce me."

Johnnie got in the truck, tossed her Wall Street Journal on the dashboard, and said, "So, what if I am. Afraid you can't handle me or what?"

Masterson pulled off and said, "How old are you, Johnnie?"

"Why Paul Masterson, a southern boy like you outta know it's impolite to ask a woman her age. Don't y'all know that, Mr. Cowboy Preacher?"

"Well, have you ever been married? Do you have any children from the marriage?"

Johnnie smiled. "I appreciate you asking if I was married before asking if I had any children, Paul. Most folk just assume a colored girl has children and no husband to speak of. I guess you're different."

"We're all different, Johnnie."

"You mean white folk?"

"No. I mean people in general. Sure, there are similarities, but we all have a different fingerprint, which speaks very loudly to our individuality."

"I bet you went to college, didn't you, Mr. Cowboy Preacher?"

"As a matter of fact, I did."

"Doesn't surprise me none. You come off like a good ol' boy, but when you want to, you're very well-spoken. So, where did you go to school?"

"Dallas Theological Seminary. I've got a Master's of Divinity degree, class of 1946."

"Uh-huh." She looked at his ring finger. No ring, but that didn't mean he wasn't married. It only meant he didn't wear a wedding ring if he was. "And are you married?"

"Almost."

"Almost, huh? Care to elaborate?"

"How about a little quid pro quo, Johnnie?"

"'Quid pro quo?'"

"Yeah, I answer a question, you answer a question. Is that fair?"

"I guess."

"Okay then, do you have a boyfriend?"

"No. Do you have a girlfriend?"

"No. Are you a virgin?"

Johnnie looked at him. "May I ask why you're asking me that?"

"Just asking."

"Yeah, but why are you asking? Are you thinking of marrying me or something?"

"I just might. You never know where these things are gonna lead."

"So, you think you should know now, before you get further involved with a black woman from New Orleans? Is that it?"

"I think I want to know everything there is to know about you, and you should know everything there is to know about me."

"Excuse me, Mr. Cowboy Preacher, but aren't you leaving town tomorrow?"

"That was my original plan. But now, I might just stick around for a while. Perhaps a week or so. Your car won't be fixed for three weeks, right?"

"Right, but how did you know that?"

"You're pretty well-known for someone who's just passing through. Isn't that what you told me last night?"

Chapter 52

"I'm going to need more time than that, Paul."

Paul Masterson pulled his Ford pickup into the parking lot of The Flamingo Den and shut off the engine. There were only a few parked cars, no Harley Davidson motorcycles. Just a few station wagons, which meant that the people inside were probably families, not riffraff looking for trouble—at least that's what he was counting on. He liked Johnnie, but it was mainly because she was very attractive. He believed that once they had a deep enough conversation, perhaps he wouldn't like her nearly as much, and then he could get her out of his mind and move on to his next preaching engagement. But he had been praying for a wife for several years. He assumed that whichever woman God would send him would be white, southern, and hopefully as beautiful as Sarah, Abraham's wife, but he knew that he never specified color. Nearly every day for four years, he had been asking for a good wife of God's choosing. The fact that Johnnie was a Negress did not automatically disqualify her. They got out of the truck and started walking to the restaurant entrance where they had met.

"So, are you going to answer my question," Masterson said. "Are you just passing through or what?"

"Originally, yes. I was going to East Saint Louis to spend some time with my father, but I don't have the correct number, or he's changed it."

"And he didn't bother to tell you what his new number is? That's strange. Are you two having problems or what?"

"It's a long story, Paul."

"Really, I'd love to hear it."

"Aren't you leaving tomorrow?"

"I might, and I might not."

They entered The Flamingo Den. The waitress that had served them the night before rolled her eyes at Masterson. She had invited him back to her place, and not only hadn't he accepted her offer, but he didn't even acknowledge that he'd even heard her offer. To add insult to injury, he was back the next day with the same black woman he had just met. She assumed that he had accepted her invitation instead.

Masterson, fearing that she might spit in their food or worse, said, "I just wanna let you know, ma'am that I'm an evangelist, and I'm preaching at a revival tonight. I heard your proposition last night, and that's why I didn't accept your gracious invitation."

Relieved, the waitress smiled and said, "I knew it had to be something like that. The way you kicked ass last night, I thought you wore the title only. I see I was wrong."

"You probably remember my friend, Johnnie. I met her last night, and again, at a restaurant this morning."

"We all know who she is," the waitress said. "Word is all over town."

"I'm wondering if we could have a booth."

"No problem, Preacher. Right this way." She led them to their seats and placed two menus on the table. "Scotty said you'd probably be back with her again today, and I was to serve you and find out when you was leavin' town."

"Scotty's not here?"

"No. But I'm sure he'll be here shortly. Let me know when you're ready to order."

"I think we're ready to order now." He looked at Johnnie. "You wanna try the chili and grilled cheese and ribs again, Johnnie?"

"Yes, please."

Masterson looked at the waitress and said, "Make that two orders, and two ice cold lemonades."

"Comin' right up," she said and left.

"So . . . let's hear that long story about your dad."

"Do you really think something is going to happen between us, Mr. Cowboy Preacher?"

"Something like what?"

"Like a romance or something."

187

"Who knows? I certainly don't."

"On our way over here, you asked me how old I was. Do you still want to know?"

"Yes."

"I'm seventeen."

Stunned, Masterson frowned. "Seventeen? Are you serious?"

"I am."

"Hmph! I thought you were twenty-seven or twenty-eight."

"Nope. I'm seventeen. Now do you still want to get to know everything there is to know about me?"

"Depends."

"On what?"

"When you'll be eighteen?"

"Next Thanksgiving, nine months from now."

"Nine months, huh? What about your mom? Where's she?"

"In a crypt."

"So, she's dead?"

"Either that, or she's very lonely in that crypt."

Masterson smiled. "I guess that was a stupid question."

"You guess?"

"Besides your dad in East Saint Louis, do you have any other relatives?"

"Yes, my dad remarried, and so I have half brothers and sisters. I also have a half brother in San Francisco, but I never think of him as a half brother. He's a famous boxer. Perhaps you've heard of him."

"He's not the Bay City Terror, is he?"

"Yes. That's him. They also call him Benny 'The Body Snatcher' Wise."

"Yeah, I've definitely heard of him. I wouldn't wanna meet him in a dark alley."

"I don't know, Mr. Cowboy Preacher. You seemed to be able to handle yourself fairly well last night in this restaurant. And there were three of them."

"They were amateurs. Benny's a professional—that ain't even the same ballpark. Those bikers were yahoos that prey on peoples fears, which made them easy. Benny can take a good punch and deliver a devastating reprisal. I wouldn't allow him to hit me once, let alone twice like I did with those punks."

"I don't blame you, Mr. Cowboy Preacher. I was in Las Vegas about a month ago, and he nearly beat a man to death inside the ring."

"I know. I was there, too."

"Really? Perhaps providence is working in our favor. So . . . tell me what happened with the woman you almost married?"

"She was my high school sweetheart. We had been going together since ninth grade. Beautiful girl."

"So, was she a virgin?" Johnnie asked, smiling.

"She was when we met, but after the prom, we ended up going all the way. We were madly in love. After that night, we were doing it all the time until she got pregnant. Her dad is a doctor. He took her to one of his colleagues, and they killed my child. I was devastated that they did it behind my back, and that I had no say in the matter. None at all. She said her parents made her do it, but I don't know if that's true or not. Our relationship was never the same after that. A lot of years passed before I was able to forgive her from the heart. In the fall, I went off to seminary in Dallas. Eventually, we broke up, and the last I heard, she had gotten married. I haven't seen her since."

The waitress brought out their chili, two grilled cheese sandwiches and a slab of ribs. Then, she put a large knife on the table to cut the ribs and disappeared.

Johnnie felt an instant connection once she heard Masterson's story. She immediately knew that he would at least understand what happened between her and Lucas. When she saw Masterson bow his head to say grace, she bowed hers, too. When he finished, she said, "What would you think of me if I told you I wasn't a virgin, Paul?"

"I wouldn't think anything of it. I just told you what happened with me and my high school sweetheart."

"Yes, but you're a man. Men have double standards when it comes to women."

"That's true. I'll try not to be judgmental, okay?"

"You'll try?"

"Okay, I won't condemn you for anything you've done."

"Thanks." She looked him in the eyes, examining him before she opened up. She wanted to see his thoughts because there was no guarantee he would ever divulge what was going on in his heart after he heard what she had to say. Still looking into his eyes she said, "My mother sold me to our white insurance man on Christmas Eve when I was fifteen years old."

Masterson was about to take a bite of his ribs and stopped when what Johnnie had said echoed in his mind. "What? Your mother did what?"

"You heard me right, Paul."

"So, this was your stepmother, right?"

"No, it was the woman who had carried me for nine months. It was my mother, Paul. My mother!"

Masterson's eyes narrowed a bit as he tried not to give away what he was thinking of Marguerite at that moment. He said, "And . . . how did she die, Johnnie?"

"She was killed by the Grand Wizard of the Ku Klux Klan, Richard Goode, a paying customer."

"A paying customer? Your mother was a—"

"Prostitute? Yes."

Masterson bit into his ribs to keep from saying harsh things about her mother. Instead, he said, "What happened. Why did he kill her?"

"She was jealous of me."

"Jealous of you? Why?"

"Because my lover, Earl Shamus, was rich and he had bought me a home in Ashland Estates. That's why. She decided to blackmail the Klansman, and he beat her senseless, and then he blew her brains out and left her on a dark road for someone to find."

"Are you being serious with me, Johnnie?"

"I am."

Masterson shook his head and started working on his chili and grilled cheese.

"Have you heard enough, Paul? Or, do you wanna hear some more?" Her eyes welled. "It really starts to get ugly from here."

"Uh . . . well . . . maybe later. I can see in your eyes how devastating it's been for you. If that's only the beginning, I shudder to think what you might tell me after that."

Even though a tear fell, she was able to laugh when he said that. "I thought you wanted to hear it all."

"I do, just later, okay? This is a lot to handle right now."

"But you're leaving tomorrow."

"I don't have to leave tomorrow."

"So, you're gonna stay then?"

"That's the plan. Now let's eat, and you can tell me the rest of the story on the way back to the Clementine."

"I'm going to need more time than that, Paul."

"I'll stick around for a while, and you can tell me everything, okay? But for now, let's just enjoy this delicious food, okay?"

Chapter 53

"You got that, Hatcher?"

Tony Hatcher walked right past Johnnie and Paul Masterson and entered the phone booth he had been in the previous night. He dialed zero and told the operator to connect him to a number in New Orleans and to reverse the charges. While he waited for the operator to connect him, he watched Johnnie and Paul. Much like the previous night, he took his warm turkey and cheese sandwich with a dill pickle on the side and some hot fries into the booth with him. He took a couple swallows of his beer before he heard Earl Shamus' voice.

"Mr. Shamus . . . Hatcher here. I have more to report, if you have time, sir."

"Let's hear your report," Shamus said.

"It looks like she's getting close to the man she was with last night, sir. They're sitting in a booth in The Flamingo Den again."

"That's the place they were in last night, right?"

"Yes, sir."

"But didn't they just meet?"

"I'd say so, yes. The man had paid his bill and left the restaurant. A few minutes later, he came back in with her. Now what you've gotta get, sir, is that this establishment doesn't serve Negroes, at least not inside the restaurant, but he said something to the owner, and the owner let her stay."

"What's his name?"

"Paul Masterson. He's a traveling preacher. He's here for some sort of revival, but earlier this morning, he had breakfast at Lucille's, where Miss Wise works. They talked off and on while he was there, and then he picked her up at 1:30 this afternoon. They came straight to this restaurant, sir."

"You say Masterson's a preacher."

"Yes, sir."

"What else do you have on him?"

"He's from Houston, sir. He preaches to the Negroes in this area a couple times a year. He's a radical, sir. The white churches won't have him preach in their churches because he preaches equality and that all races are of one blood. I'm surprised there hasn't been an attempt on his life for preaching that kind of message. Even if it's true, white people don't want to hear that. If people started believing that, it would turn the country upside down."

"Is this guy for real, or is he a charlatan?"

"That's unclear right now, sir, but what is clear is that he's obviously taken a likening to Miss Wise."

"Really? What makes you think that, Hatcher?"

"The way that he looks at her for starters, sir. Then, there's the fact that he took on three tough-looking bikers on her behalf and wiped the floor with them. The leader's going to need a lot of dental work, or his smile will never be the same. The preacher is not a man to be messed with. When they came to and tried to leave, he wouldn't allow them to until they apologized to her and she accepted. If you wanna know the truth, sir, I think Miss Wise was so flattered that the preacher did a number on the bikers that she wanted to sleep with him. That's just a guess though, sir. Also, if I'm right, and if the preacher turns out to be a charlatan, they'll probably sleep together."

"What makes you say that?"

"They're both staying at the Clementine Hotel, sir. All she has to do is let him in one night for any number of reasons. After that, nature will inevitably take its course."

"I want you and your people on the first plane to Houston. Find out all there is to know about Paul Masterson and bring it back to me before her car is fixed. It shouldn't take you more than two weeks, right?"

"It shouldn't, no, sir."

"Good. Get on it right away. Today. Now, in fact."

"What about our continued surveillance of Miss Wise? Do you want me to leave one or two of my people here to keep an eye on her?"

"No need. She's not going anywhere any time soon. If you take all of your people, you'll be able to cover more ground in Houston quickly. Besides, what if you find out that there's information to be had in another city or another state? What then? You'll have to send someone there, but I don't want the Houston leads abandoned or delayed because you found a new lead. And I don't want you to have to call Jackson and pull someone off her and have them fly somewhere when they could leave from Houston immediately. Again, Johnnie isn't going anywhere any time soon, but I want that information on Masterson as soon as possible. You got that, Hatcher?"

Chapter 54

"Forgive me, but can I be honest with you?"

Paul Masterson looked at his watch. It was almost 2:30. He knew that he needed to get back to his hotel room to study and pray before he delivered his message, but he was too interested in the young woman that he had brought to the restaurant. Her conversation earlier that day intrigued him. He could tell that she had keen intellect. He wanted to know more. Given the women that she had mentioned in Lucille's that morning, he sensed that she was what the church called a believer. Most vacation Bible school students couldn't remember a simple verse like "Jesus wept." While the average Christian might remember the verse, truth be told, most couldn't tell you what book it was in, which underscores why he was so impressed that she knew all the names of the women mentioned in Christ's genealogy. The average Christian would probably name Mary, if asked, forgetting that biblical genealogies rarely mentioned women. Here, four had been mentioned, and she remembered all four of them and their order of appearance. "So, tell me, Johnnie, why did you mention Tamar, Rehab, Ruth, and Bathsheba, the wife of Uriah, the Hittite?"

She folded her arms and leaned back in the booth. "You know why, Paul."

"I know you were testing me, but still you were very specific with those women, their names. How do you know them?"

"They're the only women mentioned in Christ's genealogy, Paul. You know that."

He leaned forward, wanting to know more, wanting to delve deeper into her heart, thinking there was an opportunity to convert her. "So, then you have some religious background?"

"I do."

"Do you mind telling me about your religious affiliation?"

"No, I don't mind. I used to go to a holiness church back in New Orleans. I loved going there. I sung in the choir, and I played piano. I was quite popular. People from other churches used to come from all over the place to hear me sing."

"Do you still go to church?"

She looked away, and then closed her eyes as she fought off the tears as a reservoir of emotions filled her heart. The question seemed simple enough, but it somehow broke through the wall of resistance that she had put up a long time ago. She could see it all now, image after image, of what her mother made her do. His hands were cold, and he had no regard for her displeasure with it all. She was bought and paid for, and so he could take her any way he wanted to. It wasn't about her anyway. It was about him, what he wanted, what he needed, his fulfillment, his pleasure.

She felt it all again, like it was happening at that very moment, the sting of pain, the blood that covered her and the white sheets when Earl Shamus recklessly entered her even though she had reminded him that he was a married man, forcing her to participate in his adultery. What made it worse was that it was her first sexual encounter, and she had heard too many sermons on adultery, fornication, and homosexuality to justify any of it. The worst blow of all had to be the sting of her mother's harsh words after she had been plundered, ripped open like a can of soup and devoured by a grown man long before she was ready.

The woman who bore her had basically told her that her purity was of no value, while at the same time making money off that very purity that she had deemed worthless. In fact, it was her purity that made it possible to charge Shamus a thousand dollars for the privilege of deflowering her. Worse than that, her mother thought that she had made a great bargain because Shamus only offered five hundred and she negotiated another five hundred, telling her daughter, "I didn't let you go cheap," as if that was to somehow make up for the loss of her purity. Never mind that her mother didn't give her any of the money.

Masterson remained quiet. He remembered that she had said that there was more ugly truth that she hadn't told him. He was ready to hear it now because whatever she was holding inside needed to come out. He knew that even though everyone has a past, secrets are hard to live with. He understood that people had to deny truth on a daily basis just to get through the day. And at some point, the hidden secrets of the heart had to surface, and they had to be dealt with in a constructive manner. So, he quietly watched her, waiting for her to open up and share her hidden truth. And when she did, he could lead her to his God.

"It's so unfair, Paul. It's so unfair."

"What's unfair, Johnnie?"

She looked at him, tears, one after another, raced down her cheeks. "Life!"

"Life, Johnnie?"

"Yes!"

"Forgive me, but can I be honest with you?"

Chapter 55

"Why haven't you done anything about this, Paul?"

Johnnie pressed her lips together and ran her tongue across them as what Paul Masterson might possibly say shaped her thoughts. She picked up a napkin and dabbed the corners of her eyes. She took a couple deep breaths and tried to compose herself, as her eyes took in all of him, assiduously contemplating their discussion and how it had progressed so far. She had heard a number of people ask if they could be honest with her and others in the past. It was her experience that asking if one could be honest was a not so subtle prelude to unpleasantness. It was the unmistakable preamble to a verbal exchange, in which most people did not want to participate. And since Masterson was a minister of the Gospel, it wasn't difficult to figure out where the conversation was going. He wanted to talk about Jesus and spiritual matters, she knew, which meant he was about to start acting like the preacher he *said* that he was. She wasn't intimidated by his desire to discuss spiritual things. In fact, she welcomed the divergent direction. It had been a long time coming. After all she had been through, after everything that had happened to her, and after the choices she made as a result, she felt like the female version of the Prodigal Son.

When they were lounging at the pool of the Savoy Hotel, sipping cool drinks on a blistering day, she had been given sound advice from Marguerite when she explained that she could be an evangelist if that's what she wanted to be. She quickly rejected the advice in favor of bilking Earl Shamus out of more of his wife's money. She had been given sound wisdom when her best friend, Sadie Lane, told her she could be anything she wanted to be. She also rejected that advice since she had acquired money and a beautiful home by giving sexual favors to a man she couldn't stand. But she had lost it all, and now, she was ready to hear whatever sound advice Masterson was about to give her. This time, she would listen. This time, she would accept whatever wisdom he had to offer. She nodded several times before saying, "Sure, Paul. Let's have it. Be honest with me."

He hesitated for a few seconds, looking into her exotic, brown eyes, captivated by them, seeing them as finishing touches of a masterpiece constructed, shaped, and painted by the finger of God Himself. "Perhaps a question is in order here," he said and paused.

"Go on," she said, encouraging him, believing that he was afraid of offending her. But she was far from being offended. Having hit rock bottom, she was more than ready to hear whatever he had to say. "I'm listening."

"Well . . . I need to ask you a question, Johnnie."

"Ask."

"Well . . . tell me . . . do you think life is unfair? Or, do you think God is unfair?"

"Um, that's *two* questions, not one." She offered a friendly smile so that he would know she was playing with him. "Of the two questions, I chose life. I chose life because God can't be unfair, can He, Paul?"

"No, He can't, but we can *think* He's unfair because of the horrible things that people do to us. In fact, most of the people I know think God is unfair, whether it's because their neighbor has something they don't or if they think they should have gotten something they didn't get. And then, there are the children of molestation. Or more specific, the children of rape. Children like you, Johnnie . . . people who have been mistreated by calculating adults who should have known better. And indeed did know better, but still raped an innocent child." He paused for a beat. "I'll let you in on a secret that will one day get out."

She leaned in as if what he was about to say was a terrible thing that should never be uttered in a public place and whispered, "What?"

He leaned in, too, and responded in like kind. "There are men of the cloth who are raping boys in the Catholic Church and nothing's being done about it."

She pulled back like she saw a punch coming at her. She inhaled deeply and exhaled, "What?"

He looked over Johnnie's shoulder and checked his periphery, making sure what he had to say was between them and no one else. "Yes. It's true. And not only is there nothing being done about it, it's actually being swept under the rug."

Floored by the revelation, she said, "You're serious, Paul?"

"I am," he said, still looking around, looking to see who might be paying attention to their conversation. "Pretty soon there's going to be an enormous bump in that very rug that the clergy, the Vatican, and the world for that matter won't be able to ignore. Don't get me wrong, Johnnie, we all have our faults. I have plenty of them, too, and we can all fall to temptation and sin . . . every last one of us, but to look the other way only perpetuates it. And if something isn't done, and I mean soon, the Catholic Church will be completely infiltrated by homosexuality and it might even invade the Vatican itself.

"Again, don't get me wrong, Christ said all manner of sin, except the blaspheming of the Holy Spirit would be forgiven, but it cannot be forgiven if it is unacknowledged and never dealt with. If it's not dealt with, it'll spread and permeate the entire church and Christians will end up with laryngitis because we can't lead the world if we're corrupt ourselves. When this kind of thing happens in the church, we should acknowledge it and help our brothers and sisters get back on the path of righteousness. That means we have to sit them down. They can't be priests or pastors until such time that they repent and completely turn away from homosexuality, adultery, or fornication. Once that happens, then we can restore our brothers to the priesthood or the pulpit, not before."

"Why haven't you done anything about this, Paul?"

Chapter 56

"Like when my aunt, Ethel, tried to kill me, right?"

Paul Masterson closed his eyes for a second or two, pressed his lips together, and shook his head as the many conversations he had with men of the cloth came to mind, followed immediately by rejection time and again, because they were afraid that if the truth ever surfaced, the church would never recover. He locked eyes with her again and said, "I have, Johnnie. I spoke up, and they took my church from me. I neither said, nor did anything wrong. In fact, I told these very truths to the powers that be in the clergy, and they called me a heretic. *Me!* Then, they forced me out of the church. That leads me to believe that not only is the Catholic Church being infiltrated, but the Protestant church is being infiltrated as well. Otherwise, how do you explain the church's hypocritical progressive acceptance of that which God's Word calls an abomination?"

"I don't know Paul, but assuming you're right, why do you suppose that is? Why do you suppose the church would turn away from its fundamental beliefs?"

Masterson took a deep breath and said, "Are you sure you wanna hear this?"

"Sure, why not?"

"What if I were to tell you that there is a war going on right now right outside this window"–he tilted his head toward the glass— "and right inside this restaurant, right now, at this very minute? Would you believe me?"

She looked out the window, and then around the restaurant. Seeing and hearing no violence of any kind, she said, "I don't see any fighting, Paul. How can I believe a war is going on right now when I don't hear any shooting and no bombs dropping and no people dying?"

"You said you used to go to church and sing in the choir, right?"

"Yes."

"Are you a Christian?"

"I am . . . I mean . . . I used to be . . . I . . . I . . . I don't know anymore, Paul. I really don't know. I mean, I've done so many sinful things that I can't be a Christian now. I mean, why would God accept me now, given all that I've done? And believe me . . . you don't know the half of it. You really don't."

"My point is that you've never seen God, yet you believe. It therefore follows that there is an invisible world, too. And if that's true, there must be evil as well. And if that's true, evil then must be at war with God whether you can see it or not. Do you disagree?"

"I never thought about it, Paul. But may I ask you a question?"

"Sure, go ahead."

"Is it too late? Will God take me back?"

"It doesn't matter what you've done, Johnnie. All you've got to do is turn away from whatever it is you're doing and turn to Him."

"I've been through so much, Paul. I'm just sick and tired of life and the way it treats me. I was a good girl two years ago. Now look at me. I've lost everything. And I've almost lost my life in the process—twice—three times when you consider that they tried me for a murder I did not commit."

"Who do you blame for the way your life turned out, Johnnie?"

Her eyes narrowed prior to saying, "My mother and Earl Shamus, that's who. They did this to me. I was innocent, Paul. *Innocent!* If they hadn't done to me what they did, none of what happened to me would have happened. I would still be in the church. There would have never been a riot. My mother would have never been murdered. There's just so much, Paul—so very much that would never have happened if those two hadn't gotten together and used me for their own base ends."

"Forgive me for asking, but are you saying that at no time did you have any choices in anything that happened to you?"

Feeling threatened, she folded her arms and said, "What do you mean?"

"Just what I said. I wanna know if you made any choices, at any time, that may have brought some of what you say happened to you on yourself?"

"No."

"Again, forgive me, but are you telling me you're perfect or what?"

"No, I'm not perfect, not at all—not even close."

"Then, you admit you've made decisions that brought destruction into your life."

She thought for a minute. The murder of Richard Goode came to mind. She had been there when Bubbles and Lucas beat him to a pulp. She had watched Napoleon Bentley castrate him. The sound of him screaming filled her mind. It was so loud that she covered her ears even though it was only in her mind. "I only did to others what was done to me or those close to me."

"But you made a choice, right?"

"I guess so."

"So, then you admit that you chose to sit on the throne of God and get your own brand of justice, right?"

At that very instant, she heard the words of her former pastor, Reverend Staples, roar in her mind when he said at her mother's funeral, *"Vengeance is mine says the Lord."* She diverted her eyes to the table, nodded, and said, "I guess."

"What do you mean you guess? You made the decision, right?"

She nodded.

"Johnnie, perhaps you don't realize it, but when you made those decisions, you set a chain of events into motion that could not be halted."

She leaned forward. "What do you mean I set a chain of events into motion? The people who did this to me set it into motion. I didn't. I only surfed, Paul. That's all I did. I just rode the wave."

"Perhaps, but you also caused a lot of ripples in the process. What most people don't get, Johnnie, is that life is like being a farmer. Do you understand?"

"No."

He laughed a little and scratched his chin. "Do you understand how things grow?"

"I think so. The farmer plants seeds, and months later, the seeds start growing, and pretty soon it's harvest time."

"Exactly! The things we do are the seeds we plant as are the things we say. And just like a farmer's field, nothing happens for a long time. If you're not a farmer, you get impatient, waiting for something to happen, thinking, what's taking so long? But the farmer doesn't get impatient because he knows that it'll be awhile before he sees the fruit of his labor. The farmer knows that something is happening with the seed. He just can't see it because it's happening underground—in the invisible world.

"And the things that your mother and the Earl Shamus guy—what a name by the way—didn't see what they were doing to you because like the Spirit of God, emotions cannot be seen. Emotions are felt, and then manifest themselves in our tears, our laughter, our anger, in our quest for revenge, or a host of other manifestations of emotions, but you cannot see them. And so, when you made whatever decisions you made, you, too, set things in motion, and believe it or not, your actions have a way of coming back to get you at the most inopportune time."

"Like when my aunt Ethel tried to kill me, right?"

Chapter 57

"Can I be honest with you now, Paul?"

Paul frowned and fell back against the booth, stunned at what he thought he'd heard. He locked eyes with Johnnie, searching her mind, looking for visible authentication of what he had just heard. Or, perhaps a smile that would let him know she was only kidding to add a little levity to a very intense conversation. But, she didn't smile. She didn't even blink her eyes. What he saw was conviction in those alluring eyes. What he heard from her was icy silence, and that was all the verification he would ever need. Her mother had sold her, and her aunt had literally tried to kill her. Then, it occurred to him that she had said that there was so much more, and that it was ugly. He wondered how much uglier it could get and wanted to ask why her aunt had tried to kill her, but thought the question might come off like she had done something that would warrant the taking of her life. Instead, he said, "When did this happen?"

"Which time? The first time or the second?"

Incredulous, he nearly shouted, "She tried to kill you twice?"

Nodding, she said, "Yes. The first time she tried to kill me was at the Beauregard mansion during Thanksgiving dinner. The second time was in a so-called court of law of all places."

Without thinking, he said, "Why?"

"It's a long story, Paul."

"I'm sure it is. But please, explain what happened. I want to understand."

"You want to understand? You say that like knowing why it happened somehow justifies the crime."

"I just wanna try to somehow make sense of it all even though it would never make sense—not in a million years."

She looked at him for a long moment, trying to decide whether she should tell him. She shook her head a couple times and said, "Because my uncle said it was okay for the Klan to kill my mother."

"What?" he blurted out without thought. Then, he realized he had gotten loud. The restaurant was nearly empty so nearly everyone there turned and looked at them with wondering eyes. Lowering his voice, he continued, "Your uncle said it was okay for the Klan to kill his sister?"

Shaking her head, she said, "I didn't say that. I said my uncle said it was okay for the Klan to kill my mother."

"Okay, but isn't your uncle your mother's brother? Otherwise, how could he be your uncle?"

"Unlike Abraham, preacher, my uncle didn't know his sister was his sister. My uncle's father had a child with my grandmother Josephine out of wedlock."

Frowning, he said, "Okay, but still, why would any Negro say it was okay for the Klan to kill any member of his own race? It makes no sense."

"Perhaps it would make more sense if you knew that my uncle and his father were white men."

If Paul Masterson's hair could stand up, it surely would have at that pivotal moment. He ran his hand down his face, as if he was trying to wake himself up from the dream world he was in. Johnnie sat there watching him fidget, trying to gather himself before he continued the conversation.

After a few moments of gathering himself, he said, "The scriptures teach that we all come from one blood, Johnnie. I hope you know that. Besides, the rules of attraction are male and female. So, I guess I shouldn't be surprised."

"Given your obvious attraction to me, I'd have to agree. I'm told that I look just like her."

"Like who?"

"Josephine . . . my grandmother."

"Forgive me for saying this, but if you look just like your grandmother, I can see why your grandfather had a relationship with her—not that I condone adultery. I'm just saying I understand when

206

men and women are attracted to each other. Sparks fly, and before they know it, it's David and Bathsheba all over again."

"Before she was killed, my mother told me that women have always been jealous of us Baptiste girls because we're pretty. I guess she was right."

"Indeed, she was."

"Paul, I think we've gotten off the subject, don't you?"

"Uh, yeah, yeah, I suppose so. I seem to have lost my train of thought. What were we talking about again?"

"We were talking about whether I thought life or God had been unfair with me. I said I thought life was unfair because God couldn't be, remember?"

He looked at his watch. "3:30! Listen. I'm gonna have to get outta here in a few minutes. I've gotta prepare for my sermon tonight."

"Okay, I'm ready to go whenever you are. I've got some things to do, too."

"Okay, all I wanted to say was that most people blame God for everything that goes wrong in their lives. I find this to be especially true of Negroes even though they are the most religious people in this nation."

"What are you saying, Paul?"

"I'm saying that Negroes, even though you'll never get them to admit it, blame God for their condition now and in the past. When a person blames their present condition on the past, they won't be able see a future because they're constantly looking over their shoulders."

Laughing, she said, "No, we don't, Paul. We don't blame God. We blame crackers! They did it, not God."

Laughing with her, he said, "I know Negroes blame us for their condition on the surface, but in places they don't want to look, dare I say examine closely, they blame God because He could've stopped it before it happened, and He didn't. And He let it go on for three hundred years. Even now Negroes unwittingly blame God because crackers, as you call us, can do irreparable harm to Negroes or even kill them, and it appears that God doesn't lift a finger to stop it. White men rape black women and don't even bother concealing their identities because they know the law won't do anything about it. White men destroy Negro families with their philandering, and then blame the Negro for why he has a splintered family. And again, it appears that God does nothing about this gross injustice. The Negro helped build this great nation, and he gets next to no credit for his substantial contributions, and again, it appears that God does nothing about this. Now . . . are you going to sit there and tell me that Negroes don't blame God, if for no other reason, doing nothing to alleviate your suffering as a race?"

"Well, when you put it that way, I guess I do blame Him for it all. I just didn't realize it."

"You also don't realize you blame Him for what your mother and Earl Shamus did to you, but listen, it's not God's fault. None of it. Again, there is a war going on that you can't see. And in any war, there are always casualties. We all wound and get wounded during the bloody mêlée even though it's an invisible battle."

"Can I be honest with you now, Paul?"

"Sure, go ahead."

"Forgive me for being honest, but it looks like God is losing. I mean, I know He's not, but it sure looks like it. I don't mean to be gross, but there are places that I can't even use the bathroom and might end up soiling myself because crackers aren't decent enough to let me use their toilet. And you're right, Paul. God does nothing about it. And you said it yourself, God's church is being infiltrated by Sodomites."

"See that's where you're wrong, Johnnie. God is doing something even though it doesn't look like it. Otherwise, the invisible war would not be raging as it does. The problem is that His people are disobedient. Do you think I'm the only white preacher who sees these injustices?"

"No. The other white preachers see it, too. They just don't care. And if they do care, only God knows they do, because I certainly don't see them doing anything about it."

He looked at his watch again. "Listen, I really gotta go. I've gotta prepare. Can we talk about this again?"

"Sure, Paul. Anytime you like. I only have one question."

"What is it?"

"What does philandering mean?"

Chapter 58

"On your feet, recruit! And you better not fall outta line again!"

Lucas Matthews and his fellow recruits had marched from the barracks to the Mess Hall. After eating a less than delicious breakfast— SOS being the main course, they marched to the processing center where they verified the identity of each recruit and started a history of paperwork that would follow them throughout their military careers, and made sure each recruit had a service number so they could collect their pay and any other benefits servicemen were entitled to. Then, they marched over to the quartermaster's office and picked up their uniforms. After that, they marched over to the Post Exchange, where they bought their toiletries and shoeshine kits. If a single individual was making all those stops, they could have gotten it all done in about an hour and a half, but there were no less than five platoons processing in at the same time, which made each stop take much longer.

Now they were on their way over to the hospital to get a battery of vaccination shots, marching at Sergeant Cornsilk's command in a cadence he set, their feet landing and rising together like they had been in the platoon for a few weeks instead of a few hours. It seemed like they had been marching forever since they now had their duffle bags slung over their shoulders with all their uniforms, an assortment of overcoats, hats and three pairs of footgear inside them. The duffle bags had gotten heavy for most of the recruits. But Lucas was in excellent shape because he worked out, doing two hundred push-ups a day and running two miles afterward while he was in Angola Prison. He smiled when he heard the men groaning as the pain in their shoulders and backs increased.

"Quit your belly achin'," Sergeant Cornsilk called out. "We're just getting started. We got four months of this. This is nuthin'. As a matter of fact, since you sissies keep moanin' and groanin' like a couple of French whores plying their trade, we're gonna pick up the pace. Double time . . . march!"

It had been like that all day long—running and then marching, running and then marching, with little to no rest to catch their breaths. It seemed like every few miles, someone would fall behind and incur the wrath of Sergeant Cornsilk, who ran along with them, but was breathing normally, like he was walking instead of running. He stopped the platoon several times just so he could yell at whoever fell behind. But Lucas was enjoying the marching and the running according to Cornsilk's cadence.

"Hut two, three, four—hut two, three, four . . . about face . . . to the rear march . . . parade rest . . . atten-hut!" Cornsilk commanded.

Lucas had no idea how much he was going to enjoy basic combat training. He thought it would be harder, but it was a breeze for him and everyone noticed. He loved being the barracks chief, and it was only his first day.

"Pla-toon . . . halt!" Cornsilk barked.

Someone had fallen out of line again, probably because they couldn't take another step due to exhaustion. There was a collective sigh of relief when Sergeant Cornsilk stopped the platoon and screamed at the man who couldn't keep up. Lucas laughed, albeit quietly. He loved when Cornsilk ripped into someone, and he had been ripping into recruits all morning for the least little infraction. The thing that seemed to drive Cornsilk insane was the fact that a few of the recruits couldn't seem to remember their left from their right. Cornsilk made a couple of guys pick up a rock and keep it in their right hands, so they could distinguish one from the other, saying to them, "You're dumb as a rock. Might as well hold one for the duration."

"You think you're tired now," Cornsilk yelled, "but you're not. Being weak . . . being physically unfit . . . will get you killed on the field of battle. You may hate me for it, but you're going to be fit to fight by the time I'm through. The alternative is too frightening to contemplate. If you don't learn what I'm teaching you today, and for the rest of your training, not only are you going to die, but you're going to get your buddies killed, too. Why? Because you couldn't march a single mile, let alone run one. You weaklings need to ask yourself one question. Am I going to get my buddies killed because I can't keep up? Am I going to get captured because I'm out of shape and end up telling our enemies our positions and strategies?"

One of the recruits dropped to his knees.

Enraged, Cornsilk ran up to him and screamed, "On your feet, recruit! And you better not fall outta line again!"

The recruit stood up, but dropped to his knees again and vomited his breakfast.

Cornsilk bent over and yelled in his ear, "You're pathetic! You know that?" He snatched the recruit to his feet. Then he put his fists on his hips, and addressed the platoon. "Your lives are in each others hands! Don't forget that! You're only as strong as your weakest link! Understand?"

"Yes, sir!"

"Double time . . . march!" Cornsilk commanded.

Chapter 59

"Do you have a problem with that, soldier?"

The platoon hadn't even gotten a half a block away when several more recruits fell out of formation. One particular recruit not only fell out of formation, but fell down and vomited, too. "Pla-toon . . . halt!" Sergeant Cornsilk commanded. "At ease!"

The platoon did as they were ordered, dropping their heavy duffle bags to the ground, bending over, placing their hands on their knees, breathing heavily, glad to get another break, even if it was only for a few minutes.

"New Orleans!" Cornsilk called out.

"Yes, sir!"

"Front and center!"

Unlike the rest of the men, sweat wasn't pouring off Lucas. He ran up to the Sergeant, came to attention and said, "Yes, sir!"

"Salt Lake City here can't seem to stay in formation. If he falls out of formation again, if he vomits one more time, it's your ass! You read me, soldier?"

"Yes, sir!" Lucas said. "San Francisco!"

"Yes, sir!"

"Front and center!" Lucas shouted.

Nicolas Lee ran to the back of the platoon and came to attention in front of Lucas. "Yes, sir!"

Lucas said, "Grab his arm and help me stand him up." Lucas looked into Salt Lake City's eyes and said, "What's your name, son?"

"Thomas Shaw."

"Thomas Shaw, what?" San Francisco screamed."

"Thomas Shaw, sir!"

"You just bought yourself some remedial running, son," San Francisco warned. "I'm gonna run you like you've never been run until you lose a hundred pounds. You understand?"

"Yes, sir!"

"You're not going to embarrass me, your barracks chief, this platoon or our drill sergeant," San Francisco yelled. "Now get your fat candy bar eatin' ass up! Let's go."

Together, Lucas and Nicolas stood up the three hundred pound man who was grossly out of shape.

Lucas looked at Cornsilk and said, "Ready, sir!"

"Are you sure?" Cornsilk asked.

"Yes, sir!" Lucas said.

"Lynchburg!" Cornsilk yelled.

"Yes, sir!"

"You're fired," Cornsilk said. "You've just been demoted, but you're still responsible for keeping the whites in line. Fail, and you'll spend two weeks in the infirmary. Understand?"

"Yes, sir!" Lynchburg said.

"San Francisco!" Cornsilk yelled.

"Yes, sir!"

"You're taking Lynchburg's place," Cornsilk said firmly. "Do you have a problem with that soldier?"

"No, sir!"

"Alright then, I expect the best from both of you. And that goes double for you, Lynchburg! Understand?"

They all screamed, "Yes, sir!"

Cornsilk called the platoon to attention, and they marched another mile or so to the hospital. "Pla-toon—halt!" He walked to the back of the platoon to talk to Lucas. He looked at Lucas and said, "New Orleans, you and San Francisco take Salt Lake City to the infirmary. He might be dehydrated. I've never lost a recruit before, and I don't plan on losing one now. Stay with him until the platoon comes in."

"Yes, sir!" Lucas said.

Chapter 60

"I could really like you, you know that?"

Lucas and Nicolas stood next to Thomas Shaw, lifted his arms over their shoulders, and walked him past five other platoons, waiting to get their vaccination shots, and then into the hospital, where they were met by several nurses, who quickly got Thomas into an empty bed and began treating him.

"So did you get your SOS today, recruit?" Lieutenant Perry said.

Lucas turned around. He saw the lieutenant standing in the doorway, looking good in her white uniform. He looked at Nicolas and said, "Stay with him. I'll be back in a few minutes."

"You know her?" Nicolas asked.

"Yeah. I met her yesterday."

Nicolas smiled and said, "Good-looking broad, man."

Lucas smiled. "Yep."

"So, did you get a piece?"

"Nope. She's not that kind of girl."

"Maybe you oughta marry her then."

"Maybe I will." He walked over to Lieutenant Perry, smiled and said, "Fancy meeting you here. Haven't we met before?"

"We may have," she said, smiling. "I oughta remember such a good-looking, tall drink of cold water like you. Refresh my memory."

"So, you remember the SOS, but you don't remember me, huh?"

Shaking her head, she said, "Vaguely. I've been experiencing memory lapses lately."

"Maybe you should see a doctor. I'm sure he won't have any trouble fitting you into his schedule . . . you being a nurse and all."

"I've seen the doctor. Several times."

"And what were his findings?"

"He couldn't explain it. He used a big word. He called it infatuation."

"Infatuation, huh?"

"Yes, do you understand that word, recruit?"

"Nope, but I like the way it rolls off your tongue though. Perhaps you can tell me the definition and how it applies to our situation when we get something the Sergeant calls liberty. I'm thinkin' the Blue Diamond Restaurant would be a lovely place to get reacquainted . . . you know . . . refresh your memory. They serve all kinds of wonderful dishes there. I'm sure you'll love it. And I've got my own car, a pocket full of money, and I just might spend some of it on you."

"You're serious, Lucas?"

"I am."

She leaned in and whispered, "Even though you know I'm not going to put out?"

"Sure, if you don't mind me trying to change your mind with a little huggin' and a kissin'. That won't turn you into a slave, will it?"

"It hasn't so far."

"Then, it won't in a few weeks when we get liberty either."

"Great! It's a date then."

"Guess who the barracks chief of the platoon is?"

"Who? You?"

"Yes, ma'am. Sergeant Cornsilk picked me out of about forty men or so. I think he chose me because I understood what the purpose of the Army was when no one else did. He's a mean SOB, but I like him just fine."

"You do, huh? He's the sergeant I was telling you about in the Mess Hall yesterday. Did he tell you all that he was a direct descendant of Geronimo?"

"Yeah."

"Just between you and me, he's not a descendant of Geronimo. He's not even an Apache. He's a Cherokee. He just tells recruits that, so that they'll fear him even more."

"Really?"

"Yes."

"Well, it doesn't matter. He's tough enough, and I think we're lucking to have him. I wanted the toughest guy. Whenever war comes again, and we have to fight, I wanna be ready. That's the only way to survive. I wanna come back in one piece to a woman I love with all my heart."

"Hmph! And who is that, Johnnie Wise?"

"You remember her first and last name, huh?"

"How could I not. It's written on the tablets of your heart. At least for now. But a few dates with me, and she'll be nothing more than a distant memory."

"Really now? You sound powerful sure of yourself, Lieutenant."

"I am sure of myself. You just need to be away from her to break the power of whatever spell she put on you. I heard about them New Orleanian women and the Voodoo they use on the men folk down there. But when you meet a real woman, a woman that's full of promise, a woman who keeps her word and is committed to you, one who loves the ground you walk on, you'll forget all about ol' Johnnie Wise. Mark my words. The woman you've met . . . the woman I'm referring to . . . Johnnie Wise won't be able to hold a candle to her. Trust me."

"So, you think you're that woman, Lieutenant?"

"Time will tell. You've got sixteen weeks of training. Let's use that time to find out. Who knows, we might just fall in love."

"You never know, but I'm willing to see where this thing goes if you are."

"I am," she said. "Now, why don't you and your friend come with me, and I'll give you your shots personally. That way you won't have to wait in that crazy long line."

"I'll tell you what, I'll come first, and then I'll send San Francisco."

"Why don't you both come together?"

"We've been ordered to stay with him."

"But there are a number of nurses who can stay with him. It won't take long."

Keith Lee Johnson

"I'm sure it won't. But orders are orders. And I have to set an example for the rest of the men. I know how these things work. I was the captain of my high school football team. The way I see it, being the barracks chief is the same thing, but different. Being in the Army is only a game when we're not on the battle field. But when it's time to fight, I have to have the respect of the men who follow me."

"But Lucas, it's just your first day. You're not even wearing a uniform yet."

"That's why it's so important that I follow orders now. San Francisco is watching me. Whatever I do, he'll think its okay to do—even now. So, let me tell him what's going on, and then we can go get those shots."

"You know what, Lucas?"

"What, Cassandra?"

Positively beaming at that point, she said, "I could really like you, you know that?"

"I feel the same way. Now, wait right here. I'll be right back."

217

Chapter 61

Paul Masterson grabbed a toothpick after paying for their meals, and they left The Flamingo Den together, like they were a couple. As a boy he had been taught to treat a lady with respect by opening and closing doors for her, by standing when she enters or leaves a room, by refraining from the use of profanity in her presence, and by protecting her from whatever evil they might encounter when they're together. He opened the door for her and waited until she was comfortable before closing it. Then, he walked around to the other side of the truck and got in, started the engine, and pulled off.

Johnnie had looked at him for a second or two before getting into the truck, searching his eyes for truth, wondering if he would try to have sex with her when they returned to the Clementine even though he had told her he had to prepare his sermon. Her experience with white men had pretty much been the same. They all found her very attractive and wanted to have sex with her as soon as they could. From the look in his eyes, she could tell that Paul Masterson wanted to have sex with her, too, but for whatever reasons, he was able to control his inclination to initiate the romp or simply take what he wanted as Billy Logan had. She admired him for respecting her and treating her the way a lady ought to be treated. What she didn't get though was that she had ceased to be a lady a long time ago, yet she thought she was.

They rode in silence for a few seconds, and then Masterson said, "Johnnie, I need to be totally and completely honest with you, okay?"

She looked at him, expecting an incredible secret to roll off his tongue, and give her a reason not to respect him as much as she did. At least that's what she thought he thought, but it wasn't true, and when he told her whatever it was he had to tell her, she would assure him that she would not hold it against him as she had a past as well. She thought that if he opened up to her, she just might be able to open up to him. She knew that a woman had to be very careful with her secrets, especially when it came to men because men had a much higher standard for the female of the species than they had for themselves. And so, in most situations, telling men things they really didn't need to know, particularly specific details of a sexual nature, wasn't an option. But she thought Paul Masterson might be different. "Okay. What is it?"

"Listen"—he paused for a few seconds—"I'm sure I probably made it sound like I was above sexual sin, but I want you to know right now that I'm not." He paused and looked at her to see her reaction, but she didn't react at all. She just continued looking through the windshield and listening. He took a deep breath before saying, "I told you that they forced me outta my church, and they did. But I only told you part of the story."

She looked at him and said, "Go on, Paul, I'm listening."

He exhaled hard. "Well . . . Johnnie . . . you see . . . there was a woman involved."

Chapter 62

"You sure you wanna see a profligate like me again?"

When Johnnie didn't respond to his confession, he looked at her intensely, trying to figure out what was going through her mind. He wondered if she thought he was a terrible person who should have known better and should have set a much better example. That's what most people would have thought in that situation, he knew. Through experience he had learned that while most people hated to be judged for the sins they committed, those very same people loved to judge others without compassion and many of them didn't even know that about themselves. He also knew that many people loved it when a man of the cloth fell into some sort of sexual sin. They thought it somehow gave them permission to be sinful, too. What he knew and they didn't was that they were already sinful and that other people's sins didn't give them carte blanche to live without restraint.

"Did you hear me?" he asked. "I said there was a woman involved."

She looked at him soberly and said, "I heard you."

Expecting to be condemned for his moral failure, he said, "Well, do you have anything to say?"

"Sexual sin is not without its rewards, Mr. Cowboy Preacher. Only virgins don't understand the allure of sexual pleasure and its vise-like grip. Yes. I fully understand."

"No. I really don't think you do."

"Of course it does, Johnnie. That's why it's so effective. And
be more effective in your lifetime. Watch and see."

Feeling the need to get the subject back on its original course,
said, "So, Delilah told the church leaders that you and her were
g at it, huh? Now that's believable."

"Yep."

"Let me guess. You knew to stop, but you couldn't, right? You
telling yourself one last time and each time you did it with her, the
e powerless you were to stop even though you knew you should."

"Yep. How did you know?"

"I had a boyfriend who had the same problem. His Delilah was
e, too. His life was on the line, and he couldn't stop either. But
vay, how did it end?"

"I had made up my mind to stop. I couldn't continue seeing her
preaching on Sundays. My sermons had lost their power. After
ile, I was just going through the motions. And I knew the congrega-
knew something was wrong, but nobody questioned me. I was their
or, so in their eyes, I could do no wrong. Anyway, I called and told
I was finished. I told her I couldn't see her ever again, but she
ded with me not to end it."

"How long had it been going on?"

"For almost a year. I thought it would burn itself out, but there
no chance of that. The thing was intensifying after each encounter.
ew that if we kept doing what we were doing, sooner or later, we
e going to get caught."

"But you let her talk you into seeing her one last time, right?"

Masterson nodded. "I remember it like it was yesterday. She
crying, and so was I. I really thought she was feeling what I was
ing—how wrong we were, you know?"

"So, you loved her?"

Nodding, he said, "Yes."

"Um."

"Anyway, I got her to swear to me it would be the last time
d call me. And it was the last time alright. We were in this hotel
n, going at it something fierce. I swear I never felt anything like it.
as like a powerful drug, and we were both addicted to it. We had
our minds, caught up in an artificial nirvana that seemed real
igh, felt real enough, but was more counterfeit than a four-dollar

"There's not much to misunderstand. She's a woman, and
you're a man. You were drawn to her, and she was drawn to you. I
mean, you did have sex with this woman, right?"

"Yes, I did, but it was far more complicated than that. You
make it sound like we were just two animals in heat."

"Were you married to this woman?"

"No, I wasn't."

"Then, that's exactly what you two were. Two animals in heat
whether you want to acknowledge that or not. You were a preacher at
the time, right?"

"Yes, I was, but—"

"Like I said, I understand."

"No, I don't think you do."

"What don't I understand, Paul? You met a beautiful woman,
and you had sex with her. It's pretty simple."

"No, it isn't. But let me say from the outset that it was my fault.
I was twenty-four at the time, and I was speaking the truth in love the
way the Bible says. I wasn't trying to bring anybody down. And I
certainly wasn't trying to bring any particular leader down. I just didn't
want the church to be brought down." He pulled into the Clementine
parking lot and shut off the engine. "That meant I couldn't look the
other way when I saw corruption in the church. Well . . . a number of
the leaders were charlatans, Johnnie. They were unrepentant profligates
who had turned the church into a moneymaking enterprise, and I was
making too much noise and shining too much light on their dark
behavior, and so they got together and decided to shut me up once and
for all."

"The church leaders were going to kill you the way they did
Jesus?"

"Yes and no. They weren't going to kill me . . . they were going
to kill my message, which was God's message by setting me up with a
modern day version of Delilah. I was young and full of myself, but I
didn't know it. Pride had me, controlled me, but it was so subtle I didn't
see it. Anyway, I had preached what I thought was a tremendous
sermon. I thought the aisle would be flooded with sinners running to the
altar who couldn't wait to be saved, but to my disappointment, only one
person came to the altar."

"The woman the leaders set you up with?"

Nodding, he said, "Yep. Now, let me be clear, Johnnie, they set me up, but I took the bait. You understand what I'm saying?"

"Yes."

"The point is, they could have sent a thousand women, one more beautiful than the previous one, but I had a choice, and I made the wrong one."

"Well, all I can say is that she must have been ten times better looking than me because you sure didn't try anything like that with me. You didn't even try to kiss me."

"Don't be jealous, Johnnie. I'm trying to do what's right by you and my God. I fell prey to that situation before, and I don't want it to ever happen again."

"Wait a minute. Was this woman black or what?"

"No. She was white."

"Well, it sounds like you're saying I'm trying to do the same thing to you, like someone is paying me like they paid your Delilah."

"No. That's not what I'm saying at all. I'm just pointing out that even though I failed the test doesn't mean that I was wrong about corruption in the church. People seem to think that when the preacher fails, it's time for the days of Pompeii to return, where no sexual restraint was common place, all under the watchful eyes of Aphrodite and her son of whoredom, Priapus. People seem to think that pastors are above temptation, but it's just the opposite. We are the targets of illicit activity. Some of it subtle and some of it not so subtle, like our friend the waitress. Let me be clear on something, Johnnie. My failure only underscores just how big a problem there is. If I could fall, and I was a sincere pastor, consider what's going on with those who are the tares of the faith, false believers in high positions, controlling the masses, deciding who to promote and who to silence. If what's going on inside the church is ever discovered by an unbelieving world, it would be wide open to blackmail, which would eventually bring about its decay and eventual destruction."

"Ah, c'mon, Paul, do you really believe the church can be destroyed? I don't."

"Okay, well, perhaps destroyed is the wrong word. It could be seriously discredited then. How about that?"

"I'm not sure I believe that either."

"That's because you're looking at it in an imm[...] rulers of darkness are committed to their cause, Joh[...] wouldn't happen overnight. It would happen twenty[...] forty or fifty years in the future. If church leadership[...] present course, the prince of this world will rer[...] irrelevant, which would open the door to all sorts of[...] worm its way into all of our institutions, including t[...] systems. What do you think'll happen if praye[...] Commandments are taken out of schools? I'll tell you[...] inside of twenty years, there will be complete and u[...] classroom. We won't be able to recognize our children[...] else?"

"What?"

"Those very same children will grow up witho[...] necessary to live in a civilized society, and eventually[...] of right and wrong. Some of those children will then [...] the legislature and change the laws that we hold so dea[...] will ensue. If evil continues to advance at its current p[...] for a woman to kill her unborn child in twenty years[...] call it killing the unborn. They'll have to call it someth[...] subtler, gentler word that'll figuratively put women to[...] won't even know what they've done to themselves an[...] In twenty years, teenage girls will start getting pregnar[...] rate and killing the unborn will become big business. S[...] the United States will lose its moral authority, and our [...] up owning us. That's why it's gotta be stopped now be[...] If the people who set me up get a firm foothold in the cl[...] and they appear to be working toward that end, we may[...] out. And people like me, people who believe this wi[...] very near future, they'll call us religious nuts. People[...] the problem when, in fact, we'll be the solution—the o[...] to do any of this, they must first silence the church. The[...] that is through ignorance—meaning the congregatior[...] read or even believe the Bible—all of this while a[...] regularly. And the infiltrators will pervert the few fou[...] believers know. Heresy will be the accepted order of t[...]

"Honestly, all of that sounds so farfetched, Pa[...]

bill. The leaders waited until we were both at the peak of excitement, screaming at the top of our lungs, and then they came into the room using the key she had given them."

"Treacherous," Johnnie said, somberly. "Just like the woman taken in adultery."

"Yep. And I knew not to go to that hotel. I had been warned by the Spirit of God not to go, but I had told her I would meet her there."

She looked at him, rolled her eyes, and said, "And you wanted your last piece, Paul."

"I hate to admit it, but . . . yes . . . I did. And since I'm being so honest with you, the real truth is I wanted it bad. Real bad."

"You wanted to get up in her one last time, hoping that the last piece would be the best piece, and you would have that memory to comfort you while you mourned the loss of the woman you loved."

Masterson exhaled softly and said, "Right again."

"And you told me all of this, why?"

"Because I didn't want you to think that I was just judging homosexuals and adulterers. I wanted you to know that I'm trying to help restore and reform the church because we are in serious trouble right now, and congregations all over this nation have no idea what's going on inside their hollowed walls. The only way to do that is to tell the truth. The leadership thought they had me. They thought they could control me, shut me up now that I had been caught in a compromising position with a paid whore who had sold her soul to them for a few thousand dollars. You wanna know the funny thing though?"

"What's that?"

"After we had gotten caught and it was all over, she still wanted to see me. She told me she had literally fallen in love with me and that we could start all over. The sad part is I almost took her up on her offer. God knows I wanted to. But I was God's envoy even though I had failed him. I was God's man even though I had become The Prodigal. So, even though I wanted to see how things would turn out with her, I made a choice and left that situation alone even though the pull of lust had a firm grip on my body, my emotions, and my psyche. In short, I was a complete mess."

"So, what happened to Delilah?"

"I don't know. I left town and haven't seen her since. To tell you the truth, I don't know what I'd do if I ever saw her again. That's what so sad. With all that I know, I don't know if I wouldn't fall right back into the trap of seeing her again. That's how powerful sexual sin is, Johnnie, which is the main reason I didn't come into your room or try to kiss you. I know my limitations, and I know my weaknesses. There's no point in even denying either of them."

Johnnie thought about a conversation she'd had with Lucas after he and Marla had come home from Shreveport. He had told her about all the things Marla had done to him when they made love. Now, she had a better understanding of why he kept going back for one last piece. "So, after they caught you two together, that's when they forced you outta the church?"

"No. Not then. Shortly afterward. Like I said, they thought they had me, but they didn't. The very next Sunday, I stood in the pulpit in front of my congregation. The church leadership had come to my church to watch the farce I was supposed to be a part of. I looked at their faces. They were relishing the moment as I struggled to find the words to make clear what I had to say. But instead of delivering a watered-down sermon, I told on myself and on the church leadership that had set me up. I took full responsibility for my part in the sexual episode, but I made it clear that the leadership had as much to do with it as I did. Then, I left while the congregation was in a heated uproar. I was loved by my congregation, and they were very angry with the church leadership. I don't know if they made it outta the sanctuary alive, but I knew I had to go on an extended sabbatical and eventually reconnect with God. Seven years later, I'm preaching at revivals. I don't think I ever want to have my own church again."

"Paul, you're a great man."

"You think so?"

"Yeah."

"I don't."

"Why not?"

"I'm an ordinary man with an extraordinary commission, fighting an invisible war that most people don't know exists."

"I think you're a little too hard on yourself. You fell, but you picked yourself up and moved forward. Not only that, but you told the truth on yourself. I don't have to tell you how difficult that is. It's so much easier to just stay down. It's so much easier to keep going left when you know you should go right. When I was a little girl, I wanted to be an evangelist. After hearing your story, I know it isn't too late for me. My mother was right."

"Well, listen, I really gotta go now. Would it be okay if I didn't see you up to your room? People might get the wrong idea."

"Sure. No problem. Am I going to see you again?"

"You sure you wanna see a profligate like me again?"

Looking into his eyes, she smiled and said, "I most certainly do wanna see you again, Paul Masterson."

"We'll see if we can accommodate you. You seem to have excellent recall of the things you learned before you left the church. Perhaps we can talk more, and maybe you'll return to Christ, too."

"I'd like that, Paul—to talk some more, I mean."

Chapter 63

"Okay, I'll see you at six."

Johnnie watched Masterson walk over to Room 107, enter and closed the door. She was disappointed when he didn't look at her one last time before shutting the world out so he could study for his sermon. The Savoy Hotel came to mind. She remembered lounging by the pool, sipping tea with her gorgeous mother, sharing her plan to make a lot of money. As it all played out in her mind again, she realized her mother had been right yet again when she had told her that nearly all the famous men of the Bible had fallen into some sort of sin, but were still used mightily by God. She really liked Paul because he was an honorable and decent man despite his moral failure.

It didn't matter that he got caught up in a bad situation and should have known better. What mattered to her at that moment was that he was man enough to admit that he wasn't perfect, but at the same time had a passion for righteousness in the church and among its leadership. What impressed her most was that he never said one bad thing about people outside the church—people like her who had left their Christian roots and lived according to their own rules, their own standards, and their own newly acquired beliefs. His main concern was those inside, specifically the leadership, which reminded her of the many sermons she'd heard Reverend Staples preach before her mother sold her.

She walked into the hotel lobby, her Wall Street Journal folded neatly and tucked under her arm, and went up to the counter. Gloria Schumacher was sitting in a chair reading an Agatha Christie mystery, much like she was doing the day before. "Hi, Gloria."

"There's not much to misunderstand. She's a woman, and you're a man. You were drawn to her, and she was drawn to you. I mean, you did have sex with this woman, right?"

"Yes, I did, but it was far more complicated than that. You make it sound like we were just two animals in heat."

"Were you married to this woman?"

"No, I wasn't."

"Then, that's exactly what you two were. Two animals in heat whether you want to acknowledge that or not. You were a preacher at the time, right?"

"Yes, I was, but—"

"Like I said, I understand."

"No, I don't think you do."

"What don't I understand, Paul? You met a beautiful woman, and you had sex with her. It's pretty simple."

"No, it isn't. But let me say from the outset that it was my fault. I was twenty-four at the time, and I was speaking the truth in love the way the Bible says. I wasn't trying to bring anybody down. And I certainly wasn't trying to bring any particular leader down. I just didn't want the church to be brought down." He pulled into the Clementine parking lot and shut off the engine. "That meant I couldn't look the other way when I saw corruption in the church. Well . . . a number of the leaders were charlatans, Johnnie. They were unrepentant profligates who had turned the church into a moneymaking enterprise, and I was making too much noise and shining too much light on their dark behavior, and so they got together and decided to shut me up once and for all."

"The church leaders were going to kill you the way they did Jesus?"

"Yes and no. They weren't going to kill me . . . they were going to kill my message, which was God's message by setting me up with a modern day version of Delilah. I was young and full of myself, but I didn't know it. Pride had me, controlled me, but it was so subtle I didn't see it. Anyway, I had preached what I thought was a tremendous sermon. I thought the aisle would be flooded with sinners running to the altar who couldn't wait to be saved, but to my disappointment, only one person came to the altar."

"The woman the leaders set you up with?"

Nodding, he said, "Yep. Now, let me be clear, Johnnie, they set me up, but I took the bait. You understand what I'm saying?"

"Yes."

"The point is, they could have sent a thousand women, one more beautiful than the previous one, but I had a choice, and I made the wrong one."

"Well, all I can say is that she must have been ten times better looking than me because you sure didn't try anything like that with me. You didn't even try to kiss me."

"Don't be jealous, Johnnie. I'm trying to do what's right by you and my God. I fell prey to that situation before, and I don't want it to ever happen again."

"Wait a minute. Was this woman black or what?"

"No. She was white."

"Well, it sounds like you're saying I'm trying to do the same thing to you, like someone is paying me like they paid your Delilah."

"No. That's not what I'm saying at all. I'm just pointing out that even though I failed the test doesn't mean that I was wrong about corruption in the church. People seem to think that when the preacher fails, it's time for the days of Pompeii to return, where no sexual restraint was common place, all under the watchful eyes of Aphrodite and her son of whoredom, Priapus. People seem to think that pastors are above temptation, but it's just the opposite. We are the targets of illicit activity. Some of it subtle and some of it not so subtle, like our friend the waitress. Let me be clear on something, Johnnie. My failure only underscores just how big a problem there is. If I could fall, and I was a sincere pastor, consider what's going on with those who are the tares of the faith, false believers in high positions, controlling the masses, deciding who to promote and who to silence. If what's going on inside the church is ever discovered by an unbelieving world, it would be wide open to blackmail, which would eventually bring about its decay and eventual destruction."

"Ah, c'mon, Paul, do you really believe the church can be destroyed? I don't."

"Okay, well, perhaps destroyed is the wrong word. It could be seriously discredited then. How about that?"

"I'm not sure I believe that either."

"That's because you're looking at it in an immediate sense. The rulers of darkness are committed to their cause, Johnnie. It therefore wouldn't happen overnight. It would happen twenty, thirty, perhaps forty or fifty years in the future. If church leadership continues on its present course, the prince of this world will render the church irrelevant, which would open the door to all sorts of evil. It will then worm its way into all of our institutions, including the public school systems. What do you think'll happen if prayer and the Ten Commandments are taken out of schools? I'll tell you what'll happen, inside of twenty years, there will be complete and utter chaos in the classroom. We won't be able to recognize our children, and guess what else?"

"What?"

"Those very same children will grow up without the discipline necessary to live in a civilized society, and eventually lose their sense of right and wrong. Some of those children will then become a part of the legislature and change the laws that we hold so dear and more chaos will ensue. If evil continues to advance at its current pace, it'll be legal for a woman to kill her unborn child in twenty years, but they won't call it killing the unborn. They'll have to call it something else, a softer, subtler, gentler word that'll figuratively put women to sleep so that they won't even know what they've done to themselves and their children. In twenty years, teenage girls will start getting pregnant at an alarming rate and killing the unborn will become big business. Shortly after that, the United States will lose its moral authority, and our enemies will end up owning us. That's why it's gotta be stopped now before it's too late. If the people who set me up get a firm foothold in the church hierarchy, and they appear to be working toward that end, we may never get them out. And people like me, people who believe this will happen in the very near future, they'll call us religious nuts. People will think we're the problem when, in fact, we'll be the solution—the only solution. But to do any of this, they must first silence the church. The only way to do that is through ignorance—meaning the congregation will no longer read or even believe the Bible—all of this while attending church regularly. And the infiltrators will pervert the few foundational truths believers know. Heresy will be the accepted order of the day."

"Honestly, all of that sounds so farfetched, Paul."

"Of course it does, Johnnie. That's why it's so effective. And it'll be more effective in your lifetime. Watch and see."

Feeling the need to get the subject back on its original course, she said, "So, Delilah told the church leaders that you and her were going at it, huh? Now that's believable."

"Yep."

"Let me guess. You knew to stop, but you couldn't, right? You kept telling yourself one last time and each time you did it with her, the more powerless you were to stop even though you knew you should."

"Yep. How did you know?"

"I had a boyfriend who had the same problem. His Delilah was white, too. His life was on the line, and he couldn't stop either. But anyway, how did it end?"

"I had made up my mind to stop. I couldn't continue seeing her and preaching on Sundays. My sermons had lost their power. After awhile, I was just going through the motions. And I knew the congregation knew something was wrong, but nobody questioned me. I was their pastor, so in their eyes, I could do no wrong. Anyway, I called and told her I was finished. I told her I couldn't see her ever again, but she pleaded with me not to end it."

"How long had it been going on?"

"For almost a year. I thought it would burn itself out, but there was no chance of that. The thing was intensifying after each encounter. I knew that if we kept doing what we were doing, sooner or later, we were going to get caught."

"But you let her talk you into seeing her one last time, right?"

Masterson nodded. "I remember it like it was yesterday. She was crying, and so was I. I really thought she was feeling what I was feeling—how wrong we were, you know?"

"So, you loved her?"

Nodding, he said, "Yes."

"Um."

"Anyway, I got her to swear to me it would be the last time she'd call me. And it was the last time alright. We were in this hotel room, going at it something fierce. I swear I never felt anything like it. It was like a powerful drug, and we were both addicted to it. We had lost our minds, caught up in an artificial nirvana that seemed real enough, felt real enough, but was more counterfeit than a four-dollar bill. The leaders waited until we were both at the peak of excitement, screaming at the top of our lungs, and then they came into the room using the key she had given them."

"Treacherous," Johnnie said, somberly. "Just like the woman taken in adultery."

"Yep. And I knew not to go to that hotel. I had been warned by the Spirit of God not to go, but I had told her I would meet her there."

She looked at him, rolled her eyes, and said, "And you wanted your last piece, Paul."

"I hate to admit it, but . . . yes . . . I did. And since I'm being so honest with you, the real truth is I wanted it bad. Real bad."

"You wanted to get up in her one last time, hoping that the last piece would be the best piece, and you would have that memory to comfort you while you mourned the loss of the woman you loved."

Masterson exhaled softly and said, "Right again."

"And you told me all of this, why?"

"Because I didn't want you to think that I was just judging homosexuals and adulterers. I wanted you to know that I'm trying to help restore and reform the church because we are in serious trouble right now, and congregations all over this nation have no idea what's going on inside their hollowed walls. The only way to do that is to tell the truth. The leadership thought they had me. They thought they could control me, shut me up now that I had been caught in a compromising position with a paid whore who had sold her soul to them for a few thousand dollars. You wanna know the funny thing though?"

"What's that?"

"After we had gotten caught and it was all over, she still wanted to see me. She told me she had literally fallen in love with me and that we could start all over. The sad part is I almost took her up on her offer. God knows I wanted to. But I was God's envoy even though I had failed him. I was God's man even though I had become The Prodigal. So, even though I wanted to see how things would turn out with her, I made a choice and left that situation alone even though the pull of lust had a firm grip on my body, my emotions, and my psyche. In short, I was a complete mess."

"So, what happened to Delilah?"

"I don't know. I left town and haven't seen her since. To tell you the truth, I don't know what I'd do if I ever saw her again. That's what so sad. With all that I know, I don't know if I wouldn't fall right back into the trap of seeing her again. That's how powerful sexual sin is, Johnnie, which is the main reason I didn't come into your room or try to kiss you. I know my limitations, and I know my weaknesses. There's no point in even denying either of them."

Johnnie thought about a conversation she'd had with Lucas after he and Marla had come home from Shreveport. He had told her about all the things Marla had done to him when they made love. Now, she had a better understanding of why he kept going back for one last piece. "So, after they caught you two together, that's when they forced you outta the church?"

"No. Not then. Shortly afterward. Like I said, they thought they had me, but they didn't. The very next Sunday, I stood in the pulpit in front of my congregation. The church leadership had come to my church to watch the farce I was supposed to be a part of. I looked at their faces. They were relishing the moment as I struggled to find the words to make clear what I had to say. But instead of delivering a watered-down sermon, I told on myself and on the church leadership that had set me up. I took full responsibility for my part in the sexual episode, but I made it clear that the leadership had as much to do with it as I did. Then, I left while the congregation was in a heated uproar. I was loved by my congregation, and they were very angry with the church leadership. I don't know if they made it outta the sanctuary alive, but I knew I had to go on an extended sabbatical and eventually reconnect with God. Seven years later, I'm preaching at revivals. I don't think I ever want to have my own church again."

"Paul, you're a great man."

"You think so?"

"Yeah."

"I don't."

"Why not?"

"I'm an ordinary man with an extraordinary commission, fighting an invisible war that most people don't know exists."

"I think you're a little too hard on yourself. You fell, but you picked yourself up and moved forward. Not only that, but you told the truth on yourself. I don't have to tell you how difficult that is. It's so much easier to just stay down. It's so much easier to keep going left when you know you should go right. When I was a little girl, I wanted to be an evangelist. After hearing your story, I know it isn't too late for me. My mother was right."

"Well, listen, I really gotta go now. Would it be okay if I didn't see you up to your room? People might get the wrong idea."

"Sure. No problem. Am I going to see you again?"

"You sure you wanna see a profligate like me again?"

Looking into his eyes, she smiled and said, "I most certainly do wanna see you again, Paul Masterson."

"We'll see if we can accommodate you. You seem to have excellent recall of the things you learned before you left the church. Perhaps we can talk more, and maybe you'll return to Christ, too."

"I'd like that, Paul—to talk some more, I mean."

Chapter 63

"Okay, I'll see you at six."

Johnnie watched Masterson walk over to Room 107, enter and closed the door. She was disappointed when he didn't look at her one last time before shutting the world out so he could study for his sermon. The Savoy Hotel came to mind. She remembered lounging by the pool, sipping tea with her gorgeous mother, sharing her plan to make a lot of money. As it all played out in her mind again, she realized her mother had been right yet again when she had told her that nearly all the famous men of the Bible had fallen into some sort of sin, but were still used mightily by God. She really liked Paul because he was an honorable and decent man despite his moral failure.

It didn't matter that he got caught up in a bad situation and should have known better. What mattered to her at that moment was that he was man enough to admit that he wasn't perfect, but at the same time had a passion for righteousness in the church and among its leadership. What impressed her most was that he never said one bad thing about people outside the church—people like her who had left their Christian roots and lived according to their own rules, their own standards, and their own newly acquired beliefs. His main concern was those inside, specifically the leadership, which reminded her of the many sermons she'd heard Reverend Staples preach before her mother sold her.

She walked into the hotel lobby, her Wall Street Journal folded neatly and tucked under her arm, and went up to the counter. Gloria Schumacher was sitting in a chair reading an Agatha Christie mystery, much like she was doing the day before. "Hi, Gloria."

Without looking at her, she said, "Hello, Johnnie. Give me a minute to finish this page."

"Okay. Take your time."

A moment or two later, she dog-eared the page, closed the book, and set it down behind the counter. She exhaled like she had just finished eating a satisfying meal and said, "What can I do for you?"

"I'm wondering if you have a typewriter."

"I do. I've been trying to write a novel with it for over ten years now. Agatha Christie and other women authors have inspired me to start writing, but not one of them has inspired me to finish. I have many ideas that would make great stories, but I can never get past fifty pages. Now . . . tell me why *you* need to use it. Is it to write about what happened in New Orleans? That would be a bestseller, I'm sure."

"So you heard about the trial, huh?"

"I did. Linda couldn't wait to call this morning."

"Okay, well, I just need to type up a stock portfolio for Lucille's husband, Hank. He's agreed to let me handle his investments for him."

"Hmph. And what is Lucille saying about all this? Is she investing, too?"

"No. She's decided to see how things go for Hank first."

"Sounds reasonable to me. Money's hard to come by, especially for Negroes. I've gotta tell ya, I'm at a loss as to why Lucille would let Hank do such a foolhardy thing with their money."

"Money *is* hard to come by, Gloria, and that's all the more reason to invest and watch it grow and set up a wonderful future for yourself. And I suppose you and Lucille might be right to wait too, but it would make more sense to do it now and save herself eleven hundred dollars. By waiting, I'll end up making twenty-two hundred more dollars to invest."

"You're not going to give her a break, Johnnie?"

"I am giving her a break, but she won't take it. If she invests now, I'll do both portfolios for a one-time payment of eleven hundred. But if I have to do the same work twice, I'll have to charge twice for twice the work. That's only fair, Gloria. I'm sure you'd have to agree."

"I guess, if you have to do twice the work, but that's an awful lot of money, Johnnie. I must say you're quite driven for a young woman of seventeen years."

"One must strike while the iron is hot or miss an opportunity that may never come again. So, may I use your typewriter?"

"I don't see why not. I'm not using it. It just sits there in my back office collecting dust. Wait right here. I'll pack it up for you, and you can take it with you."

"Thanks, Gloria."

"I assume you'll need typing paper, right?"

"Yes, ma'am."

"I'll put some in the case. That way if you wanna get started now, you can."

"Thank you. I would hate to have to walk over to Woolies, and I probably wouldn't, which means I couldn't get anything typed up until tomorrow after I get off work. I wanna take something to Hank in the morning that way he knows I'm on top of everything."

Gloria walked into the back room, and as if it were an after thought, she said over her shoulder, "What's going on with you and the evangelist?"

"What's going on with me and the evangelist? What do you mean?"

"I saw you two getting out of his truck last night," she said when she came back into the lobby. She put the typewriter on the counter and continued. "And I just saw you getting out of his truck again a few minutes ago. Did he give you a lift home from the restaurant or what?"

"Yes."

Looking her in the eyes now, suspicious of illicit activity at her hotel, Gloria said, "And where was he giving you a ride from last night?"

Johnnie lowered her head, expecting to be scolded for not taking her advice. Then softly, she said, "The Flamingo Den."

"What? You mean you went down there after I advised you not to go?"

"Yes, ma'am. I was hungry, and I thought that if I didn't cause any trouble I could buy something to eat and bring it back here."

"Why didn't you ask me for something to eat? I had plenty. You could have eaten as much as you wanted without fearing for your life."

"I started to stop by, but I thought you had been so generous already, and I didn't want to take advantage of you. I had a few dollars, and I could afford to buy a meal."

"So, you risked your life by going to a redneck restaurant instead of coming to me? Why that makes no sense at all. From now on, you'll have dinner with me, okay? I wouldn't want anything to happen to you. Plus, I'd really like to have some company. I was thinking we could discuss the books we've read. How does that sound?"

"It sounds wonderful, Gloria. And I'll be glad to pay for my meals. Business is business."

"Don't worry about paying me, Johnnie. I'm glad to do it."

"And I appreciate that, but I gotta pay my own way in life. If I didn't have any money or a job, that would be one thing. But I have both. I can't live off you."

"I understand. Dinner should be ready by six. Can you come down by then?"

"Yes, ma'am. What are we having?"

"Roast beef, mashed potatoes, green beans, and sweet potato pie."

"Sounds delicious. What are we drinking?"

"What would you like?"

"Lemonade, if you have it."

"Lemonade it is."

"Okay, I'll see you at six."

Chapter 64

The Desire to be Professional

Johnnie entered her hotel room at about four that afternoon and tossed her Wall Street Journal on the coffee table. Then she carefully set the typewriter on the dining table near the picture window. She wanted something sweet, so she tore open the bag of Brach's Orange Slices she had purchased the previous day at Woolies and tossed one in her mouth. She moved it around, sucking off the sugar, savoring the taste as she took off her clothes and hung them up. Nude now, she went into the bathroom and turned the faucets on. While the water heated to her desirable temperature, she grabbed a white towel and wrapped her hair in it. Then she put her hand under the running water—perfect. She grabbed two more towels. She laid one on the floor at the edge of the tub.

After lathering the towel, she washed herself as Paul Masterson's image came into view. She couldn't help thinking about him and the chat they had not long ago. While she admired his passion, she thought that the things he believed about the future were fundamentally off kilter. It just didn't make sense that the world and the women in it could change so radically and so quickly. According to what she learned in school, Lincoln had freed the slaves nearly a hundred years earlier, and the Negro was still catching hell—so were women. If the thinking in white America hadn't changed much in three hundred years, why would it all of sudden change dramatically by 1974, twenty years from now. That's why she didn't buy what Masterson was selling.

Then Johnnie remembered that she and Sadie had visited a fortune-teller who moonlighted as an abortionist. Her named was Madam De Mille. She had gotten pregnant, and she wanted to get rid of the child that was growing in the wall of her uterus. That's when it occurred to her that other girls she had known were having sex before she had—at least that's what she had heard in the school lavatory, where the girls openly talked about such things. She realized then that if any of the sexually active girls got pregnant, they would be faced with a similar decision. And even though the procedure was very painful, having a child out of wedlock was so shameful that having it cut out of her was more desirable than going through the humiliation of everyone knowing she was having sex and was with child.

With that in mind, she remembered that Paul had said abortion would be big business. That's where she drew the line. Sure, she had heard that a few girls at school were having sex, but the majority of the girls she knew were not. The real truth was that she hadn't seen any evidence that any teenaged girl was having sex. Looking back on it now, she realized it was nothing but talk. She knew that girls often told salacious tales on the girls they didn't like or were jealous of, saying they had sex with boys, knowing full well they were lying with the intention of ruining reputations. The boys were just as guilty as the girls who told such tales because when it got out that they supposedly had sex with a girl, they stuck their chests out, believing that having sex, even made up sex, somehow made them a man in the eyes of their peers. But the poor girl who had been lied on was called a whore—and it stuck, like the jingle of a Coca-Cola commercial.

The majority of the girls she knew were good churchgoing girls who were just as chaste as she used to be. She didn't believe that most women and teenaged girls were whores who had sex with more men than they had thumbs. That's what whores did. The only whores she knew of besides herself and her mother were men and hot-to-trot teenaged boys. And the only reason there were so many male whores was because of prostitution, not because women and girls who put out were a dime a dozen. From what she had seen, men and young boys were the ones running from woman to woman or from teenaged girl to teenaged girl, *trying* very hard to get them to go all the way.

As far as she was concerned, if her mother hadn't forced her into a relationship with Earl Shamus, she would still be a virgin. She wouldn't have even let Lucas do it to her, let alone Napoleon Bentley and Martin Winters. And she certainly wouldn't have given much thought to having sex with Paul Masterson. But now the genie, as it were, was out of the bottle, and she had needs. That's why she might have let Paul have his way with her, and then took a little for herself, just enough to make him think it was his idea, but enough to get the satisfaction physical joining engendered.

The way she saw it, there was no way girls and women were going to get pregnant so often that abortion would become legal and big business as Paul asserted. For that to happen, for women and girls to start acting like men and boys, something diabolical would have to happen; something like American Slavery or the continental United States would have to be invaded by a brutal regime like the Third Reich. If either of those historical events happened again, she just might believe it. However, as things stood at the moment, she couldn't think of anything that would make women behave like licentious men.

She let the water run all over her body until all traces of soap were gone. Then she turned off the faucets, slid the curtain to the left, and stepped out of the tub and onto the towel. She wiped the residual water off her body, careful to dry between her toes. She grabbed the hooded pink bathrobe she purchased at Woolies and went into the living room area of what she thought was her two room apartment and sat on the couch. Then, she started reading her Wall Street Journal. Martin Winters had told her that The American Stock Exchange had started in the 1800s and that Dow Jones had been around since 1882. She looked at the stocks she previously owned to see how they were doing. General Electric, General Motors, Coca-Cola Corporation, and Buchanan Mutual were all doing well. So were the rest.

She took the paper over to the dining table, sat down, and unpacked the typewriter and the paper. It was black and looked very old. A logo and the word "Royal" were stenciled on the carriage and the key well. Although she had seen Cynthia, Martin Winters' secretary, typing when she went to his office, she had no idea how to type—at least not efficiently. She just knew that Cynthia must have been really good because she typed rapidly and as naturally as she breathed. Nevertheless, she felt confident she could at least put paper into the machine and get started because she had watched Cynthia do it many times. She also knew that when she heard a bell ring, it was time to return the carriage.

234

She put a piece of paper in and turned the carriage until she could see the edge coming up, but it was crooked. It had looked so simple when Cynthia did it, but she had already wasted fifteen minutes, and now it was finally straight. She closed her eyes and visualized what Cynthia had done, where she kept her hands. They were always on the same lettered keys on the second row. She unfolded the Wall Street Journal and tried to type the words she saw. She typed a letter, and then looked at the paper to see if she had hit the correct key. She hit another and looked at the paper again. She did this for over an hour, but she hadn't made much progress. Her typing looked like the Hebrew language by the time she finished one paragraph. Undeterred, she tried again and again, but there were so many mistakes that she couldn't read any of the sentences she had typed. Frustrated, she gave up and decided to read some of Agatha Christie's *Murder on the Orient Express.* That way, if Gloria wanted to discuss it over dinner, she would have something to add to the conversation.

Chapter 65

"So, then is this Sun Tzu an Oriental like you or what?"

It had been a long, exhausting day of marching, running, and learning military protocol. The platoon had eaten its last meal of the day and had marched back to the barracks, where they were suppose to polish all three pairs of their Army issued footgear. However, Lucas Matthews, Nicolas Lee, and Thomas Shaw, who was grossly overweight, didn't have the luxury of polishing their footgear—at least not when the other recruits were polishing theirs. Lucas and Nicolas decided that Thomas needed remedial running to help him shed at least a hundred pounds. Otherwise, he would never be able to keep up. Sergeant Cornsilk had made it clear that even though the platoon was exhausted due to lack of sleep and running from place to place, the next day was when basic combat training would began.

From what Lucas could tell, he and Nicolas were in better shape than the other recruits, so they would be ready for whatever Cornsilk had in mind—at least that's what he thought. But Thomas was going to be in serious trouble, which meant that Lucas would be in serious trouble because Cornsilk would hold him responsible. They walked a block at a fast pace, and then they jogged a block alternately. Now they were on their way back to the barracks. While Thomas had to stop several times and bend over as he sucked wind, Lucas and Nicolas talked.

"Nicolas, what are your plans when you leave boot camp?"

"I'm hoping to get assigned to the Presidio."

"The what?"

"The Presidio. It's an Army base in San Francisco."

"Ah, so you wanna go back home, huh?"

"Yeah, man, don't you?"

"No. Too many bad memories in New Orleans. So, you gotta girl back home or what?"

"Nobody special if that's what you mean?"

"Yeah, that's what I mean."

"So, then you must have a girlfriend. Otherwise you would not have asked me about it, right?"

"I used to have one back home."

"But now you have one here. The pretty lieutenant at the hospital, right? You can tell me. Don't worry. I won't say a word. It's her, right?"

Lucas nodded.

"Boy, you work fast. You've only been here one day, and not only do you have a girlfriend, you've got yourself an officer. Do you think she has any friends that I could go out with when we get liberty?"

"Probably. I'll have to look into it. But liberty is a long way away, my man."

"It'll go fast. Believe me. It'll be over with before you know."

"I hope you're right, and it goes by fast."

"When it's over, what are you planning to do?"

"I've got officers training school at Fort Benning. After that, I'm going over to Germany to play football. You should seriously consider coming with me, man. I think you'll love it, too, especially since you don't have a woman back home."

"I'll give it some thought, New Orleans. I don't think they'll have any Chinese there."

"Then you can be the first of many. I'm sure one of them German girls would love to date you."

"The Fräulein? I doubt that."

"The what?"

"The Fräulein. That's what they call the single German women over there."

"Really?" He looked at Nicolas skeptically. "How do you know that's what they call 'em?"

"My grandmother is German. She taught me a few things."

"So can you speak the language pretty good or what?"

"I can speak it fairly well, sure."

"Well then you've got to come over to Germany with me, man. We'll have a ball over there, I'm sure of it."

"We helped build this country, and the whites treat us just like the blacks. I don't think the whites over there'll be any different from the whites here."

"Yet, your grandmother is German. That doesn't make sense, San Francisco. What if we get over there and we get treated better by our former enemies than we do in the land we were born in?"

"Why would you even think such a thing, New Orleans?"

"For one, your grandmother is German, and she married a Chinaman. That means that there are probably more women like her."

"But my grandparents met in Paris. Things are different there."

"Yeah but she's still German, so what I said still goes. And for two, Colonel Strong wants me to come over there and play ball for him. If things were as bad as you think, he wouldn't want me there. Besides, we have a military presence there now. The Germans wouldn't dare mess with us. We already kicked their asses twice, and there won't be a third time. They don't want no more, San Francisco, believe me."

"I don't know, New Orleans. I'll think about it, okay?"

"Great! You do play football, right?"

"No."

"What a minute. You've never played football? Not even a pickup game?"

"Not my game. Chess is my game. Do you play?"

"No."

"You mean you've never played a game of chess? Not even a pickup game?"

"I get your point, man. Don't run it into the ground."

"I'll tell you what. You teach me how to play football, and I'll teach you how to play chess. It's a good game to know if you're going to be a leader of men."

"I'll take that deal if you teach me some of that German, too. That way if you decide not to go with me, I'll know a little bit and learn the rest when I get there."

"It's a deal. What about reading? Do you like to read, New Orleans?"

"Yeah. I didn't use to, but now I do. Why?"

"You ever read Sun Tzu."

"Sun who?"

"Sun Tzu. If you're going to lead men, you've got to read that. I just happen to have a copy."

"So, then is this Sun Tzu an Oriental like you or what?"

"Yes."

"Why don't we exchange books?"

"What kind of books do you have?"

"Books about Negroes. Stuff you oughta know about us if you're gonna be my friend. I'll read yours, and you can read mine."

"Okay. We can switch when we get back to the barracks."

Lucas looked at Thomas Shaw. He was still bent over with his hands on his knees. "Alright, Salt Lake City, you've had enough rest. Let's pick up the pace. We're gonna double-time it all the way back to the barracks from here."

Chapter 66

"When I want your opinion, I'll give it to you!"

With an arm around each of their necks, Lucas and Nicolas walked Thomas Shaw into the barracks, and then over to his bed and laid him on it. They laughed because he kind of bounced when he landed. They watched him close his eyes while he tried to catch his breath. They stood at the side of his bed, looking down into his puffy reddish face. As they were about to leave, Thomas said, "I wanna go over to Germany with you guys. If I get in shape, promise me you'll take me with you. I want me one of them Fräuleins, too."

Lucas turned around and said, "We'll see, Salt Lake City. We'll see."

Lucas and Nicolas went over to the recruit who bunked next to Lucas. The recruit was sitting on the floor vigorously polishing his boots. They stared at him until they got his attention. When the recruit looked up at them, Lucas said, "Attention!"

The recruit quickly put his boot and brush down. He stood up and became rigid.

Softly, Lucas said, "Do me a favor, Fort Lauderdale."

"What favor, sir?"

Lucas tilted his head to the left and said, "I want you to switch bunks with my man, San Francisco. Is that alright with you?"

"Yes, sir!"

Keith Lee Johnson

"Outstanding. Just so you know . . . I never forget a favor. That's how we did it in the New Orleans mafia. Someone does you a favor, and they owe you a favor, understand?"

"Yes, sir!"

"Alright then. If you need anything, you let me know, and I'll take care of it. I would appreciate it if you pack your stuff. My man, San Francisco, is moving down here."

"Yes, sir."

But when the other Negroes saw it, they didn't like it. They stared at Lucas like he was a traitor. While San Francisco and Fort Lauderdale packed their belongings, ten angry Negro recruits surrounded Lucas. The leader was a man who claimed to be a ruffian from the south side of Chicago. He offered a menacing stare before saying, "We see whatcha doin', and we don't like it."

The man next to him was from the Bronx. He backed Chicago's play, saying, "Sho' don't. Not one bit."

Lucas looked at each man before saying, "Are you all in this together? Or, did Chicago here talk y'all into this?"

Some of the men looked away, but some of them continued staring at Lucas, threatening him with their numbers. Lucas noticed that the white recruits were watching and gathering around, too. This was a street thing. Chicago wanted to run the show even though Sergeant Cornsilk had given the reins to Lucas. There was about to be a show-down.

When Nicolas Lee heard the commotion, he turned around to see what was going on. When he saw that Lucas was surrounded and that more of the recruits were gathering, he hustled down there and stood next to him, ready to keep his word. He would fight them all if he had to. Lynchburg and Cheyenne didn't move. They just stood at the outer edge of the growing circle of men.

Lucas smiled when he saw that he had at least one ally even though he didn't think he'd need one. He knew most men that talked were all talk, no action. But since the man standing before him was supposedly from Chicago, he gave him the benefit of the doubt, yet he was unfazed by his bravado.

"You need to pick another second in command, New Orleans," Chicago said. "You're gonna tell the sergeant the chink's gotta go and that you want another man backing you up. The white boys got two

241

squad leaders. We want two. It's only fair. I'm sure the chink will understand since he's the only one of his kind in the platoon."

Nicolas moved forward like he was about to take on Chicago, but Lucas put his arm out, stopping his forward movement. This was his moment to shine. He was about to show everybody why he was the barracks chief and would continue to be until basic was over. Lucas said, "So who do you think I oughta pick?"

Chicago took two steps forward and said, "Me, that's who. The sergeant should've picked me in the first damned place. Not you."

"Why is that?" Lucas said.

"Because I—"

Bing! Lucas unleashed a left hook that nobody saw coming, least of all Chicago, whose eyes were now closed, and his body was about to hit the floor. Lucas caught him and eased him to the floor. This was a turf war, and he had just ended it decisively with one invisible blow.

"Atten-hut!" Fort Lauderdale called out.

All the men stiffened.

"What's going on in here?" Sergeant Cornsilk yelled, looking at Lucas.

"Nothing, sir!" Lucas yelled. "Chicago fainted, sir, and I caught him before he hit his head on the floor."

Cornsilk walked up to San Francisco and yelled, "Is that what happened?"

"Yes, sir!"

"Outstand—"

"Excuse me, sir," Lynchburg said, about to mention the racial slur. "But that's not what happened. Chicago tried to—"

Without so much as turning around, Cornsilk yelled, "When I want your opinion, Lynchburg, I'll give it to you. Understand?"

"Yes, sir!"

"That's the second time you screwed up. There won't be a third! The next time you have something to say to me, say it to New Orleans first!"

"Yes, sir!"

"You are now the fourth squad leader! Cheyenne is third now! You can't go any lower, Lynchburg. Understand?"

"Yes, sir!"

"New Orleans, there's somebody here to see you?"

"Who, sir?"

"Come and see."

"Yes, sir," Lucas said. "Give me one second." He looked at the man from the Bronx and said, "Pick as many men as you need and carry Chicago to his bed. Tell him that I said we'll finish our discussion when I return."

"You through flappin' your lips, New Orleans?" Cornsilk said.

"Yes, sir."

Chapter 67

"And after I finish with them, I'm takin' on all challengers."

After taking a few steps to the left, Lucas saw a Negro officer with brass on the shoulder straps of his uniform jacket. He was standing near the doorway, watching everything that was happening. His face was clean-shaven, and his skin was very dark, like a coffee bean. He was tall and lanky like a basketball player, easily six-two or three, but solidly built and fit. An overcoat draped his right arm and an attaché case was in his left hand. It didn't take him long to figure out that the officer was Colonel Strong. Smiling from ear to ear, he practically ran past Cornsilk to meet him.

"Slow down, son," Cornsilk said. "The Colonel isn't going anywhere."

"Yes, sir!" Lucas said, still moving quickly, nearly running over his drill sergeant.

"Sergeant Cornsilk," Colonel Strong said, "I'd like to have a word with private Matthews alone if you can spare him."

Cornsilk came to attention, saluted, and said, "Certainly, sir!"

"Thank you, Sergeant. I'll bring him back in a little while."

"Excuse me, Colonel," Lucas said. "I'm wondering if my friend, Nicolas, can come with us. I think you'll like him, sir."

Colonel Strong looked at Cornsilk and said, "Can you spare two of your recruits?"

"Yes, sir," Cornsilk said. "They're done for the day."

"San Francisco," Lucas called out.

Nicolas Lee went over to where Lucas was standing and said, "Yes, sir."

"You're coming with us," Lucas said, smiling.

"I understand you have a car, Matthews," Colonel Strong said.

"I do, sir."

"Good. I want you to drive us over to the Officer's Club," Colonel Strong said. He looked at Cornsilk. "I'll bring them back in an hour or so."

Cornsilk came to attention, held his salute, and said, "Yes, sir."

Colonel Strong returned his salute. Then the colonel, Lucas, and Nicolas left the barracks. A few minutes later, they walked into the Officer's Club. The smell of cigarettes and cigars lingered in the air. They took their seats at a table near the entrance. Strong looked at Lucas and said, "You're probably wondering why I brought you and your friend here."

"Yes, sir."

"I wanted you to see what you're up against."

"Sir?" Lucas questioned. "I'm not following you."

"Look around you, son," Strong said. "You see how angry the white officers are that we're in here? Can you feel their hatred?"

Lucas and Nicolas looked around. Not only were they the center of attention, but judging by the looks on the white officers' faces, they could tell that if they could, they would kick them out of the club violently. Unmoved by the venom he sense, Lucas returned his attention to Colonel Strong and said, "Yes, sir."

"Good," Strong said. "Don't ever forget what you see just beyond their eyes. And know that the only reason they don't come over here and voice their opinion of us being in here, in what they *think* is their domain, is because of these birds on my shoulders." He pointed at his rank. "Herein lies the lesson. Get an education, ally yourself with powerful friends, and always seek advancement in whatever endeavors you pursue. You need to understand that you . . . both of you . . . represent your race. Whether that's fair or unfair is immaterial. That's the reality of being nonwhite in America. That's the responsibility foisted upon you. You don't have to like it, but I expect you two to embrace it, and more important, carry it well. Be proud and behave like it."

"Yes, sir," Lucas said.

"Me and the Sergeant saw what happened in the barracks," Strong said.

"The whole thing, sir?" Lucas asked.

Strong nodded. "While I admire your quick solution to the problem, that's not the way to handle someone who challenges your authority. You have to leave all of that behind when you become an officer. You must learn to control your anger, or someone will use your anger against you and have you drummed out of the Army with a dishonorable discharge. Before you start officer training, you'll need to keep a cool head and still be able to dispense discipline to the undisciplined. You'll see lots of things you won't like, but you cannot solve all your conflicts with your fists. Almost any problem can be solved with your mind. Take Mr. Lee here. He knows I'm right. He's smart enough to keep his mouth shut, to listen, and to observe. He'll let you think he's an idiot until he's ready for you to know he's not. He could prove to be a powerful ally. Learn whatever you can from him and men like him, even if they're white. It doesn't matter where knowledge and skill come from. The only thing that matters is that you absorb it, and use it for advancement in the office you work in or on the battlefield."

"Yes, sir. I was wondering if you could recommend him for officer training, too."

Strong looked at Lee and said, "You haven't said much, son. Do you want to be an officer? Do you want the responsibility of being a Chinese officer in an American Army, knowing that your fellow officers may not accept you as a man, let alone as one of their peers?"

"I'm not sure, sir," Nicolas said. "I haven't given it much thought. New Orleans just asked me about it today. He told me that you were going to bring him over to Germany. Is that right?"

"Yes," Strong said. "Would you like to come with him? I could arrange it, but you need to be sure."

"Can I think about it, sir?" Nicolas said. "I was hoping to get assigned to the Presidio, but Germany sounds like a good assignment, too."

"I can get you either assignment," Strong said. "I just need to know about a month in advance."

"How long are you going to be here, sir?" Nicolas asked.

"About a week," Strong said.

"I'll let you know before you go."

"Great," Strong said. "I'd love to have you aboard, and I know Lucas would, too. Just so you know, there aren't that many Asian officers in the Army. As a matter of fact, I don't think I've met even one. The Army could use loyal men like you in its officer ranks."

"Can I ask you a question, sir?" Lucas said.

"Sure."

"How did you know I'd be here?" Lucas said. "Your letter said that I could take a couple of weeks off before I came here for basic training, sir. So, how did you know since you were in Germany?"

"Actually, I didn't. I'm here TDY. That's an acronym for temporary duty. Over time, you'll learn that the Army has lots of acronyms."

"Yes, sir, like SOS."

"Yes, that's another one. I'm here because I had to handle some administrative things, and I thought I'd check to see if you were here. I was surprised to learn that you were on post. I thought for sure you'd want to spend two weeks with your girlfriend before your training began since you probably won't see her again for sixteen weeks. Is everything okay between you two?"

"No, sir," Lucas said. "We broke up, so I decided to get started early. And it's a good thing I did. If I had waited two weeks, I wouldn't have met my man, San Francisco."

"I think he would have been okay without meeting me, sir," Nicolas said. "He's pretty good with the ladies. And he's obviously pretty good with his fists, too."

"I saw how good he is with his fists," Strong said and smiled. "And I know the Army is lucky to have you. The Army is about fighting, but not our own people. We fight our enemies."

"Yes, sir," Nicolas said. "But it appears that our enemies wear the same uniforms as we do. They live in the same quarters and eat in the same Mess Halls."

"That they do, son, but you gotta be bigger than them until the hearts of men change," Strong said.

"But the hearts of men change so slowly, sir," Nicolas said.

"That's why it would be a good idea to become an officer together. That way you two can serve together and watch each other's backs. You can't trust most of the white officers to behave like we're on the same team. That's the advantage you two will have. You can trust each other. You'll have to."

"I understand, sir," Nicolas said.

Strong looked at Lucas. "And do you understand, son?"

"Yes, sir."

"Good. Good. So, you met someone here in Columbia already, have you, Mr. Matthews?"

"Yes, we went out to dinner last night. Nice girl. Smart."

"And drop dead gorgeous," Nicolas said.

"Well, I hope it works out for you, but Germany is a long way from Columbia, South Carolina. Maybe you shouldn't let it get too serious because there are a lot of women in Germany, and I'm sure you'll find one or two that you like. Perhaps more."

"Lots of women, huh?" Nicolas said. "Put me down for OTS and Germany, sir."

Strong laughed heartily and said, "Are you sure, son? If I recommended you, I'd be putting my reputation on the line. So, I need you to be sure this is what you want."

"It is, sir," Nicolas said.

"Okay, great. It's a done deal. Now, would you like to get something to eat before we leave?"

"No, sir," Lucas said. "We've already eaten dinner."

"A drink perhaps?"

"No, sir," Lucas said. "We're fine, sir."

"Okay, then. If there are no more questions, drop me off at my quarters, and then head straight back to the barracks. I gave Sergeant Cornsilk my word."

"Yes, sir."

Thirty minutes later, Lucas and Nicolas entered the barracks. They went straight over to Chicago's bunk to confront him. Lucas said, "Glad to see you're finally awake. I think it's time we finished this thing. I wouldn't want you to think I got a lucky punch in." He looked at the man from the Bronx and said, "When I finish with him, you're next."

Nicolas said, "Let me take care of this one after you take care of him, sir."

"No," Lucas said. "I want them both. And after I finish with them, I'm takin' on all challengers. That means you white boys can get some of this, too. Now make a circle."

After Lucas knocked Chicago out a second time, he knocked out the man from the Bronx, too, but it wasn't quick. He punished him.

Chapter 68

An Inauspicious Arrival

After a wonderful meal and discussion of *Murder on the Orient Express*, Johnnie returned to her room. Gloria Schumacher was quite the storyteller. She could have regaled Johnnie for hours without running out of stories about her deceased husband's family. However, when Johnnie asked her who her favorite character in the novel was, she quickly pointed out the Belgian detective—Hercule Poirot. Gloria explained that Poirot had been her favorite because he only used his mind to figure out who committed a particular crime. When the talk of novelized murder was over, Gloria subtly switched the conversation to stock portfolios in an attempt to get a clue as to what stocks might be worth looking at. Gloria thought that since she had loaned Johnnie the typewriter, she would be more forthcoming with stock information. But Johnnie stuck to her business principles and quickly reminded her new friend that her fee was still eleven hundred dollars, and the stock market conversation came to a swift end.

It was eight o'clock when she thanked her host for the tasty victuals and gracious conversation and left. Gloria wanted her to stay longer, but she explained that she still had some work to do, for which she had already been paid a tidy sum. She sat down at her dining table again, determined to learn how to use the typewriter efficiently, but first, she had to learn how to put the paper in straight. She didn't want her first client to think she was sloppy, which would seriously undermine her credibility. It was 8:21 by the time she got the paper in straight enough to at least practice again. But there was no way she was going to give Hank a portfolio that was less than perfect. After all, his word would be the conduit for more clients. She, therefore, knew that her first portfolio would have to be spectacular. And it would be, no matter how long it took.

She started typing the words from an article in the Wall Street Journal again, trying to get a feel for the machine and how it worked. For a few minutes, she thought she had gotten the hang of it. She had even gotten into a rhythm and her speed had increased, too. But when she looked at what she typed, it still looked like Hebrew. Nevertheless, she continued typing, hoping it would get better as she went along. By the time she had gotten to the end of one sheet, it was after nine. Gloria said that she didn't go to bed until well after eleven, so she decided to go down to the lobby and get some help. Otherwise, she would be up all night, and the portfolio still wouldn't look professional. She put the typewriter and the paper back into the case, closed it, and was about to leave her room when the desire for another Orange Slice came to mind. She went into her bedroom, which was in the adjacent room. She saw the Brach's candy on the nightstand. She grabbed two of them and put one in her mouth. As she went back into the kitchenette area of her room, she realized she would have to offer Gloria something for helping learn how to use the typewriter.

At first she was going to offer her some money to type up the information for her, but she knew that if she did that, Gloria would have access to the information free of charge. She could then consult her own broker with the information she had provided. She decided to go ahead and offer to pay her even though she didn't think Gloria would take it. If she didn't, she would offer her a discount and perhaps then she could take her on as a client. But if that didn't work, she would have to tell Hank she would need another day to get his portfolio together.

She realized she could take the typewriter to work the next day, and then go to the local library and ask the librarian to help learn to use it. If she hadn't promised Hank she would have something for him tomorrow, she wouldn't bother asking for Gloria's help. She wanted Gloria as a client. And she wanted her to pay the same amount that Hank had paid. It was only fair as far as she was concerned; especially if Lucille had to pay that amount, too. Nevertheless, she admired Gloria's persistence in that she wanted a better deal than Johnnie was offering, and she had kept at it. Now her persistency was about to pay

251

off. She picked up the typewriter case. She opened the door to leave, and to her complete and utter surprise, Earl Shamus was standing there.

Chapter 69

"No, I haven't been sleeping with him."

The last time Johnnie had seen Earl Shamus was on Christmas Eve, about a month ago, before she was arrested for the murder of Sharon Trudeau. He had come to confront her about her relationships with Martin Winters and Lucas Matthews. She had answered her door, thinking it was her best friend, Sadie Lane and her children, coming over to celebrate the holiday. She had let him in, and he had reminded her of all the things he had done for her. Things had changed quickly and dramatically, she realized as her first lover, the man who had paid her mother one thousand dollars to deflower her was now standing in her doorway again.

She took a few steps backward, wondering how he had found her, scared to death of what he was going to do to her. After all, she had given him a huge piece of her mind, confessing that she had used him to get the home she owned and all the furniture in it. She had even confessed to sleeping with Martin Winters, his best friend—their stockbroker. At that time, she had all the money she would ever need. Now, however, she was pretty much broke with few options. She was about to start her own investment firm, but it took months, and most of the time, years to see substantial growth in stocks. And so, she was again at his mercy. Being at the mercy of a rich man she had belittled, a man she had taken completely apart with a truth so penetrating that all he could do was stand there and cry made her feel completely vulnerable and totally defenseless. She was certain he was there to repay her for what she had both done and said to him. She swallowed hard as she stared at him like a deer caught in headlights.

"Can I come in, Johnnie?" Earl asked politely and waited until she answered.

Nervously, she said, "Um, um, um, sure, I guess you can. Yeah. Come on in."

Earl walked into the room and closed the door. He was carrying what looked like a doctor's medical bag and a newspaper. They stood in the middle of the room, looking into each other eyes, nervous and unsure of what to say and what was going to happen next. After a few seconds, Earl said, "Can I sit down?"

"I guess so, yeah."

He walked over to the dining table and sat down. He put the newspaper on the table and the bag on the floor. He then gestured for her to sit down as well. Johnnie placed the typewriter case on the floor and sat opposite Earl, wondering what he wanted and where this was going. A measure of fear was mounting because she didn't know what to expect. His wife was dead, and she thought that he might blame her for Meredith's death. She probably hadn't been buried yet, and he was there, in her hotel room for only God knew what.

"So, how did you find me, Earl?"

"Tony Hatcher."

She leaned back and folded her arms, ready to defend herself. "The detective your wife hired to follow you around and bug my house?"

"You mean my deceased wife, Meredith? Yes, *that* detective. The same private detective that your attorneys tricked into confessing that he had bugged your home, the home *I* paid for."

"How long has he been following me?"

"Hatcher's been on your tail since you left Ashland Estates. He's been reporting all your comings and goings back to me. For example, I know that your car won't be fixed for another three weeks or so. I also know that you've been hired by the owners of a colored restaurant. Lucille's is it? I'm told Hank was an Army cook. I hear the food's pretty good there, but you seem to like the food at The Flamingo Den a lot better. I'll have to try the chili and grilled cheese and a few bones of barbecue before I head back to New Orleans to bury Meredith. I'll probably wash it all down with some of their ice cold lemonade."

Johnnie's eyes bulged when she realized that he knew just about everything she had done since she left New Orleans. She was about to say something, but he started talking again.

"Apparently, you've lost the two hundred and fifty thousand your friend, Bubbles, got from Sharon Trudeau the night he killed her." He paused for effect, knowing she was terrified of what he was going to reveal next, but also what he could possibly do with the information he was freely divulging. "It has come to my attention that you've come into a little money . . . a five thousand dollar check, most of which you deposited in the local bank here in Jackson. Prior to going to the bank, you went over to Woolworth's, where you caused so much of a commotion with Gloria Schumacher's sister-in-law that the store manager had to get involved."

She closed her eyes for a second or two, taking in all that he was saying, trying to maintain the façade of control she wanted him to think she had. But deep down, she was losing it, thinking that Tony Hatcher had probably been in her room while she was at work, going through her things, looking at her lingerie and other unmentionables. She exhaled softly and said, "What do you want, Earl?"

Trying to restrain the glee he was feeling, watching her squirm, knowing she wanted him to say whatever he had to say and leave, a burgeoning smile broke forth. He knew she wanted to know what he was going to do with the information he had gotten from Tony Hatcher; information that implicated her in the murder even though she wasn't in Fort Lauderdale when Sharon Trudeau was killed. An aggressive prosecutor just might want to charge her with accessory to murder. The prosecutor could easily make a case against her if the tapes of her conversations with Sadie, Bubbles, Napoleon, and Lucas ever surfaced.

"I'm getting to that," he said coolly, enjoying every minute of the suspense he built.

"And what's in that bag?"

A sinister smile emerged. "I'm getting to that, too. Now . . . I've come a long way to say what I have to say. I would appreciate it if you would let me finish. Unlike you, I won't be rude to you the way you were rude to me Christmas morning." He paused and watched her eyes, looking for the memory of that day and what she had said to him to surface. When he was sure she was reliving what happened, he continued in a smooth, deliberate cadence. He had been thinking about

255

what he was going to say to her for the last two days. He had even practiced his delivery, his strategic pauses, rehearsing every line as if he was going to be in a Broadway play. When he thought the moment was right for another revelation, he said, "I also know about your friend, one Paul Masterson, a native of Houston, Texas, or so he says."

"Paul *is* from Houston, Earl. He wouldn't lie to me about a thing like that. He has no reason to."

"Is that what you call him? Paul?" He locked eyes with her. "Have you been sleeping with him, too?"

The first thing that came to her mind was, *That's none of your business*, but that's not what she said. She knew Earl had the upper hand for the moment, and she didn't dare talk to him the way she had on Christmas morning. She quickly realized that he had all of his deceased wife's money at his disposal, and it was considerable, almost limitless. She believed the best thing to do was answer his question, find out why he was there, and then send him back to New Orleans. "No, I haven't been sleeping with him."

He leaned forward and looked deeper into her eyes. "But you do like him enough to sleep with him, don't you?"

"Yes," she said without hesitation. "Does that bother you, Earl? Does it bother you that I could be interested in someone other than you? Does it bother you still that I slept with your friend Martin, and you had no idea I had? Or, does it bother you that I had a boyfriend that I completely adored?"

Looking into her eyes, smiling broadly, he said, "Let's not forget the likes of Napoleon Bentley and the baby you maliciously killed the night that Sharon Trudeau was murdered."

Chapter 70

"We'll get to the bag in a minute."

Stunned that Earl knew about her relationship with Napoleon and that she had aborted the child sired by him, she looked away, trying to quickly calculate what all of this could mean for her, wondering if he was there to blackmail her or what? Abortion was against the law, and she could go to jail over that alone, not to mention that Sharon Trudeau's murder hadn't yet been solved. She said, "I've been acquitted of Sharon's murder. And even though I'm a Negro, they can't try me for her murder again. My lawyer says that's double jeopardy, which means I can't be tried for the same crime twice."

"Yes, but were you tried for Sharon's murder. You weren't tried for the bellhop's murder, were you?" He watched her intensely. Her diaphragm was no longer moving. She wasn't breathing, which let him know that no matter how calm she looked, she was terrified, and that's exactly where he wanted her. He wanted her to be scared and alone, and she was. He knew that when people were scared, they couldn't think straight, and they couldn't remember specific details. That's why he didn't call her. He wanted to surprise her and shake her up so that she would do exactly what he wanted her to do. And Jackson, Mississippi was the perfect place to confront her with the facts he had. That way anybody that could help her was too far away to do anything to save her. Armed with the knowledge he had acquired, he was her one and only savior. He thought that if he played his cards right, he would be her only savior for years to come.

He watched her searching the deep recesses of her mind, trying to remember if she had been tried for both murders or not. That was the beauty of the surprise attack. The enemy thought he was safe and slept soundly; much like Johnnie had done the last couple days. She thought all her fears had been laid to rest the moment Ethel Beauregard blew her brains out. Still watching her, he was hoping she couldn't remember if she had been tried for the bellhop's murder. The bellhop's name was never mentioned in the papers. He realized that the bellhop's death was being treated as if it were an afterthought, as if he didn't exist, like he was a Negro or any other minority or animal as far as the papers were concerned because Sharon was the target.

Sharon was the story because she was a blond bombshell, kinda like Marilyn Monroe. Her beauty gave men who hadn't known she was alive a reason to care that she was dead, how she was killed, and why. Her beauty gave women a reason to care about her and even identify with her because Sharon had made it in a man's world. Secretly, many women loved that she had the guts to steal so much money and had almost gotten away with such a high profile crime. What made the story even more sensational was that women were not known to be criminals or to even think like criminals. Nor were they the targets of assassination plots.

Johnnie knew for certain that she had been charged with Sharon's murder, and she had narrowly escaped the ultimate penalty. But she couldn't remember if the prosecutor had included the bellhop in the indictment or not. She wasn't about to find out either. She had gotten out of New Orleans in one piece. She wasn't going back to ask the prosecutor if he had tried her for both crimes. She thought of calling her lawyer, Jay Goldstein, but all she knew was that he was from Chicago, and there were probably thousands of attorneys with the name Goldstein, making it difficult to track him and the other attorneys down. The thing that bothered her more than anything at the moment, even Earl's untimely arrival, was that she could be indicted for the murder of the child she had been carrying prior to visiting Madam De Mille. Goldstein, if she found him, could quite possibly get her out of impending murder charges for the bellhop, but there was nothing he could do about abortion. She would definitely go to jail for that.

After much contemplation, her eyes found Earl's. As she looked into them, she wondered where all of this was going. She wanted to know what he wanted. He obviously wanted something. He had driven almost three hours to have this conversation.

Chapter 71

"Is that all that you came here to say?"

"**I**s there more that you have to say to me or what?" Johnnie said. "You've asked me to let you finish, but you're not saying anything. And what's in that bag?"

"We'll get to the bag in a minute. In the meantime, I think you really ought to read this article in the *Sentinel*. It's about you and your 'family.'"

Johnnie hesitated for a few seconds before she took the paper out of Earl's hand. In the brief moments that passed, she remembered the articles that had been written in the *Sentinel* and *Raven* newspapers. While Ashland Estate had survived, both articles led to a bloody riot that the poor Negro community was still reeling from. Without even looking at the article, she knew it would be inflammatory at the very least, given everything that had happened prior to her New Orleanian Exodus. She looked at the society page headline: did johnnie wise get away with murder? She looked into Earl's eyes again.

"What do you want, Earl?"

"For now, I want you to read that article, if you don't mind."

"Why?"

"I think it's quite interesting. I think you will, too. So please, humor me, and read the article."

She looked into his eyes for a few more seconds, wondering why he was being so nice, also wondering when he was going to say the vicious words she expected. She lowered her eyes to the newspaper she held, and then read the following:

Little Girl Lost: The Return of Johnnie Wise

This trial, as short as it was, was a regular smorgasbord. It had everything. It had the makings of a Hollywood production: murder, blackmail, private detectives . . . the only thing missing was Humphrey Bogart and Lauren Bacall. Some say had the trial continued the New Orleans Syndicate would have been brought into it. Well, folks, if you're wondering how a seventeen-year-old Negro girl, who dropped out of high school, constantly escapes the clutches of the law, you are not alone. No, sir. Either she is the personification of celestial brilliance and God himself is her guardian angel, or she is by far the luckiest female that ever lived. What happened in that courtroom was nothing short of legendary. And I have no doubt, no doubt I say, that this one will grow with each succeeding generation as if it were a mushroom cloud over Hiroshima, ever expanding, turning every life in its wake into a wasteland.

If I hadn't been in the courtroom, if I hadn't seen it with my own eyes and heard it with my own ears, I would have never believed it. Not in a million years. It was the most puzzling thing I've ever seen and heard in all my days. Probably the most tragic aspect of the trial was its unpredictable ending as Ethel Beauregard, one of the principle witnesses for the defense, attempted to kill her Negro niece right there in a court of law. The sound of gunfire exploded in my ears as the reigning matriarch of the Beauregard clan fired round after round, at the judge, the defense attorney, Johnnie Wise, and finally herself. All of this happened after Jay Goldstein's blistering cross-examination of Meredith Shamus, who by the way, was president of Buchanan Mutual Insurance before she got in the way of a bullet meant for Johnnie.

Mr. Goldstein had threatened to call Ethel to the stand to testify, and that's when all hell broke loose. Mrs. Shamus left the stand and ran at young Johnnie, presumably to do bodily harm after it was revealed that she had hired private detective, Tony Hatcher, to follow her husband. Well, folks, Hatcher did exactly what he was paid to do. And guess where Mr. Shamus was going? Yes, sir, you guessed it, Mr. Shamus was seeing Johnnie Wise. Mr. Goldstein asserted, by the nature of his questions, that Mr. Shamus had been seeing Johnnie for quite some time and was paying her for the privilege. Apparently, Mrs. Shamus had paid Johnnie some fifty thousand dollars to leave her husband alone, which explains where a portion of the money Sharon Trudeau stole came from.

260

Keith Lee Johnson

*If you folks have been keeping up with my articles on the Wise
and Beauregard families, you know that they are related by blood. For
the last month or so, member after member of the Beauregard family
has been killed for one reason or another. I think it's important to note
that every death in the Beauregard family happened a few months after
Johnnie's Creole mother, Marguerite Wise, was murdered, presumably
by Ku Klux Klan Leader, Richard Goode, who by the way, was paying
her for unmentionable services. Now I know what you good folks are
thinkin', like mother like daughter. I confess that I'm thinkin' that, too.
I guess these two "ladies" were running an illegal enterprise that
would have normally been found in a district that was specifically set
aside for that sort of illicit activity.*

*With everything going on, I know it's hard to keep up so let me
remind you once again that the Beauregard and Wise families are
related by blood. I don't know about you, but I've been keeping score.
The murder rate is now five to one in favor of the Wise family. But get
this folks, none of the Beauregards died until after Marguerite was
brutally murdered. Call it a coincidence if you like, but I think something's wrong. Now I know they say death comes in threes, but five
deaths in one of the Financial District's riches families over the course
of two months? Is anybody paying attention to this? If we find out that
Johnnie Wise gets the bulk of the money and the estate of her white
relatives, I think we can safely conclude that she either murdered her
own family, or she manipulated them into killing each other and
themselves, so she could inherit a fortune. Folks, I don't even think
famed mystery novelist Agatha Christie could make this stuff up.*

*Now, I know some of you good people wanted to know how
Johnnie was able to get away with killing Sharon Trudeau. I gotta tell
you folks, I'm wondering about that, too. I was sitting in the courtroom,
and I don't believe it myself. For some reason, one Jay Goldstein, a
Yankee from Chicago, was able to make the trial about the prosecution
witness, and the Judge allowed this chicanery to go on unchecked for
the better part of the trial. The trial was supposed to be about Johnnie
Wise killing Sharon Trudeau because Sharon had stolen her money, but
that assertion was somehow lost in the minutia of the prosecution's
witness's supposed extra-martial affair with the defendant.*

*Just in case you weren't at the trial, let me say unequivocally
that there was no proof presented of an affair between Mr. Winters and*

261

Miss Wise. The thing that twisted my mind into several knots was that even if Mr. Winters had an affair with Miss Wise, how would that change the fact that Miss Wise had pursued Sharon Trudeau all the way to Fort Lauderdale, knowing that she was going to kill her and retrieve the two hundred and fifty thousand dollars she had stolen, which by the way, has never been found. Consider this too, friends, with all of Ashland Estates burned to the ground, it makes one wonder if Johnnie Wise, covering her tracks, set her house ablaze, so that it wouldn't look suspicious when she left town permanently.

Now, I'm sure you good folks heard that members of a particular Holiness church supposedly went over to Ashland Estates and set the fire as retaliation for the previous riot. But I say don't even give ear to that sort of nonsense. Pay attention to your eyes. Your eyes will tell you that Johnnie is gone, only God knows where, and a quarter of a million dollars is missing, too. First, the money disappears, and then she disappears. Now is that a coincidence or what? For the life of me, I swear I don't know how New Orleans is going to survive the memory of the Wise family. Stay tuned folks, because I've got to believe that we haven't heard the last of her. I think at some point, Johnnie Wise will return to the Crescent City, if only to claim whatever monies her white relatives left her.

Johnnie looked at Earl. "So . . . they still think I killed Sharon, took my money back, and burned my house down to cover my tracks, huh?"

"Yes."

"And what do you think, Earl?"

"What I think really doesn't matter, now does it? The citizens of New Orleans think you've gotten away with murder. They don't care anything about the fact that Sharon stole your money. If they have anything to say about it, you won't get to spend one dime of it."

"But I don't have the money, Earl. None of it."

"I know that, and you know that, but the white people in New Orleans don't know that. As far as they're concerned, you're guilty of first degree murder. When I left, the atmosphere was so charged that I think they'd kill you on sight. No questions asked. I think they'd kill you because you've been so lucky with the law that they wouldn't leave it up to the law this time. This time they'd take the law into their own hands."

262

Shaking her head, she said, "So, I can never go home again?"

"It looks that way. No time soon anyway. You probably won't be able to go back home until the current generation dies out. Perhaps their children will have forgotten Sharon Trudeau, the virginal Saint of New Orleans."

"Okay, thanks for letting me know I can't go back to New Orleans for at least twenty years. Is that all that you came here to say? And what's in that bag?"

"No. That's not all I came here to say." He picked up the bag, set it on the table, and opened it. He looked at her, expecting her to look in the bag, but she didn't. She just kept staring at him, waiting for him to say whatever was on his mind and leave. "Aren't you going to look inside the bag?"

"What's in there? A Cobra?"

Laughing, he said, "No. Take a look."

Tentatively, she leaned forward, peering over the edges of the bag like she was expecting something to jump out and bite her, but when she saw the money, her eyes lit up.

Smiling, Earl said, "Count it."

Chapter 72

"So . . . what's your answer?"

There was a twinkle in Earl Shamus' eyes. It was a twinkle that Johnnie had come to know and expect when he first started "visiting" her about a month after her fifteenth birthday. She sat quietly in her chair as what he wanted slowly came into view, watching him without interruption, seeing the desperation in his eyes, and the maddening craving he had that her sexual prowess had produced. She realized that in spite of everything she had said to his face and had done to him behind his back, he still wanted and needed her to supply the opiate that her body manufactured. With that bit of knowledge, she figured out the rest. He had brought the newspaper and told her that she could be tried for murdering the bellhop. And if that didn't work, he could make sure she was tried for the murder of her own innocence. Either way, she was going to be a resident of the New Orleans penal system for a very long time as it would love to lock her up and throw away the key.

Still looking into his eyes, she realized that he had several other aces up his sleeve, a repercussion or two he had not yet revealed and probably wouldn't unless he had to. What he hadn't insinuated yet, but would if it became necessary, was that the authorities could probably get Sadie as an accessory to the abortion. And if that happened, what would happen to her children? Johnnie didn't think Mrs. Mancini would allow her husband's children to live at their mansion without their mother living on the premises with them. How would it look to have pickaninnies running around the Mancini mansion that looked just like Santino only with much darker skin? What if they, being children, slipped up and called him, "daddy" in Mrs. Mancini's presence? The other insinuation would be that Madam De Mille would be hunted down and brought to justice, too. In other words, lots of people would be hurt if she didn't cooperate. But Earl wasn't charging in like he was Genghis Khan, prepared to take whatever he wanted, knowing that she really didn't have a defense, nor did she have a choice. Not yet anyway. Instead, he would appeal to her sense of logic and practicality first. He, therefore, presented a very calm businesslike exterior, walking her through his plan, taking his time, offering what she thought was a gift that she could ill-afford to turn down at this juncture, particularly since he had the means and the motivation to make sure she and Sadie went to jail.

But for Johnnie, there was a huge level of fear mounting if she refused him. Even though he thought he hid his determination to have her no matter what, she knew that he was prepared to overpower her and force his way into her. His lust demanded fulfillment. He hadn't had sex with her for six months, and she thought he was probably thinking about it every day, wanting to take her recklessly if she wouldn't freely give him the music that calmed his savage beast. Billy Logan had coveted her for two years before he finally took what he had been hungering and thirsting for, and had given her a thorough beating in the process, damaging the organ that he had used for his pleasure. And she knew that if she refused Earl, he would take it, too. He had carefully constructed his plan to win her back, and he would not be denied. He would take what his ever-present beast demanded, and then set his judicial hounds of "justice" on her trail.

"Are you going to stare at me all night or are you going to count it?" Earl said, interrupting her logic. When he saw her hesitating, he picked up the bag and turned it upside down. The money clumped down hard on the table and was neatly wrapped in thousand dollar bundles of twenties. He looked into Johnnie's eyes. He could tell that she wanted the money. It was the answer to her dreams—his, too.

She picked up the first thousand dollar bundle and pulled off the bank binding. Curiosity demanded that she count the money, thinking the bank binding could be wrong, but also because seeing all that cash made her body betray her mind. The money made the eyes on her chest narrow as they tightened. She started counting out stacks of five twenty dollar bills until she had ten stacks. Minutes later, she had counted out twenty thousand dollars. Without realizing it, her legs were opening and closing as the heat down there began to simmer. She looked at Earl and said, "What do I have to do for this?"

"That's just for openers." He paused for a second to see how she responded to the money, hoping to see a flicker of acceptance so that he could feel confident to sweeten the offer. "I'll also build you a home, one with lots of rooms and several bathrooms, right here in Jackson. I'll buy you a brand new car of your choosing every year. Two, if you like. I'll take you on a vacation . . . anywhere you want to go at least four times a year, perhaps more. Or, I'll pay for you to go alone if I can't go with you. Depending on the time of year, one of my daughters might be graduating, and I never want to miss any event in their lives. Janet is graduating this May, so if you wanted to go, then I couldn't go with you.

"In addition to that, I'll even pay for all your medical expenses should you get sick. If you have any of my children, they'll want for nothing, and I'll make sure they get the best education money can buy. If you wanna go to college, I'll even pay for that. I can pay for your full tuition right now. You can start next semester. And since you want to be a stockbroker, I'll even set you up with an office and a secretary. You'll have plenty of privacy because I'll still be living in New Orleans. I'll only come up on the weekends. I'll also use my money to defend you if an ambitious prosecutor comes after you for any pending murder charges. If he somehow manages to convict you, I'll make sure you do minimum time." He paused again. "This is a generous offer, considering what you did to me. But at the same time, I did you wrong first. I still love you and want to get back together. What do you think? Can we please get back together?"

"What if I don't want to, Earl," she said. "What if I just want to move on with my life? Will you let me go?"

"I'm afraid not," he said firmly like he was digging his heels in, preparing for any argument she might present. "This is a one time offer, and if you refuse me, I'll be forced to use my wealth to put you behind bars for the remainder of your life. If you refuse me . . . if I can't have you . . . with God as my witness . . . no man will. And don't think for an instant that you can agree for the moment and then escape me. I'll never let that happen. Never. I'll hire every detective I can from here to Singapore to find you. I will scour the earth for as long as it takes. And when I find you, I'll make sure you stand trial for murder.

Keith Lee Johnson

"There is no statue of limitation for murder so you'll never be able to rest. You'll never have peace of mind. You'll always be looking over your shoulders, wondering when one of my representatives will inform the police of your whereabouts. When you were at work this morning, my detectives were there watching you. Can you tell me which of your customers were detectives and which were ordinary customers? You can't can you? And that's how it'll be for the rest of your natural life. Even after I die, I'll leave instructions with my attorneys to pursue you until you are caught and punished for murder. It's a good deal, Johnnie. Take it."

"Can I think about it," she asked, offering token resistance.

He looked at his watch and said, "Sure, you've got one minute."

Johnnie was deflated and elated at the same time. She wanted to take the offer. It was a good deal, considering the consequences if she didn't. Besides, he owed her all of that and more since he was ultimately responsible for her mother's death. That's what she told herself anyway. She would much rather a sweet offer like that came from Napoleon Bentley. She would gladly take his money and other gifts. But taking them from Earl? The man who had started everything? The man who had caused so much hardship and death? That was very difficult, but she was at his mercy and he wanted an immediate answer. And the thought of being brutally raped a second time made the decision so much easier.

Sadie Lane came to mind. She remembered that her friend had gotten trapped by money and ended up with three children by a man she didn't love. Even though she wanted for nothing, she had nothing she could call her own. She was totally dependent on Santino Mancini's generosity. But now, Sadie no longer had a home or the fifty thousand dollars she had given her. As a matter of fact, Sadie would probably have to live at the Mancini mansion and deal with the wrath of Mrs. Mancini on a daily basis. Even though Earl had her boxed in, she still had some leverage because he wanted to have sex right then if she was willing. And knowing that would make it possible to get the security that Sadie and her mother never had.

"Let me get this straight, Earl," she began. "You're going to do all of that for me for the rest of my life."

Nodding, he said, "Yes. I most certainly will."

267

"But what about when you die, Earl? What am I going to do then?"

"Listen, Johnnie, with you by my side, I don't plan on dying for a very long time. But, I understand your fears. They are well-founded. I'll tell you what I'm going to do. If you agree to my offer, tomorrow I'll hire a Jackson attorney and put you in my will so that what you have will always be yours, and you'll get a stipend of money every month, so that you'll always be taken care of after I die. If you ever have my children, I'll make sure they become a part of the will, too."

"And I can have an unalterable copy of the will?"

Smiling, feeling like he had been successful, he said, "You sure can. In fact, when you get off work tomorrow, we can go and get it taken care of immediately. And you can choose the attorney, if you like."

"If you're serious, why do I have to go to work tomorrow? Why can't I just quit?"

"Johnnie, you know we can't have people knowing our business. We have to keep this secret for as long as we can. You know people still hate race mixing. Some people hate it so much that they'll kill me even though I'm white. You know that. What you have to do is work at Lucille's, and then little by little, open up your business in an office. But if you all of a sudden have everything, it'll look like you have the money that Sharon stole. If you work for Lucille and Hank for about a year, then it won't arouse suspicion, especially if you have clients who have to pay your eleven hundred dollar fee up front."

Surprised, she said, "You know about that, too?"

"Johnnie, I know about everything. I even know that Lucas is starting boot camp in Columbia, South Carolina."

"I guess you do know everything. But what about the house you said you would build for me?"

"I will build it, but not right away. You've got to establish a pattern of working, saving, and building a stock portfolio. Anything less than that will arouse the suspicions of the police. One of the reason's I'm giving you the twenty thousand is so that you know I'm bargaining in good faith since it wouldn't be smart to give you everything now. So . . . what's your answer?"

Twenty minutes later, Earl's animal-like groans filled the room as she made love to him just the way he liked it. She was on top of him, in control, using her muscles to sustain him, and to ensure her own pleasure. Part of the reason she was enjoying the sex was because she knew she would never have to worry about money again. And so, she was going to make sure he enjoyed himself because if he did, he wouldn't hesitate to deliver all that he had promised. After controlling his pleasure for over an hour, she took him to the peak of excitement, and he hollered when he released. Then he grabbed at his chest for a few seconds and died with her still on top of him.

Chapter 73

Desperation

Earl Shamus was dead and Johnnie knew that there was no way she was going to get out of this one. She thought she had taken him to the peak of excitement and stifled his release with her muscles one time too many and the poor man just couldn't take the repeated intense stimulation she was putting on him. The thought of him having a bad ticker never even crossed her mind. Still on top of him, she tried desperately to wake him up. His eyes were open, and she thought there was a chance to save him. She had been accused of a murder she didn't commit. Now there would be an actual reason for the police to indict her, she thought.

After shaking him and screaming his name for twenty minutes she gave up. Earl was gone, and he wasn't coming back. She rolled off him, turned on the light, and went into the living room area of the room, and then over to the dining table. She sat down and tried to figure out what she was going to do. Shaking her head, she was thinking life was so unfair to her. She almost had everything, and now that had slipped away, too. One minute, she was high on life, and now, the high was over, and she had come crashing back down to earth like a duck that had been shot out of the sky.

Her heart was pounding as the thought of being behind bars for the rest of her life set in. A little over a month ago, she had visited Lucas at Angola Prison. She saw what being in prison had done to him in just a few weeks. Prison had made him think that he had no reason to hope that she would wait for him, that they had nothing to look forward to. That's how he thought, and he was only going to be in prison for three months. She wondered how long it would take her to get to that level of despair now that she was looking at life or the hangman's noose.

Shaking her head, she told herself that if she had listened to her mother at the Savoy, she wouldn't be in this mess. But greed had gotten to her then as it had gotten to her once again in that very hotel room. If she had just trusted her God like she had planned and told Earl that she was willing to go to jail if she had to, but there was no way she was going to do what he wanted, Earl would be alive. She had no way of knowing that the sweet deal he had offered her was laced with hemlock. She toyed with the idea of turning herself in, but she knew the police weren't going to believe she didn't kill him on purpose. Then, she thought about the twenty thousand.

What was she going to do with all that money? If she turned herself in and turned in the money, given her reputation in New Orleans and the notoriety of the trial that still had people talking, they wouldn't even bother with an autopsy. Once they found out that another death had occurred and she was involved, they would probably take her out back and shoot her in the head and be done with her. She knew her only chance was to get Earl out of that room, back into his car, and back to New Orleans. He had said that nobody knew he was in Jackson. He had sent his private detectives to Houston to investigate Paul Masterson. If everything he had told her was true, she had a chance to escape life imprisonment.

She figured that if she could just get his clothes on and out of that room before daybreak, she would be halfway home. But she was going to need help. There was no way she could lift Earl by herself. Gloria Schumacher came to mind. She thought Gloria would understand even though she was white. Given all the stories Gloria had told her earlier that night about her deceased husband, she just might be the one person who would be willing to help her. Nevertheless, she was afraid to ask for help because Gloria had told her the day she moved in that she didn't allow fornication in her hotel.

While she believed that Gloria was fooling herself if she thought unmarried people weren't having sex in her hotel, she didn't think it would go over very well if Gloria saw a naked man in her bed with semen still sliding down his leg. She was thinking, "What choice did I have?" And it didn't help that she'd had trouble with nearly every white woman she encountered. For those reasons, she was more than afraid to trust Gloria even though her experiences with her were altogether different. She had to trust somebody or it was all over. Even if Gloria refused to help it was better than turning herself in or trying to escape, leaving a dead white man in a room that was registered to her. Time was running out. She knew what she had to do. She decided to take a shower before going downstairs to solicit Gloria's help.

Just as she was about to go to the bathroom, she thought she heard somebody say, "It's time to pray." She looked around the room, wondering who was there beside her and Earl Shamus. She knew it wasn't him, and she knew she hadn't thought of praying. But the voice was so clear. And then, she heard it again. "It's time to pray." Her heart started pounding again as she looked around the room again. Seeing nothing, she realized that it was the voice of God himself—at least that's what she thought. Whether it was God speaking to her or not, the voice was right. She had tried everything but prayer. She bowed her head and closed her eyes.

Lord God, up in heaven . . . I know I did wrong, but if you're everywhere at the same time . . . that means you were here, and you saw that I didn't mean to kill him. I know I shouldn't have been having sex with him, but you heard him threaten me. What could I do?"

"You could have trusted me," the voice said.

Frowning, she opened her eyes and looked around the room again. Seeing no one, she bowed her head and closed her eyes again. She was about to start praying again when she heard, "Why are you running from me?"

She opened her eyes again and seeing nothing she closed them and listened. She felt a presence in the room, but she didn't bother opening her eyes. She knew she wouldn't see anyone. But she felt a peace that she had never experienced before. Even though she couldn't see him, she sensed that God was in her room, surrounding her, comforting her. She said, "Have mercy on me and help me."

The voice said, "I sent you my angels in the City of the Dead. And I have sent you help again."

While the voice was still speaking, someone knocked her at door. "Open up! Jackson police department! We have a warrant for your arrest!"

Chapter 74

"I need to take a quick shower first."

Johnnie's heart was about to explode. Her eyes shot open as she realized that she had imagined it all. No one was talking to her. And her prayers had bounced off the ceiling. She wasn't going to get any help from God, and if she did, it was going to be through the police. *Could they be Angels?* She took a deep breath and gathered herself, ready to face the inevitable. She figured that if God had spoken to her, He wanted her to turn herself in, and He would make sure that justice was done. But still, she was uncertain. Uncertainty made her afraid to go to the door and find out. As she slowly made her way over to the door, a single tear dropped out of her right eye, slid down to her dimple, and careened inside. She pulled the door open and stood behind it. Expecting the police to come in and arrest her, she said, "I didn't mean to do it. I swear I didn't."

"Didn't mean to do what," Masterson said, laughing. "I must have scared the living daylights out of you."

"Paul?" she said, coming from behind the door. "Is that you?"

Still laughing, Masterson said, "Johnnie, why are you hiding behind the door?"

"You said you were the police and that you had a warrant for my arrest."

He stopped laughing suddenly when he saw the tears in her eyes.

She fast-walked over to him and embraced him. Suddenly feeling safe, she buried her face into his chest and wept, repeating, "I didn't mean to do it. I didn't mean to do it."

"Do what," he said.

"I didn't mean to kill him, Paul. I didn't." She looked into his eyes. "You believe me, don't you?"

"Of course I believe you," he said, closing the door, listening intensely. "Now tell me what happened."

"Oh, Paul, just hold me for a few minutes, please. Just hold me."

He did as she asked, and then he saw what looked like the bear foot of a man lying in Johnnie's bed. He put both hands on her shoulders and gently moved her back a few feet, so he could look into her eyes. "Who's that in your bed, Johnnie? Is he dead?"

Looking into his eyes, she nodded rapidly, and then buried her head into his chest again. "Oh, God! It's Earl Shamus. He's dead!"

"The man your mother sold you to?"

"Oh, Paul, it's such a long sordid story. Will you help me, please?"

"Of course I'll help you, but you've gotta tell me what happened here."

"He came here to blackmail me, Paul."

"So you killed him?"

"No . . . yes . . . but not intentionally."

"You killed him, but not intentionally?"

"And definitely not because he was going to blackmail me."

"Well, what happened?"

She took a deep breath and exhaled. "Sit down, Paul. This is going to take a few minutes."

Masterson walked over to the dining table and sat down, shaken by what little he knew so far. He had a thousand questions running through his mind at that moment. He liked Johnnie, and he wanted to give her the benefit of the doubt, but it was hard to believe that the man who had paid her mother for sex had driven all the way from New Orleans to blackmail her. And even if he had, what was his leverage?

274

She sat at the table opposite him and looked into his eyes. She could tell he was having trouble believing she hadn't killed him on purpose. "He came here because he wanted me back, Paul."

"Can I ask you a question, Johnnie?"

She nodded.

"Is he in there naked or what?"

She nodded.

Masterson ran his hand down his face. Then he scratched his head and said, "Do I need to ask what he was doing in your bed naked, Johnnie?"

She looked away and shook her head.

"So . . . you were having sex with him?"

She nodded. "I had to, Paul. He threatened to send me to jail."

"For what?"

"It's so complicated, Paul. Let's just say he could have gotten me for the abortion I had and two other murders that I didn't have anything to do with. I was getting an abortion when they were killed."

"They? You mean more than Earl is dead?"

"Yes, my stockbroker, a woman named Sharon Trudeau is dead. So is the bellhop who was in the wrong place at the wrong time. I was tried and acquitted of Sharon's murder, and I think I was acquitted of the bellhop's murder, too. I can't remember. But I did have the abortion, and so even if they couldn't get me for the bellhop, they could get me for the abortion."

"So that's why he was here? To blackmail you into sleeping with him again?"

"Yes. But to be totally honest with you, Paul, he offered me a lot of things. And I took the offer. We were just sealing the deal when he had a heart attack and died. Now are you still going to help me?"

"Let me ask you something, Johnnie?"

"Did you ever love this guy?"

"Never, Paul. I never did, and I don't think I ever would have."

"But you accepted his offer."

"It was a great offer, Paul."

"What was on the table?"

"A mansion, tuition for school, medical bills, a brokerage firm with a secretary, money, cars, four vacations a year with the promise of not telling the district attorney's office about the abortion and the bellhop, and a strong defense if I was ever indicted."

"Don't they know about the bellhop?"

"Yes, but I'm not sure if it was a part of my indictment, and I'm not about to go back to New Orleans and find out. I didn't kill either of them, but no one would want to hear that. Just so you know Earl had detectives on us."

"What do you mean on *us*?"

"I mean he had detectives following me, and now they're on you. I don't know how many there are, but they're in Houston checking into your background, I guess."

"Are you sure they're in Houston, Johnnie?"

"That's what Earl told me."

"And you believe him?"

"Yes."

"Why?"

"Earl wouldn't lie to me, Paul."

"Why wouldn't he? He came here for sex, and you gave it to him. What makes you think he wasn't going to put the authorities on you after he left here?"

"Because he gave me money."

"How much money?"

"Twenty thousand."

"Twenty thousand? Dollars?"

She nodded rapidly.

"We still don't know if the detectives are here or not? We need to know before we move the body."

"They're not here, Paul. He wouldn't come here if they were. Frankly, I think one of the reasons he sent them to Houston was to make sure they weren't here so no one would know."

"Either that, or he was bluffing."

"I don't think he was, Paul."

"Why not?"

"There was no reason to. I told you what the offer was, and I told you what he had on me. With all he had on me, he didn't need to run a bluff. When Tony Hatcher told him that you and I were spending time together, he probably felt threatened and wanted to know who you were and if you were really a legitimate preacher. Since I'd had a bite to

276

eat with you two days in a row, he probably thought that it was now or never. So he sent them to Houston, drove up here, and made his pitch."

"Do you think he would have told the district attorney about the abortion if you hadn't given him what he wanted?"

"Yes."

Masterson frowned. "How did he know about the abortion in the first place?'"

"His wife, Meredith, hired Tony Hatcher to follow him. Hatcher bugged my house. He heard about the abortion, all my other business, and guess what else?"

"What?"

"Everything, and I mean everything, is on tape. Now that Meredith is dead, Earl has all the money and it is substantial."

"Okay. We're gonna have to move fast. You need to get downstairs and keep Gloria busy."

"You mean she's awake?"

"Yeah, that's why I didn't come up right away when I saw your light go on."

"If I have to keep Gloria busy, I'm gonna need a shower first."

"Make it quick. I'll get Shamus dressed. And when I'm sure you've got Gloria distracted, I'll bring him down."

"Maybe you should get his car first."

"Good idea. What kind of car does he drive?"

"A Cadillac. There shouldn't be too many of them out there."

"Okay, get in the shower, and I'll search his clothes for the keys."

Chapter 75

"Listen, you need to get going."

Fifteen minutes later Masterson had moved the Cadillac to the side stairs, where it would be easier to get Earl Shamus out of the hotel and into the car without being seen. He was sweating because he was nervous, but also because it was a struggle to maneuver a dead body so that he could put clothes on it. Fortunately, Earl wasn't completely naked. He still had his T-shirt and one of his socks on. It had been essential that he get Earl's underwear and pants on first, which was incredibly difficult. He sat on the bed and waited for Johnnie to come out of the bathroom. Moments later, the shower shut off, the door opened, and she came out wearing nothing but a white towel. He noticed that she had a terrific figure, beautiful skin, and he couldn't help staring at her for a moment or two. Then he said, "Could you dress in the other room. You don't have to get fully dressed, but throw something on and hurry back. When you finish, I need you to come back in here and help me put his underwear and pants on. I can put his shoes on by myself."

The whole thing seemed crazy to her, but she simply said, "Sure. No problem. I'll be right there." She grabbed a skirt and blouse combination, pulled off the tags, and took them into the other room.

He watched her leave, and then called out, "Oh, and before you go downstairs, we need to discuss the plan."

"But Paul, I thought we were in a big hurry," she said as she reentered the room.

"We are, but we better take the time to plan or we'll both end up in jail."

"What do you need me to do?"

"First, I need you to help me get him on the floor. Then, I'm going to lift his torso, and you'll have to slide his underwear on."

She looked at his naked flesh and said, "I think I should clean his thing off. If the coroner sees it dripping, he'll get suspicious."

"Good idea. But hurry up. We gotta plan this thing out and we don't have much time."

She hustled into the bathroom, wet a face towel, and put some soap on it. Then she came back and cleaned his leg and his penis off. She had cleaned Earl off many times before, but having Masterson watching her do it made her uneasy.

She took the towel back into the bathroom, rinsed it, and hurried back into the bedroom. After removing the soap, she said, "What do you need me to do?"

"Put his underwear on and pull them up as far as you can. Then, I'll hoist him, and then you can pull them up the rest of the way, okay?"

"Okay," she said and picked up his white underwear. She lifted his left foot and slid the garment over it. Then, she did the same thing to the other foot.

Looking at her, Masterson said, "You ready?"

"Yes."

"On three. Ready?"

She nodded.

"One. Two. Three." He grunted when he lifted Earl, and she quickly slid his underwear up to his waist. He eased Earl back to the floor and said, "Now the pants and we're almost home."

After putting Earl's shoes on, they walked back into the other room and sat down at the dining table across from each other. "Gloria's a smart cookie, Johnnie. What are you going to tell her?"

"I'm going to tell her I need her to help me get the paper in the typewriter straight."

"That's not going to work. She'll wanna know why it's so important to get it done tonight."

"She knows why it's important tonight. I told her earlier I need to get Hank's stock portfolio done tonight. She knows how important it is to me to get it done, but if that gets done too fast, I can talk to her about what stocks she might want to look into to keep her busy. She's been trying to get me to tell her since I got here. I told her I had to charge a fee just like she charges for rooms. I think she'll jump at the chance to get some insight on a stock or two."

"Okay, but don't force the issue. Let her lead the conversation to the stock market. Otherwise, she might get suspicious. Can you handle that?"

"Yes. How much time do you need to get him out of here?"

"Hopefully, about fifteen minutes, but try to see if you can keep her busy for twenty to thirty minutes just in case I run into a problem. Then you need to get back up here and get in bed."

"I don't think I can sleep in that bed again, Paul, if I can sleep at all."

"I understand. Sleep wherever you can, but try to get some sleep. It's important that you show up for work tomorrow and every day for the next three weeks until you leave town. Everything must look like it did since you arrived."

"What are you going to do with Earl?"

"I'm going to drive him back to New Orleans. I'll have to catch a bus back. I know I told you I was going to stay another week or so, but the smart play is for me to get outta town in the morning."

"Will I ever see you again?"

"That's up to you."

"I'd love to see you again, Paul, but just in case I don't, I want you to know how much I appreciate you helping with this. Things would have turned out real bad for me if you hadn't come up to see me."

"This is going to sound crazy, but if you want to seal this deal, we outta get married. That way if something unexpected happens, if they find something in his car or at his home that we don't know about, or if he told someone he was coming here to see you, we can't be made to testify against each other."

"Why would I testify against you, Paul? You didn't do anything."

"I'm what the police would call an accessory after the fact. I can go to jail for covering up what could be construed as a crime. And since they would love to arrest you, they'd be glad to get me, too. It'll be another sensational case with the same woman that supposedly killed her stockbroker. Only this time you won't get off. This time, they'll make sure you go to prison. But getting married is up to you. Once I'm gone, I won't be back here for a long time, so you need to let me know now what you wanna do."

"We can't get married, Paul? You're white, and I'm colored. It's illegal, isn't it?"

"Sure, we can, Johnnie. There are a number of states that'll let us get married. I've actually married a number of blacks and whites in the northern states."

"Yeah, but was it legal? Will their marriages hold up in a court of law?"

"Yes, it is legal, and it's been legal for a long time. You and most Americans don't know the law in other states."

"Are you sure? I've never heard anything like that. Since when can blacks and whites get married? This must be fairly recent, if what you're saying is true."

"It is true, Johnnie. Why would I lie about something like that? I wouldn't. But you're right, California is fairly recent. They just changed their law six years ago in 1948, but blacks and whites have been able to get legally married in Pennsylvania since 1780. The state of Iowa changed its laws against interracial marriages between blacks and whites in 1851. Some of the other states that changed their laws against it are Maine, Massachusetts, Illinois, Ohio, New Mexico, Kansas, Michigan, Rhode Island, and Washington. Now I know you black southerners like to call us white folk crackers, but who do you think changed those laws in the northern Midwest states? Negroes? No. It was decent God-fearing white folk who changed those laws, which means the Negro just might have a real future in this country—at least in those progressive states most Americans wouldn't think of as progressive."

Stunned that so many States allowed what she and others had always needed to hide, she shook her head and said, "Paul, you're not going to believe this, but seconds before you knocked on my door, I thought I heard the Lord say he was sending me help. And the help turned out to be you. But I gotta be honest with you, I don't love you. Now do you still want to marry me?"

"At this point, I can't say I love you either, but, if we wanna be sure the law can't come after either of us, I think the smart play is to get married. Besides, didn't you say you wanted to be a traveling evangelist when you were a little girl?"

"I did say that."

"Did you mean it?"

"I did."

"Well, then, I can't think of a clearer sign. Besides, I've been praying for a wife for four years now."

"Are you sure you wanna marry a profligate Negress like me?"

"If you're willing to return to the Lord, yes."

"What if I'm not, Paul?"

"You are. I think ol' Earl dying the way he did changed everything. And besides, you said the Lord told you a little while ago that he had sent you some help, right?"

"Right."

"So, do you wanna do it?"

"Yes. Let's do it, Paul. Where do you want me to meet you?"

"It's up to you. Where do you wanna honeymoon?"

"Funny you should mention where I'd like to honeymoon. An old friend offered to take me to France, but I can go with you instead."

"I'll tell you what, meet me at City Hall in Providence, Rhode Island, at 9 AM sharp the first of March, and we'll get married if you don't change your mind. I'll book passage to sail over to France. I'll take you to the Negresco Hotel in Nice, where we'll spend a couple weeks together. Do you like to travel?"

"Yes. I mean, I think I do. I think I would love to travel. I think I'd love to get out of the United States for a while. If for no other reason just so I can relax and not have to worry about white folks trying to put me in jail for something I didn't do."

"I'll tell you what then, let's travel the world together. I bet you've never been on a passenger ship that can sail from one continent to the other, have you?"

"No. My goodness, Paul, you make it all sound so exciting."

"It is exciting, Johnnie. You'll love it. I've been just about everywhere. After we spend a couple weeks in Nice, we can travel around the world on a cruise ship for the next two to three years. That way, you can see all the wonders of the world, and if the authorities try

282

to find us, we'll never be in the same place long enough even if they did try to look for us in other countries. I don't think they'll do that, but if they did, it'll be hard to track us down. They won't even know your name because it'll be Johnnie Masterson, and they'll be looking for Johnnie Wise. After two or three years of constantly moving, they'll get tired of looking."

"Oh, Paul, it all sounds so wonderful."

"It will be wonderful, Johnnie. We can spend some time in Hong Kong and visit the Great Wall of China and the Forbidden City. We can go to India and see the Taj Mahal. From there, we can go to Rome and see the Colosseum and Michaelangelo's Sistine Chapel. If you're really adventurous, we can see Kathmandu City in the Himalayas. If all that isn't enough travel for you, we can go to Egypt and see the Sphinx and the Pyramids. Personally, I'd like to go back to Greece and see the Acropolis. There are so many places to visit, so many things to do and that's only a few places in the world."

"That's going to cost a fortune. I've only got twenty thousand. I don't want to spend it all traveling. I need to make money not spend it."

"Don't worry about the cost. I've got plenty of money. You save yours, invest it, or whatever, but I'll take care of all our expenses once we get married, okay?"

"What's your family gonna say?"

"I'm not gonna tell 'em."

"Where will we live?"

"Anywhere but the southern states, especially Texas. Now listen, you're gonna need a passport. They have a regional agency in Norwalk, Connecticut where you can get a passport the same day."

"Are we really gonna do this, Paul?"

"Yes, we are. I'll call you from time to time at Lucille's to let you know what's going on, how the arrangements are coming."

"Why don't you just call here?"

"Because Gloria could be listening. I'm sure she gets bored and listens to phone calls from time to time. It's important that no one around here knows what we're doing. If you have to tell your brother, and if you ever get a hold of your father, don't tell them anything from the hotel phone. I wouldn't even say anything over the phone period unless you're going to tell them you're getting married and where we're going, okay? On second thought, don't tell anybody anything. The less people know, the less they can say if somebody comes looking for you. When you leave, stick to the story."

"What's the story?"

"You're going to East Saint Louis to see your father."

She hugged him and said, "Oh, Paul, we really are going to do this, huh?"

Laughing he said, "Yes, we are. I'll probably buy a house in Rhode Island, where we're getting married." He smiled as if to himself and said, "How would you like living in . . . get this . . . Providence, Rhode Island?"

"Providence, huh? It sounds wonderful."

"It does sound wonderful, doesn't it?"

"It does. It really does."

"Now get on down to Gloria's office and keep her busy. What time is a good time to call you at Lucille's?"

"Well, I've only worked there one day, but I think the best time to call is between 10:45 and 11:10. Don't call before or after those times. I'll be too busy to talk to you, okay?"

"Okay."

She kissed him and said, "Paul thanks so much for everything. I've never been so happy and sad at the same time."

"What are you sad about?"

"Earl's dead. I never meant to kill him. I swear I didn't."

"I don't think you killed him, Johnnie. I think he had a bad heart. The coroner will prove that, and you should be off the hook. We're getting married just in case."

"But what if we fall in love?"

"If we fall in love, that'll be a bonus. I hope to God we do. You can help me when I'm on the road going from church to church."

"Yeah. I think I'd like that, Paul. When you need a passage read from the scriptures, I can do that for you or whatever else you need done. I'll be real good to you."

Masterson looked at his watch and said, "Listen, you need to get going. Remember to keep Gloria away from the desk for about twenty minutes."

"Okay, I will."

Chapter 76

"If you hurry, she might see that you at least showed up."

After three weeks of rigorous training, and constant testing, which he passed with flying colors, Lucas had come to love the Army and had fully embraced its protocols and traditions. Even though he still had eleven weeks of basic combat training remaining, he knew that he had found his calling in life, which was to be a military officer, and nothing was going to stand in his way. Other than being a professional football player, he thought the Army had the best deal going, and he had already decided he was going to serve for thirty years—longer if they let him.

The Army had given him clothing, shoes, a bed, and three square meals a day. While the food would never compare to the delicious meals his mother, Johnnie, and Marla Bentley made for him, or any of the other food he ate in his native New Orleans, he had developed a taste for the grub the cooks prepared for him. In short, the Army had become the family he never had. Sure, he had half brothers, but the Army was different, and in some ways better. They were brothers in arms, and they all had the same father—the president of the United States, and they obeyed his will to the letter.

He had figured out early on that if he did as he was told, he would be just fine as disobedience was punished swiftly and without apology or remorse. Lots of recruits thought the rules were too strict, but he didn't think they were strict enough. He had already planned to remedy that when he became an officer. Even though racism was deeply woven into the fabric of the Army, he noticed that a man could earn respect in spite of racism's fierce bite. Colonel Strong and Sergeant Cornsilk were clear examples of this.

Having immersed himself in the culture of the Army for almost a month, he hardly ever thought of Johnnie, which was why he was stunned when a guard at Fort Jackson told him that a beautiful woman from New Orleans had driven all the way to Fort Jackson to visit him. He had been spending much of his freedom with Cassandra Perry, which helped bring closure to his relationship with Johnnie for good. They had just seen another film and had another scrumptious dinner at the Blue Diamond to celebrate his first liberty. Normally, recruits didn't get liberty for six to eight weeks after basic began, but he had impressed Sergeant Cornsilk by his ability to lead the men by example, which earned him an early weekend pass. Nevertheless, he was still impressed that Johnnie had driven nearly seven hundred miles just to see him. But at the same time, the last thing he wanted at the moment was to hear from his former flame while Cassandra was in his car pressed up against him.

The guard added, "I can't remember her name, but she left this letter for you. She said to tell you that if you returned in two hours, you could catch her at the train station."

"How long ago was that?" Lucas asked, desperately hoping it wasn't too late.

"About an hour and a half ago. If you hurry you might be able to catch her."

Lucas looked at Cassandra.

She said, "Let's go, Lucas. I hope we can catch her. I've gotta see the woman who has such a hold on you."

"Are you sure?"

"Very. Let's go."

Lucas looked at his watch and calculated that he only had about twenty minutes to get there before the train left. It was 10:35, and the train would be leaving at 11:00. He would have to get there with time to spare so that he could go inside and find her. He was hoping that the train would leave late, that way he would have a real chance of catching her. As he drove, he thought about the letter the guard had given him and what it might say. He couldn't wait to read it, but he knew

Cassandra would want to know what it said, too. He figured she wanted to read it more than he did even though she hadn't let on.

When he reached the train station, it was 10:58. He parked his car right behind Johnnie's. He looked at Cassandra and said, "She must be abandoning her car."

"Maybe she's planning to return soon," Cassandra said.

"I doubt it. Are you coming?"

"You know I am. I gotta meet her."

They hustled into the train station. The place was a ghost town. No one was in there except them. But there was a train on the tracks. They ran over to the ticket booth and asked the clerk if the eleven o'clock train had left.

"It should be pulling out at any moment. Would you like two tickets?"

"No," Lucas said, "I'm just trying to see my friend who's on it."

"Oh, you must mean, Johnnie Wise," the clerk said. "She's a beautiful girl. What happened? She waited until the last moment to get on the train. She kept watching the door like she expected you to come through it and stop her from leaving. I felt sorry for her when she got on the train and looked back at the door one last time. I think she was crying." The train whistle blew. "If you hurry, she might see that you at least showed up."

Lucas took off running, and so did Cassandra, who had pulled off her heels so she could keep pace. They blasted through the depot doors at full speed. The train was pulling out of the station. As they ran down the platform, he looked into the cars, hoping he would see her. Still running, the train was moving faster as it moved away from the station, offering a congested choo-choo as it picked up speed. And then, he saw her. She was sitting in a window seat, but she wasn't looking out of the window.

"Johnnie! Johnnie!" he called out to her, but she couldn't hear him. He was still calling her name when he reached the end of the platform. He doubled over and rested his hands on his knees, sucking in as much oxygen as he could. When his wind returned to him, he turned around, looking for Cassandra. She had given up long before he had, he guessed. Then, he made the long trek down the platform to where she waited for him.

Chapter 77

"Can we just sit here for a few minutes, please?"

"At least you've got the letter she left for you," Cassandra said with compassion, looking at Lucas as he held the letter while they sat in the front seat of his car, knowing he still had strong feelings for Johnnie. "Well . . . aren't you going to open it?" When he didn't respond, but rather sat there like he was in a trance, looking at the trunk of Johnnie's car, she snatched the letter out of his hand. "Give me that. I'll open it if you won't." She sat there, holding the letter, waiting for him to offer some resistance, but he didn't. He just sat there, stoic, staring out into the night, longing for the girl he still loved even though Cassandra was with him and had been with him for about a month. As she was about to rip the letter open, she felt something hard. She opened the letter and unfolded the paper. A car key fell into her lap. She picked it up and said, "I guess you were right."

"Right about what?"

"Apparently, she's abandoning her car if you didn't bother to come because she left you this key." She handed it to him.

"Must be the spare," he said, holding it. "What does the letter say?"

"You want *me* to read *your* letter from the woman you're still crazy about?"

Without looking at her, he said, "Sure, why not? You're just going to bug me about it until I tell you what it says anyway, right?"

Smiling, she said, "Absolutely. But I think I need more light. Let's go back inside the station, and I'll read it to you."

"Okay. Are you okay with driving my car back to Fort Jackson?"

"Yes."

They went back into the station and sat down on one of the many empty benches provided by the railroad. She unfolded the letter again and started skimming it. She wanted to have an idea of what it said before she read it to him, anticipating the worst. She was a woman, and she knew without knowing Johnnie that she didn't drive all the way from New Orleans just to say goodbye. Johnnie had driven that distance to try and patch things up. The fact that she left her car told her that not only wasn't she planning to ever return, but wherever she was going, there was a good chance that another man was involved. As far as Cassandra was concerned, even before reading the letter, Johnnie Wise had driven all the way to Columbia, South Carolina hoping that Lucas would stop her from making a huge mistake. And since she didn't bother waiting for him to return, she was on a tight time schedule, probably to meet the other man. After skimming the letter she read:

My darling, Lucas,

I'm so very sorry you had to hear what you heard in court that day. I had no idea you were out of jail, in town, and in that courtroom. I suppose that it wouldn't have made a difference had I known you were there and could hear it all because my life was at stake. All of what you heard had to come to light whether I wanted it to or not. I'm sure it won't make a difference, but I must explain why I did what I did with Martin Winters, my former stockbroker.

As you know, I wanted to learn about the stock market so that I would know how it worked and so forth, but I noticed that Martin wanted me. And foolishly, I made a deal with the devil, thinking that evil would somehow lead me to heaven on earth in the form of riches. But as you know, the devil doesn't make deals. He makes us think we have a deal when, in fact, he's the one that has the deal. We get the crumbs, and we're foolish enough to think the crumbs are a seven course meal.

Well, foolishly, I made that deal with the devil, and I got rich, but I lost you in the process. And I almost lost my freedom as well. To make matters worse, all my money burned up in my house when the white folks came and burned Ashland Estates to the ground. Had I known I was going to lose all $250,000 and end up destitute with no *money, no home, no clothes, and no shoes, I would never have made the deal. So, then I was the bigger loser. The devil and Martin Winters were the big winners.*

I thought I had everything. I thought I was going to be calling the shots. I thought I was going to parlay that money into a fortune that I could never lose. I thought that you and I were going to live happily ever after the way lovers do in fairy tales. I didn't know there was a worm in the apple until after I bought and bit into it. But I'm learning that we all get what we deserve. I messed you over, and the devil messed me over, but good.

But God is good, and his mercy is from everlasting unto ever-lasting, and I for one, am grateful. In a way, I'm hoping I don't see you so that I don't have to look into your eyes. For in them, I know I would see the disdain you now feel for me. You trusted me, and I let you down. My intentions were good, but the path I chose to goodness blinded me, and I couldn't see where I was going and I fell into a deep dark hole that only God could get me out of. I am still searching for the correct path. I'm still in need of and seeking spiritual wisdom and guidance. I think I've found it. I think I'm finally where I'm supposed to be.

I'm leaving the country, and I'll probably be gone for two to three years. I'm going to travel the world. Can you believe that? Me? Traveling the world? Perhaps, I'll send you a postcard or two to let you know I'm still alive and well. I know you're going to Germany and perhaps I'll find a way to send you something from my travels. I'm so excited about my new life and where it might lead me.

Anyway, I think I've said all I need to say. I want you to know that I love you, and that I'll always love you no matter who comes into our lives. May my God bless and keep you, and may He give you all the desires of your heart. You've been a great friend in time of need. I just wish I had been as true to you as you were to me.

Farewell,

Johnnie Wise.

When Cassandra finished the letter, she looked at him to get his immediate reaction. He just sat there, looking forward like he was in a land far, far away. "A penny for your thoughts," she said.

"She's found herself a rich man," he said, still looking forward.

"What makes you think that," she asked, testing him.

290

"All of her money burned up in the fire, Cassandra. How can she travel the world for two or three years with no money? She can't. Someone else is paying."

"Maybe she met a wealthy old woman who needs a companion to travel with her."

"You're being kind, and I really appreciate it. An old friend told me the truth about Johnnie, but I didn't listen to her. I'm listening to her now, though. It's so clear to me now. I wish it had been clear then, but it was all so foggy, while at the same time appearing to be clear. Besides, if there was an older woman, she would have said so and you know it. You're just trying to soften the final blow."

"I'm sorry. I just thought that you didn't need to know the truth right now because she hurt you one last time before leaving." She touched his hand. "If there's any consolation it would be that she came here hoping you would stop her from marrying the man she's about to marry. She was hoping to find you, but deep down, she didn't think you would give her another chance since you heard that she had sex with her stockbroker."

"Don't you mean since I heard that she was reproducing with her stockbroker."

Smiling, she said, "That's exactly what I mean." She paused and watched him for a moment. "What are you going to do now?"

"I'm going to move on. I love her still, but before today, I hadn't thought about her much, if at all. I'm going to be a soldier for the rest of my life. I'm going to eventually find a wife, get married, and have children. I'm going to travel the world, too, but, I'll be doing it the Army way. I wish her luck with her new husband. I hope it works out for her, too. I hope she truly has found what she's looking for in her God."

"I hope she does, too," she said sincerely. "I guess we can head back to Fort Jackson now."

"Can we just sit here for a few minutes, please? I still need to let this settle."

"Okay. I'll sit here with you all night if you need me to."

"Thanks," he said. "By the way, do you know anybody that might be interested in buying a car? I'm willing to sell it cheap."

"Um, how cheap?" she said, smiling and squeezed his hand affectionately.

Excerpt From Book 7: In the Line of Fire

"So, the girl knows about her father and Johnnie."

Three weeks had passed since Earl Shamus was found in his Cadillac. The coroner told Tony Hatcher that he had died of natural causes even though he found something he couldn't explain. What he found, while strange, wasn't a big enough deal to do an autopsy. The coroner signed the death certificate and released the body to the Shamus family, so they could bury their dead.

The phone in Hatcher's office buzzed. He pushed a button and said, "Yes."

"Your two o'clock is here, Mr. Hatcher," a woman said.

"Send him in," Hatcher said.

A few seconds later, his door opened and a man wearing a charcoal suit walked in. He was carrying a large envelope. Hatcher stood up and waited for the man to come to him, admiring his impeccable style, wondering how far the outfit set him back. He was thinking that the whole ensemble must have cost at least a month's salary. There was no way he could spend that kind of money for one suit.

"Mr. Hatcher," the man said, offering his hand. "I'm Seymour Collins, attorney for the Shamus family."

Hatcher offered him a seat and waited for him to sit, and then he sat, too. "I always get you and the other Seymour mixed up. He's—"

"You must mean Phil Seymour. He's the head of the Chicago office of Buchanan Mutual. You probably know the name because he's mentoring Janet Shamus to take over as President."

"Yes, that must be it. Now . . . what can I do for you, Mr. Collins?"

"I understand that you did some work for my deceased client, Meredith Shamus, some time ago, and I have reason to believe that you also worked for her husband, Earl, for a week or so immediately after her death."

Hatcher didn't respond. Who he worked for was confidential.

Collins tossed the envelope on the desk and looked at Hatcher, but again he didn't respond. He just looked at Collins, waiting for him to ask a question.

"Did you take those pictures, Mr. Hatcher?"

"What can I do for you, Mr. Collins," Hatcher said without bothering to open the envelope to see the pictures.

Collins picked the envelope up, opened it, and placed them on Hatcher's desk, facing him. Hatcher glanced at the pictures briefly and said, "What can I do for you, Mr. Collins?"

Collins exhaled hard and said, "You can tell me if you took those pictures."

They were the snapshots that he'd taken for Meredith Shamus when she hired him to follow Earl. One of the pictures was of Johnnie meeting Earl at the Savoy. Another was one of Benny punching Earl in the stomach. There was a picture of San Francisco license plates and much more.

"And if I did? Then what?"

"Meredith showed me these about six months ago when she got them from you. She thought Earl had killed the girl's mother, a Creole prostitute named Marguerite Wise. As you know, Earl was having relations with her daughter and Meredith wanted to put a stop to it. I offered to talk to the girl and offer a few dollars to keep the Shamus name out of whatever happened to her mother, but Meredith insisted on handling the girl herself."

Hatcher looked at his watch and said, "Is this going somewhere, Mr. Collins?"

Collins exhaled again, growing weary of Hatcher's reluctance to cooperate. "I've got Janet waiting in your secretary's office. I don't want her to hear the things I'm going to tell you."

"Which are?"

"According to the coroner, semen was found outside and inside Earl's shaft. There were traces of soap on his leg. Someone had obviously cleaned in the area, but they didn't think about the semen that would eventually come out and end up in his shorts."

"And?"

"The man died of a heart attack, Mr. Hatcher."

"I'm aware of that, Mr. Collins. Listen . . . I'm busy. Please get to the point. I have other business I need to attend to."

"Does it make sense to you that a man dying of a heart attack would have semen dripping out of his shaft at the time of his death?"

"Stranger things have happened. What's your point?"

"I think Earl was with this Johnnie girl when he died, and she somehow got him to his car and ran it into a ditch near the airport."

"And she did that from Jackson, Mississippi, where she's currently working."

"So . . . Earl did hire you to track her down? That means that he may have met with her."

"Let's say he did meet with her, and he did have sex with her. Are you suggesting that she dressed him and put him in his Cadillac and drove him all the way back to New Orleans, and then caught a bus back to Jackson?"

"I'm suggesting that it's possible."

"Mr. Collins, Johnnie Wise would have needed help to do all of that."

"What if she had help, Mr. Hatcher? What if Earl died in her bed?"

"What if he did? He had a heart attack. What if he had sex with her and died on the way back to New Orleans? That would account for the semen, would it not? But even if you're right, the girl is only guilty of tampering with evidence."

"She's guilty of more than that, Mr. Hatcher."

"What else is she guilty of?"

"Abortion and quite possibly the murder of a bellhop in Fort Lauderdale."

"She was acquitted of the murders, Mr. Collins."

"No, she was acquitted of Sharon Trudeau's murder. She was never tried for the bellhop. The district attorney didn't charge her with the bellhop's death. The papers only talked about Miss Trudeau's death, so that's what they indicted her for."

"But her lawyers got her off because she couldn't have done that murder."

"Exactly."

"What would be accomplished by hauling her into court again?"

"This time the district attorney will ask her where she was the night of the murder, and she'll have to say where she was. She'll have to say she was in Bayou Cane, Louisiana. And then, the prosecutor will ask her what she was doing there. And if she answers, we get her for murdering her child. If she doesn't answer, we get her for murdering the bellhop. Either way, she pays for Meredith Shamus' death."

"But she had nothing to do with Meredith's death."

"Sure, she did, Mr. Hatcher."

"I was there. I saw the whole thing. Ethel Beauregard killed Meredith."

"She made a deal with Meredith not to bring her family into this. And she broke that deal. Earl was planning to reunite with her against my advice. He told me he loved her and that he was going to try to reestablish something with her. He told me that if it didn't work out, he was going to pursue this course of action."

"So, you think he met with this girl?"

"I believe he did, yes. Did you or anybody on your team of detectives see him go into her room?

"No. We were all in Houston investigating Paul Masterson, the man Johnnie had been spending time with."

"Hmm. So he sent you and your team of detectives to Houston, so he wouldn't be seen going to her hotel room. He planned to make an outrageous offer—again against my advice. I believe the girl took it. She would have been a fool not to."

"What was the deal?"

"He was going to offer her twenty thousand cash, a newly built home, a new car every year, college tuition, several vacations every year and much more."

"And you want me to track her down and bring her back to New Orleans to stand trial for murdering the bellhop?"

"Yes."

"That's going to be really expensive."

"How much do you need as a retainer?"

"Depends on if she's still in Jackson. She should be gone by now. It's been nearly a month. Her car should be fixed, and she should be on her way to East Saint Louis by now."

"How much?"

"Assuming she's gone, I'll need at least five thousand. And that's just to start."

"Can you have your secretary send Janet in? She has the checkbook. With Phil Seymour's guidance, I think she's going to make a fine president."

"So the girl knows about her father and Johnnie."

"She found the pictures among her mother's things, Mr. Hatcher. She wants to pursue this, too."

Also By Keith Lee Johnson

The Little Black Girl Lost Series: Books 1 – 5

Faith's Redemption

Pretenses

Sugar and Spice

The Honeymoon Is Over

Hell Has No Fury

To learn more about Keith Lee Johnson
and his body of work, visit:

www.keithleejohnson.com

or visit him on Facebook and Myspace

Email the author:

keithleejohnson1@aol.com
or
d2imaginebooks@aol.com

Coming Soon from Keith Lee Johnson

Little Girl Lost: Johnnie Wise In the Line of Fire

Fall 2010

LaVergne, TN USA
17 December 2010
209199LV00012B/10/P